CHEROKEE ICE

also by
JOHN T. BIGGS

Sacred Alarm Clock
Clementine: A Song for the End of the World
The Owl of Death Row
Shiners

CHEROKEE ICE

A Novel

JOHN T. BIGGS

Bestselling Author of *The Owl of Death Row*

An Imprint of Roan & Weatherford Publishing Associates, LLC
Bentonville, Arkansas
www.roanweatherford.com

Library of Congress Cataloging-in-Publication Data
Names: Biggs, John T., author.
Title: Cherokee Ice/John T. Bigg
Description: First Edition | Bentonville: Rogue River, 2025.
Identifiers: LCCN: 2025935949| 979-8-89299-6 (trade paperback) |
ISBN: 979-8-89299-023-3 (eBook)
Subjects: BISAC: FICTION/Horror | FICTION/Indigenous | FICTION/Fantasy/
Contemporary
LC record available at: https://lccn.loc.gov/2025935949

Rogue River hardcover trade paperback edition June, 2025

Cover Design by Casey W. Cowan
Interior Design by Natalie Brianne
Editing by Deanna Adams

I'd like to dedicate this book to William Bernhardt, who helped me organize and plot it in one of his extended seminars. And Tim Tingle, who helped me by telling stories where I could hear them.

acknowledgements

I 'D LIKE TO GIVE a special thank you to Bill Bernhardt, who has had an influence in almost all literature that has come out of the Sooner State in the last twenty years. I'd also like to thank Casey Cowan, the beating heart behind the original Oghma Creative Media and the steward of its conversion to Roan & Weatherford Publishing Associates. Casey has more brilliant ideas than belong in a single mind.

author's note

THE PROTAGONIST IN CHEROKEE Ice, Danny Riley, started out as the main character in a short story, "Boy Witch." I wrote that story while I was on a trans-Atlantic cruise in 2010. I liked it, but no more than I liked every story I had written up to that time. When the cruise was over, I submitted it along with two other short stories, to Writers Digest's annual short story competition. I didn't expect to win—there were well over ten thousand entrants—but I thought a high placement might help me sell the story somewhere else.

So, without a second thought I submitted "Boy Witch" to a western anthology Dusty Richards was putting together. I didn't expect it to be accepted there either. The story had Native interest, but it wasn't a traditional western.

Well, Dusty took the story. I was absolutely thrilled about that until while I was at work, my wife received a call from Writers Digest telling her I had won the Grand Prize for the 85th annual competition. She was so excited, she didn't remember the name of the winning story.

Writer's Digest called me a second time later that evening. "Boy Witch" had won. They asked if the story had been published or submitted elsewhere.

"No," I lied, and got on the phone to Dusty Richards as soon as I hung up.

"You caught me just before we were about to send that anthology off the printer," he said. Many publishers in that position would have told me I was out of luck, but Dusty told me to email another story about the same length to him and he'd substitute it. If it hadn't been for his generosity, I doubt I'd ever have written *Cherokee Ice*.

prologue

NELVA RILEY UNFASTENED HER seatbelt and scooted close to Richard Daniels. "Children are a blessing." She gave him her best smile, kissed him on the cheek, and tried to remind him how much he liked her before she told him what he didn't want to know.

Richard kept his eyes on the road and his foot on the gas pedal.

"The Laguna people say family is the most important thing." Nelva sounded so much like her mother. She cleared her throat and tried again.

"The Laguna people say...." Exactly like her mother.

Nelva had been trying to get away from her mother and *her people* as long as she could remember. That was almost impossible in New Mexico, where every Indian wanted to know your tribe, and white people would hardly talk to you.

Richard finally broke his silence. "You were supposed to do something. Pills, a diaphragm, whatever." He sounded mean, not like when he put the baby inside her. Told her he'd love her forever. Gave her a gold wedding band that used to belong to his mother. He promised her, "This ring means it's forever." Didn't say one thing about pills or diaphragms.

He turned north on U.S. 491—onto the Navajo Reservation. He drove past Yah-ta-hey going eighty-five. If he'd been going any slower, Nelva might have jumped out. Maybe she'd do that anyway if he didn't settle down.

"We'll go to Oklahoma," Richard said, not calm, but moving in a calm direction like he'd made his mind up about something but hadn't worked out the details. "You know. To meet my family." He tried to smile but couldn't get it right.

He turned the radio on and flipped through the news and religious programs until he found a country-and-western station.

As soon as Richard's hands were back on the steering wheel, Nelva switched the radio off.

"This ain't the way to Oklahoma." She pointed east, as if he'd forgotten his directions. As if he wasn't making plans for a careless girlfriend and an unwanted baby.

Lots of empty space on the Navajo Rez. Plenty of room for something bad to happen to a sixteen-year-old Laguna girl, who should have known better than to hook up with a man like Richard Daniels.

"Someplace we need to go first." His voice turned flat, like a banker who'd decided Nelva couldn't open a checking account. "Something I have to do."

THEY WERE TWENTY MILES FROM Naschitti when she told him she had to pee.

"That's how it is with pregnant girls," she said. "They have to pee all the time, and if you don't let them, they'll pee all over your front seat."

That was logic an angry boyfriend could understand. Nelva gripped the door handle. As soon as the car stopped, she was out.

Lots of rocks on the shoulder beside U.S. 491, and Nelva picked up a big one before she started running. There were boulders and creosote bushes a hundred feet away. If she made it that far, he'd never catch her. No way Richard Daniels would chase her through the scrub.

Nelva broke left, then right—the way rabbits run from coyotes—so she could look behind her without slowing down. What she saw scared the hell out of her, but it came as no surprise. Richard held a black, square-barreled pistol in both his hands and steadied it on the roof of his car, getting ready to drop his problem like an out-of-season deer.

She turned in a tight circle and headed back toward him, long enough to wind her arm up like a big-league pitcher.

You'll put an eye out. That's what her mother would have told her, and that's exactly what she meant to do. This was how a Laguna girl played hard to get—hard to hurt, hard to kill—when she was in a family way.

Nelva knew her aim was good as soon as the rock left her hand. Just like she'd known she was pregnant when Richard rolled off her and went looking for a cold beer.

Woman's knowledge. Had her mind always been so cluttered with Laguna ideas?

Richard squeezed off a shot before her rock turned his left eye into ketchup. His bullet drew a red line across Nelva's cheek and took away a dime-size piece of her ear.

She didn't stop to think about how much it hurt or how much blood dripped off her chin or what the boys might think of a girl with a funny-looking ear and a scarred face. There'd be time for all that later. After she got away.

Nelva ran through the reservation scrub, where a one-eyed Oklahoma Indian wouldn't follow her. A few more wild gunshots and his bullets were all gone.

Nelva was done with Richard Daniels forever. She stopped running and watched him get into his car. Watched his car get smaller as it headed north toward Gallup and the nearest hospital.

Ten minutes passed, then twenty. Not a single car went by, but Nelva wasn't worried. A Laguna girl is never really stranded in the desert, even in the Navajo Nation. A Laguna girl can always find a ride, even if that girl is pregnant and dirty and her bloody face is not so pretty anymore.

She put her hands over her belly, protecting her baby who was barely there, because "family is the most important thing." That's what the Laguna people say.

1

THE NEW-CAR SMELL HITS Danny Riley in the face the moment he climbs into Sammy Begay's GMC King Cab truck. He's never been inside a vehicle this nice—crack-free, tinted windshield, leather interior, aftermarket radio with a digital clock that says it's 6:01 a.m. Pretty accurate for the reservation.

No music. Maybe Sammy will put on a CD when they come to an understanding, but right now he's got both hands on the steering wheel, and his right foot's doing a little tap dance on the brake pedal. It's Sammy's truck, so Danny starts the conversation.

"It's like this...." He tries to work up to what he has to say—Navajo style—but he's never been any good at that, so he tells Sammy, "I really need to get off the rez. You know?" Blurts it out the way a white man would.

That's no way to bargain with one of the Diné. They like to pace their conversations. Start off with clan relationships, then move on to family. An Indian is nothing without his family, and everybody knows Danny doesn't have one. Except for his mother, of course. Every man in the Western Agency is on a first-name basis with Nelva Riley, but they don't like to talk about her much.

Danny tries to think of friends he and Sammy have in common, but the truth is the only friend he ever had was a timber wolf that didn't belong on the rez any more than he did. Probably best not to bring that up.

"Tried to leave a dozen times, but something always happens." Like when his bus broke down in Tonalea, right on the edge of the Hopi Nation. Or when the tribal cops pulled him off a Greyhound to ask questions about something he might have done a long time ago.

"It's like there's some kind of magic spell keeping me here." Danny puts a fifty-dollar bill into Sammy Begay's hand. Way too much for a trip to the New Mexico side of the rez, but that's what happens when a half-breed Laguna buys a ride from one of the Diné.

Sammy folds the fifty and sticks it in his shirt pocket behind a pack of Camel Filters. Danny's not sure he's got a ride until the engine turns over.

"Ain't nothing magic about tribal cops." Sammy puts the GMC in drive and eases onto the road, slow and easy, like he still might change his mind.

"Cops have yellow notepads. They write things down—things you did and things they only think you did."

Like the sack full of money Danny took from a Circle K—allegedly, as they say on TV—and a couple of minor drug transactions and Nathan Balance's unfortunate accident.

Danny's famous around the Western Agency, even though no such person as Danny Riley officially exists. His name isn't on any government paper, except for a couple of police reports. No birth certificate. No Social Security number. No listing on any tribal roles. Nothing that would give him any rights. "Think we could listen to some music?" He reaches for the radio but stops, his hand an inch from the knob because Sammy Begay could still kick him out of the truck if he wanted to.

"Rather listen to the quiet," Sammy says. A typical Diné answer. He uses his automatic controls to roll the windows down.

Danny doesn't complain loud enough for Sammy to hear him over the wind. He's got two good reasons for getting off the rez today—Ed and William Balance. Hitchhiking is no good when the Balance brothers are looking for you. Busses are no good when it's the cops. He's hoping the Sammy Begay Express will take him as far as the great state of New Mexico, where nobody's heard of Danny Riley yet. From there, who knows?

SAMMY TAKES THE BACK ROADS. Danny figures that's because he has legal troubles of his own.

"Surprised you stuck around this long." Sammy's got his elbow out the driver's window, steering around chuckholes he's memorized from driving across the desert in the dark. A Navajo would never do that unless he had a good reason.

This is one of those Indian Country roads that hasn't earned a name. Two ruts wind around boulders and washouts across the edge of Chaco Canyon National Park, where people aren't supposed to go but no one stops them if they do.

"How come we didn't go through Gallup?" The back roads there are paved, some of them anyway. They could go fast enough to roll up the windows and turn on the air conditioner. Danny's tired of breathing dust, and he's tired of looking into the morning sun. It's 8:03 a.m., according to the digital clock on the radio Sammy won't turn on. Digital Indian time.

The Diné like to get an early start. First thing after sunrise, if they can, so there's plenty of time to get back home before the reservation ghosts come out. The *chindi*—spirits made of things too bad for a man's soul to carry all the way to heaven.

Chindi come out when the sun goes down. So does Danny Riley. He likes to walk under the moon and the stars and listen to coyotes sing. That's another reason Navajo don't trust him.

Danny puts his hand over his heart, the way people do when they've got indigestion. He pats his chest like he's trying to loosen a gas bubble, so Sammy won't notice the bulge underneath his shirt—his good luck charm. It's a thin leather bag made of the skin of a red-tailed hawk. Danny killed the bird with a slingshot and cured the hide himself. Inside the bag are little pieces of his history—a wedding ring his father gave to Nelva before he disappeared, the canine tooth of the timber wolf that wasn't wanted on the rez any more than Danny, an empty cartridge with a fingerprint cooked into the brass. According to Nelva, Danny's father tried to kill her with that bullet.

The leather on his good luck bag is thin enough he can feel the sharp edge where the slug used to be. He can feel the indentation in the primer. He can't feel the fingerprint, but he knows it's there. According to Nelva, that's the only thing his father touched that didn't leave a bruise.

Sammy asks, "You ain't gonna get car sick, are you?"

Danny pats his chest again. A pretend belch is his only answer. Easier to keep quiet than explain.

EVERYBODY KNOWS DANNY RILEY DOESN'T belong on the rez. Everybody knows he can't be trusted, and a lot of people—the Balance brothers, in particular—think he's some kind of witch. That's the reason Danny doesn't say anything about the dust devil that crosses the road in front of Sammy Begay's pickup truck.

"That's a counterclockwise devil, ain't it?" Sammy stops and lets it by. He crosses himself, even though he's not Catholic, because every Navajo knows counterclockwise dust devils are bad luck. Men like Sammy use signs and rituals to help them get over being afraid of things they don't understand. And men like Sammy don't understand much of anything.

"Never really thought you was a witch," he says. "Not a Skin Walker, or a Two-Heart. No kind of witch at all."

"Even after everybody blamed you for Nathan Balance." Sammy crosses himself again. The Diné can't lie worth a damn.

"Diabetes killed Nathan Balance." Danny had something to do with it too. So did whiskey, and fast food, and Danny's mother, Nelva. "Chased me into the desert," he tells Sammy, even though everybody in the Western Agency knows the story. "Took his insulin. Didn't eat breakfast." Danny watches the whirlwind draw circles in the dust and disappear.

"I think that one was a good luck whirlwind." He locks eyes with Sammy Begay, like a dog that's trying to be boss.

Sammy looks away. He crosses himself again. "A pure and simple accident," he says. "Like Nelva told Nathan's brothers."

Nobody thought Danny's mother was a witch, just a pretty Laguna girl who never learned to say no, even to a man like Nathan Balance, who'd rather die than leave her boy alone.

Sammy takes off easy so he won't dig himself into the sand. He's been coming around to Nelva's trailer off and on for a couple of months. Not her boyfriend yet, but heading there. Sharing six packs, acting friendly, the way they all do in the beginning. Sammy figures she'll be more fun if Danny's off the rez—and she's already a lot of fun.

Nelva Riley has a way with men, but she likes the bad ones best. Married ones, drunk ones, men like Sammy Begay, who know every back road on the rez because they transport dope across the checkerboard of tribal lands that straddle New Mexico and Arizona, where nobody's sure of jurisdiction.

"Just like Nelva said." Sammy pats his shirt pocket to remind himself of the full pack of cigarettes and the fifty-dollar bill.

Danny realizes Sammy would have given him a ride for nothing, just to get him out of Nelva's trailer. He tries to think of some way to get his money back, but he doesn't get past the first word.

"Sammy—"

A white horse comes out of nowhere and trots beside Danny's open window. It glides across the hardpan without effort—high, fancy steps like horses in military parades. Its hide is brilliant white, dappled with grey spots like the ones that paint a face on the full moon. The horse passes Sammy's truck as he steers around a group of pig-sized boulders that don't have any logical reason to be there. It stops behind the rocks and looks at Danny, the way Danny looked at Sammy a few minutes ago to see if he was telling the truth. It bolts toward a mesa that looms ahead of them about a quarter mile away and disappears into a perfect vertical break in the volcanic rock.

"Well, would you look at that?" From the front seat of Sammy's truck, the space where the horse disappeared looks like a solid pillar of light supporting the morning sun.

Sammy says, "That's got to be a sign." He revs his engine and starts his tires spinning. He ignores the digital clock on his radio and looks at his watch, which has said ten o'clock ever since the batteries ran down.

He guns the truck again and digs in a little deeper. The rifle on the gun rack across his rear window shakes loose and bounces off the back seat onto the floor.

"This whole damn park's infested with Pueblo ghosts." He tells Danny to get out and push.

"Sure thing, Sammy." Danny reaches over the back of the front seat and grabs the rifle. "Never can be too careful, what with counterclockwise dust devils and mystery horses." It's a Winchester .44-40 with lever action, the gun cowboys used to take land away from the Indians. Perfect.

Danny puts his shoulder against the tailgate and rocks the truck, while Sammy tries to roll onto solid ground. As soon as the tires take hold, the truck picks up speed and pulls away, toward the break in the mesa where the horse disappeared.

Maybe it *was* a sign.

Sammy Begay might drive off and leave Nelva's boy-witch son in the desert, but there's no way he'd leave him with a perfectly good rifle unless he was sure he was going to get it back.

That means trouble for Danny Riley. Balance brothers trouble.

He aims the Winchester at Sammy's right rear tire. The first shot sends the truck into a skid. One more shot and a front tire goes flat.

Sammy hops out of the truck and runs toward the sun. A perfect black human silhouette, like targets on firing ranges where law-abiding white men learn to shoot fleeing felons in the back.

Danny considers the possibilities, but he's no murderer—even if he did kill Nathan Balance indirectly. He thinks about it long enough for Sammy Begay to get past his range of accuracy. Geronimo would have taken Sammy's life. So would Cochise and Victorio and Chato. All Apache. He takes a minute to see if he can remember any Laguna warriors.

None. Danny figures he has just enough Laguna blood to keep his finger off the trigger.

An old pickup truck drives out of the split in the mesa where the horse disappeared. A Ford F350 with dual rear wheels. Danny knows that truck. The Balance brothers, out on witch-killing business. It isn't the first time they've come after him, but it's the first time they've recruited help from one of Nelva's would-be boyfriends.

He kneels on the hardpan, eases his weight onto one knee, and uses the other as a rest for his elbow. Long-distance shooting—a hundred yards—closing at a rate of four yards a second. Easy to miss a moving target. More difficult than hiding in a blind and shooting an unsuspecting whitetail that doesn't know what's coming, especially when the shooter is being careful not to kill.

The Balance brothers weave around the double ruts that are as close as anything comes to a road in this part of the rez. The old shock absorbers bounce and shudder, slam the body of the truck onto the frame, and send the front wheels skittering. They could get killed if Danny's shot goes high—one of them, at least. Would he stop with one? Would it be so bad to leave his troubles for park rangers and FBI agents to sort out?

Laguna warriors think too much. He takes aim, holds his breath, and squeezes the trigger, anticipating the recoil so he won't flinch because even an inch of rise could send his bullet into the windshield instead of the radiator.

Nothing happens for a count of four. Then a little steam drifts through the seam between the right front fender and the hood.

Two more shots in quick succession. Danny thinks this Winchester holds nine bullets, but he can't be sure.

The truck hitches to a stop. Two Balance brothers roll out the way they've seen gangsters do on television. One has a black boxy-looking semiautomatic pistol—useless at this distance. He starts firing it immediately. The other has some kind of AK 47 clone—a witch-killing weapon, probably picked up at a gun show in Arizona.

Danny's never been too good at math, but he knows how to count bullets. Sammy Begay's rifle has four shots left, presuming he was right about there being nine to begin with. Nowhere near enough for a full-fledged gunfight. The Balance brothers aren't too smart—especially Ed—but they'll figure it out if he gives them time to think.

Danny starts walking backward away from the disabled trucks, firing a shot whenever a Balance brother shows himself. Danny's a good runner, especially when two men are chasing him with guns, but he wants plenty of lead. His head start is one hundred fifty yards so far, and growing. An AK can easily kill a man at that distance, but it usually doesn't when the shooter has nervous hands and a slow mind.

The pistol-wielding Balance brother steps out of cover long enough to empty his weapon. Brass cartridges sparkle in the sun like a stream of urine. He's a left-handed shooter, so a couple of hot empties hit him in the face and tumble into his shirt. He does a little dance that reminds Danny of a Hopi rain ceremony.

The pistol locks open, the way semis do when they are out of bullets, but the Balance brother keeps pulling the trigger.

It must be Ed.

Danny sends a bullet toward the truck. Doesn't really aim. He doesn't take cover—not that there is much cover in this part of the desert—even when the AK gets into the action. He waves his empty rifle in the air, the way Geronimo used to do. A defiant act of bravery to impress any warrior spirits who might be watching.

AK clones aren't all that accurate and William Balance is afraid of the noise and the recoil, so his shots are all wild misses. No worries for a boy who is regularly shot at by his mother's boyfriends at much closer range.

He points the empty rifle toward the truck, and William Balance dives into the dirt. Danny watches him scoot backward, pretending to be paper thin, pretending his butt isn't poking into the air. Geronimo would have saved a bullet for William Balance's ass.

Danny pulls the trigger and says, "Bang." No harm done. He probably would have missed anyway, but the image of William Balance with a bloody ass calls for a war cry.

It's a manly yell. A yell that would scare the hell out of Danny if it came from a Balance brother. It bounces off the mesa and comes back at him, as if he has spirit allies behind his enemies.

They huddle behind their ruined truck with Sammy Begay, talking about crooked spirits, Navajo Skin Walkers, and Pueblo Two-Heart witches. The wind brings enough of their conversation Danny's way, so he knows they think magic is afoot. They think he's tricked them into the desert instead of the other way around. Sometimes the desert wind chooses sides. Secret plans, bits and pieces of conversations are carried to ears that weren't meant to hear them, and other sounds too. Sounds that can't be explained, like the sound of the beating hearts of three cowardly conspirators hiding behind a ruined pickup truck. Danny's eyes stay locked on the truck, waiting for the Balance brothers to realize he's out of ammunition, but his ears reach out and grab the heart sounds that are growing louder with each passing second.

Too loud for a human heart, or even three human hearts beating like war drums. When Danny looks up from his enemy's hiding place, he sees the white horse from before, galloping toward him, kicking up dust like a bad luck whirlwind. The Balance brothers and Sammy Begay stand up to watch the horse speed past them. It makes a circle around Danny Riley and stops beside him.

Danny's never ridden a horse, but it doesn't look too hard on television. The animal doesn't move away when he throws his leg over its back and presses his knees against its sides.

He holds the horse's mane with one hand and the empty rifle with the other.

"Giddy up!"

It must be the wrong thing to say because the horse bolts toward the truck—toward the Balance brothers who have stepped from behind their cover. Ed is trying to change the clip in his pistol and William is taking aim with his clone AK.

William squeezes off a shot that whizzes past Danny's ear, but the horse charges straight ahead—between the Balance brothers.

Danny swings Sammy Begay's empty rifle as the horse makes an impossible turn. The barrel catches William's chin, hard enough to send a jolt all the way to Danny's shoulder.

The horse circles and rides back toward the brothers. Close enough for Danny to smack Ed with the rifle this time around, counting coup, the way the Plains Indians did in *Cheyenne Autumn*.

The horse rears up and holds steady long enough for Danny to let out another war cry. It's not so manly this time, more like a little girl who's been frightened by a spider, but the Balance boys are unconscious, and Sammy Begay looks impressed.

Danny wants to get off the horse and demand his fifty dollars back, but the horse has other ideas. It charges due west, only it doesn't follow a pair of ruts made by Diné poachers and drug mules. It races across the desert over gullies and washouts, around boulders and mesquite. Danny's legs strain against the animal's sides like a ring of cramped muscle. Too hot and painful to hold on, but the horse is moving too fast to let go, and the desert is looking less friendly as counter clockwise dust devils sweep the path clear in front of him.

Maybe the Balance brothers have been right all along. Maybe Danny Riley is a witch. That's the last thought Danny has before he can't hold on any longer. He lands with a thump hard enough to shake the world. He bounces once and skids until he stops under an acacia bush. The kind with thorns, but Danny's lucky, and nothing sticks him. He lies there long enough to decide whether bones are broken, whether any internal organs have exploded, whether he's so hopelessly lost he'll wander the desert until the night falls and the *chindi* come for him. Ghosts seem a lot more real after a white horse gallops out of the desert and saves your life—then leaves you for dead.

"Hey there." A woman's voice—young, not friendly or unfriendly— just a woman's voice wanting to know what the hell Danny's doing under an acacia bush, but she's too polite to ask right off.

"I'm Claudia Tso." She moves around so Danny can see her. Young, pretty, long black hair in a single braid, a Lakota style that's taken hold on the Navajo rez in recent years.

"Slow Talking Clan," she goes on with the introduction the way any well-bred Diné girl would before asking whether Danny is some kind of criminal who's come around to take... what?

He crawls out from under the acacia, picking up only a few thorn sticks to add to his scrapes and bruises. The girl is looking at his rifle.

"Empty," Danny Riley tells her. "Unloaded, you know? My name's Danny Riley." It's always nice to have a clan name ready for a Big Rez introduction, but what's a half-breed Laguna boy to do?

"So why are you under a cat's claw bush with an empty rifle?"

"I'm Laguna," he tells her, as if that explains everything. And maybe it does because there's a traditional hogan right behind Claudia Tso that Danny hasn't noticed until now, and Papa Tso isn't charging out, armed to the teeth, demanding Danny Riley get off his land.

"Looking for a way back home," Danny says. "Out in the Western Agency. Close to Tuba City. Trade you this rifle for a ride."

That's the cue for Claudia's father to come out. He takes the rifle from Danny. He examines the barrel for scratches, jacks the lever, and runs a hand over the stock. Satisfied with the deal, he carries the rifle into the hogan. It takes him at least five minutes to return.

Claudia and Danny Riley stand in silence, looking everywhere but at each other until her father joins them. Then all three stand quietly together long enough to satisfy the requirements of a culture that's gotten rigid over the last thousand years.

There's no point in trying to rush a Navajo. Danny pretends his scrapes and bruises aren't killing him. He pretends it's the most natural thing in the world to stand around looking at rocks after he's traded his rifle for a trip back to his mother's trailer.

After the appropriate number of polite minutes have passed,

Claudia's dad says. "I'm Charley Tso." No clan name is necessary for a Laguna. "Truck's over the rise." He points and starts walking.

As they crest the hill, Danny sees the white horse beside Charley Tso's rusty green pickup truck. The horse is grazing on a plant so dry and brown it doesn't look like it would keep anything alive.

Danny asks, "That animal belong to you?"

"Nope." Charley Tso climbs into the truck, leans over, and opens the passenger door.

"Get in," he says. "Want to get back here before dark."

2

CHARLEY TSO ONLY ASKS for directions once, which makes Danny wonder if the old Navajo has made the trip before. He doesn't look familiar, but there have been so many men over the years.

Charley stops a respectful twenty yards from the front door and waits for Danny to get out. He doesn't respond when Danny thanks him for the ride. Doesn't wait to see what happens when the trailer door opens. Doesn't turn his head to watch Danny get smaller as he drives back to the Eastern Agency. Charley Tso has no interest in Laguna business. Danny will never figure these people out, and they're the only kind of people he's ever met.

There are no trucks parked anywhere around Nelva's trailer, but Danny knocks on the door anyway before he goes inside. He calls out, "*Ya'ah'tee,*" the only Diné greeting he knows, and a large percentage of his Navajo vocabulary.

Nelva throws her arms around him as soon as he steps inside. "Somebody you've gotta meet." She gestures to the African American man sitting on the couch in front of the television set that's not turned on. He's dividing his attention between the blank screen and his iPhone.

"You're gonna love him, Danny," Nelva says. He can tell she already does.

This is the first black man Danny Riley has ever seen who wasn't on TV or inside a car driving by at sixty miles an hour or filling up his gas tank at a Circle K. His first up-close African American. Danny has heard they can be sensitive, so he decides to practice his Indian ways and not say anything to this stranger until he figures things out.

"John Horse," Nelva says. "He's a Black Seminole from Oklahoma."

"Black Seminole?" Already Danny's lost track of his Indian ways. He's heard of Black Seminole. Buffalo soldiers from the Wild West days. They helped the U.S. Army take away Indian land. One more reason nobody on the rez likes Oklahoma Indians.

John Horse rises from his seat carefully, as if he's balanced on a narrow ledge. He runs his fingers over his black man's hair and shows Danny his black man's smile—exactly like on television, down to the space between his two front teeth. John Horse's skin is the color of the Bisti boys' rugby ball that Danny never got to play with. John Horse's face is rugby leather, right down to seams and cracks and rough patches.

"Pleased to meet you." Danny extends a hand and expects the Black Seminole to lead him through some African handshake calisthenics.

John Horse doesn't take his hand. He takes a step back instead, smiles a little wider, and exhales a heavy breath laced with something that smells like lighter fluid. He looks suspicious and humorous at the same time, the way a man looks when he thinks someone's setting him up for a surprise birthday party.

"This here is my son, Danny," Nelva says. "He's never met an Okla-homa Indian before, even though his daddy was one."

"Cherokee." Nelva makes a face. "You know—Cherokee."

John Horse looks Danny up and down, filling the space between them with so much lighter fluid vapor Danny is afraid the air will catch on fire.

"Pleased to meet you." Louder this time, in case Oklahoma Indians are hard of hearing. Danny sticks his hand out a little farther, as if Nelva's new boyfriend might not have seen it yet.

John Horse stares at him—not like any Indian Danny has ever met. One of his eyes is the color of blue turquoise and the other is brown with scattered golden flecks. The irises are thin hoops around oversized pupils that reflect Danny's face like funhouse mirrors.

"Better not shake hands right now," John Horse says. "The touch is coming on pretty strong."

"John's a holy man," Nelva says. She leads Danny into the kitchen and shows him a mound of shredded plant stems soaking in a bowl of liquid that smells like John Horse's breath.

"Cat's claw acacia," Nelva tells him. "Grows on the rez. John collects it. Turns it into visions."

"Ain't the plants," John Horse walks up behind them. Careful not to touch Danny. Not so careful around Nelva.

"It's the ants that does it. The ones that live inside acacia stems." He reaches into the bowl and stirs the shreds with his fingers so Danny can see the dead ants floating to the top. John Horse nets the ants in a metal tea strainer, picks them off, pops them into his mouth, and grinds them with his back teeth.

"Drown them in Red Devil lighter fluid," John Horse says. "My insides turn them into visions."

"Some kind of drug?" Danny knows all about the Native American church and how they use peyote. He also knows about methamphetamine. This doesn't look like either one.

"Starting to reach its full potential." John Horse's pupils have swallowed the unusual color of his eyes. Beads of sweat form on his face like condensation droplets on a cold can of beer.

Nelva kisses him on the lips, holding it long enough to make Danny uncomfortable.

"Black Seminoles are the only Oklahoma Indians worth a damn," she says. Her voice is louder than usual, and her speech is a little slurred.

John Horse walks her to the couch and plumps a pillow for her back.

He says, "You'll get the picture—Danny, ain't it?—when the hippies start coming around."

"Rumor brings them." He looks at the place on his wrist where his watch would be if he wore a watch. "Rumors travel quick on the Big Rez." He does something to the front of his iPhone. "'Specially when you start 'em on the Internet."

There's a knock on the front door. Two white women and a Native American man are there when John Horse opens it. The man gives him three twenty-dollar bills. John draws a finger across his own sweaty brow and prints a moist X on the Indian man's forehead. He does the same for the two women.

"Fifteen minutes for a forehead touch," he tells the visitors. "Don't be driving when it hits." He asks Danny, "Ever been to Tahlequah?"

The three visitors stumble away like sleepwalkers, like fifteen minutes went by already.

"What kind of dope is this?" Danny points to the mound of plant shreds and insects floating in the lighter fluid.

"Ain't no kind of dope until it runs through John Horse," The Black Seminole opens the door again and trades perspiration X's for twenty-dollar bills with four white people.

"They always know where John Horse is selling touches." He answers the question before Danny Riley has a chance to ask it. "Don't suppose you ever met Wilma Daniels?"

"What's it do to them?" Danny wants to know. "The touch, I mean."

"Different every time," John Horse says. "How 'bout Tommy Bracken? Ever heard of him?"

"Don't you just love John Horse?" Nelva slides off the couch and sits on the floor. She crosses her legs yoga style.

"He don't yet, but he's gonna," John Horse says. "Ever been to Oklahoma City?"

"Never been off the rez," Danny says.

John Horse tells him, "I was you, I'd go to Oklahoma. There's something special waiting for you there."

The Black Seminole answers a question he sees on Danny's face. "Special in a family way. You'll figure it out if you ever get there."

Danny glances at Nelva to see if she's going to object. She usually does. Any time he talks about leaving the rez. Any time someone mentions his Oklahoma connection. But she's caught up in her vision. Remembering things that never happened. Talking to people who aren't there.

"Family has its own peculiar magic," John Horse shifts his smile into high gear. "That ain't the ants talking either."

Nelva interrupts the discussion with a revival song she heard on one of the preacher shows she watches Sunday mornings. High volume. Plenty of vibrato. She stares at the ceiling of the mobile home like she's looking at the face of God.

"That kind of thing is pretty normal," John Horse tells Danny. "Sometimes people sing when the ant magic gets in them. Sometimes they dance. Sometimes they fall in love." He starts to put a hand on Danny's shoulder but pulls back before it's too late.

Chapter 3

TOMMY BRACKEN SITS IN the front seat of his 1965 classic, lemon-yellow Mustang and practices his double Ls and Rs.

"*Tengo un carro de color amarillo.*" I have a yellow car. He smiles at his reflection in the rearview mirror. It's dark inside the parking garage. The dim illumination deepens his complexion. That won't last once he's in full sunlight, but for now, it's reassuring. Tommy's skin will turn a lighter shade outside the garage, but his expression will become more humble. So humble, no one will suspect he has murder on his mind.

"*Venganza.*" Revenge—His undocumented immigrant smile blossoms into a snarl.

That will never do. Tommy takes a deep cleansing breath and imagines a wave of relaxation starting at the top of his head. It sinks like the mercury in a thermometer on a cold December day until every bit of rage pools in the soles of his feet. It won't leave him completely. Without it he wouldn't be Tommy Bracken. People wouldn't be afraid of him. And when people aren't afraid, bad things happen.

Bad things used to happen to Tommy Bracken all the time. Not anymore. Nobody's done bad things to Tommy since....

"*Descanza en paz, madre.*" Rest in peace, mother.

He feels tears pushing up behind his eyes. Missing her, the way a man misses an extracted tooth that made him miserable for days. The pressure will give Tommy Bracken a focal point. Somewhere he can put his doubts, the way his mother put him inside the punishment box at the foot of her bed to remind him how things were.

Today, he will remind the Oklahoma City Police how things are. He feels the tension in his shoulders slip into his arms and dribble off his fingers.

He slumps into the posture of someone who stands out because he desperately wants to blend in. Someone who has worked too long for too little and sees small problems growing large on the horizon. His smile isn't scary anymore. It's convincing enough to get him reported to *inmigración* by concerned citizens who want people like *Señor* Tommy Bracken to cut their grass and get out of the U.S.A. when the bill comes due.

Humble, fearful—the transformation isn't perfect, but it's close enough.

"*Es lo mas parecido al rock-and-rol.*" Close enough for rock and roll.

Spanish is an aerobic language. The words are difficult for Tommy to twist his Irish-Oklahoman tongue around, especially with a modified tuberculin syringe hidden in the fold between his molars and his cheek like a pinch of Skoal.

The needle cap wobbles on the tip when he stretches his mouth around Castilian vowels. He should have shortened the syringe more, but now it's too late. He'll have to suffer the consequences the way he did when his mother was alive.

"*Consecuencias.*" The OKC police will be suffering the consequences soon. Tommy has a special consequence for Detective Lalo Rivas.

"*Ahí voy*, Lalo." I'm coming, Lalo. Tommy puts his hand on his cheek and resists the temptation to secure the needle cap on the shortened tuberculin syringe. He needs to keep it loose, the way he needs to keep his posture loose, like a man who is too tired to run. Too exhausted to be dangerous. Someone who could be ignored if he didn't have to be arrested.

Tommy walks out of the parking garage in the center of Oklahoma City, across the street from the Oklahoma County Court House, where numerous warrants have been recorded authorizing his arrest on complaints of murder, drug manufacturing, and racketeering.

Detective Lalo Rivas's name is on many of them.

Tommy thinks of Lalo's warrants as suicide notes. Only a dozen people in the world know Tommy Bracken on sight. Today, Lalo Rivas will be one of them. For a short time.

THE POLICE STATION LIES HALFWAY between the Oklahoma City Metropolitan Art Museum and the county jail. An architectural barrier between OKC cultural extremes. Lalo Rivas's office is on the second floor. A private room, where he can conduct interviews that don't look like interrogations. Set aside from the rest of the detectives because of the progress he's made on the Cherokee Ice that Tommy Bracken has spread over the state of Oklahoma like a plague of locusts.

Drug labs closed. Distributors arrested. Cooks chased out of state. Snitches paid embarrassingly small sums of money to put Tommy Bracken's head on Lalo Rivas's platter. As if it would be so easy.

There are no policemen on the streets. A cruiser here, an unmarked car there. Obvious and unoccupied. Where are the cops when you need them?

A white cop is what Tommy needs today. Black or Native American will do in a pinch. His Spanish isn't authentic enough to convince a native speaker. He should be safe. There aren't many Hispanic cops in OKC, and most of them will be on the southeast side of town rounding up stray Juaritos gangsters or out on I-35 intercepting drug shipments from Sinaloa. Eliminating Tommy's competition—like there is any real competition for Cherokee Ice.

Once Lalo is out of the way, and Tommy gets his Cherokee Ice production back online, his superior product will sweep the competition like a Kirby vacuum cleaner. First, he needs to get himself arrested.

It should be easy. Nobody could look more suspicious than Tommy Bracken, walking past the expensive condos built around the center of town since the Oklahoma City bombing. The police station occupies expensive real estate now. How long will it be until an entrepreneur with political clout moves it to a part of town where crime still wears blue-collared shirts?

Tommy checks the condos out the way a hungry man looks at cakes behind a bakery store window. He's put a rock in his left shoe, so he limps without giving it a thought. A limping, impoverished foreigner in a rich white neighborhood is low-hanging fruit for a cop, but no one comes for him.

It's a sure sign of sensitivity training. Probable cause is usually something reserved for the privileged class, and when it's not, the reason is usually litigation.

"*Abogados malditos!*" Goddamned lawyers! Tommy says it loud enough to attract attention but still no uniforms appear.

He stops in front of the Oklahoma City Museum of Art, where the tallest blown glass sculpture in the world grows behind a three-story wall of windows like a hothouse plant. The people behind the ticket counter show him uncertain smiles when he walks into the lobby.

"How may we help you, sir?" A male voice speaks to Tommy's back. There are two ticket clerks—a man and a woman—so it's not exactly the royal we. The woman is on the phone, probably calling security. Probably telling them to get rid of the scruffy Mexican in the lobby without making the museum look anti-Hispanic. Telling them to do it quickly because the immigrant's hand is reaching toward the sculpture as she speaks.

Tommy points his index finger the way Adam extends his finger to God on the ceiling of the Sistine Chapel. He wonders if the ticket clerks recognize the symbolism. It would make a nice detail on the incident reports they'll have to write.

He reaches over a narrow reflecting pool that makes the sculpture appear even taller than it is and brushes his fingertip across a piece of blown glass that looks like a bright yellow dead goose tangled in a pile of summer squash. How can that be pretty? But it is.

"Step away from the sculpture, sir."

The glass is coated with a fine layer of dust that was invisible until Tommy drew a line across it.

He turns away from the sculpture and teeters for a moment, like he might be about to fall into the glass column.

It's a real cop. Not a security guard. He has his hand on the butt of his pistol. Tommy sees him coming to an understanding about the velocity and mass of bullets, the stopping power of an undocumented Mexican body, and the cost of the world's largest glass sculpture.

"*Soy* Don Quixote." Tommy smiles at the white cop, who doesn't look like a student of the classics. He raises his hands halfway between a shrug and outright surrender.

"Step away from the sculpture, Don. Nice and slow." The cop points his free hand in the general direction of the ticket counter, while his other hand unsnaps the strap that secures his sidearm in its holster.

The female ticket clerk says, "*Despacio.* That means slowly. I took Spanish in high school." She smiles as if she has no part in this thing anymore. Like a good citizen who called animal control on the stray dog in her neighborhood and just realized what happens in the pound.

"*Aqui, señor.*" She taps an index finger on the counter that, until now, has protected her from the foreign intruder but will become his refuge.

Tommy smiles and walks to the counter. He places his hands on it in a way that suggests he's been arrested in city art museums before.

The cop handcuffs him. Conducts a short body pat down that does not discover the handcuff key taped to his left forearm and does not include a search of even the most G-rated body cavities. He finds a wallet in Tommy's back pocket. Two hundred dollars cash. No driver's license, but there is a business card. An OKC detective's card.

"Detective Lalo Rivas," The cop reads the name aloud. He flips the card over and reads a name written on the back in neat Catholic School Palmer longhand. "Tommy Bracken."

"You got information about Tommy Bracken?" The policeman's words come out slow and loud. Easy for a Spanish speaker's brain to process.

"*Le conozco bien.*" Tommy shows the female ticket clerk a smile that is far too well-maintained for an undocumented immigrant.

"He says he knows him well." She looks into Tommy Bracken's eyes, hoping to bond with her first illegal. Two people, equal in every way except that one of them is handcuffed.

"*Gracias,*" he tells her, exactly like they said he would in Putnam City Central, Spanish I.

"*De nada,*" she answers, smiling at the thought of a high school education that wasn't a total waste of time.

TOMMY RELISHES THE FEEL OF the handcuffs double locked around his wrists.

"You're not under arrest." The cop sits him in a cheaply upholstered chair in a room full of handcuffed people who are also not under arrest. He shows Tommy a laminated card with Miranda rights written on one side in English and the other side in Spanish.

"*No puedo leer.*" Tommy knows the cop doesn't understand his declaration of illiteracy, but when he tells him, "*Necesito ver a* Lalo Rivas," the message is received loud and clear.

"Wait here." He leaves Tommy sitting in the large intake room without looping his handcuffs through the chair back. A vote of confidence. He disappears up a stairwell beside an elevator that's being loaded with people who are under arrest.

Tommy touches the key taped to his wrist, reassuring himself he can unlock his cuffs any time he chooses. He learned that trick, the same way he learned everything useful to his criminal enterprise—from Mom.

DISCIPLINE WAS THE THEME OF their relationship. It varied from a spanking to a beating to being tied or cuffed and locked inside a box too small for Tommy to stretch out to full length. She eased him into a tolerance of small spaces without intending to. Tommy was a growing boy, and the box was always the same size.

By the time he was ten years old, he could slip out of most knots, pick a set of handcuffs with a paperclip, and open the punishment box's simple lock from the inside in total darkness. Escape was a matter of survival because sometimes Mom forgot she had a son locked inside the chest she kept at the foot of her bed.

It started as a hope chest. She told Tommy all about it one day in a rare period of remorse. Young women kept wooden chests like hers in days gone by, collecting things they'd need when they were happily married. When Mom lost hope, the chest became something else.

But it still contained a vestige of hope. When she put Tommy in the box, it meant the beating was over. The temperature of her anger lowered to a simmer. The box was uncomfortable but safe. A refuge from her fury.

Handcuffs and plastic cinches gave him a feeling of security too. His hands pressed together in an upside-down backward prayer—perfect when the supplicant knew better than to pray for mercy. Restraints meant his mother no longer had to worry he would escape. Benevolence replaced her rage after a while. Her lips kissed him instead of scolding. Her hands caressed him instead of slapping.

The pain of the restraints was comforting, even sensual. It was a perspective on relationships most people would never understand. Beatings were like foreplay—satisfying in a way Tommy didn't care to understand—and the box was the most complete consummation ever.

The only problem was the spiders. Brown recluses liked the inside of the punishment box. The bites were painful—so Tommy had heard—

potentially deadly, and Mom didn't believe in doctors. He checked the box every day when he was a boy. Sprayed it when he could because he never knew when Mom would have one of her anger spells.

TOMMY LOOKS UNDER HIS CHAIR to make certain no spiders have followed him into the OKC Police intake room. He knows it's a phobia, but that doesn't change the way spiders make him feel. The fear is sensual in a way. Not as sensual as restraints, or slaps, but still... Spiders are the only thing Tommy really fears anymore. Spiders make him remember how sweet it felt to be locked inside a wooden box by a woman who had the power of life and death. Not the only woman he ever loved, but the only woman who ever really loved him—in her own unusual way.

The cop says, "Lalo wants to see you. Better have something to tell him, Don. Lalo speaks perfect Mexican."

"*Estoy listo.*" I am ready. Tommy stands slowly as if arthritis has robbed him of the potential of escape. His limp is exaggerated because the rock in his shoe has moved underneath his heel. By the time they reach the top of the stairs the policeman is convinced his prisoner is a harmless man. He ushers Tommy into Lalo Rivas's office and stands at the doorway.

"*Buenos días,*" Rivas says.

Lalo's Armani suit is wrinkle-free. His black hair is parted in a line so straight and clean it might have been cut with a razor. He wears a pencil-thin mustache more suited to David Niven than Emiliano Zapata, but his skin is the beautiful bronze color of Sonoran Mexico and his voice resonates with authority.

"*Buenos días.*" Still morning, a lucky break for Tommy. The *R* in *buenas tardes* would have pegged him as a fake. Lalo Rivas is the real thing. No second-generation Mexican American who knows enough Spanish to impress the EOC.

"Says his name is Don Quixote," the cop behind Tommy Bracken says. "He one of your confidential informants?"

Lalo Rivas smiles at the alias. He watches Tommy Bracken for any sign he understands English. "*Conoce a* Tommy Bracken?"

"*Quiero susurrar algo.*" I want to whisper something. Tommy's double Rs feel clumsy. Lalo sits up straighter in his chair.

"He's going to come around to my side of the desk," Lalo Rivas tells the officer. "Watch him. His Spanish sounds a little off."

The cop checks Tommy's cuffs again. "Secure." Gives him a little push in Lalo Rivas's direction.

Tommy stumbles forward and watches Lalo Rivas watching him. Still suspicious but the detective shows no signs of fear. Tommy stands beside Rivas, casting a nervous glance at the cop who brought him here.

"Okay, *amigo, dígame.*" Lalo turns his head so Tommy can pass his secrets across the inches that separate them.

It takes Tommy Bracken less than one second to remove the cap over the needle of his modified syringe with his tongue. A few drops of phencyclidine mix with his saliva. That could be bad. This is a concentrated mix of the powerful dissociative anesthetic. Undissolved granules float in the tap water Tommy used to cook the suspension earlier this morning. He'll have to take care of things fast before the drug passes through his digestive system and makes his senses unreliable.

He holds the short syringe between his incisors so the needle protrudes enough for the cop at Lalo's door to see it—if he looks. Tommy distracts him by wiggling his fingers behind his back. The movement is much more interesting than a twenty-five gauge needle that almost blends in with scratches on the wall behind Lalo.

Tommy plunges the needle into the detective's jugular vein, then pushes the plunger with his tongue. The phencyclidine solution sets fire to Lalo's brain while the solid particles lodge in capillaries and cause miniature strokes. They dissolve in turn like chain reaction improvised explosive devices.

"*El Diablo!*" These are the last two words Detective Lalo Rivas says before the drug freezes his body in place and lets his mind run wild.

Tommy spits the syringe onto the floor. "I think it's a heart attack," he says in perfect English.

His arresting officer doesn't notice. He races to Lalo Rivas's side.

"You okay?" he says even though it is very clear Lalo Rivas is not. He takes the detective's carotid pulse without the slightest idea what he'll do with the information.

"What...?" All the cop's attention is focused on the tiny drops of blood on his fingertips.

He rubs the blood between his fingers and looks for its source on Lalo's neck while Tommy Bracken unlocks his handcuffs and finds a large glass paperweight on the detective's desk. He hesitates a moment because there's a Tarantula frozen inside the transparent sphere.

Scary, but Tommy brings the tarantula and its glass house down on the officer's head and watches him collapse on the floor. He wipes the paperweight on his shirt and returns it to the desk.

"Guess you know I'm Tommy Bracken." His eyes are inches from Lalo Rivas's. Close enough for him to see into the depths of the detective's pupils to the place on the *other side* where Lalo's soul will be headed in a matter of minutes.

Not heaven. Tommy knows that place doesn't exist. Someplace dark and close and uncomfortable where you go when the beatings are finished.

"Tell Mom I still love her," Tommy says. "Wish you were with me, Mom." Even though at this moment, he's pretty sure she is.

He pinches Lalo Rivas's mouth closed. Pinches his nostrils closed and waits until the detective has finished with his trip. Lalo's pupils contract into pinpoints and then open into empty black pools.

Tommy takes the detective's gold shield. That might come in handy later and walks out of the police station like a citizen who's come in to lodge a complaint.

The parking garage isn't far away, but Tommy fights the urge to run. He has to get there before the hallucinations start. And the paralysis.

Phencyclidine works fast, and by the time Tommy has reached his car, he can barely remember the magnetic box that hides his key in the left front wheel well.

Phantom spiders lunge at his hand as he runs his fingers over the underside of the fender. He opens the trunk, climbs in, and shuts it.

He's safe, like he was inside his mother's hopeless hope chest. He sprays the trunk regularly for brown recluse spiders, but he curls into a fetal position just in case. He hears his mother's footsteps outside the car. Far away but coming closer. In the middle of a rant. Tommy knows it's a hallucination, but it feels real. Real enough to make him wonder if he's made her proud, but not quite real enough to ask her.

Chapter 4

"**A**N ART FAIR IS a good place for a holy man," John Horse tells Danny Riley. "Folks come here lookin' to feel special." He licks the tip of a finger and draws an X between the eyes of the white man who drove them all the way to Shiprock.

"Paid in full." John Horse is starting to smell like lighter fluid. His pupils are fully dilated. Visions gather on his forehead and dissolve in beads of perspiration.

"Who wants to talk with the Great Spirit?" People flock around the Black Seminole, their eyes full of wonder, their hands reaching for money. White people mostly—men with ponytails, women wearing squash blossom necklaces.

"Twenty for a touch. A hundred for a kiss," John Horse says, "Free if you're a really pretty girl."

Several girls in the crowd look pretty enough to Danny, but they all pay their money and go away with perspiration X's.

"Shouldn't have said *really* pretty," John Horse says. "Girls never think they're *really pretty*. Even ones that are." He stuffs the money in the side pockets of his jeans and removes a glass container shaped like a can of Skoal.

"Vision ants." He pops the lid and carries a pinch toward Danny's mouth the way a priest offers Holy Communion.

"Open wide."

The dead insects burn Danny's tongue like jalapeno pepper seeds.

"Heat passes in a minute," John Horse says. "Don't tell your momma—about giving kisses away for free, I mean. You know how women are."

"Not really." Danny isn't used to sharing secrets, but talking eases the hot feeling on his tongue, and John Horse is a good listener.

"Not many Laguna girls on the Rez." Danny feels hotter and stickier than he did before the girl talk started. He watches the Black Seminole draw crosses on three more foreheads. White people who've come to the Shiprock Art Fair to learn what it's like to be an Indian. When they figure out that isn't going to happen, they start looking for a vision. People just naturally know John Horse is the man to see.

The Black Seminole flashes a victory sign, rakes his fingertips across his brow, and touches a bearded white man on the eyelids. "Double vision, no extra charge."

"Twenty dollars is a bargain," he tells Danny. "Some folks see God. Some folks see Elvis. Some folks see something like this." He stops in front of a wooden sculpture that looks like one of those six-hour erections Danny's heard about in Viagra commercials.

"Acacia plus ants plus John Horse." The Black Seminole counts off the three parts of touch-magic on the fingers that send people to vision land.

"My grandpa could do it, but not my dad. The holy man business skips a generation." He uses his pinky finger to transfer a crystal clear drop of hallucinogenic sweat to the tip of the wooden penis sculpture. It dries quickly into an obscene blotch of white powder.

"Hey there." A female Navajo tribal cop steps out of the crowd. "Don't touch the artwork, sir."

"Pretty girl. You think so, Danny?" As if the lady cop can't hear him.

"Sure." The Diné cop looks extra tall and slender standing there in front of the supersized wooden erection. Her uniform hugs her natural curves. The pistol and the can of mace hanging from her utility belt exaggerate the flair of her hips. She shifts her posture the way television dancers do to strike a line.

"Wow." Danny wants to say more, but the first word out of his mouth sounds so stupid, there isn't any point. Things are changing in his body like they do when he's all alone thinking about the female clerk in the Circle K who calls him "sweetheart," or Leslie Nacomis, who he once saw swimming naked in the San Juan River, or the girl in the MacDonald's commercial who looks almost as sexy in her uniform as this Navajo policewoman.

He tries to move away from the cop, tries to fade into the crowd like he does when he has something in his pocket that doesn't belong to him, but Danny's legs won't follow orders. Neither will his voice. He hears himself say, "*Really* pretty." It sounds a little like a cat purring before it climbs into your lap, a little like a dog growling before it bites, and a little like a half-breed Laguna boy before he turns into a real live holy man.

Danny's mouth switches from being dry to being so full of saliva he keeps swallowing or it will run down his chin. His face and arms break out in a flow of perspiration as if he's full of fluids that must find a way out before they drown him from the inside. His mind is full of the Navajo cop, who has just turned full-fledged beautiful instead of merely pretty.

Her name is Sarah Benally. He doesn't know where that came from, but it must be true because he says, "Sarah," and she says, "Yeah?"

Her voice is pretty, too. It keeps on coming even when her lips stop moving—bright-red lips that promise to taste as sweet as wild strawberries. They're shaped exactly right for Danny Riley's first kiss.

Her voice says, "Do it, Danny." Clear and concise, right from the mind of a very pretty Diné girl who doesn't know exactly what she wants quite yet. But in a moment, she will. Before Sarah Benally can object, Danny kisses her.

There's a hint of lighter fluid on Sarah Benally's breath—or is that coming from him? The world contracts around them, squeezes them into a bubble of time and space that no one else can see except for John Horse—and he doesn't matter.

Danny and Sarah Benally are invisible, like spirits drifting through a reservation night, like the double souls of a Two-Heart Pueblo witch that floats away on his dying breath.

Sarah Benally leads Danny Riley to her Navajo police cruiser parked in the shade of a cottonwood tree growing beside a river that is as dry as Danny Riley's mouth was right after his first taste of hallucinogenic ants.

Sarah Benally's eyes are full of solid black pupils that are locked on Danny as they walk. She tells him things no one's ever told him before as their feet tap out a rhythm on the hardpan that sounds like the hoof strikes of a magic white horse with gray dapples.

"Like the face on the full moon," Sarah Benally tells him, as if she can read his mind. "Just sayin'."

He understands exactly what she's "just sayin'." Danny has been in the backseat of a police car several times, but this is the first time the doors have been left open.

He knows his rights, even though nobody has read them to him from a card. He has the right to touch this tribal cop's perfect body anywhere he wants. He has the right to lose himself inside her. He has the right to remain silent, but neither he nor Sarah Benally can.

"Oh God," she says, and Danny hears God's answer. He speaks a language that only magic ants can understand. It sounds a lot like Navajo. The world fades to black the way it does on Netflix movies.

WHEN THE WORLD COMES BACK, Danny Riley is in the backseat of another car. This one is a Mercedes, driven by a woman with hair the color of copper wire.

John Horse is unbuttoning Danny's shirt over the good luck pouch nobody knew about until today. The Black Seminole holy man gives the pouch a thump and calls it an "Amulet bag." He waves the Skoal-shaped glass container filled with dead acacia ants in front of Danny's face, loosens the drawstring on the bag, and slips it in.

"You got the touch," John Horse tells him. "That's what I thought, the first second I laid eyes on you." He hands Danny a bottle of Perrier sparkling water, cold and covered with condensation. Magic, Danny figures, like everything else about Nelva's newest boyfriend.

"Drink up," John Horse tells him. "Witchery is thirsty work."

Chapter 5

"SAMMY BEGAY GOT ANOTHER brand-new truck." Nelva Riley is still sleeping with John Horse, but Danny recognizes the early signs of romantic slippage.

"Better than the last one." She's talking about Sammy's midnight blue Chevy Silverado, but relationships are on her mind. Nelva knows they don't last long. Like cartons of low-fat cottage cheese, when the one in your refrigerator starts tasting funny, it's time to shop for a replacement.

The Sammy Begay project is still in the planning stages, but soon, Nelva will feel the need for solitary walks in the desert and come home smelling like Camel filter cigarettes and the inside of a brand-new truck.

"He drove by the trailer three days in a row." Her voice hovers on the edge of a song. "Comes closer every time. Maybe today he'll stop and visit like he used to."

Like he used to before John Horse came along. Before Sammy drove Danny Riley into a Balance brothers ambush. Nearly got him killed. Danny wants to tell her all about that, but she doesn't want to listen.

She says, "Best let bygones be bygones," but Danny tells her anyway.

"I paid him fifty dollars for a ride." He doesn't tell her he was leaving the reservation. Best to save that detail for later, maybe write it on the back of a postcard mailed from someplace far beyond the Western Agency like Santa Fe or Albuquerque.

Dear Mom,
Wish you were here. By the way, I'm gone.
Your loving son,
Danny Riley

He tells her, "Sammy dumped me out by Chaco." He tells her, "Ed and William Balance were already there." He holds his breath and waits for Nelva's serious look. When he can't hold it anymore, he says, "With guns."

"Just a misunderstanding is all." According to Nelva that happens a lot with men like Sammy Begay. "He might even give your money back if you ask him nice."

Danny starts to tell her it's not about the money, but Nelva would never believe anything isn't about money or love. Instead, he tells her about the white horse that rode out of nowhere and the Winchester lever action rifle he "borrowed" from Sammy and traded for a ride back home after he'd emptied it shooting tires and radiators.

"Sammy loved that old rifle." Nelva kisses Danny on the cheek. "Maybe he'll keep the fifty after all."

John Horse looks up from the kitchen counter where he's busy grinding acacia stems in a marble mortar and pestle. "Your Momma's getting restless."

He dumps a baseball-size mound of pulp into a metal pan and douses it with a stream of Red Devil lighter fluid. Magic ants struggle to escape, but the lighter fluid works too fast.

"Red Devil works the best," John Horse says. "Cheapest too. A holy man has to watch his pennies." He puts all his supplies on a shelf under the kitchen counter where Nelva would keep her pots and pans if she ever did any cooking. It doesn't hide the smell completely, but it helps.

John Horse says, "Your Momma likes bad boys. Gets used to one kind of badness, then goes on to worse."

"I understand that kind of attraction. Got a touch of it myself." John Horse can get away with talking like that in front of Nelva because he's a holy man. But then he goes too far. "You've got to get clean off the rez, Danny. Before one of those Balance brothers *misunderstandings* gets you killed."

Nelva's smile flickers like a bad fluorescent light bulb.

"Don't talk that way." She cups her hands and holds them out as if she's waiting for a convincing argument to fall from the sky.

John Horse says, "People start in on witch-talk, it's time to move on."

"My boy…." She looks at the ceiling of the trailer and finds a stain where rain leaked through last month, a brown splotch that looks like a petroglyph of Spider Woman. The Pueblo goddess is no help at all.

"My boy won't ever leave me." She looks straight at Danny and holds her stare so he'll know this is his cue to swear allegiance to his mother. When he doesn't, Nelva cries.

Danny's seen her cry over electric bills she couldn't pay, and boy-friends who don't come around anymore, but this is the first time it's been for him. Big tears as round and regular as marbles roll down her cheeks and splash on the indoor-outdoor carpet. There are sound effects too, so it doesn't do any good to look away. She hitches and sobs like a bathtub drain that's suddenly come unclogged. She throws her arms around Danny and soaks his shirt in saltwater.

"If those tears were dollar bills," John Horse says, "They'd buy a brand new truck as good as Sammy Begay's."

Danny pats Nelva on the back until she calms down.

"I'd better go to the powder room and freshen up," she says. "You boys don't talk about me while I'm gone." Her good mood is on the way back. Nelva Riley has confidence in her tears.

"Don't say nothing unless it's nice." She leaves the bathroom door open, so Danny has to whisper when he tells John Horse how some-thing weird happens every time he tries to get off the reservation.

"If it ain't the cops, it's the Balance brothers. If it ain't the Balance brothers, it's a flat tire or a flash flood." Danny's never been past the four sacred mountains that fence off Diné territory from the outside world, and he's not even Navajo. "It doesn't make any sense."

John Horse says it's family magic. By now, Danny knows that's the only kind of magic the Black Seminole holy man thinks is real. He says mothers have a special kind of power over their boy babies.

Danny's heard how Navajo mothers hold their sons with a piece of umbilical cord hidden in a special place. A lock of hair can do it too, or a matchbox full of baby teeth. Or Maybe Nelva collected dirt from one of his footprints and stored it in a mason jar. That's the kind of magic Danny knows about. Reservation Magic.

John Horse tells him all those things are nothing more than styling. "All for show, like a woman dressing up a special way to attract a man who really wants to see her naked."

"A mother's power is like a rubber band," John Horse says. "Stretches so far, then draws her boy back where he came from unless something catches hold of him that's just as strong." That's why Danny couldn't get any farther east than Mount Blanca no matter how much he paid Sammy Begay to drive him. "Everything comes down to family in the end."

Danny knows he's got family somewhere in Oklahoma. Way beyond the sacred mountains and his mother's little trailer in the Western Agency. He wants to talk about it, but Nelva walks out of the bathroom.

A smile has worked its way onto her puffy face. She blows her nose into a Kleenex and stops at the picture window. "Looks like Sammy's come for a little visit."

It's a brand new midnight blue Chevy Silverado all right, but Ed and William Balance hop out. Both are strapped with old-time six shooters worn in fancy hand-tooled holsters slung low and tied with strands of rawhide above the knee.

"Like the goddamned gunfight at the O.K. Corral," John Horse says.

Nelva tells him, "Watch your language around my boy."

WILLIAM BALANCE TAKES THE TIME to roll a cigarette and light up. Ed strokes the butt of his revolver, checks how much force it takes to break it free in case things come to a quick draw contest.

"Ed's a lefty," Nelva says. "Never noticed that before."

The Balance boys walk toward the front door of the trailer. Ed, the lefty, is in the lead, and William, the smoker, brings up the rear. They hold their arms away from their sides like a couple of muscle-bound bodybuilders who've let their bellies get out of control.

"Walking mean," John Horse says.

"Cute, ain't it?" Nelva says. "How Ed has that little swagger."

John Horse asks, "Any guns in the house?" but he already knows the answer. "Cause if there ain't, Danny better hide."

There's an aluminum emergency escape hatch in the kitchen roof that leaks a little when it rains. Danny considers it for a moment but decides the roof of a trailer is too exposed.

He tries the bathroom. The toilet wobbles. Maybe if he rocks it, he can make a hole in the floor big enough to get into the crawl space. He leans against the float tank and the commode tips. There's a cracking sound, and the base of the toilet pulls free, but the floor is still intact. The drain is exposed, which is a good thing, because the water running from the cold water feed has some place to go.

"Danny!" Nelva has forgotten all about the armed men who are knocking at her front door now that her boy has ruined the only toilet in the trailer.

Danny runs into the kitchen and climbs onto a counter because the emergency escape hatch is looking much better now. But it's stuck tight—too tight to break free in a real emergency like two killers who won't have any trouble getting through a rickety trailer door.

He jumps off the counter and considers the possibilities. The smell of lighter fluid reminds him of the empty space below the sink where John Horse is drowning vision ants. He crawls into the space, which is way too small for comfort.

Lighter fluid vapors choke Danny like a swarm of gnats. They fill his eyes with tears and fill his mind with thoughts of mortal combat.

Facing the Balance brothers might be a better choice than hiding here—if he can only find a weapon.

He knows there is nothing, but he searches the darkness with his hands. He finds a jelly jar with a metal lid and a handful of rubber washers that never quite stopped the faucets from leaking. He knocks John Horse's can of Red Devil lighter fluid over and struggles to pick it up before it makes the air too thick to breathe. The little red plastic cap that covers the spout is gone. He traps the fumes inside the can with a fingertip.

The Balance brothers are in the house.

"No forced entry," is what the police will say because Nelva let them in. No point adding a broken door to all her troubles.

Danny hears her explain about the uprooted toilet. She doesn't make any more sense than John Horse, who is telling the Balance boys about family magic and "peaceful co-existence."

"What's that friggin' smell?" William Balance's voice. The word, *friggin'* gives his identity away. William is the polite one. The one who won't use the word *fuck* in a woman's presence while he kills her son. His footsteps shake the trailer as he moves toward the kitchen.

Danny tries to shrink to the size of one of the drowned ants floating in the pool of lighter fluid that is bringing William Balance right to him.

"Smells like a goddamned refinery. Pardon my French, Nelva."

Danny clutches the can of Red Devil in one hand and the jelly jar in the other. Neither one will stand up to an old-time cowboy pistol, but still....

William pulls the cabinet door off its hinges. Doesn't pay any attention when Nelva tells him, "You're going to have to fix that."

His cigarette bobs in his lips as he tells Danny, "Say your prayers, you little asshole." French again, but this time William doesn't apologize. He holds his pistol in his right hand, closes his left eye, and sights down the barrel. He takes his time because he can't miss at this range, and Nelva's boy has no place to go.

There's no room to hide, and Danny is as small as he'll ever be, so he points the open spout of the Red Devil lighter fluid can at William and squeezes.

Flames spread out from William's cigarette, over the narrow zone of male pattern baldness onto his hair. His shirt catches fire. He drops the pistol, which discharges and puts a dime-size hole in the escape hatch in the trailer's roof.

"Shit!" He doesn't have time to apologize for his language. He's busy slapping the blue flames. After a few swats, his hands catch fire. He runs for the trailer door, which Nelva is already holding open for him. He screams something long and complicated, but Danny doesn't think it's French.

"William?" Ed Balance steps aside, the way people usually do when somebody is on fire.

John Horse tells Ed, "Runnin's the worst thing for a burning man. If my brother was on fire, I'd go after him."

Nelva shouts advice at William's flaming backside. "Stop, drop, and roll, Bill. That's what they always say."

"Ed is faster than he looks." John Horse watches Ed roll William on the hardpan until the flames give up. He helps his brother into the truck and drives off without so much as a goodbye to Nelva, who is waving both hands furiously.

"Who's gonna fix my kitchen cabinet? Who's gonna patch the bullet hole in my roof? Where am I supposed to pee now that my toilet's broke?"

Danny walks into the front yard, still clutching the little jar he didn't have a chance to throw at anybody. There's something black and shriveled inside, something that looks like it should have been put out with the trash twenty years ago.

"Where'd you find that?" Nelva reaches for the jar, but Danny holds it over his head.

"What is it?" he asks.

The little jar catches sunlight and bends it into a rainbow that circles Danny's feet.

Nelva steps away from the rainbow circle. She's learned that much from living with a holy man.

"What is it?" Danny asks again.

"I thought that thing was lost for good." Nelva reaches her hand toward the rainbow circle but pulls it back as soon as the color shows on her fingers.

"It's your umbilical cord," Nelva says. "Don't know why I saved it."

"I do." Danny slips the jar into his pocket. He looks around for John Horse, but the holy man is back inside the trailer, fixing Nelva's toilet.

Chapter 6

BOTH OF TOMMY BRACKEN'S hands are cuffed around the intake water pipe of the radiator in Wilma Daniels's living room, so he can't massage the welts on the backs of his legs. He'll have to do something about the handcuffs soon because she's left the front door open, and he's naked.

Wilma sits in a lawn chair on her front porch tapping her foot in time with Tommy's moans. He picks up the tempo a little to remind her he's still there. He doesn't want to be too intrusive because Wilma is drinking Jack Daniel's and smoking a Marlboro cigarette. Those things have never been good for her state of mind.

He watches a spot of light dance in front of the open door—reflected from the shiny metal hip flask given to Wilma by her no-good-meth-addicted son, to make up for stealing her wedding ring.

It wouldn't do to start her thinking about that again.

"LAST THING HE GAVE ME before he died," Wilma told Tommy, after the final stroke from the Teaching Stick, "except for that little half-Laguna bastard grandson."

Tommy could see her considering the wisdom of launching into another beating, but she hung the stick in its special place in her kitchen and lit a cigarette. Wilma inhaled deeply and blew smoke into Tommy's face.

Something that had been inside her. Something that satisfied Wilma Daniels the way Tommy never could. She dribbled ashes onto his naked body and walked out the door.

"Got to visit Cousin Jack." She reached into a secret pocket sewn into her skirt and withdrew the flask of sour mash Tennessee whiskey that shared her last name. She stood on the front porch for several minutes, swallowing noisy gulps of sipping whiskey and enjoying the afterglow of beating the hell out of her lover. Tommy knew she'd enjoy it more if he didn't like it too.

"You lay there and think about all the things you've done." From the sound of Wilma Daniels's voice, Tommy knows she's sitting down. He hears the smoke and whiskey in her vocal cords meshing with her anger like the teeth on a set of ancient gears.

God, there's nothing like an angry woman. The way she walks. The way she talks. Her tone of voice that stings almost as much as the Teaching Stick.

No woman in the world is as angry as Wilma Daniels. She says it's part of her heritage as a Cherokee matriarch of the Long Hair Clan. Tommy has met lots of Cherokee in his time. Some of them were angry, but none of them could wield a stick like Wilma.

A car drives slowly down the street. Teenagers. Loud music and laughter, bordering on hysterical. Tommy's mother used to laugh like that. He catches a green blur as the car drives by and wonders if they saw him cuffed to the radiator.

Tommy tries to summon up a little shame, but that part of his brain is temporarily out of service. The sweet spot—he remembers the sensation.

The runaway emotion that comes from knowing your secrets no longer have a place to hide, and it doesn't do any good to care.

Tommy Bracken's pleasure and his business both involve handcuffs and bruises. It's a delicate balance when you love what you do almost the same way you love what's done to you. The only difference is who inflicts the pain.

A knife has a handle and a blade. Tommy likes the feel of both. He hears Wilma shift in the lawn chair on her porch. He stops moaning for a moment because he doesn't want to attract her attention now that she's had time to visit with her favorite "Cousin Jack."

Tommy pulls himself around so he can check behind the radiator for spiders. Nasty little creatures that fill you up with poison just when you think you're safe. Recluses are bad, but black widows are the worst. They spin their webs around water pipes. There's a red hourglass on their bellies that shows you how little time you have left after a bite as tender as a kiss.

His breath stirs a dust bunny or two, but there are no spiders. He spits a handcuff key into his right hand. Always good to have one close when you live like Tommy Bracken. He doesn't think Wilma would let anyone come in and see what she's done to him, but with Wilma, a man can never be sure. If people saw what Tommy let her do, maybe they wouldn't fear him so much. And if people aren't afraid of Tommy Bracken... well, that doesn't bear considering.

Wilma steps into the doorway and watches Tommy grimace as he pulls his clothing on over his abrasions. The look she gives him hurts almost as much as the beating did. He can tell, she's thinking how to put him in his place now that the stick is hung up and his clothing covers the evidence of her work. She flips her half-smoked Marlboro at his chest. Watches it explode in a shower of sparks.

"Clean that up." She takes a pull from her flask. Looks at her reflection in its polished metal surface. "Hoover's in the closet."

She smiles. Tommy figures she's remembering J. Edgar Hoover's special needs. No less embarrassing than his.

"Got some business in Muskogee," Tommy tells her while he's cleaning up her mess. "Want you to come with me."

Wilma crosses her arms underneath her breasts and lifts them so they point at Tommy like a pair of headlights—her way of showing attitude because she can't say no when Tommy asks her to do something. Wilma is the angry one, but they both know who the killer in the room is.

She thinks he might murder her someday. Tommy can see it in her eyes. It will happen after one of their sessions—if it happens at all—after he's licked his wounds and tasted satisfaction.

TOMMY LOVES HIS LEMON-YELLOW 1965 classic Mustang almost as much as he loves Wilma. He keeps it just the way it came off the showroom floor, the same year he was born. The Mustang is one of those things that reached perfection at the end of America's golden age. Between the JFK assassination in 1963 and the RFK/MLK double-header in 1968. When the world started going bad, and the drug business started getting good.

Wilma holds her hip flask in her hands and rubs it like there's a genie inside who'll grant her three wishes.

Tommy knows what the first wish would be—her no-good-meth-addicted son is alive again.

The second would be Tommy Bracken, out of her life for good. That might happen, but not the way Wilma imagines.

The third, John Horse comes back from where he's hiding and falls in love with her again.

Tommy could go along with the John Horse wish—except for the "in love" part—because John might be the only man who knows the secret of Cherokee Ice. And without Cherokee Ice, Tommy Bracken is just one more top-rung meth dealer.

When people smoke meth, they get high, but when they smoke a John Horse batch, they get visions. Wilma says John is a holy man.

It doesn't matter that Cherokee Ice is the most addictive speed in the entire world, or that it kills people, including Wilma's son. Holy things always kill people, and nobody goes around blaming Jesus. Some of them blame that upstart Mohammed, but it really isn't his fault either. It's man's nature to kill people and break things.

"People are no damned good," Wilma tells him. Two great minds sharing the same twisted thought. She stares at him, so there's no doubt about the comment being personal.

"No damned good at all," Tommy agrees. He doesn't rule out the idea of holy men. He doesn't believe in heaven but there's *someplace* people go when they leave this world. He's watched it dozens of times. It's easy to see if you look into dying eyes at the right moment. The pupils get big and black, and something glides through the darkness like a shark waiting for a moonlight swimmer.

The "Mother Place" is what Tommy likes to call it. Dark and close. The place you go to hide when you've had all the pain you can stand, even though it's not exactly safe. His lips form the words, Mother Place, but he doesn't add sound because there are some things about Tommy Bracken that Wilma Daniels doesn't need to know.

A TEMPORARY SOLUTION TO THE CHEROKEE Ice problem lives on the outskirts of Muskogee—a city named for a Native American language. Four of the five so-called "Civilized Tribes" speak a Muskogee dialect. All but the Cherokee, who—according to Wilma Daniels—are the most civilized of all.

Tommy pulls into the cinder driveway leading up to the wood frame house that's painted the same color as his classic Mustang. The lawn is full of dandelions. Tommy can see rusted remnants of farm equipment in a fallow field that abuts the back yard. He sniffs the air. No hint of ammonia. Meth isn't manufactured here.

"From now on, I'll be Skip," Tommy tells Wilma Daniels as he steps out of his Mustang. He walks around the car and opens her door, practicing an exaggerated limp. He turns his instep at an acutely uncomfortable angle and walks on the side of his shoe. He's done this often enough to abrade the leather from the toe box to the heel.

Tommy's shoulder blades shift into a jumble that suggests a serious skeletal malfunction is written into his DNA blueprints.

"Skip." Wilma repeats Tommy's alias so she'll be sure to get it right. He's explained how all this works many times before.

"Nobody is afraid of a cripple," he reminds her. "Everybody is polite."

Men aren't naturally afraid of women, either. Especially a woman Wilma's age who still has a straight back and is shaped like the hourglass on a black widow's belly. Men are put off balance because of being sexually attracted to someone who reminds them of their mothers.

Tommy knows she'll go along with him because bad things are about to happen inside the lemon-yellow house, and if she doesn't want them to happen to her, she will pretend to be a cripple's wife, at least until they get inside.

He exaggerates his pretend handicap as he leads Wilma across the lawn because he knows the people inside the house are meth dealers. And meth dealers—especially the ones who use—are as dangerous as pit bulls with sticks of cinnamon up their asses.

"They're watching." Tommy points his lips toward a set of curtains flopping back into place. "Trying to figure out if we're customers or Jehovah's Witnesses."

Rumors fly around the drug subculture the way they move around a prison yard, and rumor has it John Horse sold this pair a load of Cherokee Ice.

John did that a lot before he went away. Not polite. Since Tommy Bracken has the franchise. Not polite at all. Of course, Tommy will forgive John, since he might be the only one who knows how to make the product, but he won't forgive his competition.

Wilma asks, "Do they know where John is hiding?"

"Maybe," Tommy tells her. Sometimes rumors are just drug-addled bullshit, but Tommy's pretty sure that these dealers at least have a supply of Cherokee Ice, and if he can't get John Horse, at least he'll corner the market on what's left of John's product.

Wilma stands beside Tommy/Skip, smiling like a mother who

doesn't have a Teaching Stick hanging in her kitchen and a hip flask full of Cousin Jack hidden in her skirt.

After three knocks a man's voice behind the door says, "What you want?"

"Howdy. My name's Skip." The door opens a couple of inches. It's hard to tell if the gaunt face in the shadow belongs to a man or a woman. He can't see any hands, but he'd be willing to bet that one of them holds a pistol.

The door opens another inch. The man—now Tommy can see it is a man—winces at the light. He shades his eyes with one hand, which does, indeed, hold a pistol.

A revolver. An old-school cowboy gun. The man in the shadow sees Tommy's eyes focused on the pistol and realizes he's lost the element of surprise.

"If I was a crippled cop, I would have brought back up instead of my wife," Tommy says. "Me and Wilma are in the market for some Chero-kee Ice. We hear you've got some. We'll pay top dollar."

The addict looks at Tommy's fake clubfoot like it holds the secrets to the universe. He turns things over in what's left of his mind and says. "You'd have to tell me if you was cops. Right? You'd have to tell me."

"Not cops," Wilma speaks up. "You might say Skip and me are the opposite of cops."

The man in the shadows opens the door wider and steps back out of the light.

"Well, come on in." He sticks the pistol into the waistband of his dirty jeans and scratches at the line of ribs that show through a thread-bare T-shirt with a "Dare to Discipline" logo.

If Tommy believed in omens, that would probably be a good one.

"I'm Darryl." The skeletal man points to a woman who might be his fraternal twin. "This here's Cindy"

Cindy stands with her arms folded across the concave groove where her belly used to be. She holds a semiautomatic pistol in one of her hands in the absent-minded way senile smokers hold lit cigarettes before they catch themselves on fire. She looks like the kind of woman who had a nice shape once upon a time, before the big bad wolf came around and turned her into a speed freak and a prostitute.

She's wearing a wife-beater T-shirt and a pair of grimy jeans that droop over her hips to reveal a spider tattoo on the chicken wing of one pelvis.

Tommy extends his hand toward Cindy, the way businessmen do before they try to cheat each other. She uncrosses her arms and looks at the unfriendly weapon in her hand.

"Sorry 'bout that." She looks for a place to put the pistol, but every surface in the room is covered with candy wrappers and Mountain Dew cans.

Tommy turns so Darryl can't see the two-shot .22 caliber Derringer in his hand. In one easy, non-crippled movement, he puts the pistol barrel behind Cindy's ear and pulls the trigger.

She stands there, moving her head back and forth like a metronome, keeping time with a funeral song playing in her head, while Tommy walks over to Darryl and shoots him in the foot. He snatches Darryl's pistol while the meth addict hops around the trash in the room, screaming. He hands the gun to Wilma and says, "Keep Cindy covered till she drops."

Cindy's head continues its harmonic motion, but now she's saying something. A poem she probably learned as an obnoxious child. Tommy is curious, but he can barely hear over Darryl's screaming, so he reloads his Derringer, points it in Darryl's general direction, and says, "Shut up, or I'll kill you now and find the dope myself."

"Chinese, Japanese, dirty knees, look at these," becomes Cindy's death mantra stuck in replay mode. If she notices Darryl's predicament, she doesn't care.

Tommy would like to look into her eyes while the life leaks out of her, but Darryl is flopping around on the floor, and there's so much trash scattered in the room that he's bound to find something he can use as a weapon sooner or later. So Tommy gives Cindy a little shove and watches her collapse. She finishes her life with the word Chinese.

Tommy stands over Darryl and points his Derringer at the addict's knee. The same leg as the gunshot foot. That way Darryl might harbor some hope of walking with a limp one day.

"Where is John Horse?" Tommy keeps his tone as friendly as possible under the circumstances.

Darryl moans and shakes his head.

"You know what happens next." Tommy pulls one of the hammers back on his little pistol.

"Don't know where John is," Darryl tells him. "Really, Skip."

He thinks about that for a second. "Really, Mister Skip."

Tommy fires a shot into Darryl's knee. When the addict starts to scream, Tommy points the Derringer at his groin.

Darryl goes quiet. Tommy knows the addict hasn't had a use for that part of his anatomy for some time, but men always feel nostalgic.

"Please, Mister Skip. I'd tell you if I knew. John sold us some Cherokee Ice but didn't tell us nothing."

Tommy steps away from the bloody addict. Surveys the room. The only clean places are a pair of aquariums in opposite corners. Both are lit. One holds a rattlesnake. The other holds a pair of tarantulas.

"Dope's hid in the glass cages," Darryl tells him, but Tommy already knows that. He walks over to the rattlesnake cage. Shoots the snake. Watches it writhe for a few seconds. Then he reaches inside and pokes around until he finds a plastic-wrapped bag of methamphetamine. He penetrates the plastic with his index finger. Catches a few granules on his fingertip and tastes it. Green apples and lighter fluid. It's Cherokee Ice all right. He walks back over to Darryl, places the pistol barrel behind his ear, and pulls the trigger.

Tommy watches Darryl's methamphetamine-engorged pupils constrict and then open again. He looks into the Mother Place.

He can see her face looking out at him.

"Here's another one, Mom," he says. "Tommy still loves you best of all."

He feels heat from Wilma's body standing close enough to hear. For the first time in a very long while, Tommy feels ashamed. It's as good as he remembers.

"What about the spider cage?" Wilma lights a Marlboro. Holds the match up in a Statue of Liberty pose. Shadows of trash flicker over the bodies. The tarantulas wave their front legs in the air, trying to read the future.

"Won't touch spider dope," Tommy says. "You know what to do."

Wilma tosses a lit match onto a pile of candy bar wrappers. In minutes, a blaze grows to the ceiling like a magic beanstalk.

"This is the part I like the best," she says.

Wilma points Cindy's gun at him for a moment. Then she tosses it on the floor.

Chapter 7

"**W**ASN'T AS GOOD AS last time." Officer Sarah Benally promised to drive Danny off the reservation, but now that she's made love to him in the back of the police cruiser, it looks like she's having second thoughts. "No offense intended."

"None taken." Danny scoots as far away from the policewoman as he can get.

"Kind of quick," Sarah Benally says. "Kind of clumsy too. Just sayin'."

She wanted all his clothes off this time. The only thing she didn't insist he remove was the amulet bag, so all this talk about quick, clumsy sex makes him feel vulnerable.

Sarah Benally is naked too, and that's kind of interesting. Danny's only seen one other naked girl who wasn't his mother, and he was hiding behind a boulder near the San Juan River at the time. This is better—even after the not-so-good sex is finished—and he's sitting there trying not to stare at things he's never seen up close before, trying not to scratch himself in embarrassing places that usually don't itch this much.

"What's that?" Sarah Benally worries Danny for a while until he realizes she's looking at his amulet bag.

"Good luck charm." He opens it so she can see what he keeps inside.

"This is the ring my father gave my mother before he ran off to Oklahoma." He tries to fit it onto Sarah Benally's finger, but she's just traditional enough to believe that sort of thing is bad luck.

She takes the ring from him. Looks inside where a name is engraved. "Who's Wilma Daniels?"

"Maybe that's the jeweler. Or maybe all wedding rings have Wilma Daniels's name engraved inside them." Funny how he's never noticed the engraving before.

Sarah thinks maybe it didn't work out with Nelva and Danny's father because he tried to give her a second-hand ring.

"The worst kind of bad luck," she says. "Curses a romance. Everybody knows that."

Everything is good or bad luck on the Big Rez. Bad luck that Danny's mother has a sweet tooth for the worst kind of men. Good luck none of them have killed him yet. Bad luck everybody thinks he's a witch. Good luck that maybe he does have a little of the witchery way—just enough to talk a pretty policewoman into driving him off the rez—unless the sex was so quick and clumsy she doesn't want to anymore.

"What's this?" Sarah Benally holds the Skoal-shaped glass container of dead vision ants John Horse gave him, takes the lid off, and winces at the lighter fluid smell. Danny can see she thinks it's some kind of drug, and she's sort of right.

"Something magic," Danny says. "John Horse gave it to me."

"He's got papers on him," Sarah Benally crosses her arms under her breasts. Lifts them up in a way that makes Danny wonder if leaving the reservation is such a good idea. "Wanted in Oklahoma for manufacturing methamphetamine."

She crosses her legs. Danny wants to touch the one on top, but he holds off because he knows that might lead to something more, and he probably couldn't follow through unless he chewed up a couple of magic ants. So instead, he shows her everything inside his amulet bag.

"Here's the brass cartridge from when my father tried to kill my mother."

"And this," he says, "is Queenie's tooth." He tells her about the timber wolf turned loose on the rez by a group of white environmentalists.

"Never was quite wild enough," Danny says. "She'd mind me like a well-trained dog. Scared the hell out of everybody."

He tells Sarah how one of the Balance cousins shot Queenie. "But not before she tore him up pretty bad."

"Buried her behind Nelva's trailer. Had a marker for a while, but Nelva said it made her boyfriends nervous. This tooth is all that's left." He tries to stop crying, but it's already too late.

Sarah Benally doesn't mind. In fact, she seems to like it. Before long, the two of them are at it again in the back of the police cruiser, and from the look on the policewoman's face, it's every bit as good as the first time.

Sarah says, "Oh God." He must be listening because the sun moves over a chip in the windshield and casts a rainbow across her face.

Danny kisses her on the red part. No lighter fluid taste, just crest toothpaste and spearmint chewing gum.

A few minutes of Diné silence go by, and the rainbow moves onto Sarah Benally's breasts. "I'll take you as far as Albuquerque if you still want to go."

"Guess I'd better." Danny wonders if the rainbow marks the brand-new border of Nelva's power over him. Reaches his hand across it just to be sure he can.

"But we don't have to go right now." Sarah watches his hand move on her body. "Just sayin'."

Chapter 8

RICHARD DANIELS'S HANDS HARDLY shake at all as he packs his rehab wardrobe into the cheap Department of Corrections suitcase. Plenty of room inside for his two pairs of pants, six shirts, and the eight-by-ten photograph of Mary.

"All for you, baby." He holds the picture frame in both hands and kisses Mary's image on the lips. His breath bounces back into his face and repulses him. Rotten teeth, a wrecked marriage, and a slight tremor that never goes away. Three good reasons for a methamphetamine addict to turn things over to his higher power.

Fifty-six days' worth of clean and sober. Like two Februaries back-to-back—one in a locked-down rehab and one in the halfway house recognizing things he's powerless to change. Rehab bullshit, but it's working. Richard is mostly back to normal now, except for the bad breath, the shaky hands, and memories of how it used to be for the first few seconds after he filled his lungs with smoke.

"Everything good comes flying back." The counselors all make the same promise. Identical, like they're reading from a card. "The best part of your life is like a boomerang. Can't throw it away no matter how hard you try."

So here is Richard Daniels packing his clothes, muttering the Serenity Prayer, hoping his boomerang won't hit him in the ass when he isn't looking. His appetite is back already, especially for sweet things like Skittles and Mountain Dew, for salty things like cheese curls and barbequed Fritos, and for spicy things like chili with pickled jalapeno peppers. Meat still tastes a little funky, but it's getting better. Green vegetables have always been nasty—especially lima beans—but potatoes are pretty good and corn with lots of salt and butter.

Richard's counselor says, "Sensory progress is in-cre-men-tal." He stretches out the spaces between the syllables. Slows them down to, "Com-pen-sate for neurological damage." He promises Richard's sexual urges will return in-cre-men-tally too.

"A penis always remembers." The counselor gives Richard an exag-gerated wink as if they are sharing a moment, as if the counselor's penis is forgetful too. "Just you wait and see." Another wink. This one's quick and efficient, like an exclamation point at the end of a sentence.

Richard's waited for fifty-six days—and his penis still hasn't got it figured out. When those old feelings come for a visit, memories of his grandma chase them away.

Grandma Wilma Daniels. How fucked is that? Too fucked to tell a counselor, that's for sure.

Richard starts off remembering things he and Mary used to do before the Cherokee Ice froze his libido all the way to absolute zero. Mary. Wild girl, crazy girl, naked girl, who would do anything Richard wanted, even if it was weird. And things got pretty weird—had to be pretty weird to keep his interest once the big freeze started, and all he could think about was getting high.

Tweaking is still on Richard's mind, but now he thinks of Grandma too. Mary's image flickers in his imagination like a string of Christ-mas lights with a bad connection, but Grandma Wilma Daniels is as solid as a hundred and fifty pounds of petrified dinosaur shit. God, how Richard hates that bitch.

God, how he loves Mary. He's convinced her to take him back at least as far as her guest bedroom. "No farther till I prove myself." He starts doing that first thing tomorrow when he talks to Mary's dad.

"Really, Mister Bailey, I'm not the asshole I used to be. Fifty-six days of court-mandated rehab has wrung the evil out of me." Richard Daniels snaps the latches on his suitcase like a pair of quotation marks around a sworn statement to his father-in-law just as a counselor knocks on the frame of his open door.

"Somebody here to see you, Richard. Somebody very strange."

Richard never bothers with counselors' names. People come and go so fast in rehab there isn't any point.

"Maybe I should send him away," the counselor says. "Your visitor has a tongue that's split on the end like a snake's. Lots of tattoos." He touches different points on his face and names cartoon characters. "Wylie E. Coyote, Tweety Bird, Bugs Bunny." He draws an imaginary line across his forehead. "Four words right here. Written backward."

"Back-ward." He breaks the word in two so Richard won't miss the implications.

"Violators will be Toad," Richard says. He points to his forehead so the counselor will know it's a translation. "Toad's his street name. Everybody in the life has got one."

Richard's street name is Two-Heart. According to Grandma Daniels, that's some kind of Indian witch. She should know. Grandma Daniels is a Cherokee. Member of the Long Hair Clan. The most full-blooded old Cherokee bitch he ever met. Richard's not even a half-breed according to Grandma. His blood's mixed up because his daddy wasn't careful, and his mother was a Laguna Pueblo whore.

"Means your spirit's mixed up too," Grandma Daniels told him. "Means you'll never amount to nothing."

Looks like the counselor agrees with Grandma. His eyes shift from Richard to the DOC suitcase back to Richard again, like he's watching a game of beach volleyball. He doesn't say Richard shouldn't hang around with friends who are so easy to pick out of a police lineup because Richard "Two-Heart" Daniels isn't on probation after today and doesn't have to account for his friends and acquaintances to anyone. But the counselor knows meth addicts don't usually make it, and the ones who do stay clear of men with split tongues and tattooed faces.

"Toad's not as bad as he looks," Richard says.

"Couldn't be." The counselor checks his watch like he is making note of the exact moment Richard Daniels started to lose it after his mandatory rehab had been served.

"HEY NOW." RICHARD GIVES TOAD the standard Grateful Dead greeting they exchanged back when they were coming up. Toad started off so weird, meth couldn't make him worse. That's why Richard likes him. Good old Toad, always strange but always strange in the same predictable way.

"Tried to call you, dude." The split ends of Toad's tongue explore the exterior surface of his upper lip like a pair of octopus tentacles. "Your phone turned off?"

"Maybe." Richard takes his phone out of a side pocket. "No chargers in rehab." Not talking to people like Toad is part of getting well. The counselors all tell him that. Mary thinks so, too, and she's been paying for the service since the phone was in a property envelope at the Oklahoma County jail. A sign that she still loves him, but also a way she can keep track of him.

Richard switches the power on. "Battery's low." Four missed calls from Toad, none from Mary.

"Looking for some Cherokee Ice." Toad doesn't waste time on small talk. A dealer never knows when somebody will drive by and end his life with a bullet or change it with a ride in the backseat of a police cruiser.

Richard shrugs, wide and gangly, the way a baby pelican stretches his wings. "Stayin' clean, you know. Moving back with Mary later on today." He tells Toad how she gave him one last chance. How he can't let her down this time because she's already lost so much. "Like me, for instance, and her mom."

Mary didn't lose her mom, exactly. Ellen just sort of ran away when Mary went off to college. Still calls now and then, but Richard doesn't want to get into that.

"I love her, man. You know?" Richard wants to explain, but talking about Mary makes him think of Grandma again, so he sums things up in a single word. "Love." He says it loud and points at the sky because it's one of those things he's powerless to change.

Toad looks at the knuckles of his left hand where the word "LOVE" is tattooed in block letters. Toad doesn't know much about love, but he knows all about Cherokee Ice. The best meth ever supplied by the meanest motherfucking dealer in the state, the evil and mysterious Tommy Bracken.

Toad also knows that Richard "Two-Heart" Daniels was the assistant cook, a student of the infamous John Horse who gave Tommy Bracken's meth a mellow, euphoric edge like you get from ecstasy. Nobody else in the world knows how to do that except for maybe Richard Daniels.

"Ten thousand dollars," is what Toad is willing to pay for a standard load of product. "One time only. That's a promise." Once Toad takes over the Oklahoma City market, Tommy Bracken will sell to him directly. "Tommy's lookin' to branch out now that John Horse went missing. Wilma Daniels told me."

Richard's mouth fills up with stomach acid at the sound of Wilma's name. Richard's bitch of a grandma, one of the few people who ever met face-to-face with Tommy Bracken and lived to tell about it.

"I won't come to you no more." Toad's split tongue causes him some trouble with *Ns* and *Ts*, but Richard understands.

"Thing is...." Richard Daniels knows how to cook meth, all right. It's not rocket science. It's barely even chemistry. But John Horse is the only man alive who can make Cherokee Ice. The secret ingredient is John himself. A drop of his urine, a sweat-soaked filter paper, a dribble of saliva. There's something in John Horse that turns his meth into a visionary drug.

When John Horse is full of visions, he can pass them on with a touch. A sweaty hand on the forehead, kisses for the girls. Even Wilma

Daniels woke up when John Horse kissed her. Until he finally figured out she wasn't worth the trouble.

"One more batch won't kill you." Toad smiles at Richard because he knows getting killed is a real occupational hazard in the methamphetamine business, especially when you're trying to steal a franchise from somebody who doesn't believe in competition.

"Little Bits." Richard whispers the name of Tommy Bracken's number one sales rep in Oklahoma City. Top of the pyramid, like the best Amway salesman ever. Everybody in the metro works for him. The people who don't, get killed. He doesn't look like much. African American dwarf, twisted, superstitious, and mean. Almost as dangerous as Tommy Bracken.

Almost.

Richard considers telling Toad there's no way in hell he's getting back into the business, but instead he says, "Let me think about it." Tells him about the meeting with Mary and her father, Jack Bailey, at the Art Museum Café. "Lunch tomorrow. I'm kissing his ass as an appetizer. Bring the ten thousand, and I'll let you know for sure."

He's still planning to say no, but if things don't work out like he hopes, it's nice to have an alternative.

EVERYTHING REMINDS AN ADDICT OF being high. A flash of light, static on a car radio, the fresh plastic smell of the brand new shower curtain in Mary's bathroom.

Richard told her, "Cleanliness is next to Godliness." Narconon wisdom, like sixty meetings in sixty days, the Serenity Prayer, turning things over to a higher power.

Cleanliness is in there somewhere. Richard wants to wash off the stink of mandatory rehab in a real bathroom with a lock on the door and lather himself with a bar soap that's free of pubic hair. But he knows things aren't going to go his way when he gets a whiff of Mary's brand-new shower curtain.

The scent is stronger when he's standing naked in the tub.

"Attention, Kmart shoppers." He pushes the fabric of the curtain against his face and inhales through his mouth as if there's a glass pipe in his lips. The taste and smell are so close to Cherokee Ice.

He turns the water on and lathers his body as though he can wash away the memory of what it feels like to suck the air out of Heaven one breath at a time. Maybe when every speck of rehab grease is washed away with lavender-scented soap the craving will be gone. He pictures Mary standing under the running water beside him. Pretends it's her hand instead of his, touching him in places she touched so often until he blew it.

In-cre-men-tally, like the counselors say.

Lust is almost strong enough. Another few seconds and the ice-craving will change directions like a weather vane in the schizophrenic Oklahoma wind. If he can hold the image of Mary, smiling at him the way she always smiled just before—

The memory of Grandma Wilma Daniels pushes into Richard's mind, holding the stick she used to beat Cherokee ways into him, "So you won't turn into a no-good Two-Heart witch like your whore-momma."

"Nel-va Ri-ley." Wilma always spit when she said Nelva's name, as if she couldn't stand the taste of witch-tainted saliva.

"Two-Hearts whore. No better than a wart on a Cherokee's ass." Her words stung him more than the stick, but only by a little.

Richard turns the water off and finds his reflection under the layer of steam that coats the mirror of Mary's medicine cabinet. Maybe she has a little something in there to help a recovering addict forget the first time he heard his mother's name. He was ten years old. His father's overdosed Cherokee spirit was already in the Darkening Land.

Huffing spray paint and gasoline were the only way Richard could get away from Grandma until John Horse came to live with them. He was a Black Seminole, the product of two races. Not as good as a Cherokee, but close. He'd lived with Wilma Daniels once before when Richard's father was born. So long ago it was hardly more than a legend.

There's a bottle of Xanax in the medicine cabinet, three tablets remaining. Richard swallows two, hoping Mary's lost count of the pills the way she lost count of all the times he let her down. All the times he flew into a rage like Wilma Daniels did when Richard reminded her of Nelva Riley.

"Two-Heart witch," Grandma told him. "Hid her mixed-breed bastard on the Navajo Reservation until my boy took you home to Tahlequah."

Wilma's lips flattened into a straight line as she told Richard how his father shot his mother dead. "But the last laugh belonged to her. Death curses are what a Two-Heart does best." Grandma wiped an imaginary tear from the corner of one eye and told him, "My boy should have killed you both." Then she got the stick and started Richard's Cherokee lessons.

John Horse changed things for a while. Taught Richard a trade. Gave him a dog. Fucked Wilma Daniels into complacency—the way he'd done a long time ago before he disappeared for so many years people stopped believing he was real.

Richard reaches for his amulet bag. He's left it hanging on the towel rack, so it won't get wet while he's washing away dirt and old memories. The pouch holds pictures of everyone he's ever loved and everyone he's ever hated—Mary, his father, Wilma Daniels, John Horse.

"John Horse was real, all right."

Richard considers the last Xanax. Figures that's just one more thing Mary will forgive. She's good at letting bygones be bygones. Momma Ellen ran away. Daddy Jack started drinking. Richard lost his slippery grip on Cherokee Ice.

But Richard's turning things around, stayed clean for fifty-six days. Can do it a little longer if he wants. One day at a time, like Narconon says.

"One fucking day at a time." He looks at the ceiling, waiting for his higher power to do something, and it better do something fast because Xanax is like water to an Ice addict. He shakes the plastic bottle and listens to the last lonely tablet rattle like a snake warning him to "stay away if you know what's good for you." He tips the prescription bottle and slides the pill into his mouth, like the last ice cube in a glass. With all the things Mary's had to forgive, one more Xanax shouldn't make a difference.

Grandma Wilma Daniels is still in his head, but she's farther away. So far away Richard can barely hear her complain about the Two-Heart witch, Nelva Riley, who cursed her only son all the way to the Darkening Land.

But after a few deep breaths and a string of heartbeats that hiss in Richard's ears like a leaky compressed air hose, Grandma's voice gets strong again. The shower curtain smell is stronger too. Richard looks at the ceiling again, waiting for his higher power to come back from its coffee break, and he remembers something he wishes he didn't.

There's a trap door to the attic crawl space he can reach easily if he stands on the toilet seat. There's a canvas pouch lying on a ceiling joist. It's green with U.S. Army stenciled in black on the cover flap. Inside are a thousand paper envelopes full of Ice. There's a scorched glass pipe and a butane lighter that makes a flame so pure it's practically invisible.

Richard might feel better if he holds the pouch and thinks about all the things he'll lose if he starts smoking Ice again.

"Just for a little while," he tells himself as he climbs onto the toilet seat and pushes the attic door open.

"I can do it." He opens the pouch and looks inside. He remembers loading every envelope with exactly the right amount of crystal meth to make him forget Grandma Wilma Daniels.

He licks a fingertip and picks up a crystal in the moisture, transferring it to his tongue. Candied green apples and a hint of Red Devil lighter fluid. A sure sign of a John Horse batch.

Richard's hands move as if Wilma Daniels is controlling them. Before he has time to think about it, the Ice is in the pipe. The pipe is in his lips. A butane flame is turning the crystals into smoke that Richard realizes isn't really anything like plastic shower curtains.

Fucked by his higher power.

Maybe this is the way it's supposed to be. Recovery is one day at a time—that's what they say at Narconon. Maybe it's time for a day off. Richard looks at the trap door in the ceiling where his higher power lives. He promises, "Cold turkey tomorrow for sure." He'll restart recovery before he kisses Jack Bailey's ass in the Art Museum Café. The Ice speeds up his brain and creates excuses at the speed of light. Wilma Daniels is a distant memory, no more important than a parking ticket he forgot to pay.

Richard's senses are tuned to his higher power's frequency. Short waves, microwaves, waves of pleasure wash through him, following laundry instructions from the fancy side of heaven.

He's full of confidence. Chemically enhanced optimism that you can't get from climbing the twelve steps to sobriety. He's ready for something life-changing to take him by surprise, the way the best things always do.

His phone vibrates in a wrinkled pile of clothing on the bathroom floor. His telephone, that's been on since he met with Toad. One of those coincidences people confuse with miracles?

Caller ID says it's Nelva Riley. His dead mother... calling from the *other side.*

"*Hello, Richard,*" she says as soon as he accepts the call. "*John Horse gave me your number.*"

Richard's thoughts skip around like a twenty-two caliber bullet ricocheting off the inside of his skull.

Chapter 9

MARY ALWAYS SEEMS TO know when Richard is high. This time it's because he's crying.

"Where did you get it, Richard? Where did you find the dope?"

He wants to tell her she's imagining things, but if he does, she won't believe him. That will make him angry, and one thing will lead to another, so he cries a little harder. Maybe she'll feel sorry for him—sorry enough to forgive him like she has before.

Richard is deep into one more thing he's powerless to control. He feels the meth all the way from his toes to his hair follicles because it's been fifty-six days since he's had a taste. His heart thumps like a bowling ball rolling down a flight of stairs. His lungs struggle to keep up. His temperature rises. The polar ice caps are in danger. An explanation is on the tip of his tongue if he can get it to break free.

He wants to tell Mary that his mother is alive—that she called him five minutes ago and said he was her favorite, told him he had a brother who'd turned into a wolf, or maybe she didn't because he connected just as he reached the peak of Cherokee Ice Mountain. And reception there is mostly imaginary.

"Grandma Wilma...." All the bad things Richard has to say about Grandma Daniels get stuck in the back of his throat. They make it hard to breathe.

He's just remembered how Grandma Wilma Daniels killed his dog. Had her killed, really. Had Tommy Bracken kill Queenie while Richard went to Frenchy's Market for a can of lima beans.

"Never will eat lima beans again." He hopes Mary's mind will shift from methamphetamine to vegetables. "Green Giant lima beans!" His voice is so loud, Queenie would turn her ears back if she were alive, but she's not. Not alive like Nelva Riley.

Mary backs away from Richard, as if he might fly into a rage and hit her any moment. He wants to tell her he would never do that, but of course, he's done it before.

And the bitch won't let him forget it. Anger rises around him like floodwater, and he should do something besides hit the only woman who ever loved him. He must do it quickly. He runs out the front door, looking for a good place to put all the energy that's built up in his muscles over the last fifty-six days. There's Mary's vegetable garden. Full of tomatoes and beans—no lima beans, thank God—and crows picking things to pieces. He screams at them and charges through the garden, careful not to step on anything, careful in a way that only a man on crystal methamphetamine can be.

It's a weird house Mary lives in. Built at the end of the only remaining one-lane road in Oklahoma City, separated from everything by woods maintained as a city easement for reasons Richard can't remember because his mind is moving too fast for answers to hang on.

The woods fade into a natural stone wall, as if the earth shifted to make a special pocket where a man is protected from the curious eyes of nosy neighbors. Where a man could walk naked into his front yard, and no one would notice.

Richard realizes he *is* naked. One more reason Mary knows he's high. Richard has been carrying his clothes since he came out of the shower because clothing is just one more way society has of dragging a man into slavery. The cloth is as rough as a cat's tongue and as hot as the anger he feels when the crows fly back into Mary's garden.

"Scarecrow."

The genius of Einstein at the speed of light—a few well-placed rips in the shirt and pants. A couple of knots beyond the scope of the *Boy Scout Handbook*. Bundles of weeds pulled from around the drainage ditch that borders one side of Mary's yard the way the Grand Canyon sprawls between Utah and Arizona. A rope from the back of Richard's pickup truck that has been parked in Mary's driveway for fifty-six rehab days.

He opens the door carefully because wasps have built a nest between the cab and the old, dented camper shell in the bed—a paper nest the size and shape of Richard's fist. He hears the insects buzzing, sees them crawl over the surface like guard dogs protecting his old blue GMC pickup truck. They watch the world through compound eyes that never close, even when they sleep.

Ideas fly through Richard's mind faster than wasps attacking an intruder, faster than the speed of comprehension. Before he can say "Scarecrow" again, he's hung a man-simulacrum over Mary's tomato cages, and he's sliding down the sloping wall into the drainage ditch where there are piles of rocks he wants to see arranged in a grave-size rectangle in Mary's yard.

Scratched and skinned by the process, but still full of energy, Richard realizes he's finally made a grave for Queenie, even though she died many years ago. That's who he's been crying for. He had to wait until now because a Two-Heart witch never cries in front of his bitch of a grandmother.

He runs back into Mary's house, hardly noticing the little black revolver she's pointing at him, in case he has murder on his mind—and he does. Just not Mary's murder. He sorts through a junk drawer in the kitchen until he finds a red Sharpie and a three-by-five recipe card. He writes *Wilma Daniels* on the card, book-ended by two hearts.

Pleased with the symbolism, Richard retrieves his U.S. Army meth pouch, puts the card inside, and buries the whole thing under the rectangle of rocks he doesn't remember arranging. Done with Grandma, done with meth, even if Mary is done with him. His energy is coasting to a stop the way it always does with Cherokee Ice, but there's still enough for him to find some lumber and some paint in Mary's garage and make a cross for Queenie's grave.

The warm tide of methamphetamine recedes, leaving a cold, empty, mudflat of depression behind. If Richard could stop crying, he would go inside and plead with Mary to shoot him or forgive him. It doesn't really matter which. He hardly notices when a black Cadillac pulls into the driveway and parks next to his truck.

Two men's voices rumble at each other about the Queenie cross and the hanging scarecrow and the naked tweaker with his bare ass sitting on the lawn. Richard can tell from the way they sound, one man is white and the other is African American. He looks toward the footsteps that are moving apart and moving toward him at the same time, like a pair of tweezers coming for a splinter. The white man is a giant—or maybe he just looks like a giant—because the black man with him is a dwarf.

"Little Bits." Richard recognizes the number one meth dealer for greater Oklahoma City. Little Bits jingles when he walks because he wears a string of Mercury dimes around his left ankle to ward off evil spirits.

Everybody knows Little Bits is afraid the ghosts of all the men he's killed will come for him one day. He pulls a flask from the inside pocket of the blue blazer he always wears and takes a sip. Some people say it's holy wine. Others swear it's holy water. Everybody agrees on the holy part. Little Bits wears a jumbo silver crucifix around his neck, which he kisses from time to time, reminding himself that Jesus has a safety net ready to catch sinners no matter how far they fall.

This is as close as Richard has ever been to the little man. Never wanted to be any closer because Little Bits is dangerous. Even a tweaker-meth cook knows that much.

The giant crosses his arms over his chest. Richard knows he has a pistol under his jacket. So does Little Bits.

"John Horse has done run off again." Little Bits crosses his arms like a fun house mirror image of the giant.

Richard doesn't say anything more until Mary opens the front door and walks out holding her pistol.

"Go back inside, baby." Would she kill for him? Waves of love sweep his depression away as he watches Mary risk her life. She walks up to the giant, the pistol at her side.

"Get out of here," she tells him. That's how little Mary knows. She thinks leaving is up to the bigger man. She brings the pistol to chest level, not pointing it, showing everybody how much trouble she can cause if they don't do exactly as she says.

Clouds move across the moon, carried by the Oklahoma wind fifteen thousand feet above their heads. Mary is lost in darkness for a moment and then bathed in moonlight when the clouds move on. Moths the size of hummingbirds hover around her. Moonflower moths. They seem to hang by invisible strings over her shoulders.

Richard understands they are floating in thermals created by heat from Mary's body. They are drawn by her scent that's filled with pheromones and the perfume of night-blooming flowers.

"I'm not in the business anymore," Richard tells Little Bits. "Don't cook meth. Never could do it like John Horse."

"You ain't done till I say you are," Little Bits tells him. "Gonna cook till I say quit. That day may never come." He points a stubby finger at Mary. The giant backhands her. He knocks her to the ground, draws his pistol, and points it at her head.

"Okay, Mister Two-Heart." Little Bits flashes him the peace sign. "C'mon and go with us, now that you know how things are."

Little Bits walks Richard to his car, opens the back door, and tells him, "There's gonna be hell to pay if my backseat smells like ass."

LITTLE BITS HOLDS A GLASS pipe so Richard can see it. "You get a taste when I get my Cherokee Ice." He drops it on the floor and crushes it under the heel of his wingtip shoe. The little man won't give Richard any dope. Doesn't have any clothes for him either. He calls it "motivation."

"Motivation" is why he put a bag over Richard's head as soon as they were in the backseat of the Cadillac and didn't take it off until they were inside a dimly lit basement that was going to be his "brand-new meth lab."

"Motivation" is why the giant white man waits outside the only door, safe from fumes and flammables, while Richard works his magic.

"He'll check on you every hour or so. Kick your ass if he ain't satisfied. And he's kind of hard to please, so you'd better work fast."

Little Bits taps his jumbo silver crucifix against a glass beaker. "Everything you need." Electric range, filter paper, funnels, bags of lye, barrels of ammonium nitrate fertilizer, bottles of phenyl-2-propanone, gallon jugs of muriatic acid, cans of toluene brake fluid.

Little Bits holds the crucifix over his head so Jesus has a bird's eye view. "Lots of ways through the woods. I got them all right here." He struts around the basement, talking about what will happen to Richard if things don't go exactly right. "I might even go back and visit with your little girlfriend."

"Let her momma tell you what happens then. Come on in here, Ellen." The door opens, filling the room with light that's way too bright for Richard's dilated pupils. A silhouette stands there for a few seconds, a slutty female silhouette like a sign over a gentleman's club.

Ellen Bailey—Mary's mom—walks into the dim light where Richard can see her clearly.

"Ellen?" She is dressed in the best call-girl fashions—a pleated skirt that makes her look cheap instead of young, four-inch heels that make her ass sway when she walks—and she walks a lot—and a satin blouse the color of arterial blood. It matches her lips and her nails. Rubies dangle from her ears like signs over the doors of a whorehouse. The sight of Ellen Bailey sends a rush through Richard's brain like a lung full of John Horse's special batch. It goes right to his penis.

"Hey there, Richard." Ellen left Jack Bailey long after most women would have decided it was way too late. Now here she is, all decked out in her upscale call-girl wardrobe, hot enough to make Little Bits's ammonium nitrate explode.

"Glad to see me?"

He tries to hide his feelings with both hands but gives up after a couple of embarrassing seconds. Ellen looks like Mary only older—a few more worry lines at the corners of her eyes, a touch of anger in her smile. Richard doesn't dwell on those things because there's not an ounce of fat on her butt or a square inch of sag in her breasts. Legs like a fashion model. Good profile. Excellent from behind, and she knows it. Best slut walk he's ever seen.

"You could have tapped this." Ellen looks back at him over one shoulder and lets one hand run over contours his fingers want to touch.

He's looking all right, exactly as she wants him to look, feeling like she wants him to feel. Ellen flirted with him shamelessly while he and Mary dated. Handed him a card with a motel name written on the back—room number and time. She slipped a pair of her panties into his hands, still warm in case there was any doubt. All that happened right before she disappeared.

She bends over and kisses Little Bits on the lips. Richard can't make up his mind whether to watch the kiss or the two halves of the delicious butt stirring the pleats of her skirt like tectonic plates sliding into an earthquake. Where is Wilma Daniels when you need her?

Chapter 10

THE AIR SMELLS STALE for the first few days Danny Riley's off the rez. Colors aren't as bright. Shadows stretch out longer. Dust is dustier. But survival is the same as always. Whether Danny is in Tuba City, Arizona, or Amarillo, Texas, or Oklahoma City, Oklahoma, it all comes down to stealing food.

He learns the rules quickly. It's easier to walk the check in a restaurant than to snatch a hot dog from a Circle K. Restaurants with waiters and tables are easier than restaurants with counters and booths.

Fancy places like the Oklahoma City Art Museum Café are the easiest of all.

The first thing he needs to do is go invisible. That shouldn't be too hard because people in art museums like to look at pretty things, and nobody likes to look at a young mixed-blood Native American man like Danny—especially not in Oklahoma City where there are so many mixed-blood Indians another one doesn't make anybody curious.

Danny slumps a little. Walks like he might be drunk. Looks at everyone in glancing blows. Sniffs the air like he's casting for the scent of spare change. His lips move as if he's gossiping with an invisible friend. Familiar words are best. The "Happy Birthday" song works well or "America the Beautiful" or "Eenie Meenie Miney Moe." Anything, as long as there's no air behind the words.

People step around him like he's a wad of sticky-wet Double Bubble chewing gum. Hard to shake loose if they make contact. Noticeable, but only long enough to avoid. That's how going invisible works. Danny learned all about it on the reservation. Maybe he didn't learn enough to be a full-fledged witch, but he learned enough to make everybody wonder.

It's easy to go invisible if you only steal things nobody wants, like clothing from the Goodwill store or items put at the curb on big trash day or food that doesn't really belong to the people who are watching it.

Money is different. People watch dollars like they might catch on fire at any moment. They hide them in safes and fanny packs and cash registers that won't open without the code.

Money has its own special kind of magic. Dollar bills turn into imaginary numbers full of decimal points and commas. Fortunes hide in cyberspace and on magnetic strips and microchips. Capitalist magic. The magic of being able to walk into a store and trade your signature for food.

If you know the PIN code, then pop! Ones and zeros turn into groceries and gasoline and rooms at Motel 6. That's not the kind of magic Danny learned on the rez. He'll have to learn about PIN-code magic someday, but right now he's pretty hungry, so going invisible will have to do.

Magic lives in everybody's mind. Where they look when they walk into a room, what they love, what they hate, what they think about when nobody's watching—Danny has understood this kind of magic since he was ten years old.

What everybody wants to look at in the lobby of the OKC Museum of Art is a three-story tall glass sculpture mounted in an inch-deep reflecting pool.

Danny touches the water with his finger. People pretend they don't see him do that because he's not supposed to. He's invisible all right.

The only problem is it's hard to keep his mind on stealing lunch when he's standing next to a tower made of glass bubbles hanging onto each other like crookneck squashes. They're mostly yellow and orange, but they throw the sunlight around the room so much it's hard to tell where the glass stops and the universe begins. Not much difference between art and magic, as far as Danny Riley can see.

Anyone can come into the lobby for free, and lots of people do, so Danny isn't noticed while he stands among the artsy crowd and wonders how in the hell something like this got here.

A little girl stands next to him. Danny guesses she's eight years old—no parents anywhere in sight. She's found a spot where the sculpture breaks the sunlight into a rainbow. Colors spread over her face like a peyote hallucination. Like a holy figure on a Navajo sand painting. Like the rainbow that fell across Sarah Benally's breasts when they made love in her tribal police car one last time, when he reached the border of his mother's hold on him.

Magic?

People on the rez talked about visions all the time—spirit animals, ghosts, angels, prophesy. Danny always wanted a vision, but now isn't a good time. He tries to pick out Rainbow Girl's features, but the colored lights make it difficult. He examines her as closely as he can with his peripheral vision because staring directly at a spirit leads to trouble—that's what he's always heard.

She walks out of the swirl of color. She points to the glass tower and says, "Magic beans are how it's done."

She looks real enough, but you can never tell with visions, so Danny says, "Good to know." As few words as possible, the way Navajo people talk on the Big Rez. The way criminals talk while they're waiting for their court-appointed lawyers.

Nobody ever gets in trouble by keeping quiet. Every word is testimony to be used against you later, whether you are having a vision or walking the check in an art museum café, which he needs to do pretty soon because he's really hungry.

Danny's stomach rumbles loud enough to make Rainbow Girl

laugh. How long since he had a meal? Indians fast before vision quests. Does missing breakfast qualify? Danny's not clear on the rules.

He turns his attention to the entrance of the restaurant. It opens into a corridor that leads past a movie theater and a gift shop, then to the glass sculpture that grew from magic beans in the museum lobby. This is the route he'll take when he pretends to look for the restroom. He'll hold his belly like a character in a restaurant manager's training film.

Fellow diners will try to read their future in Danny's leftovers. Waiters will know that tackling a runaway patron is no way to secure a big gratuity. The manager will review the security video later and wonder if Danny was a thief or a victim of food poisoning, going off to die like a sick cat.

He'll walk the check past a movie theater featuring a Czech art film. Danny Riley takes the pun as a good omen. *Walking Fast* is showing— even better. He can't help looking for signs and omens, but he also takes inventory of potential problems, pretends he's just a fan of art museum lobbies and not some pain-in-the-ass mystical Indian who steals gourmet food from four-star restaurants because whether it's a hamburger or filet mignon, walking the check is still a misdemeanor.

The café is understaffed. No security anywhere. No one will stop him because he looks too Indian, even for Oklahoma City, and nobody fucks with Indians in an art museum café.

The waiters weave through tables like tightrope walkers carrying big silver trays with over-priced specials and little silver trays with bills enclosed in gold-embossed leather folders. Skinny fine arts majors work off college tuition in a sensitive environment, living off tips from the whitest of white people, who are way too enlightened to call the police on a minority fleeing felon.

"You know about magic?" The Rainbow Girl tugs at Danny Riley's pant leg. She has blonde hair that looks like it's made of spun sugar. She has eyes the color of the sky over the Chuska Mountains. Her smile includes every muscle of her face. Danny falls in love, but it only lasts a second because he can't take the chance of being spell-struck.

"Yes."

He knows about magic, but right now he's got to keep his mind on food. Danny throws a hard look at the elevators behind the ticket counter. Nothing there, but Rainbow Girl turns around to see for herself, and Danny Riley steps outside the museum.

Poof! Danny Riley's gone. He learned to do that on the Navajo Rez, where a half-Laguna half-Cherokee boy might as well be a witch because everyone will think he is anyway. Danny learned to disappear so well he did it permanently four weeks ago.

The number four is a sacred number. Four directions, four seasons, and four letters in almost every curse word in the white man's English language. Something special might happen in this art museum café now that the fourth week of Danny's reservation-free life has finished—or it might not. You can never be too sure.

He steps away from the glass-front of the museum and wonders if all little girls believe in magic beans.

Oklahoma is a lot different than Danny thought. His mother said the state was chock-full of Indians who learned to be mean from white men.

"Chock-full," is how she put it because Nelva Riley likes the feel of consonants on her tongue. "Chock-full of Indians who studied the white man's cruelty and took it to the next level."

Nelva told him how white people put Cherokee and Choctaw in charge of Pueblo Indian schools.

"They made us look them in the eyes," she said, "like dogs trying to decide which hand to bite. They beat us for speaking the Laguna language."

Nelva was good at remembering things that never happened to her. Very good at holding grudges for wrongs that weren't commit-ted—against her, anyway—like smallpox the reservation Indians caught from sleeping on BIA blankets.

"The worst things came a lot later," Nelva said. Bad teeth from drinking Coca-Cola. Diabetes from Hershey bars and Fritos. Fat butts from Big Macs and fries. The very worst thing had something to do with Danny's Cherokee father, who got Nelva pregnant and then went back to live with his mother in Tahlequah, Oklahoma. Danny's evil, nameless grandmother.

"Meanest Cherokee in the world," according to Nelva Riley. "Gave birth to the second meanest." That would be Danny Riley's evil, nameless father.

Two strikes against Oklahoma Cherokee. There was something more. Something even worse, but whenever Danny asked about it, Nelva pointed to a notch in the top of her left ear that looked more like a blemish than a scar.

"Made by a nine-millimeter bullet." That's as specific as Nelva Riley would get. Danny suspected she mixed up every bad thing ever done to her with Oklahoma Indians.

"Meanest Indians in the world," she told him. "Can't hardly tell them from white people."

"Civilized Tribes." She didn't spit on the ground when she said "Civilized Tribes" unless she was outside her trailer.

As far as Nelva was concerned, all Danny Riley needed to know was this. "Your daddy is a no-good, bastard Cherokee who knocked me up and gave me an ugly ear."

Case closed.

DANNY LOOKS THROUGH THE PICTURE windows into the restaurant, but he keeps an eye on the reflections of people walking behind him. The streets are full of men and women dressed in uniforms and suits and jeans and T-shirts. He can't tell how many of them are Cherokee in disguise.

One of the reflections leans on a parking meter separated from Danny Riley by a sudden flow of pedestrians wearing addled expressions and jury duty pins. The Parking Meter Man looks hard at Danny Riley's back and mumbles something that might be a prayer or just schizophrenia.

He stares at the Parking Meter Man's reflection, the way he would never stare directly at a real person. Bad manners don't bounce off glass.

Danny has no idea how that knowledge was acquired. He has no memory of many important things, like what it was like to be a sperm swimming through a Cherokee penis toward a Laguna egg that was waiting there to turn him into a half-breed boy who didn't belong on the Big Rez.

Bad things happen when you're not paying any attention, so Danny keeps his eyes fixed on the Parking Meter Man's reflection as it grows bigger and clearer—coming Danny's way with its head jerking sideways, like a chicken walking across an open yard. Nervous men do nervous things, and this one's walking Danny's way. The reflection turns sharper with every step, and Danny doesn't like what he sees. The Parking Meter Man's face is inked over with words and pictures, like a witch trying to soak up spirit energy through his skin.

Danny understands the power of skin, but the pictures inked onto this stranger are mostly images of cartoon characters—Woodstock, Snoopy, Road Runner, Daffy Duck. Some he doesn't recognize. Cartoon characters, four words written across his forehead, and symbols scattered over his skeletal contours like debris from a plane crash. The symbols are easier to see when the man stops a couple of feet behind Danny—five-pointed stars, triple sixes stacked like pyramids, power spirals, and crescent moons. The words are too small to read, and Danny doesn't want to. He doesn't want to run tattooed words through his mind because they might be a spell.

"Richard." The Parking Meter Man throws the name, but Danny doesn't catch it. It's too early to tell if it's mistaken identity or magic. He thought magic would be less common when he left the rez, but here in Oklahoma City, magic is everywhere. Rainbow Girl and Parking Meter Man. A glass tower growing in an inch of water.

"Richard Daniels." Parking Meter Man reaches out a hand but stops before it touches Danny's shoulder. The words on his face are clear enough to read in the reflection now. They race through Danny Riley's mind before he can stop them. The words aren't backward, the way mirror writing usually is—a sign of magic or a sign the ink is self-applied by a person who doesn't understand the nature of reflections.

The forehead words say, "Violators Will Be Toad."

Danny says, "Toad?" aloud without meaning to. That's how a spell takes hold of you. Words come out before you know it. They claim knowledge you don't have and make promises you won't be able to keep.

"Toad." Danny says the magic word again as he turns to face the Parking Meter Man.

The ink on the stranger's face distorts around a smile filled with rotten teeth. "You know me, Richard. Old Toad will be late to his own funeral."

Skinwalkers on the rez turn into wolves. Choctaw witches turn into owls. Cherokee wizards take the form of ravens. Danny has become a Richard. He's not sure what that means, but when you are caught in a magic current, the safest thing is to go where it takes you.

Toad says, "Glad you waited, man."

The tip of his tongue is split down the middle, forked like a snake's. It gives his D's a soft, wet sound, like the hiss of a copperhead hiding under a log. The effect loses its power among the stumps of rotten and broken teeth. Toad squints at Danny, waiting for a response, afraid of empty air filled with the background noise of automobiles and footsteps.

Danny crosses his arms and nods, like an Apache warrior who's not sure whether an enemy is brave enough to fight. When in doubt, always pretend to be Apache.

"Just sayin'." Toad reaches behind him and produces a yellow business envelope packed so full its glue has begun to fail.

"Like we talked about." Toad weighs the envelope in one hand and holds it out for Danny to see.

"Ten large." Toad pushes the envelope into the grabbing zone, one foot in front of Danny. Green edges of U.S. currency poke through loose flaps of yellow paper that was never meant to hold so much treasure.

"Hundreds." Toad holds the envelope within Danny's reach. He stares at the space between his shoes. He tries to think of words to fill up the conversation-free atmosphere that's settled between the two men. The only thought that finds its way to the split tip of Toad's tongue is half-finished.

"Like I said...."

Danny takes the money because that's what hungry, half-breed Laguna men do. He doesn't say thank you, the way Nelva taught him. He doesn't run down the street, the way he'd like to. He puts the envelope into his back pocket and turns to face Toad's reflection in the restaurant plate glass again. He locks eyes with the reverse image, safe from everything except the backward words.

Toad says, "When can I expect to see product?"

Danny crosses his arms again. He wonders if Toad will snatch the money out of his pocket if he doesn't speak.

"Soon." As if he understands the question.

Toad says, "Sorry about your troubles," as if someone Danny loved has died. "Hope everything works out." Toad's reflection shrinks as he backs away, smooth as a dancer in a Night Chant ceremony.

"Me too," Danny says when he's sure Toad is too far away to hear.

Tires screech as brakes lock when Toad backs into the busy street behind the row of parking meters where this whole thing started out.

Danny doesn't look to see if his benefactor was hit. He's a hungry man with a pocket full of money. The art museum café is open for business, and magic is going his way.

Chapter 11

JACK BAILEY CHECKS HIS watch for the fifth time since the maître d' seated him almost ten minutes ago. He's eaten the two complimentary muffins on the little plate beside his water. Brianna, the waitress who has already introduced herself to Jack three times, promises him more.

"Soonest." She smiles, thrilled with her use of the superlative. She points her collagen-enhanced lips in the general direction of an exceptionally good-looking young man, who is stacking bite-size pastries onto a tray with a giant set of silver tongs. He turns his head away from the muffins, as if his breath might contaminate the tray with flesh-eating bacteria.

Maybe that explains why the process takes so long. Every human being in the restaurant is moving too slowly for Jack Bailey. Oozing like organic slime trying to organize itself into creatures intelligent enough to transport complimentary miniature muffins across the room.

"Rudy's new." Brianna shows Jack her sympathetic smile. The one she learned in the twenty-minute training film that came with the job.

She takes his drink order, "A glass of Wild Ass Cabernet." She doesn't blush but doesn't write it down either. When Brianna walks away, Jack isn't even tempted to watch her butt. Instead, he counts the minutes on his Breitling Chronometer Emergency watch that keeps perfect time within six picoseconds every thousand years.

Twelve minutes since he came into the art museum café—still counting. The second hand starts on circuit number thirteen. Thirteen fucking minutes and still no overpriced glass of red wine with an embarrassing name. He taps the crystal of the Breitling and thinks about the transmitter inside—capable of alerting first responders within a one-hundred-mile radius if Jack remembered how to turn it on.

Two more Breitling Chronograph Emergency minutes and Brianna's back. No sign of Mary, but Jack saw Richard Daniels earlier, looking into the restaurant accompanied by one of his ne'er-do-well tattooed friends. Jack didn't wave. Didn't try to catch Richard's attention. No sense spending any more time with the worthless bastard than necessary. Mary says Richard kicked the meth habit during his last stint in rehab. Jack has his doubts. Recovering addicts show up on time when their fathers-in-law want to talk to them about working things out.

Jack grabs Brianna by the wrist before she can slip away and drinks his cabernet the way he used to chug Keystone Beer when he was in college 10,512,000 Breitling Chronometer Emergency minutes ago— give or take a picosecond. She is too refined to struggle.

"Will there be anything else?" She calls him "sir," after a couple of beats, but she means "asshole." Jack can tell.

"Bring me another." He points at his empty glass. He thumps the naked muffin dish with his middle finger—deeply symbolic if he's not mistaken. "And a couple more of these goddamned things, if Rudy's not too busy." He releases the waitress's wrist, and the Good Ship Brianna backs into the sea of tables. He thinks she says, "My pleasure," but curses sound a lot like gratuitous compliments when they are said in a soft voice surrounded by the refined white noise of an art museum café.

Jack hopes to have a pretty good buzz on by the time he plays marriage counselor for his daughter and the no-good son of a bitch she chose over his objection.

Marriage counselor. That's a laugh. Jack's loving wife, Ellen, is "in the wind," as the police are fond of saying. Gone, but not officially a missing person because she's an adult with no medical problems or mental deficiencies, other than a strong desire to be free of Jack Bailey. Her email account is alive and well.

Jack, don't try to find me.
Jack, try to find someone else.
Jack, I never want to see you again.
Fuck You, Jack. Go Away.

All signed "Love, Ellen." What a joke.

It's sort of Mary's fault. Everything is sort of Mary's fault because everything was fine until Mary went away to college and met Richard Daniels instead of getting her degree. That's when Ellen remembered about being sexually frustrated. Midlife crisis when it happens to a man, and "second heat" when it happens to a woman.

Brilliant. Jack will try to figure out a way to work that into the conversation if Mary and Richard show up.

"Second heat," he says, as Brianna returns with his second glass of wine and a smile that looks like the expression on the face of an alpha female in a troupe of chimpanzees. She's brought Rudy, who is prettier than Brianna. He has a tray of muffins balanced on one hand and a highly polished set of tongs in the other. He waves them around like a bandleader's baton.

Jack wants to say something clever that can't quite be construed as anti-gay, but nothing comes to mind, so he says, "Fuck," and looks at his watch again.

"Retails at ten thousand dollars," he tells the muffin man, who's handling blueberry pastries with his tongs as if they are plutonium. Gay men like fashionable watches, don't they?

"Got it for three thousand, five hundred nineteen dollars and twenty cents." Jack bolts his second glass of wine and tells Brianna, "One more Wild Ass, please." A fine spray of pink saliva fills the air between them.

Ellen said Jack knew the price of everything and the value of nothing. That may be true, but he knows the value of Richard Daniels, who he's pretty sure had an affair with Ellen back when she was sleeping with everyone but Jack.

Correction. Back when she started sleeping with everyone but Jack—because she's still doing that as far as Jack Bailey knows. He checks his watch again. Looks at the bar to see how Brianna is coming with his Cabernet. Twenty-four dollars' worth of wine so far. He could buy a bottle for that and drink it at home while he watches the Discovery Channel in the hope of learning how long it took man to evolve from apes into creatures that aren't as sensible as apes, and why Ellen doesn't love him anymore.

And there's Richard Daniels, walking through the front door of the restaurant like the king of the world.

Thinking of Ellen at the same moment Richard arrives is proof—as far as Jack is concerned—the two of them had an affair. Not logical, but after two glasses of Wild Ass Cabernet, who needs logic? He checks his watch again. Twelve twenty. He'll make it a point to remember that, although he's not sure it makes any difference.

"Richard!" Jack waves at his no-good bastard of a son-in-law like he's a game show host, and Richard is a contestant who's been chosen to "Come on down."

"Richard!" Everybody in the restaurant is looking at Jack Bailey except for Richard.

"Goddamn it, Richard, over here!"

Brianna's headed Jack's way with a third glass of wine, but she might be having second thoughts.

"Pardon my French," he tells the café patrons. That's as close to an apology as anyone is going to get until he drinks another glass of wine and makes Mary understand that Richard Daniels needs to go.

The muffin man takes Richard by the elbow and walks him to Jack's table the way a prom queen walks beside the captain of the football team.

"Where the hell is Mary?" Jack doesn't give Richard a chance to answer before he asks him the same question a second time—louder in case Rudy the muffin man didn't hear it.

Brianna wants to take Richard's drink order, which gives Jack exactly enough time to down his third medicinal Cabernet.

"Sparkling water," Richard says, like a member of the goddamned trashy British Royal Family.

"Sparkling water?" Jack's not sure whether he slurred the words or not, but he doesn't really care at this point because when he asks, "Where the hell is Mary?" for the third time, Richard acts like he doesn't have the slightest idea who Jack is talking about. The blank expression on his face looks real enough. No dislike, no disdain, no sign of recognition. Maybe he really has put the past behind him—or maybe methamphetamine has wiped his mental slate clean.

"Is San Pellegrino all right?" Brianna asks. She looks at Jack and takes a step away when he points to his empty glass again.

Richard thinks San Pellegrino is perfect, and Brianna suggests Jack try some too. "Until you get something on your stomach," she says. "Food, you know?"

"F-o-o-d." the word oozes through another of Brianna's mechanical smiles. There's a speck of drool on her lower lip, but she leaves it there for Jack to stare at while he comes to a decision.

The room is spinning slowly, and the floor is starting to tip toward Richard Daniels. So the insufferable, wet-lipped Brianna is probably right.

"Hokay." Agreeable. Jack will be so goddamned agreeable that nobody will blame him for breaking up his daughter's marriage to this goddamned methamphetamine addict who watches Brianna pour his goddamned sparkling water like it's a cup of drug-free urine that will keep his parole officer happy for another week.

Jack has a whole speech worked out about how if two people really love each other, they should really break up for a little while to be sure.

Trial separation. He mouths the words without putting any sound behind them, making sure he won't slur the vowels and consonants.

Trial separation. Perfectly executed. Now that his lips are moving, Jack decides this is the perfect time to launch into the little speech he's been working on for several days. He tries to remember it, but all that comes to mind is "Mary."

He feels a Wild-Ass-Cabernet-sob hitching a ride from somewhere in his chest, all the way to his eyes. Pressure builds up the way it does every time he mixes alcohol with thoughts of Mary and Richard together. Or thoughts of Ellen and Richard together. Or thoughts of Ellen and Jack not together anymore.

"Mary had so much promise." Jack pronounces the letter *S* the way Sean Connery did years ago in an interview with Barbara Walters, where he said it was all right for a man to *sh*trike a woman with his open hand—on occasion. Jack thought that was a terrible idea until Ellen went into her second heat, and he sort of thought Sean Connery was on the right track after all. Then Mary started showing up with bruises, and he thought Sean Connery was an asshole all over again.

"Ash-hole." Jack takes a sip of his San Pellegrino and says something about Mary and meth addicts and spousal abuse and how she shouldn't expect to find Prince Charming in the county jail. And that bastard Richard looks like he finally gets the picture, and he doesn't take it personally.

"Mary likes bad boys," Richard says, as if he isn't the bad boy Jack is talking about. "Gets used to one kind of badness and then goes on to worse."

Like he's quoting some radio talk show host who calls himself doctor somebody. Doctor Oz. Doctor Phil. Doctor Laura. Come to think of it, Dr. Laura was pretty much right on target. Jack doesn't think she would approve of Richard at all. She probably wouldn't approve of Jack Bailey either, but she'd approve of Ellen even less.

Jack's no-good son-in-law gets one of those flat arrogant smiles like a movie star who's just converted to Scientology. He turns quiet, like somebody's just read him his Miranda rights and he hasn't decided yet if he needs a lawyer.

Jack decides that Mary's husband is good-looking in a rugged Native

American sort of way. Like Lou Diamond Phillips, who Jack suspects is Mexican.

Richard says something about the mysterious forces that keep the world in balance and how it takes all kinds of people to do that. How good and bad are two sides of the same behavior coin. Total Native American, New Age bullshit.

Jack's no-good son-in-law waves a finger at Rudy, and two muffins are delivered to his plate in less time than it takes for a Breitling second hand to make another circuit.

"The best kind of magic," Richard says. "A hand motion and food appears." He takes a bite that's way too small to be manly and doesn't complain when Jack reaches across the table and steals a muffin. He doesn't complain at all, and that pisses Jack off.

"Fuck you." The muffin and the Wild Ass Cabernet and the sparkling water and the bitchy waitress and the gay muffin man and Richard's smiling face turn up Jack's temper thermostat.

"Lou Diamond Phillips is a Mexican." Jack recognizes the warning signs he learned in the court-ordered Anger Management Classes he took right before Ellen wanted to be free more than she wanted him.

Richard sips his sparkling water and nibbles a blueberry mini-muffin that's only big enough to satisfy a methamphetamine addict's appetite, and asks, "Is Lou Diamond Phillips Mary's boyfriend?"

Jack is trying to decide between a fistfight and a shouting match when Mary arrives.

Brianna wants her drink order. Rudy wants to give her muffins. Jack wants to know how she got the swollen lip and the bruise over her eye that she couldn't quite hide under concealer.

"What are you doing here?" Mary stares at Richard. She puts her hands on the back of the chair selected for her by Brianna while Rudy tongs a perfect pair of muffins onto her plate. She points at her swollen lip. She touches her bruised eye and winces. "I mean it, Richard. What the hell are you doing here?"

"Not really sure," Richard says. He takes a sip of sparkling water. He tells Mary something about a little girl who looks like a rainbow and a glass beanstalk that's growing in the lobby of the art museum and a tattooed man named Toad who's buying lunch for everybody if Mary will just take a seat. He smiles—like a felon who's finally been accused of something he didn't do—and says, "Everybody has to be somewhere."

Jack thinks Richard is about as charming as a male prostitute at a national meeting of the Red Hat Society, but Mary smiles like a single mom at a third-grade talent show. Forgetting all about the bruises, the methamphetamine, and Richard's dalliance with Ellen. Mary is falling under his spell again.

Nothing for Jack to say but, "What the fuck?"

Mary slides into her chair, possibly willing to see the world from Richard's perspective even though one of her eyes is almost swollen shut. Maybe even ready to kiss and make up, if her lip doesn't hurt too much.

Jack sees that Richard was right. Mary likes bad boys. She gets that from her slutty mother, who never thought Jack Bailey was nearly bad enough. Even when he was drunk, like now.

"No way." Jack's voice is loud enough to turn every head in the restaurant his way. Lots of witnesses. Normally, that would slow him down but after three glasses of Wild Ass Cabernet and not nearly enough muffins....

"No way you are going to hit my daughter and get away with it."

Mary puts a hand on Jack's shoulder, like that will stop him from getting up and kicking Richard Daniels's ass. He tries to shrug it off, but Mary is stronger than she looks. He pushes her hand away so hard it strikes her in the bruised eye. The table shakes. Richard stands. His San Pellegrino crashes to the floor.

Mary bursts into tears.

Brianna shouts, "Call nine-one-one!"

Jack spouts a string of curse words so fast his tongue can't keep up.

Richard steps out of a sparkling water puddle.

Muffin man points his tongs at Jack. "Calm down."

But Jack is already halfway around the table, shouting at the top of his voice about Richard fucking Mary, Richard fucking Ellen, and Richard fucking up the lives of everyone around him.

"Bruises! Apologies! Asshole!" Even Jack doesn't understand what that means, but every word makes him feel less like a father and more like an executioner, and that slimy little wife-battering Richard Daniels doesn't even have the decency to look ashamed. Mary's prick of a husband holds his hands up in what might be a gesture of surrender or an Asian meth-addict fighting stance. It doesn't make any difference to Jack. He's ready to kick some Native American ass all the way to the art museum gift shop.

"Stand away from the table, sir." A woman's voice, too authoritative to be a member of the wait-staff.

Jack is already on Richard's side of the table. Already so close there's no way he can miss a punch if he acts fast enough.

Richard catches the first blow in an open hand.

"Step back, sir."

Jack throws another punch. This one connects with Richard's nose. A little blood is a good start.

"Sir!"

Jack turns his head far enough to catch a glimpse of a slender female form in blue. Policewoman? There's no way Jack can resist getting a better look when she says, "Sir!" again.

The nametag on her uniform says Laura Pepper. Corporal's stripes on one sleeve. Black hair, probably shoulder length, but it's pulled back in a severe ponytail. She's holding something that looks like a cross between a gun and a transistor radio.

"Let me see your hands."

Jack's hands are still made into fists. Still ready to swing at Richard Daniels's face. Ready to spill more Indian blood with everybody watching. Any remnants of white guilt evaporate much faster than the puddle of San Pellegrino on the floor. He's not at all sorry about killing the buffalo, or Wounded Knee. He hopes Leonard Peltier rots in jail forever.

"You've been warned." Corporal Laura Pepper's Taser darts catch

Jack in the chest before he comes to his senses one half of a Breitling second too late to do him any good.

He falls into the puddle of San Pellegrino and broken glass. Sparkling water and electricity are a very bad combination, but the police officer is kind of cute, even in the middle of a seizure.

Jack Bailey tries to call Mary's name, but what comes out is, "Shit!"

Chapter 12

EVERYBODY'S EYES ARE LOCKED on the forty-something white man at the end of a pair of Taser wires and the sexy policewoman who works him like a remote control grand-mal action figure.

Nobody in the art museum café wants to look at Danny Riley. He glides among patrons like Michael Jackson moonwalking through a chorus line of *Thriller* zombies. A reggae tune plays on the sound system—"Lively Up Yourself" by Bob Marley, if Danny isn't mistaken—barely loud enough to hear over the gasps and whispers in the circle of diners gathering around the convulsing man.

The policewoman tries for one more jolt of electricity but her batteries are dead.

"Show's over, folks." She nudges her disabled perpetrator with the spit-shined toe of her regulation boot in perfect time with the Jamaican music.

Danny steps and turns on the syncopated beats and wonders why Indians never played drums like that. Until the policewoman came on the scene, he was pretty sure he was caught up in a vision. The Rainbow Girl who told him about magic beans, the Toad Man who named him Richard, the mysterious white man posing inscrutable questions, the beautiful girl. What could be more mystical?

The girl liked Danny more than most girls did. Smiled at him the way Sarah Benally smiled at him in the backseat of her police car. Not quite the same, but close.

Mary—she tried to stop the white man from attacking him. Didn't she? A pretty white girl, who never set eyes on Danny Riley before today. That kind of thing never happened on the Big Rez.

Except for the bruised eye and swollen lip, Mary was pretty enough to be on TV. Refined, like the girls on the evening news. Hot, like the girls in beer commercials. And totally white. The first girl like that who ever smiled at Danny Riley.

Maybe he should take a souvenir, something small he could put into his amulet bag. Something to tie him to this moment. He doesn't see anything except for sugar cubes and croutons—things that can't be magic because they turn to crumbs.

Danny threads his way through latecomers who are anxious to witness their first arrest before proceeding to the permanent display of Chihuly glass or the collection of American Impressionists on loan from Dallas.

Mary. Danny blows her a kiss and she keeps her smile. She watches as he backs away. She touches her lip. She touches her eye. She glances at the man on the floor as the policewoman cuffs his wrists and recites a list of rights so fast no one could take them seriously.

Danny could be gone by the time Mary looks his way again. He could dance out of the museum on the notes of the nearly subliminal reggae tune. Step between the words of the late great Bob Marley and be on the street, but he wants to see her face one more time.

Her eyes remind him of his mother's. Blame, guilt, and something else that isn't exactly love but it's close. None of those things can be meant for Danny, but he feels as if they are.

Love. Danny's heard Nelva talk about it all his life. Something that happens just before a disaster. Something that makes you walk slowly when you ought to run. Something that makes you say yes when you should refuse, make promises when you should practice your Indian ways. Sex is involved, but Danny's not sure exactly how.

Danny Riley shines like a searchlight when he ought to be invisible, gives Mary a chance to see he's not such a bad guy after all, and smiles like someone is about to take his picture—someone who's not a police photographer.

He gives Mary a little finger wave, the way he's seen Nelva do to boyfriends who never wave back. Is Mary some kind of shape-shifter's reward? Does she come with being Richard? Nobody's ever told him what to do when this kind of magic happens.

Mary whispers something that can't be heard over the list of Miranda rights. "Why do I keep doing this?"

Danny can read the question on her lips easily because his mother asked it at least a hundred times—after every black eye and every bloody nose, and every proposal of marriage that didn't work out because there was already a wife. Nelva never saw the error of her ways until it was too late. Until her lover's promises popped like soap bubbles in her face and left her asking, "Why do I keep doing this?"

Danny's invisibility is nearly complete by the time he reaches the rear entry to the restaurant, where he'll walk past the movie theater and the gift shop and leave the scene of the crime through the museum lobby the way he planned. Only it isn't his crime scene, and instead of a full stomach, he has an image of Mary's bruised face and a feeling he can't quite place.

He wonders if Nelva Riley feels like this when she begins a brand-new romance. Danny's pulse keeps time to the reggae beat even though he's well beyond the reach of the restaurant speakers. Fantasies sweep through his mind featuring a pretty girl named Mary with a black eye and a swollen lip that somehow make her even prettier.

Mary's image moves across Danny's mental stage fully clothed—not a typical fantasy for a healthy reservation boy.

His feet carry him on a path his mind is too distracted to figure out, as if he's guided by a supernatural GPS. Maybe this is how the spirits operate where the Civilized Tribes hold sway. He almost stumbles into the reflecting pool where the glass tower is still growing, but Rainbow Girl warns him, "Look out mister." She's bathed in the sun's broken colors again.

"Magic beans," she says. "Remember."

"I remember." Danny steps out of the museum. He checks the envelope in his back pocket. The Toad Man's gift is still there. Spirits are always giving gifts in Indian legends—a magic talisman, a special power—but never money. Never "ten large."

Danny crosses the street to avoid the two police cars and the ambulance parked in front of the art museum café.

On the rez, holy people show up in visions—White Shell Girl, Talking God, Changing Woman. Maybe in Oklahoma City it's cops like Corporal Laura Pepper. Holy people ask for acts of faith and bravery. Cops want to see a driver's license. Danny puts as much distance between himself and the police as quickly as he can because he doesn't have a driver's license. He doesn't have a photo ID of any kind. According to reservation records, Danny doesn't exist. Wasn't born in an abandoned hogan in the Short Mountains. Didn't live in an ancient Airstream trailer near Tuba City with a Laguna mother who'd sleep with any man who wasn't Cherokee. Danny appeared on the Navajo Nation, stayed long enough to cause trouble, and then vanished, the way *witch-people* do.

Good enough for the Navajo, even if Danny hasn't been initiated by robbing a grave or murdering a sibling. Even if he had no relatives who could teach him the *Witchery Way*.

Danny's stomach rumbles loud enough to make him visible to post-lunch hour pedestrians headed back to wherever people go in Oklahoma City when the excitement is over at the art museum café.

Can a person with ten thousand dollars in his pocket starve to death in Oklahoma City? Danny sees a pair of yellow arches. No blueberry mini-muffins or sparkling water at McDonald's, but right now he'll settle for a Quarter Pounder.

THERE ARE FOUR LINES AT the counter, filled with people who can't make up their minds until they ask a lot of questions. People who don't know whether they want large fries, or if Coke will be all right since McDonald's doesn't have Pepsi. Women think out loud about 'healthy options,' but they settle on fried meat and potatoes. Children want happy meals with *Star Wars* figures. Men cluster around the condiment dispenser filling tiny paper cups with ketchup, putting the smallest amount of ice possible into their drink cups. The air is so full of grease and noise that everybody in McDonald's is invisible to everybody else, except for the uniformed clerks behind the counter who say, "Welcome to McDonald's. How may I help you?" It's the least supernatural place in the whole world.

Adult customers pretend they don't see the African American dwarf enter the McDonald's, but everything goes quiet all at once. Danny recognizes the signs of Oklahoma City magic slipping into gear. The clerks don't remember their lines. Children don't remember it's not polite to stare. People who've waited patiently in line look at their watches and decide to live off their fat until dinnertime.

Not a pigmy. Danny knows all about those little guys. They are completely proportional. They speak with clicks and grunts. They live on the Serengeti Plain. All facts Danny learned from a movie, *The Gods Must Be Crazy*, that Nelva made him watch while she rolled around on the only double bed inside their beat-up mobile home with her latest after-market man.

This dwarf has arms that are too short, fingers that are too thick, and a pristine bald head that's at least two hat sizes too large. He wears a blue blazer—like British schoolboys on PBS mysteries—only this blue blazer has a pistol-size bulge under the left lapel. The jacket is tailored perfectly to fit the abnormal curvature of his spine without hiding it.

The little man has glazed-gray coyote eyes that don't approve of anything. People dodge out of his line of vision as he sweeps the path in front of him with a slow oscillation of his head.

Danny is all the way up to the counter, but the dwarf's coyote eyes have paralyzed the clerk. Danny says, "Excuse me," but the young man in the stained uniform stands as still and lifeless as the freeze-tag champion of the world.

Powerful magic. Danny never expected anything like this in McDonald's. He can feel the dwarf's eyes on his back like the laser sight of a sniper's rifle ready to open an escape hatch for his soul. Dwarves are wizards, everybody on the rez knows that. Like a flowering bush with all its buds pinched so every ounce of power concentrates in a single flower. A reproductive outlet—the most powerful kind—and this dwarf is black. Danny knows all about stereotypes. Surely they can't all be wrong.

Lots of supernatural legends about dwarves buzzed around the rez. Ancient heroic stories that trickled down from grandfathers, and modern twisted romances told to Danny by his mother.

Nelva's stories were mostly about the same dwarf, an architect who designed the Ute Mountain Casino and fell in love with her while he waited for a labor dispute to end. A real bastard with a gambling problem, a womanizing problem, and warrants for failing to pay child support in Arizona. An evil witch, who always found a way to make his troubles disappear—then reappear again in somebody else's life.

"Close Magic," is what Nelva called it. "The most dangerous kind of witchcraft where lovers are concerned."

The dwarf staring at Danny's back is close all right. Hate radiates from the little man like a miniature space heater.

"How the fuck did you get away?" The dwarf has an edgy Muppet voice, nothing like the little guys in *The Wizard of Oz*. He jingles when he walks—some kind of ankle bracelet, like a grass dancer in a plains Indians powwow.

Danny turns around, hoping for a case of mistaken identity. No luck.

"What you doing here?" The dwarf clutches a giant silver crucifix that hangs around his neck. Squeezes hard enough to make Jesus cry for mercy.

"What you doin' here, Richard?"

Richard again. Oklahoma City sprits have a one-track mind.

Will Mary make another appearance or Rainbow Girl? Will the police chase this vision away with Tasers and Miranda Rights? Will the dwarf give Danny a gift of ten large, like Toad Man?

The little man works his hand under his jacket, the way a snake closes in on a cornered mouse. His too-thick fingers touch the pistol bulge for a second then move lower. The hand is holding an iPhone when Danny sees it again. An oversized finger pokes at the screen.

"Richard Daniels is right in front of me. Get in here and kill his ass right now."

Not a friendly spirit. Not a spirit who is afraid to declare his intentions in front of witnesses either, and there's no back way out of this McDonald's.

Two giant economy-sized thugs crowd into the entrance at the same time. Big guys who don't look anything like spirits.

The clerk in front of Danny is starting to breathe again, making up for lost time like a distance runner who's picked a course that's too long and too steep but still plans on crossing the finish line.

"Quarter Pounder with cheese. Large order of fries. Medium Diet Coke," Danny tells him. Perfect McDonald's etiquette.

The clerk punches the order into his computer like a horse trained to tap an answer to a math problem when the proper signal's given.

Now for an act of bravery. Danny fishes a hundred-dollar bill out of the Toad Man's envelope and hands it to the clerk. He heads for the men's room, like he's suddenly remembered eating a half-dozen prunes.

He hears the dwarf tell his spirit helpers to "Get the son of a bitch."

He hears one of them ask if they can wait till he comes out.

"Fuck no!" as the door closes.

No back way out of the restroom either, but a half-Laguna boy who grew up among the Navajo always has a plan.

Three sinks with three plastic soap dispensers kept full of pink antibacterial cleanser by order of the Great Franchise God of McDonald's.

One at a time he empties the soap dispensers in front of the restroom door. He wedges a stall door shut with toilet paper—all the better if it looks suspicious. He crosses himself the way he's seen superstitious non-Catholic Navajo do when they are just about to do something dangerous and don't have time for a proper Indian offering.

Danny flattens himself against the wall next to the entry door on the side opposite the stalls, where the thugs won't look because the first thing they will see is a wad of toilet paper stuck between the stall door and the jamb like a piece of cheese in a mousetrap. Practical magic for a witch who doesn't know spells.

It's too late to see if his reflection shows in the mirror over the sinks. Too late to wonder if he could have leaped over the counter and run out through the kitchen. Too late to wonder if the clerk will have his order ready to go. Danny Riley is as hungry now as when he hunted for rabbits on the rez with his pet wolf, Queenie.

He crosses himself again when he thinks about the wolf released on the rez after she'd learned to depend on humans. One more reason the Navajo thought he was a witch. One more reason he was in a men's restroom in an OKC McDonald's hoping the dwarf's thug spirit helpers are as stupid as they seemed.

The door pulls open—in keeping with the city fire codes. A pistol is the first thing to come through.

"Don't see his feet." Another pistol joins the first, like a pair of pistol puppets discussing what to do next.

"Probably standing on the seat." The thugs crowd through the door at the same time, off balance, guns pointed at the imaginary half-Laguna, half-Cherokee boy standing on a urine-splattered toilet seat.

They pop through the door like a double-barreled zit that's reached its full potential, already sliding when Danny pushes them across the soap-slick floor.

A pistol discharges as he runs out the door. Then three more shots and a scream. Danny steps around the dwarf and collects his order from the clerk.

"Keep the change." Not a typical Native American offering, but a substantial one. "Call nine-one-one."

In less than a half-minute he's on the street again listening to police sirens howl like a lonely timber wolf that has no business on the rez.

13

THE MIXTURE OF AMMONIUM nitrate and phe-
nyl-2-propanone smells like an overcooked home permanent.
Time to turn down the heat. Richard spits into the mix, the
way John Horse used to do. The master meth cook's body was a regular
drug factory. He sweated love potions and urinated miracles.

He told Richard, "It's something in the blood." John Horse came
from a long line of Black Seminole medicine men. "Daddy couldn't do
it, but Grandpa could. I got it, but my son… I guess we'll never know."

The Black Seminole is the result of two lines of witch doctors separated by an ocean. Or maybe that's just some John Horse bullshit.
Maybe Richard's saliva will work magic too. He spits another glob into
the pot—can't hurt anything—and waits.

The first crystals out of the toluene bath look as much like Cherokee Ice as anything Richard Daniels has ever seen. He crushes one the
size of a three-carat diamond in a mortar and pestle, moistens an index
finger, and rakes the powder across his tongue.

No big amphetamine rush—there never is with oral ingestion—

but the candied sour apple taste is perfect. He tries a little more and chews the crystals like rock candy. The texture feels like broken glass. The acidity burns his throat. His heart plays a familiar tune against his breastbone—Seminole war drums—and his mood rises like a hot air balloon. He's got it right.

Little Bits will be as pleased as people like Little Bits can be, but maybe Richard doesn't have to worry so much about Little Bits anymore. Ideas take root deep inside his brain, push their way to the surface like seedling redwood trees moving toward heaven one millimeter at a time. The temperature inside Richard's mind drops into the cool zone. As cool and steady as a Cherokee Ice glacier. His senses go to high alert because an opportunity might walk through the door, the way it always does if you wait long enough.

He hears the lock tumblers turn over. Hears the door slide open. Hears four-inch stiletto heels on the cement floor, moving quickly, like a whore who wants to get business taken care of so she can move on to other clients.

"Hey now, Richard." Ellen stands away from the electric range top, wrinkling her nose at the boiling cat piss cloud of anhydrous ammonia that's too much for the vent. "How are things going?"

She turns sideways, cocks a hip so Richard will start wondering what she looks like underneath the skirt, but Cherokee Ice has put his sex drive into suspended animation, frozen it so solid it might take fifty-six more days of mandatory rehab to wake it up again.

"Hey there." Richard's penis doesn't say hello. Good distraction. Little soldiers usually stand at attention when Ellen walks into the room. He takes a cautious step in her direction, the way an animal control officer approaches a stray cat. Richard doesn't want a foot chase now that he's figured out what to do.

"So why did you leave Jack Bailey?" Richard really doesn't want to know. Just something to turn Ellen's attention to herself, where it naturally goes. "He seems like a nice enough guy." Richard takes another step, smiles at Ellen the way Jesus smiled at the dessert course of the last supper.

"Too nice for a girl like me," Ellen tells him. "Not strong enough, not mean enough, not dangerous enough." She's so lost in memories of Jack Bailey, she doesn't see that Richard is almost close enough to grab her. Doesn't remember Richard is *not* too nice for a woman like Ellen.

"Jack's never been in a fight. No one's afraid of him. Especially not me." Ellen's busy trying to sort through the short circuit between love and fear. There's no reaction when Richard puts his hands on her shoulders.

Ellen says, "Jack whines instead of shouting. Wrings his hands instead of using them... you know?" She looks into Richard's eyes to see if someone finally gets it. To see if someone finally understands why she likes men who are so unlikable. She doesn't resist when Richard Daniels proves he's one of them, by covering her lips with his. She lets his tongue push past her teeth and fill her mouth with the taste of candied green apples and a hint of lighter fluid.

Ellen decides—as Richard knew she would—she'll do anything he wants. Anything at all, at least until his kiss wears off. Not every woman would be this easy. Richard understands that very well. But it's Ellen's nature to be seduced by men who'll treat her badly. Until someone worse comes along, and right now Richard Daniels is the worst man in the room.

He takes Ellen Bailey away from Little Bits as easily as John Horse seduced Wilma Daniels.

Richard holds a beaker of muriatic acid by the rim. It's reached the boiling point. Hotter than a cup of McDonald's lawsuit coffee, ready for an unsuspecting customer.

"Scream." Richard touches Ellen's bare arm with the hot beaker to ensure authenticity.

She shrieks like the heroine in a slasher movie. She dances away from Richard and rubs her arm, not sure what's going to happen next. But she's still sure she likes violent, dangerous men like the one waiting with a beaker of boiling acid for Little Bits's white giant bodyguard to come through the door.

The beaker is too hot to hold, but the nerves of Richard's hand are coated with a layer of Cherokee Ice. Blisters raise on his fingertips and pop open. They spill Ice saturated fluid over the glass surface. Make it slippery as a promise to stay sober. He switches hands, once, twice, like a game of hot potato, while the tumblers turn inside the lock on the basement door and the giant white man's silhouette appears in the same rectangle of blinding light where Ellen stood minutes ago.

Like a target on a firing range, concentric circles form around the giant's head, not quite solid enough to break through the hallucination barrier but clear enough to focus all of Richard's strength on his pitching arm.

The beaker tumbles twice before it shatters in the giant's face.

He covers his eyes—like a three year old trying to hide from monsters. Acid fumes mix with screams. Hair turns to ash. Thick folds of skin flake off the giant's face like lead paint inside a condemned building. He inhales acid fumes rising from his shirt. Foam flickers from his nose and mouth. He charges forward because he can't think of anything else. Falls over the electric range. Tips a pot of ammonium nitrate onto the burners, where it mixes with a pool of spilled toluene brake fluid.

Richard doesn't know what will happen next, but he knows it's best to be far away. He grabs Ellen by the arm and runs out the open door, onto a street of abandoned houses that once was fraternity row on the campus of Oklahoma City University.

"Run!" Richard shouts, but Ellen is already running from the smoke rolling through the door to the basement of the old Tri Delta sorority house. He wants to tell her that delta is the Greek symbol for change, but he's not sure how he came by that information. Maybe from his higher power, who has not been all that reliable lately.

So he says, "Run," again, just as he remembers he's still naked.

Orally ingested Cherokee Ice comes on slowly but lasts a very long time. Much longer than a kiss from a man in the direct line of Black Seminole medicine men. Richard doesn't have time to do the arithmetic, but he's pretty sure John Horse is his grandfather. Why else would a man like that come back to Wilma Daniels?

That explains a lot, and there is a lot that needs explaining.

A police cruiser pulls up behind Richard and Ellen, turns on its light bar, and squeals the siren. A woman's voice shouts at them over a speaker system that vibrates her voice like the number-caller in a bingo game.

Richard knows a naked man is never going to blend in, even on a college campus, so he comes to an abrupt stop as the female cop steps out of her car and puts her hand on her weapon.

"Fraternity prank." The perfect excuse comes to him right before she draws her pistol.

He looks around for Ellen, but Mary's mom has sat in the back of a police car many times and doesn't want to do it anymore.

"Show me your hands." The female cop comes close enough so Richard can read her nametag. Corporal Laura Pepper. Exactly the right number of stripes on her shoulder to let her ride around Oklahoma City in her very own cruiser, arresting naked men with blisters on their hands.

"Those look like burns," Laura Pepper says, moving cautiously because the closer she comes to Richard, the less he looks like a fraternity boy. Especially now that she is close enough to catch the strong scent of ammonia on his skin.

She's almost chosen between her sidearm and her Taser. Richard sees Corporal Laura Pepper's hand drifting toward electronic apprehension, away from the lethal force that requires so much paperwork after every authorized use. Neither the pistol nor the Taser is very good for him, so he spits directly into her extra wide, hyper-observant eyes.

"Sorry, officer." Always best to be polite when you've done an unforgivable thing. He backs away because he wants to see how long it will take for medicine man saliva to soak through a policewoman's eyes all the way to her brain.

Not long. Corporal Laura Pepper looks into the sky. She doesn't notice her perpetrator has slipped away and disappeared into a drainage ditch.

Flood control highway. He knows that every drainage ditch in Oklahoma City is connected. Knows it with the same certainty that every person on the planet knew the earth was flat for centuries before they knew it wasn't. It doesn't matter if you're right or wrong if, when you're so full of certainty, there's no room for doubt.

Now all he needs to do is figure out which way to go. Graffiti covers the sloping cement drainage ditch walls but none of it tells him, "This way to Mary's house."

He's temporarily forgotten about the burning meth lab full of chemicals getting ready to explode until a solid thump shakes the ground, as if God smashed a cosmic croquette mallet into the planet. Richard turns toward the shock wave, waiting to see if the world is coming to an end just when he's finally got a handle on things.

A mushroom cloud of meth-laced smoke rises in the air. Most of it blows away, but some of it settles on the OCU campus like the ghost of Timothy Leary. It drifts over political science students and philosophy students, accountants, and engineers. It seeks the lowest geographical point for the same reason floodwaters look for an escape route. For the same reason Richard Daniels found the drainage ditch.

Inside the flood control channel, the cloud becomes a hallucinogenic ice storm. Visions swarm inside Richard's brain like Africanized killer bees. He crawls into a man-size pipe that opens into the side of the ditch. Mosquitos don't come near him because of the ammonia smell, but the visions don't subside until after the sun goes down.

RICHARD DANIELS'S PUPILS ARE THE size of Mercury dimes, so large he squints against the light of the crescent moon. He leaps over debris in the drainage ditch—almost like he does in flying dreams where each step is higher and longer than the last.

There are wings on Richard's heels, another concrete connection with Mercury, the messenger of the gods. Human sacrifice was all it took to bring Mercury to life—Little Bits's bodyguard, cooked through and through in a methamphetamine explosion, frozen in a block of Cherokee Ice like a Neanderthal man. Embalmed on the spot from the outside in, a mummy that doesn't need pyramids and wrappings.

Richard uses the stars to navigate his route to Mary's house. Distance and time are interchangeable. His heart rate is a drumroll so fast it's a continuous pulse of energy, like alternating current lighting up the gas inside a fluorescent tube.

Claws scrabble across the cement behind him. Maybe feral dogs, maybe his imagination. They can't catch him because his winged feet are charged with Cherokee super fuel. The world has been running on Indian time since the Ice cloud settled on him. How many days of recovery will it take to get that out of his system?

The soles of Richard's feet turn into mats of blood and embedded debris, loaded with bacteria that, fortunately, can't survive in an environment of Cherokee Ice. How does the messenger of the gods stop running?

"Help me!" he calls out to his higher power. One endless methamphetamine-minute passes, and another starts. A clatter of cans and bottles tumbles down the sloped side of the drainage ditch in front of him.

The wings on his feet won't hold him up a second longer. The right foot lands on a forty-ounce empty. The left one stays airborne until his bare ass slides through the pile of trash. Richard lies on his back and flaps his arms, forms the impression of an angel in the cans and bottles. Wonders what it looks like from his higher power's point of view.

"What you lookin' at, *pendejo?*"

Until Richard Daniels heard those words, he hadn't been looking at anything, but now he's staring at a shirtless man shaking the last scraps from his garbage can into the drainage ditch.

"You naked motherfucker?" The kind of accent that comes with a green card.

Richard wants to answer, but his saliva is too thick, and his mind is too busy sorting through the complicated way his higher power chose to stop him. He rises from the pile of cans and bottles, careful to leave his trash-angel intact as an offering. Richard turns his back on a string of Spanish obscenities. He scampers up the side of the ditch opposite his cursing brakeman. He sees his old, blue GMC pickup truck. He sees Mary's car. He sees the Queenie cross, the hanging scarecrow, and Mary's house with a light on behind every window.

He turns and waves to the shirtless man on the opposite side of the ditch.

"Fuck you!" The man extends an arm and flips his middle finger up like the blade of a switchblade knife.

MARY'S STANDING IN THE KITCHEN, talking on the telephone. Richard walks past her to the kitchen sink, puts his mouth on the faucet, and runs the water full speed across his lips. He swallows as much as he can hold, then retches into the sink and repeats the process.

"Charming," Mary says, but Richard is pretty sure she doesn't mean it.

She finds her little pistol on the telephone stand. Four suitcases sit on the floor beside her like a pack of pit bulls threatening to charge if he comes any closer.

"Mary."

Richard wants to tell her that it's not his fault, but what comes out is animal noises. He wants to tell her, "It's not me. It's the Ice," but his hands are knocking dishes off the counter and tipping over chairs because he can't stop moving.

His legs and arms are so full of energy they'll explode if he tries to hold them still. His brain is hot enough to singe his eyebrows. He needs more water. He needs to climb inside the refrigerator to cool down, but as soon as he opens the door, he realizes he isn't going to fit.

Chapter 14

BLOCKED NUMBER, POPS OVER the face of an enthusiastic female narrator on Jack Bailey's television screen. He doesn't curse the caller right away because of the extra-large swallow of Budweiser beer that feels like the beginning of a heart attack.

"*This place is called the Red Slough,*" the narrator tells him from behind the caller ID rectangle. "*Bet you've never heard of it.*" She walks across the screen but not far enough to escape from the BLOCKED NUMBER sign.

"Damn." Jack keeps his curse well below the mortal sin threshold. No point in taking chances if his chest pain turns out to be something more serious than foam.

The announcer says, "*Africanized killer bees, rattlesnakes, exotic birds, and—can you believe it—alligators. Right here in Southeastern Oklahoma.*" Her left hand stretches out in the most feminine gesture Jack has ever seen and points at something in the water that looks like one of the artificial logs in his gas fireplace.

"Alligators, folks!" She says something else, but Jack can't hear it over the first eight bars of "Hanky Panky" sounding on his telephone.

"Damn it to hell." Ellen installed the ringtone on their landline before she decided things weren't working out.

The pressure eases in Jack's chest, and he thinks about how much he wants to hear about Oklahoma alligators, and how much he doesn't want to hear the first eight bars of the worst song Madonna ever recorded.

The ringtone coaxes Ellen from the back of his mind like a gigantic alligator crawling out of the Red Slough to bite him on the ass.

The girl announcer peeks at him from behind the BLOCKED NUMBER sign. Her voice sounds so much like Ellen's, Jack tries to cover it up with super loud beer-swallows, followed by a belch that goes on long enough to recite half the alphabet. The way he used to in his charming college days when his future seemed bright, and Ellen seemed....

The TV girl has a body like Ellen's—slender, sexy, screaming to be touched—and probably has her face, too, once the caller ID rectangle goes away. She absolutely has an Ellen hand, with her wrist bent just so and her delicate index finger pointing at an ugly reptile that, *"Never attacks people, so I'm told."*

The answering machine kicks in and a recording of Ellen's voice tells the caller, *"We can't come to the phone right now, but if you'll leave a message, we'll get back to you."* Another promise she won't keep.

According to the digital readout on Jack's DVR, it's 8:45, which means the caller is probably a collection agency. When Ellen left, she packed everything but her bills. Credit card and PayPal charges, mostly negligees from Victoria's Secret that Jack never saw, hotel rooms he never slept in, a dating service or two, and a cash advance for Abraham's Bail Bonds.

Jack points the remote control at the TV screen. He punches "record," so he can learn all about Oklahoma alligators later. He punches "mute," so he can hear what the secret caller has to say right now—because there is the off chance it might be Publisher's Clearing House Sweepstakes telling him he's already won ten million dollars.

"Pick up, Jack." It's the real Ellen. Her voice hasn't changed much in two years. Still ordering Jack around. How long has he waited for this call? Jack looks at his Breitling Chronometer Emergency watch, which probably has a calendar function if he could figure out how to use it.

"Two years!" He shouts at the telephone. He's been sitting in a La-Z-Boy recliner long enough to drink four thousand three hundred eighty Budweisers, waiting to tell Ellen, "You've got a lot of nerve!" but now that doesn't seem like the right thing to say.

Not after she orders him to, *"Pick up Jack,"* using a tone of voice hostile enough to make a pit bull hide under the bed.

He recites a string of curses, relying heavily on the f-word. He begins a sentence with "bitch," and ends it with "whore." He accuses Ellen of having an affair with their daughter's husband, which is no more than a hunch.

Jack finishes his beer, crushes the aluminum can, and walks over to the telephone. He yells a few more curses at Ellen's voice, which is now telling him to, *"Pick up, you son of a bitch. I've got to talk to you about Mary."* A nasty demand, but the tone has almost turned friendly.

Almost.

Jack touches the telephone with his fingertips, remembering all the things he's wanted to tell Ellen since she walked out on him two years ago, but none of them seem all that important now that he has the chance.

"Please, Jack." Like she's asking him to pass the green bean casserole.

"We need to talk, Jack. It's important."

Important, like when Jack came home from selling insurance to find Ellen gone with most of her things and some of his. He wants to throw that in her face, but he wants to do it without picking up the telephone because Jack is pretty sure there is no way he'll refuse the real live Ellen anything—especially after she said please.

"Jack... pick up. I know you're there." As if she's trying to coax a puppy through a pet door.

He knows all of Ellen's tricks, but that doesn't mean they won't work. He picks up the phone but can't remember which button to push. All the gravity in her voice makes him too heavy to move, too slow to think things through.

Inertia. Jack learned all about it on a NOVA program just last week. A husband at rest tends to remain at rest unless acted upon by an outside force, like his wife saying, "I still love you, Jack."

But Ellen stops short of saying that, and Jack's answering machine is about to beep. The message opportunity has passed. Ellen has time to say just two more words, and the ones she chooses are, "*Fuck you!*"

Jack snatches up the phone after he knows it is too late.

He says, "Oh yeah!" to the dial tone.

He's glad she's not able to hear him.

Jack is a little drunk and very tired, and it's a long walk back to the La-Z-Boy recliner. He's wondering if Ellen's call will be the first of many. Will she leave messages when he's not at home? Will she make an offer of reconciliation—for Mary's sake? Was her call really about Mary, or is that just the last remaining link between the two of them now that the credit cards are canceled, and they don't have sex?

Jack doesn't want to think about Ellen anymore, but he's halfway through Discover Oklahoma, and all he remembers is the telephone call. His beer has turned as flat and bitter as his life, and the foam inside his stomach is now a serious case of heartburn.

He's kept a buzz on for two years now. Wine and beer, so his liver deteriorates at the slowest possible rate. He watches documentaries in high definition, so maybe something will soak through the haze and improve his mind enough that Ellen will want him back—if she ever comes to her senses.

A mallard duck swims across the television screen. It's pulled under-water by an alligator. The duck never saw it coming. Just like Jack, who should have known Ellen was going to leave him but didn't.

If he had another chance….

BLOCKED NUMBER pops onto the TV screen again. Jack's prayer is answered, and he hadn't even realized he was praying.

He says, "Thank you, God," even though he's agnostic. That's an atheist without the courage of his convictions, according to Ellen, who is probably calling him back now that he played hard to get.

He's out of the La-Z-Boy just as "Hanky Panky" starts to play. One step follows another, carefully, as if Jack is one of the flying Wallendas crossing Niagara Falls on a tightrope after happy hour.

Ellen's recorded voice has already told the caller to leave a message when Jack picks up the phone and pushes the green button.

"Ellen!" Jack is not sure what comes after that, but *Ellen* is such a good start he says it again. Ready to forgive everything, at least until she's safely back home. But he's already thinking of things a man shouldn't have to forgive, like when his wife told him she never had a real orgasm with him—not even once—and she had lots of them with other men. Men who were shorter, men who were fatter, men with zero fashion sense, men with small penises, and even smaller bank accounts. She had orgasms with a couple of women, and with a Swedish hand massage vibrator—"and nobody uses those anymore."—and once she had one sitting all alone on the washing machine in the laundromat on Northeast 23rd and Classen.

She told him, "Never with you, Jack. I faked it sometimes, but usually, I didn't bother. Surely you noticed."

So, the first word out of Jack's mouth is, "Whore." He's powerless to stop it.

"Dad? It's Mary."

Jack says, "Mary! I didn't mean to call you a...." He can't say whore when he knows it's Mary, so he goes quiet enough to hear Richard screaming in the background.

Lots of expletives. Most of them are worse than 'whore.'

Furniture crashes. Dishes break. Something heavy falls.

"Richard has gone sort of crazy," Mary says. *"Way crazy. He's back on meth. Mom thinks I should leave."*

Jack tries to think of something to say, but this is the second time the telephone has caught him by surprise today.

"I'm coming home, Dad."

Her no-good bastard of a husband is screaming—high-pitched, like a woman who is too hysterical to know if she is angry or afraid. Murder is the only non-curse word Jack understands.

"Your mother...." Probably not a good time to talk about Ellen, but she and Richard are stuck together in Jack's mind like two dogs mating who can't pull themselves apart, even if a classroom full of children is watching.

"*If I'm not there in fifteen minutes, call the police,*" Mary says.

"The police?" Jack almost turns the sentence into a question, so Mary tells him again.

She screams the word. "*Police!*"

She shouts, "*Get back!*"

A gunshot. It sounds like a very large balloon popping near the telephone. Then another and another.

"*I told you,*" Mary says. Everything is quiet in the background.

Jack doesn't ask what happened because he doesn't want to know.

"*Fifteen minutes,*" Mary tells him. "*Starting now.*"

Jack checks his Breitling Emergency Chronometer watch.

A male enhancement commercial comes on the TV. A smiling man, a smiling woman, better living through chemistry. Jack listens to penis measurements quoted in centimeters, which makes everything sound big and scientific. When the commercial fades to black, he takes it as a sign he needs another beer.

Fifteen minutes. If Jack hurries, he might have time for two.

Chapter 15

THE GUNSHOTS SOUND LIKE sonic booms inside the little room. Richard Daniels checks his body—no bullet holes, no bloody places he didn't have before, no lancinating pain, except for the sensation Mary's eyes send to his skin.

She tells him something and then fires another shot. He watches the bullet streak past his head, hot and spinning, moving too fast to see except through the time-lapse lens of Cherokee Ice.

She's hanging up the telephone while she takes aim again, saying bad things about Richard Daniels, who is standing naked in her kitchen, struck dumb by the chemicals in his blood. If he doesn't say something soon, Mary will be done with him. The pistol is a sure sign. He sees the emotion in her eyes. Two decisions perched like identical twins on a teeter-totter. Anything could tip the balance, a hiccup, a belch, a leaf falling from the sky.

"Two-Heart," he tells her. Growls it out like a stray dog on the snare end of a catchpole. It's exactly the wrong thing to say.

There are lots of things he could tell her about being taken prisoner, about a cloud of methamphetamine that struck him like a hammer. So many things Richard needs to tell Mary, they all try to come out at once.

"I've got to pee," he says. Calm and collected and one hundred percent true. He walks into the bathroom and shuts the door like the polite gentleman he wants her to believe he is. He sits down on the seat because the world is starting to spin in two directions at once. It's a good thing he's already sitting down because he can't feel his legs. His arms turn into strands of spaghetti. He leans against the wall beside the toilet, closes his eyes, and turns things over to his higher power.

"Help me!" he says again for the second time tonight. Two prayers in four words. That's probably some kind of record. When he opens his eyes again, the room has stopped spinning. When he walks out, Mary is gone. She's laid out a pair of pants, a shirt, even socks and underwear on the kitchen table. His wallet is there too and his cell phone.

"That means there's still a chance, doesn't it?" Richard's language skills are back again. Maybe Mary will come back too. He turns the cell phone on, thinking he should call her. Thinking he should log onto his Apple Store account and buy an application for fixing marriages, but Mary wouldn't answer, and there is no such application, and the batteries are low.

Richard's personal batteries are low too. He sits at the kitchen table and wishes for a higher power who takes a more personal interest. He closes his eyes and listens to the world go by. An owl calls to its mate in one of Mary's trees. The shirtless Hispanic neighbor dumps another load of cans and sings a Spanish song. One corner of Mary's house settles a millimeter into the Oklahoma caliche clay. The front door opens.

Richard hears the jingle of an ankle bracelet of Mercury dimes. Mercury again.

Little Bits carries a semi-automatic pistol at his side. Richard likes to think of it as a Glock—no reason, he just likes the word.

The Glock has a laser sight attached under the barrel. Little Bits raises the pistol so a little red dot dances on Richard's shirt as he stands up.

The clothes come as a complete surprise. His zipper is up. His buttons are all in the right places. His arms smell of lavender soap. He runs his hands over his face—clean-shaven. When did this all happen? Everything would be perfect if the visitor were Mary instead of Little Bits.

Richard watches the little red dot circle the place where his heart is beating much closer to a normal rate now. Still too fast, but not fast enough to turn the little laser dot into a light show.

"Hey now, Two-Heart."

Richard is at a loss for words.

"You killed my bodyguard."

The red dot draws a figure eight on Richard's chest. The number burns itself into Richard's retina like a sparkler image. A backward, upside-down eight is still a number eight.

"Palindrome." He tells Little Bits the name for words and numbers that look the same from different points of view.

"You blew up my meth lab." Little Bits doesn't say anything about running off with Ellen. Maybe he doesn't know, or maybe it isn't important to him.

Richard shrugs. There are enough amphetamine molecules still flowing in his blood to make him believe things might still work out. He's been shot at once today already. He's already killed a giant, inhaled a cloud, and run through Oklahoma City naked.

"Help me." Richard's third two-word prayer rolls out like snake eyes three times in a row. It doesn't seem like superstition because he keeps it simple.

"Say what?" Little Bits reaches for his jumbo silver crucifix. Kisses Jesus on the lips the way Judas kissed him at the last supper.

The way John Horse kissed Wilma Daniels.

"Kiss me." Richard moves toward Little Bits with his arms held out, the way lovers do when they run toward each other in slow motion at the end of romance movies.

Little Bits keeps the Glock pointed at Richard Daniels's heart. The red dot dances wildly, but the little man doesn't need a laser at six feet.

Five feet, four feet, three feet. Little Bits fires.

The flame from the discharge scorches Richard's shirt and singes his skin. The bullet smacks him like a baseball bat. Rib splinters fly into his lungs like a handful of darts. Not pain, exactly. That will come later, if there is a later.

"Two-Heart witches are really good at death curses." Richard locks his lips over Little Bits's, covering them with bloody foam like a madhouse makeover specialist.

"Shit!" Little Bits pushes Richard away. Holds his crucifix between them as if Richard is a vampire. He points the Glock at Richard's face, in case Jesus isn't really on his side.

Richard's eyes fill with fire from the muzzle blast. He feels the impact on his skull at the same time he hears the explosion.

Little Bits's Mercury dime anklet jingles like a belled cat as he runs out the front door of Mary's house.

No pain yet, but Richard can feel its shadow fall across him as he lies on the kitchen floor, waiting for his higher power to arrive in the nick of time.

"Hey now, Richard." His higher power has a dreamy female voice like the Krishna Consciousness girls who sell smiles for a dollar. She takes his spirit by the hand and pulls it free before the pain sets in. Methamphetamine molecules clatter on the floor as they tumble off his soul.

He tries to ask her, "What's your name?" But he's left his vocal cords behind.

"Cherokee Ice," she tells him, but she doesn't have to. Richard Daniels knew that all along.

"Time to go," she says. "It's just a short trip to the other side."

Chapter 16

MARY PULLS INTO THE empty side of Jack's double garage with five minutes to spare. Not a hair out of place. She points to four large bags in her backseat.

"Sorry, Dad. They're kind of heavy." That means Jack has to carry them.

Mary is almost as good at giving orders as Ellen. She looks like Ellen too, standing beside the car. Slender girl, blonde hair verging on red, little black dress not quite short enough to be slutty but close.

Mary points at her suitcases the same way the pretty girl in the Red Slough documentary pointed at the alligators. She dabs the corners of her eyes with a tissue, soaking up tears that collected during the short drive across the city. She still cares about her husband. That's the big difference between Mary and her mother.

Beer blurs the image but not before Jack understands that Richard is still in his daughter's life. He'll be in her life, even after the divorce. And there will be a divorce. Jack is certain he can talk her into that right after he explains why he called her a whore when she phoned him ten minutes ago.

"BLOCKED NUMBER." Jack Bailey remembers four things about the Red Slough—Africanized killer bees, rattlesnakes, alligators, and BLOCKED NUMBER.

"I'd help you carry them, but…." Mary ignores the blocked number comment. She steps around the beer-breath fog that floats in front of Jack like a low-hanging cloud.

Jack strains to lift the largest suitcase. "What's inside? A body?" Then he remembers the gunshots. Maybe Richard won't always be in Mary's life.

He carries the bags to her room, one at a time to minimize the damage to his back. Mary's old room is exactly as she left it when she went to college. Ellen insisted they keep it that way—like a shrine because Ellen always knew it wouldn't work out between Mary and Richard.

Mary sits in the family room while Jack wrestles with her luggage, taking stock of her life and watching HGTV. *Property Virgins*—her favorite show. To hell with *Discover Oklahoma*. Some of her tears have gotten too heavy to hold back.

She's ignoring them. Jack isn't.

"I see how it was with you and Mom," she says when Jack finishes his assigned duties. Forgiving him, finally, as if there were something to forgive.

"I love you, Daddy," Mary tells him for the first time in more than two years.

"I love you back." Jack hasn't said those words either—hasn't thought them for so long he wonders if they are still true.

After an uncomfortable, post-vulnerability silence, Jack wants to know, "What happened?"

"You know." That means Mary isn't ready to talk about it, but maybe after *Property Virgins*, when Brad and Ginger finally decide on house number one, two, or three. She turns the volume higher.

"I think they should take the one with the big back yard and the view," she says. "Even if it adds twenty minutes to Brad's commute." Mary makes a face when she says Brad's name. He doesn't look anything like Richard, but Jack knows Mary is mulling over things they have in common—surplus testosterone, five o'clock shadow, smart-aleck attitudes, and erections at inappropriate times.

No undertones of guilt in her conversation, so maybe she didn't shoot Richard after all.

"Men." She sniffs at her fingers. Shows them to Jack. "Gunpowder residue."

Not something he thought he'd ever hear his daughter say. He wonders if the gun is in one of the suitcases he just carried. Was it the pistol he gave her the first time she and Richard separated? A .38 caliber, Smith & Wesson, five-shot revolver, registered to Jack but exactly the right size to fit in his daughter's hand.

"Gunshot residue?" Jack thinks there might be two more beers in his refrigerator. He's hoping for a two-beer answer, something troubling but not devastating. A devastating answer will require a trip to the grocery store, and Jack's a little bit too tipsy to drive.

"My nails are chipped." Mary shows Jack her left hand. Her wedding ring is still there. "Mom leave any nail polish when she... you know." Tears have left salt trails down both cheeks and moisture in the tiny creases at the corners of her lips.

Jack shrugs, exactly the way Brad does on *Property Virgins* when Ginger explains why his opinion doesn't matter.

"Check her vanity." He tries to strain all the unpleasant maleness from his voice. It's easier than he hoped. "So, what's up with Richard?"

Mary points the remote at Jack's TV and raises the volume. "Even though the kitchen will need a complete remodel, I still like house number two."

Pools of serotonin-laced salt water in her sinuses make Mary's voice as thick and nasal as a summer cold. The sound triggers a protective urge in Jack that he hasn't felt for a very long time. Makes him feel strong and masculine. Ready to drive over to Mary's house and beat the shit out of Richard Daniels like he should have done at the wedding when the minister asked if anyone present knew a reason these two people should not be joined.

"Is it possible he might call?"

Mary turns the TV volume up a notch.

"Should I answer if he does?"

"House number three has potential, too," Mary says. "Do you mind if I DVR this program? I need to unpack right now." She rubs her fingertips together and smiles at the gritty feel of nitrates in the whorls of her fingerprints.

"Warning shots," she tells him. "A sure way to get a man's attention."

Jack remembers how quiet it got right after Mary fired her pistol.

What came after the warning? Was she carrying the .38 around the house? How did she manage to pack four heavy suitcases and transport them in less than fifteen minutes? Planning ahead? Maybe Jack should ask, but it's clear she won't answer. That's the way conversations always went with Mary. That's how they'd gone with Ellen too. All the women's magazines say women like to talk. To be fair, they don't say women like to answer questions.

"Can we talk about this later?" Jack looks at his Breitling Chronometer Emergency watch, as if all he needs to do is name the perfect hour. "Tomorrow, maybe?"

Mary fiddles with Jack's remote control. Screens change. Red colors highlight programs.

"Done," she says. "You want me to turn back to the Discovery Channel?"

"Guess not." He's still looking at his watch. The second hand moves more slowly than usual, the way Albert Einstein said it would when everything else was moving fast.

"Sorry to shake things up, Dad."

He tries to fake a yawn, but it feels more like a petit mal seizure.

Mary walks out of the room before Jack can think of a clever response. Something sensitive and ironic, with just a touch of cynicism.

Maybe next time.

TWO A.M. IS WHEN ALL the worst things happen. The small-numbered hours when it's morning but it's going to stay dark for a very long time. Jack sits in his La-Z-Boy recliner, wondering if he can watch a cable news channel without waking Mary, wondering if the police have already investigated the shots fired in Mary's house, wondering if they are talking about a murder on secret police radio frequencies.

How can Mary sleep while Jack can't? He'll ask her first thing in the morning when she walks into the kitchen and complains about the coffee being too strong.

Jack doesn't turn the TV on, but he watches the digital clock on his DVR so he knows it's exactly two a.m. when a rock crashes through his living room window.

Breaking glass, like sound effects from the documentary on Crystal Night he saw right after Ellen left him. The night of breaking glass, when the Germans spoiled their reputation for the rest of the twentieth century.

"Damn!"

It's not Jack's first broken window. Somebody broke a few of them right after Ellen left him. Could have been her. Could have been one of her *special friends*. Anyway, he's had too many beers to get emotional.

Tires squeal on Jack's pressed concrete drive, the way they always do after broken living room windows.

"Dad?" Mary calls to him from her bedroom. Not excited. She's had experience with the sound of broken things. Dishes, furniture, a marriage—must run in the family.

"It's probably Richard." Barely loud enough for Jack to hear as he walks from the television room, where he spends most of his life, to the living room, where he does almost no living at all, and considers the possibility his daughter isn't a murderer after all.

Good news, he tells himself. The positive side of a broken window in the middle of the night.

There's a slightly elliptical softball-size stone lying in a scattering of glass shards on the hardwood floor, like a hard-boiled ostrich egg on a platter of shaved ice. Ellen had the floor installed one year before she left him. "Easy to clean," she promised, "and durable." According to Ellen, wood floors lasted practically forever, and scratches only added to their charm.

But scratches made by broken glass don't look all that charming.

"Call the cops, Dad." Mary shouts loud enough to overcome Jack's beer inertia.

He follows orders—as usual. He doesn't wait for warning shots. He practices what he's going to say a time or two because he wants to make a sober impression on the emergency operator, but his speech loses all its polish when the operator says, "Nine-one-one, what's your emergency?" A woman, naturally. Jack wonders if she's pretty.

"It's like this...." He tells her everything that happened for the last two years, except for the gunshots he heard on the telephone and the gunshot residue on Mary's hands. The operator has a friendly voice. She's a good listener. Jack isn't accustomed to that. He thinks the 911 operator likes him just a little and probably doesn't notice his S's are slurred and his consonants are soft, but when he asks her name, she tells him, "We're not allowed to give out that information, *sir*. Is there anything else?"

Sir. Polite and efficient, but not friendly after all.

"Nothing else," Jack tells her. He stands by the front door and waits for the police. It'll be the first time they've come to his house since Ellen went away.

JACK WATCHES THROUGH HIS BROKEN window as a police car squeaks to a stop in his circular drive right in front of his door. Checks his Breitling Chronometer Emergency watch. Two eleven a.m. Pretty good response time for the Oklahoma City cops, but Jack's responses are blunted by the last beer he drank just before the Chrystal Night re-enactment. He slaps himself in the face, which brings him back to reality enough to realize he shouldn't be doing that in front of a broken window with a police car in the driveway.

Radio chatter fills the air as the cruiser door opens, and a policewoman steps out. Tall, with wavy, black, shoulder-length hair that reflects the outdoor lighting like a sable coat. She checks the snap over her holster, adjusts her cap, walks to the door like she's got all the time in the world, and knocks.

Familiar. Jack has had lots of experience with policewomen in the last few years. Was even Tased by one in the art museum café after he poked Richard in the nose. Drunk and disorderly was the charge. Nothing but a fine because the judge had an ex-wife and a no-good son-in-law too.

This might be the same policewoman, but it's hard to tell because women in uniform all look the same after they Tase you. Angry, pushing your face into the floor, reading a list of rights that sound like accusations. They look especially similar after a few glasses of art museum wine.

She knocks on the door instead of ringing, the way cops always do. Lots of knocks, like a drumroll before the winner of a game show is announced. She continues the knocking motion for a couple of seconds after the door is open and there's nothing to knock on but air.

Like a mime. Jack debates whether to say something about this but finally decides not to because he sees the Taser in the policewoman's utility belt and is pretty sure she's the one from the art museum café.

She asks, "Have I been here before?" Her badge catches the reflection of Jack's porch light. The glare makes little yellow spots dance across his eyes.

He's about to apologize for his pre-tasing behavior in the art museum café, but it's hard to make a positive identification behind all the yellow spots.

She looks over Jack's shoulder and holds her mouth, like she smells something rotten and is pretty sure the source is Jack. Every policewoman Jack has met holds her mouth like that, so it doesn't mean this one has anything personal against him.

He isn't interested in talking about the past, so he tells her, "The rock-throwing incident was about thirty minutes ago." He checks his Breitling Chronometer Emergency watch, thinks about telling her its retail value but decides against it.

"About two o'clock in the morning, a vehicle pulled into the driveway, and the driver tossed a rock through the living room window."

"Have I been here before?" The policewoman pushes the front door wider, shoves Jack aside with her hip, and eases herself into the foyer.

"Wow," Jack says before he can stop himself.

The policewoman's ID tag says her name is Laura Pepper. She isn't talking about Tasing him in the art museum café—which can't be anything but good—and she has a nice firm butt, which he can't help noticing when it slides into the perfect spooning position for about half a Breitling Chronometer Emergency second. He hasn't been in that position for a very long time.

"It was a blue GMC pickup truck," Jack says. "It belongs to my daughter Mary's husband. She left Richard early last night, so I know it was him. Even if I didn't exactly see the vehicle." Which means Richard isn't dead. Which means Mary isn't a murderer after all. Which is why Jack is smiling like an idiot.

Where is Mary, anyway? Probably on the telephone leaving nasty messages that will bring Richard back for another window.

"Yeah," the policewoman says. "I've been here before. I recognize the crappy prints in the hallway—no offense."

"You might want to go to Mary's house and check things out." Now that Jack knows Richard is alive, he thinks it would be nice if the cops found him surrounded by broken furniture. "You might want to take back up." Jack recites the address three times before he gets it right, but that doesn't matter because the policewoman isn't writing anything down.

"Richard Daniels is his name," Jack says, even though the policewoman isn't interested. "His friends would call him Rick if he had any friends, which he doesn't because he's so damned crazy."

Jack points at the rock and the glass shards on his hardwood living room floor and makes a sweeping gesture with his hand, like a football referee calling for a penalty and wants everybody to know it.

Instead of paying attention to Jack's complaint, Officer Laura Pepper executes a perfectly lovely three-hundred-and-sixty-degree turn, takes in her surroundings, and gives Jack a thrill at the same time. Her uniform is tailored. Every curve pops, like a *Playboy Magazine* photo shoot. Jack wonders if Officer Pepper might like a cup of coffee.

"It was a domestic disturbance," she tells him.

There had been so many of those right before Ellen left. Jack sort of remembers Officer Laura Pepper coming to their home. She'd cuffed Jack's hands behind his back—"For my safety and for yours"—and then after a little while, she'd pepper-sprayed Ellen—for her safety and for Jack's.

Ellen was going through her costume phase back then. Dressed as a cheerleader. That had been one of her best looks, but teen spirit got the better of her and she screamed loud enough to make the neighbors call the cops. It was amazing how fast a little Mace brought Ellen to her senses.

Officer Laura Pepper makes another three-hundred-and-sixty-degree turn. She hadn't looked this good back then. Maybe she'd been working out.

A lot of women look better to Jack since the divorce. Older women look younger, and younger women look old enough. Things like that happen to middle-aged men—so Jack has been told. One more nasty rumor, true like all the others.

Time to think about something else. Jack gestures to the broken glass on the living room floor. He points out the rock lying in the glittering slivers. Jack picks it up when Officer Laura Pepper doesn't. It's a glacial stone that has no business in Oklahoma, elliptical and smooth, like a woman's breast. Lots of things remind Jack of those since Ellen left.

Two Valentine hearts are painted in red on opposite poles of the elliptical stone, and between the hearts, the words "Fuck You" are printed in crude red block letters. Ellen's last words to Jack before he knew she really did want to talk to him about Mary.

He shows them to Officer Laura. "Rick's handwriting. I'd know it anywhere. It says Fuck You." Jack's saliva production increases when he says those words. He sprays the policewoman a little. He thinks about repeating them to see if they come out dryer the second time but doesn't.

"I see." Officer Laura takes a step back. Still not writing anything. "Is your wife home?"

"In the wind," Jack says, the way FBI agents talk on *Criminal Minds.*

Officer Laura Pepper does not look impressed with the police jargon. She takes the rock from Jack. She scratches at the letter F and says, "This is fingernail polish."

She twists the stone under the overhead ceiling light in the foyer. "Milani Neon-Red Nail Lacquer, if I'm not mistaken."

Jack wants to ask her if fingernail polish forensics is part of police training, but before he does, Officer Laura Pepper gives the rock a sniff.

"Fresh," she says. "What shade does Richard Daniels wear?"

Jack wants to sniff the rock, but Officer Laura Pepper pulls it away. She holds it over her head, well out of olfactory range.

"Go find your daughter. Now!" Leaving no doubt about how fast Jack should walk back to Mary's room.

Scurrying feels wrong, but he does it anyway. He knocks. He calls out, "Mary, could you talk to the police officer?" He opens the door.

"Coming in," pacing himself so she can cover herself or tell him, "Just a minute." But none of that is necessary because she isn't in the room.

"Mary," he calls out, in case she's hiding under the bed or inside the closet. He looks both places to be sure.

He searches Mary's bedroom and the guest bedroom and finds the partially used bottle of Milani Neon-Red Nail Lacquer in the bathroom off the hall. Mary apparently found it in Ellen's vanity.

He checks the garage. Her car is gone. Did she really call him last night, interrupt a Red Slough documentary with gunshots over the telephone, and show up ten minutes later with four heavily packed bags? Jack can't think clearly with all the impatient cop vibrations coming from the foyer.

"She was here a moment ago." Not running back but walking fast. Jack notices the loose leather strap over the policewoman's baton— that's new. He tries for a winning smile, but it feels like the one on his driver's license photograph.

"Sorry."

"Fraudulent nine-one-one calls are a crime," Laura Pepper says.

Jack takes it as a good sign that she isn't holding a can of Mace in the ready position. He points at the glass shards in his living room and shrugs. It seems less confrontational than words.

"Somebody did this," he says. "Probably Richard. Maybe Ellen. Definitely not Mary." The Mary denial comes out as a whisper.

"Not really what you'd call fraudulent," he says. "Not with the broken glass and all—right?"

The sneer on Laura Pepper's lips is personal now, but maybe Jack can save the day.

"It's just that Mary left her husband and came home, and then there was this broken window and the rock you're holding in your hand," he says, building an explanation out of random words. It isn't really working, and the policewoman's sneer is turning more sour by the second, and her foot is tapping double-time—maybe triple.

This is one of those times it would be nice to know more about women. Perhaps a compliment? Women like those, don't they?

"You were definitely here before." He hopes she doesn't remember how weird things turned out then. "I didn't recognize you right away because I think you've lost some weight." He stretches his smile as wide as it will go. "You look really good."

Laura Pepper stares at Jack as if she'd like to see him inside a chalk outline at a murder scene. She twists the stone in her hands so he can read the "Fuck You" sign painted in Neon Milani Neon-Red Nail Lacquer—Ellen's shade. She turns and walks out the door.

"Later." Jack wonders if that's the right thing to say at the end of a police visit. He wonders how the police report will read.

Chapter 17

DANNY RILEY STANDS IN the shadows between two buildings and tries to get Mary off his mind. Not working.

Streetlights are on. Stores are closed. Police cruisers patrol the city looking for people who don't belong. Danny moves a little deeper into the darkness. No one belongs less than him.

The sanitation department dumpster he leans against is warm to the touch. Something lives inside, rustling through the cast-offs of a day in Oklahoma City. Cats, probably. Rats for sure. Cats and rats are survivors, like Indians. They always find what they need at exactly the right time.

John Horse told him, "Living off the land is real, and magic is mostly imaginary." He's a Black Seminole holy man, so he should know.

Danny might be a holy man too, but it's still a little early to be sure. He pats the amulet bag underneath his shirt and listens to the sound of his own breathing. Waits for something mystical to happen. He tries his best to clear his mind so he'll be ready. Doesn't even count his breaths because mathematics can tie a vision in knots.

But Danny Riley's mind won't clear because a pretty, white girl is caught in his soul like a barbed fishhook. *Mary*. That's everything he knows about the girl of his dreams. More than she knows about him. Maybe more than she wants to know.

It's time to live in the moment. Let his Indian ways take over. Danny needs a place to sleep and a good long shower. The last one was in a Jesus House shelter. It's worn off, and pretty girls don't like boys with skunky airs.

Mary. Everything that pops into Danny's mind takes a direct path to her. Fighting it is useless, even though there's no way on earth a girl like her could fall for a guy like him. Except... with magic, anything can happen.

Danny's got ten thousand dollars in his pocket and a new name—Richard—that sounds good when Mary says it. There was the Rainbow Girl, the dwarf that jingled when he walked, and a man with backward writing on his forehead. John Horse might have a logical explanation for all those things, but as far as Danny is concerned, they're magic. Old fashioned, reservation magic, like people have been telling him about ever since he can remember.

Magic... Mary. There she is again, popping up like a rabbit out of a magician's hat.

Danny hears a struggle inside the dumpster. Squeaks and thrashing and then a low-pitched growl, like an electric motor running down. Not everything survives. In the end, nothing does. A boy should be careful even if he's full of reservation magic. He needs a roof over his head and walls around him, and a bath would be nice too.

Lots of construction in Oklahoma City. Buildings coming down. Buildings going up. Failure and success trading places. He'll find a building that's nearly done. Law firms are the best. Large private offices, complete with showers and kitchenettes. More luxury than he had on the rez even though he'll have to sleep on the floor.

Something without furniture, waiting for the final fixtures because lawyers are particular. No burglar alarms until contracts are signed. Easy to break in because blue-collar workers are careless with other people's property.

Of course, he has alternatives. There's an Embassy Suites down the block, a Marriott, and a couple of transient hotels where nobody cares if you give a false name. Danny can afford a hotel easily.

Profit from a case of mistaken identity. That's what John Horse would call the ten thousand dollars in Danny's back pocket. But it feels a lot like magic.

The movement inside the dumpster ends. The cats and rats sense danger from outside—someone nearby who isn't Danny Riley.

He freezes in place and breathes slowly so he doesn't stir the air around him. He fades into the background like a cutthroat trout sinking into the deepest part of a stream. Impossible to see unless you know exactly where to look.

"Richard?" A man's voice. The D is mushy.

"That you, Richard?" No hard edges on the consonants. Danny Riley has heard this voice before. A hunched figure moves in front of the alleyway, backlit by a halogen light. His shadow reaches like a finger into the darkness and then disappears, the way Danny Riley has disappeared.

"You're scaring the shit out of me, Richard. It's Toad."

The man with the tattooed face and bad teeth who gave Danny Riley ten thousand dollars for, "product." The first man in Oklahoma City to name him Richard Daniels.

"So, how'd it go with Mary? She going to take you back?"

Danny has already started gliding toward a junction of escape routes. Lots of back-ways out. There always are with alleys. Hard to trap a man in a place like this. But when Toad asks about Mary, Danny stops.

Not so hard to trap Danny Riley using the answer to his prayer as bait. Danny hadn't known he was praying. That's how magic works.

Danny's mother always told him, "Never turn your back on miracles," and he wouldn't think of it, especially now that finding Mary has become a distinct possibility.

"You know her?" He's out of the alley before Toad realizes he has moved. "You know Mary?"

Toad jumps. "How the fuck you do that, man?"

"You know where Mary lives?" Danny stands so he'll have the street light at his back.

Toad squints, trying to bring him into focus. Two vertical creases in his forehead divide the backward sentence tattooed over his eyebrows

DOAT EB | LLIW / SROTALOIV

"Why you ask me that, Richard?" Toad scratches his ribs and shifts his weight from one foot to another as if he is keeping time to a methamphetamine withdrawal tune that only he can hear.

"Same old place she's always lived. Right?" As if this is a test Toad needs to pass in order to get his product.

"Can you take me there?"

The worry lines on Toad's forehead fade away now that Danny's asked a question he's absolutely sure he can answer.

"Sure thing. Right? Old Toad's your man."

He stands there, confident he's passed the test, until Danny tells him, "Now, I mean. I want to see her now."

"It's kind of late." Toad looks at a tattooed watch face on his wrist. "Almost midnight."

When he looks up again, Danny has moved out of his line of vision without making a sound, the way the moon disappears behind a cloud. Danny feels a little guilty about scaring the strange man with the forked tongue, but scared people lose their curiosity, and Danny doesn't feel like answering questions.

"WEIRD HOUSE." TOAD DOESN'T WANT to drive all the way down the single-lane road that leads to Mary's place. "One way in. One way out. A man could be trapped real easy."

Toad is wrong about that. Mary's house is bordered by a natural stone wall that would be simple to climb, crowded against a copse of trees with minimal undergrowth. A drainage ditch forms one border of the property, as flat at the bottom as a subterranean super highway.

Toad watches Danny assess the possible escape routes. "For a car, I mean. No easy way out for a car. So maybe I should turn it around, you know? Point it in a get-away direction."

"Possessions—" Danny is ready to repeat what every holy man who's ever lived has to say about the material world, but Toad doesn't let him finish.

"A car is nice to have when you want to get someplace. Like Mary's house."

Holy men have plenty to say about women too, but Danny doesn't really want to talk about things like that with Toad.

He says, "I'll walk the rest of the way."

"Maybe you should call first, Richard. Maybe no one's home." Toad sounds hopeful, but lights are on inside the house.

Danny doesn't know if Mary will be glad to see him show up unannounced in the middle of the night, but he's pretty sure she won't be glad to see Toad. He steps out of the car. He leaves the door open, so Toad sits bathed in the interior light while Danny vanishes into the darkness down the one-lane road, into Mary's drive.

The property has no visual connection with the city, but highway sounds leak through the woods and blend with the Oklahoma wind. Not natural, but no longer completely mechanical. Vehicle noises mix with shifting branches, night bird songs, and insect mating calls. They sound mysterious. Mystical. Scary. Even John Horse would be impressed.

"Holy shit." Toad has followed Danny after all. He shuffles through the grass like a tribal dancer who's had a stroke but still thinks he can make it rain. "Goddamn, would you look at that?"

Toad is pointing to a black, late-model Cadillac parked beside an old blue GMC pickup truck with a camper shell, but Danny is more interested in a cross embedded in a rectangle of stones in the middle of Mary's yard where nothing like that belongs.

A name is written on the cross, but the moonlight isn't bright enough for Danny to read the letters.

"We've got to get out of here, Richard!" Toad's voice sounds like a whiskey-ravaged prayer. He waves one hand in the general direction of an unconvincing scarecrow hanging from a tree over a collection of tomato cages, the old truck, and the Cadillac with the glossy-black finish that reflects the full moon like a mirror.

Danny isn't going anywhere now that he is close enough to read the name on the cross. "Queenie."

"Really, Richard. We have to go right now." It takes Toad's halitosis a second to cross the space between him and Danny. "Really, dude. That's Little Bits's car."

"Queenie." Danny's voice cracks when he says the name a second time. Still painful to think about the wolf who was his only friend. So many years ago.

He pushes Toad away. Gathers rocks from the cairn. Tosses them aside.

"Not a real grave." He sees that right away. No wolf buried in Mary's yard, but still…. The cross has the inexplicable, mysterious feel of magic. It tips as Danny uncovers a canvas satchel with "U.S. Army" stenciled on it in black letters.

Danny opens the satchel. A glass pipe falls to the ground, along with a butane lighter, paper envelopes—several hundred of them—and a white three-by-five card.

"Holy shit." Toad scrambles for the envelopes and the paraphernalia. "Gimme that satchel."

"Wilma Daniels." Danny reads the name bracketed between two Valentine-style hearts. "Who's Wilma Daniels?"

Danny can't remember where he's heard that name before. He nudges Toad with the toe of his boot, but the tattooed man is too busy crawling around the fake grave to answer. Rooting out every envelope, stuffing them back into the pouch like a scavenger postman.

"Cherokee Ice." Toad looks up at Danny like a dog who's hoping not to be kicked. "This ain't ten thousand dollars' worth, but it's a good down payment."

He stands up and dusts himself off as if his appearance suddenly makes a difference. "You know this ain't all, right?"

"Who's Wilma Daniels?" Danny puts one hand on the satchel as if he might take it back if Toad doesn't answer.

Toad pulls the satchel closer to his body. "Long as you know this ain't all I'm gonna get."

When Danny doesn't speak, Toad tells him. "Wilma's your grandma, Richard. Did they brainwash you in rehab or what?"

A gunshot from inside the house. Danny's heartbeat turns erratic. Pain races across his chest and travels down his left arm. Another gunshot. He almost can't hear it through the wall of heat that settles over his face.

Danny feels moisture on his cheeks.

Blood? His fingers recognize tears right away. Gunshots have never made him cry before. But….

"Mary!" Danny takes a step toward the front door, ready to die for a woman whose last name he doesn't know.

The door swings open. An African American dwarf runs out, brandishing a pistol.

"Two-Heart!" The dwarf levels the pistol at Danny. Fires a shot that comes out in a soccer ball-size bubble of flame. The noise is no louder than one of the Black Cat firecrackers they sell just beyond the Arizona border of the rez.

"Why ain't you dead?" The same dwarf who confronted Danny in the McDonald's. The same one who called two thugs in to kill him. He levels the pistol at Danny again. Drops onto one knee as if he's praying, and maybe he is because Danny can see the large silver crucifix dangling from the chain around his neck.

"Fucking witch!" Steadying his hands with curse words.

Danny has seen other men with guns do that. Guns that were pointed his way, just like this one. He stoops down and picks up a rock from Queenie's grave. Draws back while Little Bits is steadying his nerves with a string of hateful words. Throws an eighty-mile-per-hour pitch into the strike zone. Catches Little Bits between the eyes.

Another bubble of fire. Another Black Cat firecracker report. The gun flies out of Little Bits's hands, and lands among the tomato cages.

"Help me, Jesus." Little Bits runs to his Cadillac and skids away down the one-lane road, away from Mary's house.

"I hope that little bastard don't hit my car." Toad holds his satchel under one arm like a businessman.

"See you later about the rest of the product." He walks backward down the one-lane road, exposing his rotten front teeth in a twisted moonlit smile.

THE GUNPOWDER SCENT IS SHARP inside Mary's house. It concentrates in Danny's tears and stings his cheeks. The sense of loss closes around him and squeezes all the air out of his lungs. His heart stutters between beats and aches as if his soul is trying to pull free.

Danny stands in a lingering cloud of smoke and waits for the smell of blood to break through. Someone has died. Someone important. Maybe someone even more important than Queenie.

"Mary!" He shouts the one word that sums up everything he knows about the girl of his dreams, who might have turned into a nightmare. Vision blurs as his eyes sweep across the living room, looking for something he doesn't want to see.

Living room.

The hum of violence hangs in the air like vibrations from a high-tension line.

"Mary, it's...." She doesn't know anything about Danny Riley yet. Now, maybe she never will.

"It's Richard, Mary. Are you okay?" He waits for an answer.

"It's Richard," he says again. Calmer this time. His breathing and his heart rate are almost normal, but the tears keep coming. He doesn't try to stop them.

Strains of a Spanish song find their way through the door Danny forgot to close. A real holy man would know what that means, but Danny will have to search the house to find out. Rumors of a dead human have already spread through the insect kingdom. Flies and mosquitoes are the first to arrive. They head straight for the kitchen. Danny follows.

The rich metallic odor meets him as he steps onto the tile, sweet and nasty, like the drain in a butcher shop after a very busy day. A dead man sprawls on the floor. Probably average size, but he looks like a child in death. Innocent, helpless, faceless, his arms are spread into the beginning of an embrace. Large caliber, soft-nosed bullets have erased his identity and made a golf ball-size hole in his chest.

Not Mary. Danny is relieved, but the insects are indifferent.

A pool of blood circles the dead man's head like an angry halo. Splatters have turned his face and his shirt into a painter's drop cloth. Chinese-red splotches. Rust brown at the edges. Danny's eyes are stuck on the murder scene, but his ears are everywhere else. Nothing but flying insects and the continuing refrains of "Cielito Lindo."

Crawling insects are on the move too. Going for the soft, injured parts. Danny can't tell whether the dead man's eyes are open because of all the blood, but the ants can. Already here before the body cools. They've lived in the woodwork, eating crumbs until real food came along.

What could John Horse do with ants like these? What visions would they bring once he drowned them in lighter fluid and swallowed them? Danny's right hand strays to his amulet bag. Magic didn't bring him here without a reason.

There's a small lump under the dead man's bloody shirt. Not big enough to be a weapon, not wet enough to be an injury. Danny unbuttons the shirt with his left hand while his right closes around his amulet bag. At this moment, he believes in God more than he ever has before, but the God who's watching him search the dead man isn't the white man's God.

It's Skeleton Man. Massau'u, Pueblo spirit of the dead, who Danny doesn't know anything about except he's watching—taking notes on the activities of a clanless Laguna boy who is in way over his head.

"Forgive me," he tells the body, just in case the Christian God is watching too.

The dead man wears an amulet bag. Something like Danny's—no… exactly like Danny's. He feels the hide between his fingers and measures it with his eyes. The same shape as Danny's amulet bag. The same size. Made from the hide of a red-tailed hawk inexpertly cured.

There's no spent bullet cartridge inside it. No glass container full of acacia ants. No ring. The dead man kept pictures.

A picture of a young Danny Riley with John Horse—a younger John Horse than Danny Riley has ever seen. Impossible. Danny never met the Black Seminole until earlier this year.

A picture of a dog—not a wolf—not Queenie, but a lot like Queenie.

A picture of Nelva Riley, taken years ago. A teenage picture of Danny's mother taken before an Oklahoma Indian got her pregnant.

A picture of that Oklahoma Indian. Danny knows that as surely as he knows the man on Mary's kitchen floor is dead. The Oklahoma Indian looks a lot like Danny Riley—only older. He looks a little like John Horse—only younger. More Indian. Less African. He has a patch over one eye and an unhappy smile on his lips.

There's one more picture in the bag. A pretty woman, middle-aged, proud, with good posture and the same grim smile as the Oklahoma Indian who ruined Nelva Riley's life. It's hard to make her features out because someone has drawn an X across her face. Danny turns the picture over. "Fuck You, Wilma Daniels," is printed on the back. The letters have the same shape as the ones on the white card in the satchel in the Queenie grave. The same shape Danny would make if he printed Wilma Daniels's name. Exactly the same shape.

A pair of headlights feel their way across the windows of the kitchen and the living room. They stop, find their way into the open front door, fill the room with an alien light, and make the kitchen look dark by comparison.

Danny searches the side pockets of the dead man's pants. He leaves the change and the facial tissues but takes the iPhone. It vibrates in his hand like a live cicada. Wilma Daniels's name and number flash onto the screen. Neatly printed in indifferent electronic letters.

An omen? Danny's never owned a cell phone before, and he doesn't have time to experiment because the car lights are still shining in the front door. He pockets the phone and rolls the corpse enough to remove the wallet from his back pocket. Pops it open. A picture of Mary smiles back at him and a picture of himself on an Oklahoma driver's license. The name on the license is Richard Daniels. Now he knows the reason for his tears.

Twins are the strongest kind of family magic. One spirit with two hearts.

Richard Daniels was the other half of the mystery Danny has been trying to work out all his life. He closes the billfold like a Bible at the end of a church service. His picture and Mary's come together, face to face, in a photographic kiss.

Danny Riley's tears stop flowing the moment he knows the truth— the reason he felt the pain and the pull on his spirit when the shots were fired.

"I'm Richard Daniels now."

The knowledge clears his mind and cools him the way a feminine spring rain cools the desert back on the rez. Who could doubt him now that he has Richard Daniels's amulet bag, Richard Daniels's ID, and Richard Daniels's cell phone that's finally stopped vibrating in his pocket? He's certain he's got Richard Daniels's soul as well. A big piece of it, anyway.

"I'll try to take good care of it," he tells the body on the floor. "I'll take good care of everything." *Especially Mary.*

He leaves the crime scene without saying goodbye and walks out the front door into the illumination of the headlights as if he's an entertainer making his first appearance on the Ute Mountain Casino stage. He isn't surprised to see Mary step out of the car.

Everything my brother had is mine.

Chapter 18

DANNY RILEY SHUTS THE door behind him and stands in the double beam of lights as if he's waiting for a drum roll.

"Mary." His mouth won't fit around the name now that it belongs to *her*. He stretches it into three syllables and follows it with an involuntary swallow that sounds like a belch.

"Mary." He tries again. Better this time. The lights on her car turn off with a click—like the sound of a deadbolt being thrown. Mary stands beside the car and doesn't speak until her image solidifies on his retinas.

"Richard?" As if she knows that Richard Daniels can't be standing there. As if she knows about the insect feast behind the front door that is shut but not locked.

The brand-new re-animated Richard Daniels takes a step toward her. She takes a step back.

A cloud passes over the full moon and plunges the yard into darkness for a few seconds. Danny can still see the fake Queenie grave with the tipped cross and the scarecrow hanging over the tomato cages where Little Bits tossed his pistol.

The cloud moves away. A spark of moonlight flashes off of the murder weapon. Bright as a lightning strike in the San Juan Mountains when the Hopi call rain to the Big Reservation.

"Is that you, Richard?"

Danny's hand goes to the driver's license in his back pocket that makes it official. He turns his head away from the moon's reflection on the pistol in the garden. Waits for his pupils to tighten their grip on Mary's face.

Pretty girl. The thought is so strong he wonders if Mary can hear it.

"Talk to me, Richard. Are you okay?"

The new, improved Richard Daniels is very much okay. New name. New future. New girlfriend. New cell phone vibrating in his pocket again. He'd shut it off, but he doesn't want to do anything to distract Mary.

"Sure, I'm okay." All his life Danny Riley struggled with his Indian ways. Now that he's Richard Daniels, things are different. Now he doesn't want to talk. All he wants to do is stare at Mary, who looks worried—but still beautiful—in the light of the full moon.

"I'm fine." He takes a careful step in her direction, the way a half-breed Laguna boy tames a wolf.

"Never been better." Richard Daniels, now and forever. That will take some getting used to.

A large moth, white in the moonlight, hovers over Mary's shoulder like a hummingbird checking out a trumpet vine.

"Richard Daniels," he reminds himself. Not Danny Riley anymore. Now Danny Riley is a secret name, like the war name given to a Diné boy when he reaches puberty. A secret between Skeleton Man and the brand-new Richard Daniels. A name too secret to be said out loud.

He points a finger at the moth that has landed on Mary's hair, feasting on her scent, drawn to her the way flies are drawn to the smell of blood.

"Hawk moth," Mary tells him. "Moonflower moth. You remember. Big and harmless. They like datura nectar."

"They like you too." Danny watches the moth take flight. Moon-flowers grew on the reservation. Filled with alkaloids that tune a man's ears so he can hear spirits sing. Maybe this moonflower moth hears the spirit of Danny's twin brother singing his death song from Mary's kitchen floor.

"They've always liked me." Mary brushes the spot on her head where the moth used to be. "Have you forgotten?"

"I've forgotten everything," he tells her.

The way a newborn baby forgets the struggle through the birth canal, he thinks but does not say. Instead, he says, "Everything you were afraid of is gone."

He takes another step. Mary flinches but doesn't retreat. So much like a wolf that would rather lick his hand than bite him.

"I came to see if you're all right." Her turn to take a step. Two moon-flower moths fly between her and Danny and hover like a pair of hum-mingbirds

"Earlier, you were so...." The tension in her shoulders rolls down her arms with a shudder and tumbles from her fingers. She shakes her hands to rid herself of the remnants. "Now you're...."

Mary's tension doesn't return, even when Danny Riley stands right in front of her. He's only been with one other woman. When he was someone else. When he lived on the Navajo Reservation, where the rules were different.

"I fired a shot at you," Mary says. "Three shots, actually, but...."

"You missed." Danny holds his hands up in a victory sign to prove his point. It doesn't matter now whether the African American dwarf killed the original Richard, or if Mary's bullets did the job.

"Alive and well." He turns in a circle, like a boy modeling a pair of jeans for his girlfriend. His new identity is a perfect fit. Anyone can see.

"You're not stoned," Mary says. "I can always tell. Not stoned, but different."

He puts his arms around her. Feels a ripple of muscular contraction in his fingers like noodling a catfish, pulling it out of a mountain stream with his bare hands so gently it won't resist.

Different than Sarah Benally. Warmer, more vulnerable, a perfect fit against his chest. She knows what comes next, but Danny Riley doesn't. Will the tenderness turn into passion the way it did in the backseat of a Navajo tribal police car? Skeleton Man is no help at all, and the white man's God probably doesn't approve.

"Richard Daniels," he reminds himself and Mary.

The name makes her flinch again, but it only lasts for a second.

He holds Mary as if they are stuck in time. As if they can stay that way forever. As if there isn't a dead man in the kitchen and a pistol between the tomato cages. He's been with Mary for ten minutes, and already there are secrets.

Danny looks at the full moon and whispers a silent prayer loud enough for spirits to hear, but not loud enough for Mary.

"Help me." A simple, familiar prayer. It seems as if he's used it before, but he can't remember when.

A moonflower moth hovers in front of his face, floating on the scent of Mary's hair. A spirit sign so certain even John Horse couldn't explain it away. He opens his mouth like an observant Catholic waiting for the priest to place a wafer on his tongue. The way Danny Riley received acacia-ant-communion from John Horse the day he was with a woman for the first time. The moth lands on his tongue. Doesn't struggle as he crunches it between his teeth.

He holds Mary in his arms and waits until spiritual guidance is throbbing in his temples like the hooves of a white horse galloping across the hardpan in Chaco Canyon. Like the smiling face of a Rainbow Girl in the Oklahoma Museum of Art.

"Touches work fast," he tells Mary, "but kisses are faster." She doesn't resist when he places his lips over hers.

Danny remembers how it felt to be loved by Mary in another life he never lived. It doesn't matter if the memory is magic or one of those mysterious twin phenomena that only seems like magic. The identity baton has been passed, and so has Mary. She melts in his arms like a handful of jeweler's wax. Flows into every crevice of his sparkling new soul.

There is no empty space between them, and they know exactly what to do.

"Let's go inside." Mary pulls away and gazes into his eyes, where Danny is sure she sees a double image of the moon. She licks her lips and kisses him again, refreshes his desire and hers with shared saliva, bolstered by datura that has been processed first by a moonflower moth and then by the descendent of a Black Seminole medicine man.

She doesn't know about the dead Richard Daniels, whose *chindi* roams her kitchen.

"Let's go inside." Mary looks at the lights behind a window in the front door of her house.

"Not there." Danny breaks away long enough to find an alternative. The old GMC pickup truck with the camper shell? Better than the backseat of a police car, but who knows what he might find inside.

"Your car," he says. "The backseat of your car."

He watches thoughts turn over in Mary's mind. The bed inside is more comfortable, but the car is closer, and they haven't done it in a car since...

Danny doesn't know what memories his twin took with him when he left this world, but making love in the car is one of them.

"Please," he whispers through lips that are still shaped like a kiss.

He knows she expects him to make demands rather than ask permission, but the brand-new Richard Daniels is different from the old one. He leads her to the car as if he is in control, but they both know it's Mary. A tug here, a tremble there, and Danny moves accordingly. He thinks what she wants him to think, needs what she wants him to need, as if she's shouting orders through a moonflower moth megaphone.

Until the brand-new Richard Daniels is all used up. Not one ounce of passion is left inside him, no unfulfilled desires from his previous life.

They sit together in the backseat of the car, looking at the garden where, according to Mary, hornworm caterpillars feed on beans and tomatoes until they're big enough to spin themselves into scrotum-size cocoons and turn into moonflower moths.

"You're different," she tells him.

"Yes."

"Really different," she says. "Your lips feel different. Your hands are different." She takes his right hand in both of hers. Explores his knuckles with her fingertips.

"You kiss differently. You touch me differently. Your saliva doesn't taste the same." She opens a door so the interior light comes on. She squints at the new Richard Daniels the way a banker evaluates a suspicious hundred-dollar bill.

"Different." Mary's clothing is in disarray, but her mind is straight. "But still Richard."

His new identity has been consummated in the nick of time. Moth magic has run its course. The white horse no longer gallops in Danny's chest. Mary doesn't feel it either. She's looking at the world through pupils that aren't dilated with spirit power. Her senses are honed to a fine edge by sex.

She steps out of the car—not a good sign—and walks over to the garden, where she can see Little Bits's pistol shining in the moonlight like a neon vacancy sign for a cheap motel. Danny is right behind her, trying to think of a good explanation for the pistol.

Fell out of the sky.

Hatched out of a moonflower cocoon.

Don't know how it got there.

But here is Danny standing near a weapon where no weapon used to be. A shrug doesn't seem good enough, but it's all he has. His Richard Daniels identity feels tight around his chest.

She picks the pistol up. Shows it to him. Points it at him for a second, then turns the killing end toward the ground.

"It stinks," she tells him. "This is what guns smell like after they've been fired." She doesn't point the weapon at him again, but she holds it in a ready position, halfway to a threat, then drops it between the tomato cages.

"Maybe you're not as different as I thought." Mary moves fast, like she's been energized by the violence that still radiates from the pistol. Danny moves sluggishly, like a blue bottle fly that's been trapped on a windowsill for days. Can't really go anywhere because all his places are used up.

"I don't know, Richard. I just don't know." Somehow Mary is behind the steering wheel of her car. The engine turns over. It lurches toward the driveway.

Going.

Going.

Gone.

A moonflower moth hovers in front of Danny and floats in a body-temperature thermal filled with the scent of Mary. It doesn't try to escape when he reaches for it. Good to have one handy, when he meets with Mary again. Danny Riley has no doubt that will happen soon.

He turns his attention to the GMC pickup with the camper shell. Automatic transmission. Keys in the ignition. Driver's license in his back pocket.

A new identity, a pickup truck, and a girl, although the girl seems sort of up in the air. Still…. Not bad for his first night in the world as Richard Daniels.

His cell phone vibrates in his pocket.

Chapter 19

DANNY'S "NEW" PICKUP TRUCK smells of mouse droppings and mold. It shakes and rattles so much he hardly notices the minor scrapes with parked vehicles or the bumps when he drives over curbs. He knows about ignition keys and automatic transmissions and how to kill the lights and accelerate away from an accident, but nothing about rules of the road. Lucky for him, Oklahoma City closes during primetime television hours and stays closed until after the morning news.

Convenience stores are open—7-Elevens, Circle K's, and Love's truck stops. So are strip clubs. They light up the night with neon signs, which must be the best advertising ever. Their parking lots are full. Nobody will notice one more beat-up truck parked among all the others crowded around the Red Dog Tavern.

A flashing neon girl dances over the entryway. She wraps her body around a flickering pole that used to be the color of brass but now looks more like blighted corn. Two cowboys throw wild punches at each other near the front door.

A big, alien-looking bouncer grabs the brawling men by their collars. He shakes them the way a cat shakes a rat when he hasn't decided between a broken neck and disembowelment, and tells them, "Take it to the back of the parking lot, assholes."

When Danny Riley parked his truck so he could figure out how to answer his new cell phone, he had inadvertently chosen the most suitable location for mortal combat.

One of the cowboys calls the other a "goddamned cocksucker."

The cocksucker answers back, "Fuck you," just as Danny Riley accepts a call from Wilma Daniels.

"*Hello, Richard.*" A woman's voice, full of cigarette smoke and authority, followed by a pause that demands an answer.

"Hey there." Richard Daniels's amulet bag is on the seat beside him like a silent accusation of fraud. The identity swap might be more complete if he combined it with the one he wears around his neck, but now is not the time. He removes the picture with Grandma Wilma's head crossed out and "Fuck You" written on the back. No way he'll hang something like that over his heart.

"*What do you want from me, Richard?*" Wilma Daniels starts off sounding educated and difficult—those two things always seem to go together. She has a pretty face, as far as Danny can see under the red X. Elegant, sophisticated, a noble Native American woman who's maybe even a little bit hot in a slightly over-the-hill sort of way, like an older version of Pocahontas in the Disney movie Nelva rented for him when he was a little boy.

"I'm not really sure." Danny's mind hasn't settled into his new identity yet. He's circling it like bathtub water going down a slow drain. Trying to get there without taking any of the scum along—like the picture of Wilma Daniels with the red X and the dirty words.

He hears a swallow, followed by a rapidly expelled breath of air, the way Nelva's boyfriends sounded when they did tequila shooters.

The cowboy fight reaches the rolling stage. They tumble across the dented hood of Danny's pickup truck and call each other motherfuckers loud enough for Wilma to hear it over the cell phone.

"*Wha's goin' on, Richard?*" Slurred, except for Richard's name. That's crisp and clear, but the D lands with a thud. Danny Riley heard lots of men talk like that on the rez. He's heard Nelva talk that way when she was with someone she thought wouldn't try to ease his intoxicated, guilty conscience by beating the hell out of her.

"Tequila shooters?" he asks politely.

"*It's Jack, you little bastard.*"

The Tased man from the art museum café?

Wilma Daniels swallows so loud, it sounds like a toilet flushing over the phone. "*You know I always drink Jack Daniel's.*"

One cowboy bashes the other's head on the hood of Danny's truck. Their hats are gone. Their noses are bloody. They show their teeth to each other like angry dogs. Both have gaps.

"*Cousin Jack, I call it,*" Wilma Daniels says. "*'Cause of the last name, you know?*" In case Danny forgot his brand-new last name.

She tells him, "*Tommy Bracken's got his eye on you.*"

He looks around, but the two brawling cowboys are the only ones in the parking lot. He thinks about the name Tommy Bracken for a while. He's heard it a couple of times before—once when he was Danny Riley on the rez and once outside the art museum café when the Richard Daniels transformation was just beginning.

"*Warning you about Tommy 'cause you're blood,*" she says. "*Even if you're bad blood.*

"*Don't act surprised.*" Wilma sounds angrier than the fighting cowboys, even over the tiny iPhone speaker. "*You know how Tommy is.*"

"Well—"

"*Nobody ever knows when he's around.*"

"I guess—"

"*Tommy can be anywhere. Can be anybody. Irish, Mexican, Italian, even colored, when he wants.*"

"A shapeshifter." Danny finally gets it. "A witch."

Another shot of Cousin Jack fills Wilma Daniels's vocal cords full of metal filings. "*You know all about witches. You and that Laguna whore.*"

"Wilma?" Hard to know how to address a raving drunk woman who doesn't sound like anybody's idea of Grandma.

"John Horse was the only man I ever loved. Left me before your daddy was even born." Her voice chews the words like an angry dog that is so pissed off at the world it doesn't care who it bites.

"Don't matter that I tried to shoot him. Pregnant women do that sort of thing. Everybody knows."

The rest of Wilma Daniels's rant turns into high-speed curses heavily laced with fucks and assholes and familiar names. Like Nelva Riley, the whore who blinded Wilma's boy in one eye. And John Horse, who left Wilma Daniels for no good reason other than a half-assed attempted murder.

Wilma takes another swig of Cousin Jack. Talks about making love to Tommy Bracken. *"Ain't exactly ordinary, but Tommy's a special case. Addicted him to me the way he addicted my boy Richard to meth."*

Danny figures Cherokee grandmas are a different sort.

"My boy Richard." Another loud swallow. More descriptions of sexual activities Tommy Bracken liked a lot, but Danny is hearing about for the first time.

"Stole my ring." Hard to tell who Wilma is accusing now that she's so drunk she's dropped the telephone. Sounds like she's shouting from the far side of a canyon.

"Gave it to that whore."

Danny's hand goes to his amulet bag. He thinks about the ring Nelva gave him long ago. Remembers Sarah Benally reading the name engraved inside, after they made love in the back seat of her Navajo Tribal Police cruiser.

"Brought back a little half-breed Two-Heart bastard for me to raise."

"Fuck everybody." The last words Wilma Daniels says. Followed by a thump. The sound a body makes when it hits the floor.

Danny ends the call as the cowboys finish their brawl. They lean quietly against his truck. Not exactly apologizing but not calling each other assholes anymore, either.

The front fender is a diplomatic zone where enemies learn tolerance. Where bloody fists scab over while split lips turn into lopsided smiles. But things can always go wrong. Like when a wasp flies out of nowhere and lands on one cowboy's neck.

Who knows how insects make their choices?

The stung cowboy shouts, "Goddamned motherfucking cunt." He slaps his neck. Jumps back. Picks up his string of curse words with cunt and carries it through the alphabet.

The other cowboy draws a pistol from some place Danny Riley doesn't see. Fires a shot that lights up the space between the trucks.

The first bullet double-thunks through the camper shell. The second shot double-thunks the wasp-stung cowboy's head. Sends him sprawling and bloody across the hood of Danny Riley's truck.

Danny turns the ignition key. The engine grumbles twice and catches hold. He throws it into reverse. Accelerates fast enough to send the gunshot man sliding, but there's enough life in his arms to grab a windshield wiper.

The truck slams into something hidden in a blind spot beside the camper shell and propels the gunshot cowboy onto the windshield. His nearly-dead eyes are open. His nearly-dead mouth struggles with last words.

Danny lip-reads the message from the border checkpoint at the land of the dead. "Tell my wife I love her."

"Sure thing, cowboy." Easy promise to ignore since Danny doesn't know the cowboy's wife, and Richard Daniels probably didn't either. The cowboy's widow might hold a grudge over how and where her husband died, but Danny doesn't mention that. He lets the man's soul go off to cowboy heaven without reminding him of the naked pole dancers inside the Red Dog Saloon with his paycheck tucked into their G-strings. A man should die with family on his mind. Danny is still a reservation boy at heart.

"She'll be relieved to get the news," he tells the cowboy, just in case his spirit is still hanging around. It takes four days for a Navajo soul to find its way to heaven. Probably longer for a cowboy at a strip bar.

Danny guns the truck into a hard turn, and the cowboy's body slides off with a thump. Like God pushed the END CALL rectangle on his sacred iPhone screen. He looks in the sideview mirror, but the dead man is already out of sight. Oklahoma City is a lot more dangerous than he expected. It's probably full of evil spirits looking for a boy fresh off the rez walking around in a previously owned identity that isn't broken in. Fortunately, there are plenty of turns and intersections sure to confuse any *chindi* looking for trouble in the Red Dog parking lot.

A few drops of rain splatter on the windshield. Not enough to wash away the cowboy's blood, but maybe more will come. Oklahoma storms are something new to Danny Riley, like grandmothers and wives and African American dwarves with pistols.

And Tommy Bracken—the Irish, Mexican, Italian, *colored* witch who might be watching him right now. At least according to Wilma Daniels and her favorite cousin Jack.

Lightning flashes fill the western sky, as furious and sudden as an artillery attack. Loud thunderclaps follow, then torrents of rain spray the truck like a cosmic car wash. Windshield wipers are useless. Streets turn into rivers as high in places as the pickup's bumper.

Masculine rain. That's what the Navajo would call it, but only because they don't have a better description. This kind of storm doesn't happen on the rez.

Wind and rain make it impossible to tell if the truck is standing still or moving until the front wheels roll over a curb. Driving blind is dangerous, but stopping in the middle of the road is even worse. Danny catches glimpses of parked cars and trees in lightning strikes as bright and hot as sparks from a welding torch.

Thunder disguises the sound of his bumper raking against doors of parked cars and metal posts of traffic control signs until, finally, he comes to a dry place underneath an overpass.

A homeless man is sleeping there on a bed of cardboard and rags, wedged under the steel girders that support the highway. He doesn't acknowledge Danny's wave.

Maybe it's because he's between identities. Not quite Danny Riley anymore. Not quite Richard Daniels, either. Until he comes to terms with that, he's no better than a *chindi*. Lost among the intersections of a strange city designed by devious Cherokee engineers.

Chapter 20

"I DON'T LIKE TO COMPLAIN, but..."

Mary can't make up her mind whether to focus negative comments on the torrential rain or Jack's coffee or the questions he's asking her like, "Where did you go last night when the policewoman came?"

"I mean, first you show up with four bags packed, and then there is a rock through the window, and then you tell me to call nine-one-one, and then...." Jack can't come up with anymore "and thens," and Mary hasn't answered any of them.

She tips her head forward, as if she's looking at him over a pair of non-existent glasses, exactly the way Ellen did before she told an outrageous lie.

Jack knows he ought to let it go because it's going to be his fault in the end, but instead of doing that, he sums everything up in a single word.

"Policewoman."

He thinks about repeating himself, maybe with a gesture for effect, but Mary's lips are starting to move, and her story won't be far behind.

The expression on her face tells Jack she's about to say, "I went out to make sure Richard was still dead," or "I went out to move the body," or "I went out to dispose of the murder weapon," but what she says is, "I just went out."

Mary sniffs at her coffee, wrinkles her nose, and takes a sip.

"I have a lot on my mind in case you haven't noticed." Her voice is thick with Jack's extra-dark German roast coffee. "Don't know what I'm going to do... yet." Another sip. "In case you haven't noticed."

It's Jack's fault, all right. Maybe that's something Mary learned from Ellen, or maybe it comes attached to that extra X chromosome all women carry around like a poorly concealed sidearm. Mary sets her coffee on the kitchen table. She turns her back on Jack—the way her mother used to do—and stares at the rain that's coalesced into drops the size of cocktail onions. She wraps her arms around herself in an imitation embrace. As if Richard Daniels's ghost is seducing her from the other side.

"Is Richard...?" That's as far as Jack can go. Is Richard? Philosophical. Concise. Shakespeare never did it better. Is he or isn't he?—that is the question.

"I don't know." Mary turns to face him again. Holds her coffee mug in both hands as if she needs the warmth to keep from freezing.

"Something happened last night that left me wondering...." The silence of a decision waiting to be made. "Mom thinks I should have Richard served." Another sip of coffee. Another wrinkled nose. "The house is mine, you know. I need to keep it that way, just in case. Get him out."

She takes another swallow of coffee that must be cold by now as well as bitter, but this time her nose doesn't wrinkle. "Even if I don't go back right away. Richard needs to be somewhere else."

Mary licks her lips and smiles as if she's savoring the taste of something sweet that's survived the onslaught of Jack's coffee. "Know what I mean, Dad?"

Jack has a pretty good idea.

"Be good to see how Richard's doing," she says. "Make sure there won't be any trouble." Mary's eyes are clear and steady, the way Jack imagined they were when she fired the pistol shots he heard on the phone.

"So...." she says as if that ends the discussion.

"Maybe I should check things out." Jack watches his daughter's eyes go soft. He's executed his lines perfectly. Exactly as Mary planned.

A rolling thunderclap shakes the dishes in the kitchen cabinets. Lightning flashes like supernatural paparazzi taking photographs at the beginning of the new and improved world-ending flood. Storm warning sirens blow. High winds are on the way. Maybe even a tornado.

The rain stops momentarily, turning up the volume on the sirens. They blow for thirty seconds more and then go silent, as if the danger has already passed or else it's too late to take cover.

"Is there anything else you should tell me—about Richard?" So many things go without saying, but Mary doesn't answer questions that Jack is afraid to ask—or, for that matter, questions that he's not afraid to ask.

"Anything you need to tell me? Anything at all."

"He'll be served day after tomorrow. Somebody Mom's boyfriend knows."

Mom's boyfriend.

"She'll take care of it unless I tell her different." Mary pours herself another coffee, dilutes it with two percent milk, downs it in a single gulp, and goes for another cup.

"The cops will be there, too," Mary tells him. "Just in case."

She evaluates her Milani Neon-Red Nail Lacquer under the flickering kitchen lights. "You know, Mom has taste for shit."

Jack wants to believe the comment is aimed at the nail polish but he's believed so many things that have turned out to be false.

"I'll drop by your house as soon as it stops raining."

Another flash of lightning. A crack of thunder. The power goes off for a count of ten. Then the electricity is on its feet again, ready for another round.

LIGHTNING FLASHES TURN JACK'S CAUTIOUS movements into stroboscopic zombie jerks as he leaves the safety of his car and walks across the drenched lawn that hasn't been mowed for at least a couple of weeks. It's five p.m. according to his Breitling Chronometer Emergency watch, but cloud cover makes it dark enough for a flashlight.

The rain has turned into a faint mist that puffs Jack's hair into a brown fright wig. Thunder rumbles in the background like an old-time locomotive. Jack catches himself singing a tune he hasn't thought about for twenty years.

"The worms crawl in. The worms crawl out. The worms play pinochle on your snout."

The song coats his tongue with the taste of rusty iron. Jack wants to spit, but he's fresh out of saliva. He coughs instead. That stops his singing, but the lyrics play in the background of his mind like subliminal music in a supermarket.

Horror-show-isolated. That's how Jack thinks of Mary's place. In the middle of the city, but without close neighbors. The lack of urban planning and the demands of a fifty-year flood plain have trapped the little house at the end of a one-lane street surrounded, by wooded easements, a natural sandstone outcropping, and a deep concrete drainage ditch, like a moat around a medieval castle.

Jack shines his flashlight into the ditch. No more than a trickle of water at the bottom, despite the heavy rain. Flood control, Jack supposes. Not used unless things get desperate. Until then, it's a secret passageway, a hidden route traveled by stray dogs and teenage gangsters. Graffiti decorates the sloped cement walls—bloody, complex murals by Diego Rivera wannabes. Names are scrawled between angry spray-paint figures. Some names are circled. Some are overlaid with black X's. An accounting system for the doomed.

Something rolls down the sloping wall of the ditch directly across from Jack. Round and heavy. Jack catches a bowling ball in his flashlight beam as it bounces on the bottom of the culvert and rolls past the mouth of a concrete pipe as big as a railway tunnel. Three pairs of wild, green eyes inside the pipe reflect Jack's flashlight beam, then disappear before he can identify the owners.

A trash bag scoots down the steeply sloped wall, slow and easy, like a fat kid on a rusty sliding board. A crack in the slab snags it for a moment, but gravity finally wins out. A cascade of beer bottles and broken glass follows. Jack turns his flashlight onto the source. A Hispanic man with no shirt and a belly large enough to hold a full-term baby dumps a basket full of cans.

"What you want, *puta*?" The shirtless man extends his right hand and raises his middle finger.

Jack waves back as if he doesn't understand the gesture. He steps away from the ditch and plays the light over Mary's yard. Piles of compost in various stages of decomposition—Jack doesn't like that word. A scarecrow dances from the end of a rope like a hanging victim over a garden consisting mostly of tomatoes in wire cages.

A dog's grave is the crowning glory of Mary and Richard's landscape. A stone cairn—at least Jack thinks that's what it's called—and a plywood cross with the name Queenie written on the cross member in childish purple letters. The grave would be weird even if Richard and Mary had ever owned a dog, but they hadn't.

Kids tell stories about places like Richard's and Mary's around campfires before eating s'mores and going to sleep among frog noises and mosquitoes—the house at the end of the lane where Queenie the ghost dog stands guard.

Richard's rusty, blue GMC pickup truck with the camper shell is nowhere to be seen. No lights behind the windows anywhere in Mary's house. That doesn't mean anything. Electrical power has been battling with lightning all over Oklahoma City.

Knocking on the door is always good, especially when you are going into enemy territory and trying to play a father figure—the voice of reason and understanding. Jack leaves the extra-large garden trash bags in the car for now, as well as the bleach, spackle, and touch-up paint—things a father needs when covering up his daughter's felonies. Best to keep his suspicions to himself for now because Richard might greet him at the door, and explaining bleach and ersatz body bags could make small talk difficult.

Jack tells himself that all his suspicions are unfounded. Richard and Mary's marriage will be dissolved by an ordinary divorce, the way more than half of all marriages end in the United States of America, where matrimony doesn't have to wait for death to "do us part."

"Anybody home?" A louder knock, with the "Shave and a Haircut" rhythm Jack learned as a child. His way of showing Richard that Jack Bailey is an all right kind of guy who's only here to do a job—whether that job is a crime scene cleanup or the preliminaries to a formal eviction the day after tomorrow.

Maybe Richard will be alive and well. Maybe he'll invite Jack in for a beer. It feels strange being sober after five p.m. Jack is usually halfway to his drunken plateau by now. Sober feels less complicated than he thought it would. Who'd have thought there was a functioning mind underneath that layer of Budweiser foam? Sobriety is good for a change, even when it's tainted by fear.

Another "Shave and a Haircut" knock.

"Hey there, Richard. It's Jack Bailey." You know, good old Jack Bailey who never thought you were good enough for his daughter and wonders if you're dead.

"Dropping in to see if you're okay." Not here to hide your body, that's for sure. Not looking for your dead body one little bit.

One more whimsical knock. One more non-aggressive greeting and Jack tries the door. Unlocked. Could be good. Could be bad. Nothing left to do but go inside and see.

"Olly olly oxen free," Jack calls, then listens for an answer. Thunder rumbles in the background, loud, but not loud enough to drown out the dead silence from the dark interior of the house. Lightning flashes project the shadow of the dangling scarecrow into the living room. The clandestine Hispanic trash man sings "Cielito Lindo" from across the drainage ditch.

"Better than 'Worms Crawl In.'" Jack steps inside.

"Richard! It's Jack." The wind slams the door, like an evil spirit sealing Jack's doom.

"Richard?" Jack tries for a shout, but all he can manage is a whisper. The air smells like the inside of a freezer after a power failure. Serious bad odors aren't here yet but the invitation has been sent. Bluebottle flies float in the beam of Jack's flashlight like hot air balloons, mostly in the kitchen where they take turns landing on something big and dead and human lying on the tile floor.

"Richard?" Flies don't land on living things—not in those numbers. Jack is sure of that, but he still asks, "Are you all right, Richard?"

Flies learn the bad news before anybody else. They know the exact second when a man is dead enough to turn into a maggot factory.

Jack points his flashlight at what's left of the dead man's head and steps closer. The scene is eerily familiar. He's seen it a hundred times on *Law and Order* and *CSI: New York*. But television doesn't include the smell of clotting blood and the sounds of celebrating insects.

The pool of C-battery-powered light tightens into a circle around the corpse's face, but positive identification is impossible.

The lights flash on all over the house at once, burning a reverse color image of the bullet wounds into Jack's retinas.

"It'll go away," Jack tells the body on the floor. "When my eyes adjust to the light, it'll go away." But he knows the image will never completely go away.

Jack knows he's supposed to leave everything alone and call 911. But he knows whose crime scene this is, and he's pretty sure everybody else will know, too, so he finds a jar of Raid under the kitchen sink. He fills the room with a mist of poison that makes flies fall out of the air like hailstones.

The body on the floor is decomposed more than Jack would have thought possible. The bullet through the head got things off to a good start. Richard's shirt is pulled open as if Mary thought about doing CPR, then changed her mind. A second bullet hole in Richard's chest makes Jack think of a dead prostitute's vagina—God knows why.

A pistol is on the kitchen counter by the telephone. The five-shot .38 caliber Chief's Special Jack gave to Mary long ago for just this purpose—though he never realized it until now. He pops the cylinder open. Three shots fired. The body looks like there were more, but it's best not to think about that until all this mess is cleaned up.

He always knew things would work out something like this—a big mess that Jack Bailey has to clean up. And here he is, part of his own self-fulfilling prophecy.

"Told you so." Jack finally gets to have the last word. He thinks of all the things he never said to Richard.

"Always thought you were a son of a bitch." He gives Richard a chance to reply. Five seconds timed on his Breitling Chronometer Emergency watch, which cost substantially more than Richard's beat-up GMC truck.

What the hell did Mary do with that?

For that matter, what did she think would happen when they came back with a process server and a cop?

Dad will fix it. Jack Bailey smiles. He's always been the go-to guy. Started off small with things like concert tickets and flat tires. Worked himself up to crime scene clean-up and conspiracy. He owes her an I-told-you-so. Diplomatic. Fatherly. Maybe just a touch of arrogance. Plenty of time to work on that while he cleans up Mary's latest, greatest mess.

Jack runs a fingertip over the crystal of his way-too-expensive watch with the emergency feature that can alert first responders at one hundred kilometers. He considers setting it off, the way a man standing beside Niagara Falls considers jumping in. Because deep down, Jack Bailey doesn't think he's up to concealing a murder. He can bag the body, mop the floor, and patch the walls, but keeping secrets is something he's never been good at. Especially when Miranda rights are involved, and detectives who know a lot more about murder scenes than good old Jack Bailey.

"Wish me luck," he tells the late Richard Daniels, who is getting later with every Breitling Chronometer second. "I'll need it."

THE VERY FIRST THING JACK does is take the murder weapon out of the house. The pistol smells like his daughter's fingers. His mind is spinning too fast to think of a good hiding place, so he pops the trunk and wedges it in the well beside his spare tire.

Temporarily, Jack promises himself. Everything is *temporarily* until the crime scene clean-up is complete. The first part is easy. Two extra-large lawn trash bags, one inside the other, and Richard inside both. Cinched at opposite ends to seal the odor in. Jack doesn't know how long it takes rigor mortis to set in and go away, but Richard is as loose and slimy as a marionette that's been dipped in butter. Hard to slide dead Richard into the first bag but easier to slide bagged Richard into the second. Jack figures on dreaming about this for years to come.

His late son-in-law is heavier than Jack expects. One eighty, at least—dead weight.

Murdered weight.

Jack drags him out the door and through the wet yard, past the scarecrow and the dog's grave. He sings "Cielito Lindo" as he slides his ersatz body bag into the drainage ditch right in front of the concrete pipe that will make a perfect temporary resting place for Richard until he thinks of something better. No green eyes are staring at him from inside the pipe this time, but Jack imagines they haven't gone far. He hopes they don't mind a little company.

"It won't be long," Jack promises the creatures that live inside the pipe. "Fish and guests stink after three days. Even if the guest is inside a body bag."

Chapter 21

DANNY FEELS OLD AND wilted after spending a night underneath an overpass. His silent homeless companion packs his cardboard and rags into plastic trash bags, loads them into a dented Aldi shopping cart, and leaves without a word.

Doesn't say, "So long, it's been nice."

Doesn't say, "It's not you, it's me."

Not even a finger wave goodbye. The way Nelva Riley's boyfriends always left when their business with her was finished.

Nelva Riley. Whose memory is that? Danny's or Richard's? Still flashing back and forth, like a skip image coming through on satellite TV. The downside of being an authentic *Two-Heart.*

He removes a picture from Richard Daniels's amulet bag without looking. The way a priest draws a raffle ticket from a goldfish bowl to see which lucky boy has won the chance to play Jesus in the Easter Passion Play.

A photograph of Nelva Riley in her youth—too young to be a mother but old enough to get pregnant by a no-good Cherokee meth addict drifter.

The smile on Nelva's face looks innocent, like there are still things she hasn't learned about men. Cherokees, especially. There's a smear on the photograph where Richard Daniels's lips have touched it hundreds of times. Stealing kisses from a mother who only existed in two dimensions.

Is that a memory, or just something Danny knows? The way he knows the people in all the amulet photographs. His family. His and Richard's.

Because when you're a Two-Heart, anything is possible. Two people separated by a state line and four hundred miles can have the same mother and the same father. They can both have dogs named Queenie—even if one of the dogs had been a wolf. They can have the same amulet bag made of the same skin of the same red-tailed hawk that has the same faint smell of spoiled meat because both bags were improperly cured the same way.

Picture of John Horse, Richard's and Danny's grandfather. Wilma Daniels's lover.

Picture of Wilma Daniels. The meanest grandmother who ever lived.

Important parts of Danny's family—whether he wants them or not. Passed on from the old Richard to the new one like a bedbug infestation. Maybe other things were passed down, too, like how to find his way around Oklahoma City.

The streets are laid out perpendicularly. No geographic barriers to go around. No mountains, not even an impressive hill. But, the roads take occasional mystical twists or end without good reason and change their names without notice. Not as hard as finding your way through Canyon de Chelly back on the rez, but Danny can't remember what Richard Daniels must have known. Every street he takes pulls him into the downtown area the way gravity pulls mountains into the desert—but a lot faster.

Destiny, or just bad luck. He always winds up where he started out, around the Art Museum, the County Courthouse, and the County Jail—the grim building with glass bricks instead of windows couldn't be anything else.

The jail is surrounded by impound lots, police cars, and bail bond businesses with signs that advise literate perpetrators how to use their one free phone call.

Get out of jail almost free, according to the mural painted on the wall of Abraham Bail Bonds. Clever. A monopoly man caricature is posed with an old-fashioned telephone, reminding hapless perps they can't call cell phones collect.

Cell phones. Danny pulls into an empty lot where a sign promises a brand-new 7-Eleven will be built soon.

Cell phones have all kinds of useful things, don't they? Like apps that tell you how to get from where you are to where you want to be. He knows about apps and icons from television, but when he looks at Richard Daniels's phone, the old familiar screen is gone.

Instead, he sees *Missed Calls.* On that screen is Nelva Riley, a name he never expected to see on an iPhone. Beside Nelva Riley is a number in red.

So far, Danny has held Richard Daniels's cell phone only twice. Once when he took it from his dead twin's pocket and once to answer Wilma Daniels's call in the Red Dog parking lot where a man was killed. One touch after a man died, and one before, so Danny hesitates when he places the tip of his index finger on Nelva Daniels's name. He touches it lightly and pulls his finger back.

One fearful touch is all it takes. After a little cyberspace spirit noise, his mother's voice says, "*Hello, Richard. I hope you can talk a little longer this time.*"

"How did you know it was me?" Then he remembers the rectangle with Wilma Daniels's name on it from the parking lot of the Red Dog strip bar. He looks around quickly, but there are no cowboys with guns.

"*I haven't seen you in so long,*" Nelva says. "*How do you feel? How do you look? Show me.*"

"Don't know how."

"*Are you hiding something?*" Danny Riley can hear Nelva's tears taking shape on the other side of the cell tower connection. They pull him completely out of his new identity.

"New phone, Mom. Don't know how to use it yet."

"*Can't lose you again,*" she says. "*Not after John Horse brought us back together.*"

"John Horse did what?"

"*William Balance is gone.*" Her words are full of tears because crying is what Nelva Riley does when she's happy or when she's sad or when things might go either way. "*Everybody says Danny witched him.*"

"John Horse brought us together?"

Nelva's full of magic tales. Indian legends about her boy Danny, who turned into a wolf. "*The way he did once before. Only I never believed it.*

"*I hear him singing to the moon. Coyotes answer. You know how the Diné feel about coyotes.*"

She tells him about hunting parties and trappers hired from Montana, and then she says something she would never say to Danny Riley. "*I always thought your daddy stole my very best baby.*"

"Best baby?"

"*One twin's always smartest,*" Nelva says. "*One twin walks first. Talks first. Loves his momma more than the other one.*

"*A mother always knows. Don't know how your dad found out.*" She changes to a whisper. "*If one of my babies had to turn into a wolf, I'm glad it was Danny.*"

"Got to go." Danny feels tears pushing at the edges of his lower eyelids. Not crying for Queenie this time, or for Mary, or for Richard Daniels. This time he's crying for himself. "Good to talk to you, Mom. Good to hear your voice."

He fumbles when he tries to end the call. It takes a second too long, so he hears his mother say, "*Later, Richard. I always loved you best.*" In case there was any doubt.

The Danny to Richard transition is far from complete when he says "Goodbye" again. He still has Danny Riley's heart breaking in his chest.

Chapter 22

THE HOUSE AT THE end of the lane isn't scary in the morning light as Jack and Mary pull into the gravel driveway. The dog's grave looks more eccentric than horrifying, and the dangling scarecrow looks more like a scarecrow and less like a hanging victim. Everything has been washed clean by the rain, even the police car and the perfectly restored, lemon yellow, 1965 Mustang parked among the puddles.

"The process server." Mary points first at the Mustang, and then at the statuesque policewoman standing beside her cruiser. "I was hoping for a man."

Jack recognizes the officer right away. "Corporal Laura Pepper."

The prettiest cop who ever read him his rights looks good at eight o'clock in the morning, as good she looked in his foyer at two a.m. And this time, Jack is stone-cold sober.

Corporal Laura Pepper leans against the police cruiser, posing like a model who'll lose bits and pieces of her uniform all the way to the centerfold. Like the models in the stack of vintage magazines Jack has hidden in his closet. God bless Hugh Hefner.

Do women like Corporal Laura Pepper understand the effect they have on men? She runs her finger through her shoulder-length black hair that has reacted to the rain with waves and curls that look decidedly post-coital. Of course, they understand.

"She came to our house to investigate the rock incident." He doesn't remind Mary about the Tasing in the Art Museum Café, or mention his prior history with Officer Laura Pepper after his marriage reached explosive stage.

"Pretty," Mary says. "Not many cops look that good in a Kevlar vest."

"Hot," Jack says a little too loud for Mary to ignore. He considers turning on the air conditioner as cover, but he can tell from her expression it will never fly.

"It's the coffee talking," Jack explains. He usually starts the day with a beer or two, but now that he's an accessory after the fact, he's switched from alcohol to caffeine. It's left him with a low-grade headache, a mouth that tastes like vinegar, and a mental process that is filter-free.

Officer Laura Pepper parked her cruiser sideways in the drive, a barrier between Mary's house and the rest of the world. The flap over her service pistol is unsnapped, and the cruiser's driver's side window is open. The police radio is chattering inside. Something about floods. Something about fires. Something about a robbery in progress. Incomprehensible gibberish followed by, "See the man," followed by more incomprehensible gibberish. Jack would bet anything that Officer Laura Pepper understands every word.

She produces a small spiral notebook and makes an entry. Something about the dangling scarecrow and the dog's grave, Jack is sure of it. He notices the drag path across the wet grass. It's the exact size of a body in a plastic bag leaving a crime scene without permission. Laura Pepper follows the drag path with her eyes. Writes something down.

Anything could make a path like that. Jack tries to think of some examples he can offer later if it comes up. Garbage dragged over to the drainage ditch. Illegal dumping is a misdemeanor. That's a step in the right direction. He didn't think about a drag path yesterday—not that he had any alternatives—and besides, the storm should have washed away the evidence.

Clouds are beginning to clear, but lightning flashes in the southwest as reinforcements gather for the next deluge. Six inches of rain, according to the morning weather report, from three a.m. to seven.

Too much water vapor in the air for evaporation to dry things out. The cross over Queenie's grave is dripping. The water level in the drainage ditch is rising. Laura Pepper's hair turns more X-rated by the minute. Jack wants to get this process-serving charade out of the way while he can still get to Richard Daniels's temporary resting place.

A little man with poor posture slides out of the Mustang. He stretches, fans himself with a stapled set of legal documents, salutes Corporal Laura Pepper, and limps over to Jack's car. The process server has what people used to call a clubfoot back in the days when cripples were less sensitive. Jack tries not to stare while he considers politically correct synonyms. There aren't any. Not staring is a total failure, but the attempt takes his mind off the rising water in the drainage ditch.

Live people sink, but dead people float. Jack can't remember where he heard that.

"Name's Skip." The process server taps on the driver's side window, then backs away from the car far enough so Jack can step out. He waves at Mary, then shakes Jack's hand. He turns his head enough to check out Officer Laura Pepper in his peripheral vision.

Jack nods and silently contemplates the fantasy life of a crippled process server.

Skip says, "Your boy must have priors." Still shaking Jack's hand. "Policewoman's wearing her bulletproof vest. Left mine back at the house. How about you fine people?"

Jack pulls his hand away. Wipes it on his shirt. He shrugs, trying to act nervous about his *boy with priors* who might be waiting inside the house with a gun.

Acting innocent and afraid is harder than he thought. Mary is doing a better job of it. She fidgets with her purse, checks her make-up in a compact mirror, and rearranges misplaced locks that have become unruly in response to the weather, but not as unruly as Corporal Laura Pepper's.

The policewoman has spent the last few minutes studying the interactions of Mary and Jack and Skip, but now she turns her attention to Queenie's grave.

"What's that?" She points a finger like a pretend pistol, throws her question into the air, and waits for someone to catch it.

"That's Richard being weird," Mary tells her.

Jack doesn't miss her use of present tense. He bets Laura Pepper doesn't miss it either. Mary is good. How will she react when they go inside?

She tells the policewoman about Richard's dog, Queenie, who died when he was a boy.

"Guess he never got over it," Mary says. "A boy and his dog, you know?"

Officer Laura Pepper walks over to the grave. Kicks the stones. Pushes on the cross, checking its stability.

"Lot of work for a dog that isn't buried here." Laura Pepper locks her gaze on Mary and doesn't say another word. She waits for the silence to become so overwhelming Mary will fill it up with words that may be used against her later.

So Jack comes to the rescue. "He really loved that dog. Always going on about good old Queenie."

"What kind of dog?" Laura Pepper has a notebook in one hand and a ballpoint pen in the other. At least she hasn't reached for her gun.

"What kind of dog?" Jack repeats the question, the way lying witnesses do on Court TV. He hasn't got the slightest idea about Richard's dog, but based on the size of the cross and the size of the cairn, it must have been a big one.

"Richard never said." Jack holds his hands out, palms to the sky like a little boy pretending he didn't steal the cookies.

Mary's turn to come to the rescue. She stands in front of the policewoman like a little girl making demands from an aunt who hasn't learned to refuse.

"Can't we get this thing over with?" She tells Laura Pepper about all the time she's already wasted with Richard. Talks like a woman who's already made up her mind about the future.

A good sign, but Jack knows how temporary Mary's decisions about Richard usually are.

"I don't want to waste another second," Mary says. "I want to serve these papers and get my life on track again."

Mary looks at the cross on Queenie's pretend grave. Moves her lips in silent prayer for a second or two. Wipes a finger under one eye as if she's catching a stray tear and says, "Please."

The magic word is a cue for the process server, Skip, to step forward. He shows Jack the stapled set of papers, which will order Richard out of the house in five days.

"All I got to do is touch him with it." Skip rolls the papers into a tight cylinder and pokes Jack in the arm like a two-year-old with a pretend sword. "Won't take long if there ain't no gunfight." He looks over at his '65 Mustang for a few seconds, trying to determine if it's in danger, then goes back to poking Jack with his paper sword of justice.

Officer Laura Pepper walks Mary to the front door. She tells the process server, "You're pokin' the wrong man with that paper, Skippy."

"Skip," he corrects her and hobbles quickly to the door, not exactly skipping, but close.

Laura Pepper puts her right hand on the grip of her sidearm as Mary knocks.

"This house ain't even listed as Richard Daniels's last known address," Skip tells Mary as he fits himself into the space behind Officer Laura Pepper's Kevlar vest.

Jack backs away even though he knows there is no possibility of a gunfight. He stands behind Queenie's cross and tries to strike a balance between looking like a law-abiding citizen and a coward.

Mary tries the front door. Unlocked the way Jack left it. He waits for her reaction when she steps inside. Maybe he should have told her about moving the body, but maybe she should have told him about killing Richard. Tit for tat seemed logical when there were still a few

Budweiser molecules bouncing around his system, but caffeine makes him see things differently.

Jack aims a silent prayer at the Queenie cross and makes a few vague promises to God if he and Mary can pull this thing off. Not that God has been much help so far. He makes the sign of the cross, the way French Canadian Hockey players do before they go on the ice and beat the crap out of the opposing team. It seems appropriate to Jack in his present caffeinated state, with the water in the drainage ditch already up to the level of the pipe where Richard Daniels will hopefully rest in peace a little while longer.

Mary can pull it off. Jack is sure of it. She's a consummate liar, like her mother. Always believes her own stories until the witnesses have left the scene. "Richard," she calls out. "It's Mary. Don't do anything crazy."

Laura Pepper is the first to go inside.

Five minutes later, she comes out. "You'll have to serve by posting, Skippy."

"I prefer Skip." He follows Mary inside. "Any tape in here? I got to stick these papers where Richard Daniels is sure to see them. That's what posting's all about."

No Kevlar vest, no tape, Skip didn't bring any of the tools of his trade, just an immaculate 1965 Mustang and a limp. Jack thinks the limp is less pronounced as Skippy crosses the threshold into the crime scene. His deformed foot settles evenly on the ground. Is it an affectation? A way for a process server of small stature to diffuse violence?

Laura Pepper walks over to Queenie's grave. She circles the cairn, waiting for her suspicion to crystallize into something solid.

A wall of water rushes behind Jack in the drainage ditch. He turns to see. Thousands of gallons released in accordance with some urban flood control plan that wasn't included in Jack's prayer. Tree limbs and plastic bottles float on the muddy swirling water. Shadowy objects tumble underneath the surface. Is Richard floating among the trash? Will he sink to the bottom or catch on a snag? Will someone find him weeks from now, miles from home, a murder victim bagged and dumped like a Sicilian message? Richard Daniels sleeps with the garbage.

Officer Laura Pepper says, "Something's not right."

Jack turns away from the drainage ditch and tries to strip emotion from his face, as if standing beside a dog's pretend grave with a beautiful lady cop is the most natural thing in the world. Laura Pepper stands behind the Queenie cross. A rainbow arcs across the sky behind her, and dirty water rushes in the concrete ditch behind Jack. He's never believed in omens, but now he's not so sure.

A Yellow Cab sticks its dented nose into Mary's driveway. It skids to a stop when it's far enough inside to see the police car.

"Who's that?" Officer Laura Pepper puts a hand on the butt of her sidearm. She adjusts her Kevlar vest, making sure it covers all the strategic places.

"I don't like surprises." She takes a few steps toward the cab but stops when it starts to back away. She tugs at her sidearm, checking to see exactly how hard it's going to be to draw when the time comes. The expression on her face tells Jack, and anyone else who cares to look, that time could come at any moment.

The cab's back door opens with a rusty metal sound. Ellen steps out. The last time she and Jack and Laura Pepper were together, Ellen wore a cheerleader costume. Now she's wearing jeans, something from the French Cowgirl that fits so well Jack forgives her for everything she's ever done.

Laura Pepper releases her grip on the pistol but she keeps her hand close. She flicks her head in Jack's direction but keeps her eyes on Ellen. "Move over here so I can keep an eye on you." Brushes her fingers across the holster.

Ellen follows Officer Laura Pepper's orders because standing by Jack is what she'd planned to do all along.

Jack has no plans. He stands beside the Queenie cross and waits to see what will happen next. Something always happens next when Ellen is around.

"Mary told me she was serving Richard today," Ellen says. "I knew you'd come with her, Jack. You always were *dependable*." She chokes on the word.

Her attitude might change if Jack told her he's an accessory after the fact in a homicide, but Officer Laura Pepper is watching, and she still has her shooting hand close to her sidearm. A hard, flat expression spreads across the policewoman's face. The flatness offsets her curves in a very appealing way.

Jack looks at the drainage ditch instead of telling Ellen about Richard's body. Like he knows about something hidden there, something that would make Ellen see him in a whole new bad-boy light. Maybe he'll be able to tell her later if Laura Pepper finally decides her job is done at Mary's house.

"Sorry I missed your call." Jack looks at Ellen's fingernails and thinks the color is close to the FUCK YOU printed on the stone that broke his window. "Got your message."

"Sorry about the broken glass, Jack. You know how I get sometimes." She shrugs so Jack will know this is something he shouldn't expect her to control. "Guess that's just who I am."

Laura Pepper runway walks to the place where the yellow cab used to be. The place where Ellen stood and passed money through the driver's side window to a cabby who was almost nervous enough to work for free. She bends over—charming—and picks up a glassine envelope full of white powder. Walks over to Ellen and shakes it two inches in front of her face. "What have we here?"

"Not mine," Ellen tells her, like guilty people always do.

"No way to prove that's mine." Quick correction to let the policewoman know this isn't the first accusation that's been pointed her way. "Known drug dealer's place of residence, you know? Cabby with dilated eyes. Everybody saw it." Ellen's sweeping gesture takes in Jack, Mary, and Skip, the not-so-crippled process server, as if they were a cast of thousands. "No way to make it stick, so...."

In a moment, Laura Pepper has Ellen's hands cuffed behind her. The policewoman's hands run over Ellen's legs the way Jack's hands did on their honeymoon. The search gets most thorough at the inner thighs and under the breasts. Laura Pepper reaches into every pocket but finds nothing. She checks the back pockets twice.

Jack asks Ellen, "Where have you been for the last two years?"

"Don't talk to her." Laura Pepper shoehorns Ellen into the backseat of the police car. She smooths Ellen's ruffled hair the way a lover might. She runs the tip of her tongue over her lips as if she's getting ready for a very wet kiss.

Jack can't help thinking about a movie he once saw about a women's prison. *Chained Heat*—he thinks it was. Catchy title. A series. Jack watched them all on HBO right after Ellen left him. He still thinks Laura Pepper is hot, but after watching her search Ellen, he understands things will probably never work out between them.

Ellen asks Jack, "Bail me out, will you, please?" before Laura Pepper shuts the police car door.

Of course, Jack will bail her out, after he takes care of a couple of details. He walks over to the drainage ditch and wonders who will bail him out when Richard's body finally comes to rest. When the cops find his fingerprints on the bag within the bag that holds Richard Daniels's mortal remains.

A dead coyote floats in circles in front of him, caught in a vortex, the way Jack is caught in Ellen's vortex. Its eyes are open. Jack thinks they would reflect green light if a flashlight found them in a concrete pipe after the sun went down.

"Where does it all go?" Jack isn't asking anyone, but Laura Pepper answers.

"There's an overpass at Northwest Thirtieth." An official voice from the giant blind spot directly behind Jack Bailey. "A chain-link barrier catches most of the debris," Officer Laura Pepper tells him.

"Cleanup crew will remove it once flood control quits releasing water." The policewoman goes silent, letting Jack wonder if she's still there. Daring him to turn around and lock their eyes until one of them looks away.

Jack can't stare at the drainage ditch forever. He'll have to turn around soon, and if Laura Pepper is still there, he'll have to say something. Something incriminating if the cop has her way. Plenty of room in the backseat of her cruiser for another perpetrator.

Mary saves the day. She calls to Jack from behind a large pile of things she can't live without for one more day. She doesn't look surprised to find Richard's body missing. She doesn't look surprised to see her mother in the backseat of a police car either.

"Got to help my daughter," Jack tells Officer Laura Pepper. Her stare feels like a spider crawling on the back of his neck. He wants to wipe it away, but he's afraid a sudden move might end in gunfire.

Chapter 23

WET BODIES DETERIORATE FASTER than dry ones. Jack is pretty sure of that. How fast? Even Google can't tell him. Thank God Richard is double-bagged.

What Jack needs is an old-fashioned Oklahoma drought. Even a temporary let-up would help, but things moved from drizzle to deluge and back to drizzle again with no end in sight.

According to the meteorologists, hurricane Ellen has settled in the Gulf of Mexico, fifty miles east of Corpus Christi. It's wet now. It will be wetter later. The best time to retrieve Richard's body is now—provided the water level in the drainage ditch is low enough. Provided it doesn't rise again and sweep Jack and all his troubles into the wire debris trap under the Northwest Thirtieth Street Bridge.

Hurricane Ellen. Now that Jack believes in omens, they've started popping up like Internet advertisements.

He pulls his car into Mary's driveway so his headlights point toward the drainage ditch, but first, they swing past the hanging scarecrow and the Queenie cross. More omens. The scarecrow twists slowly in the breeze. The Queenie cross tips as his lights pass over it, like a graveyard movie trailer for a *Hammer House of Horror* production.

The water level in the ditch is down to a trickle at the bottom. No relationship to the amount of rain that fell in the last few hours. No way to predict when a civil servant in central flood control will pull a lever and send the next wall of water rushing through.

Jack checks his Breitling Chronometer Emergency watch as if he has an appointment with Richard and doesn't want to be late. A nearby lightning strike lights up the ditch. The accompanying crack of thunder jumpstarts his heart. The flash illuminates the graffiti mural on the far wall of the ditch, highlighting old graffiti buried under layers of spray paint. Two words stand out, three feet tall, written in red block letters. FUCK YOU. The afterimage stays on his retinas for several seconds. Milani Neon-Red, the color of Ellen's fingernails. It's another omen.

Jack steps out of the car into a light mist that's almost nothing more than extra-strength humidity. He wonders if there is beer inside Mary's refrigerator. Keystone would serve his purpose right now, even one of those dark foreign beers that look like bloody urine. Maybe he'll check it out after all of this is over, but not until Richard's body is safely in his trunk. Not until he has a plan.

Jack hopes God is watching as he straightens the Queenie cross before heading for the drainage ditch. It's hard to stay agnostic when you're looking for a body on a stormy night and you really need a beer.

The drainage ditch wall is slicker than Jack expects. He falls onto his butt immediately and drags it across the cement like a dog with a worm infestation—over the spray-painted face of a cartoon Hispanic gang banger and then across a caricature of the Virgin Mary.

At the bottom of the drainage ditch, a cloud of gnats hovers at eye level, floating on the top of a stench layer—the smell of wet dead things.

Jack's flashlight beam catches a dozen sparkling rat eyes posed behind the carcass of a potbellied pig, lying on its back in front of the pipe where he stashed Richard. The pig's snout is pressed against a bowling ball, the sight of which triggers the memory of "Cielito Lindo" for reasons he doesn't understand.

The rats disappear when a soggy cat—black, of course—hops out of the drainage pipe where Jack stored Richard's body. Feral, he supposes, living off carrion and things that eat carrion. He shines his flashlight into the pipe. The beam bounces off broken glass and aluminum cans throwing spots of light inside Richard's temporary tomb like a disco mirror ball.

No Richard. He's been washed away, carried on the top of dirty floodwaters inside his double trash bag. A disrespectful parody of a Viking funeral. He'll wind up in the South Canadian River instead of Valhalla unless he's stopped by the chain link barrier Corporal Laura Pepper told Jack about. The Northwest Thirtieth overpass is only a few blocks away.

Jack feels something nudge his leg. Almost soft enough to be his imagination, but it bumps him again, harder the second time. The black cat pushes its face against his shin and threads itself through his legs as if it has found its long-lost owner standing beside a dead pig in a death-saturated ditch. Nothing has touched Jack with this much affection since before Ellen left him. He reaches down to stroke the cat—careful, not because he is afraid of the animal, but because of the slime and germs on its fur.

He holds his hand so it can sniff his fingers. It does so with the delicacy of a Persian long-hair sampling caviar from a silver spoon. After it is satisfied Jack is no threat, it rakes its claws across his hand, too quickly and too forcefully for the attack to have been unplanned. Five perfectly straight parallel lines just above his knuckles, like a music score waiting to be filled in with notes.

Jack hears a string of curses echoing in the tunnel where Richard used to be. It takes him a minute to recognize his own voice.

The cat retreats fifty feet down the ditch. It circles back, returning to Jack like a boomerang he doesn't dare try to catch. He picks up the bowling ball beside the dead pig's snout and rolls it at the animal. No contest. The cat steps around it easily, heading for more affectionate leg bumps and another vicious scratch that's sure to get infected. The cat has almost reached him when a circle of light catches Jack from the upper edge of the ditch on the side that borders Mary's yard.

"What the hell are you doing?" The voice of Corporal Laura Pepper.

Jack squints into the flashlight beam and tries to think of a good reason for a grown man to be in a drainage ditch bowling for cats.

"Well…." Jack holds his hands where the policewoman can see them because he'd bet anything that Laura Pepper has her free hand on her pistol grip.

"Rescuing my daughter's cat." It is out before he realizes it makes no sense at all.

"The one you just tried to kill?"

"Changed my mind," Jack tells her. "Cat's gone feral." He holds his scratches up for Laura Pepper to see, even though he knows she's too far away.

"Went feral quickly," Jack tells her. "Happens that way sometimes. Looked it up on the Internet."

The cat is bumping its head against him again, calling him a liar in its peculiar feline way.

"So how about you get your ass on up here," Laura Pepper says. "And bring the feral cat."

Can Laura Pepper be a cat lover? She doesn't seem like the type, but Jack can't be sure. Is there a law against using a cat for a bowling pin? One more thing Jack can't be sure of, so he reaches down and tries to snatch the animal by the scruff of its neck, like a cat whisperer who has lost his edge.

Who would have thought a cat could levitate? Certainly not Jack. Certainly not Corporal Laura Pepper. Claws catch Jack in places he'd have thought impossible to reach. The cat flies over his head toward the drainage pipe where Richard Daniels used to be, ricochets off the concrete, and heads for Jack again like affection is the last thing on its mind.

Laura Pepper keeps the animal in her spotlight as it springs off the dead pig.

Jack doesn't see what happens next because he's distracted by a pistol shot. When he locates the cat again it's missing a sizable portion of its chest.

"Glaser safety rounds." Laura Pepper admires her work from the edge of the drainage ditch.

"They don't look all that safe," Jack says.

"Get on up here, Spanky. It's starting to rain again."

THE FRISK PROCEDURE FEELS PRETTY good. Better than being mauled by a cat, anyway. Laura Pepper puts Jack in the front seat of her police car, right next to a shotgun and a radio. He wonders which buttons control the siren but doesn't ask. Laura Pepper finds a first aid kit under the driver's seat and sets to work dressing his injuries.

Thunder rumbles. Lightning flashes. The rain picks up for a few minutes. A gust of wind rocks the police car and tips the Queenie cross. The violent weather passes as quickly as a cat attack ended by a Glaser safety round.

"I suppose I can rely on your discretion about the shooting?"

"Okay." Jack examines his facial scratches in the police car's rear-view mirror. Laura Pepper has coated them with Mercurochrome. Bright red, like the FUCK YOU graffiti Jack saw just before he slid into the drainage ditch.

"The thing is, Spanky, I still want to look inside your car." She gives him a short time to consider this, then walks around to his side of the car, pulls him out, cuffs his hands behind his back, and puts him in the backseat of the cruiser.

The perpetrator seat.

"You're not under arrest at this time," she says.

Jack feels under arrest, especially when she shuts the car door. Laura Pepper must have taken his keys during the frisk because she's opening all four of his car doors, letting the drizzle blow in. She crawls through the car like a feral cat looking for a rat. She pops the trunk, shines her light around inside, and comes up with the pistol he hid in the spare tire well.

Oops!

Laura Pepper carries the pistol by looping her index finger through the trigger guard, so she won't smudge any fingerprints. Like she already knows it's a murder weapon.

She has a quick conversation over the police radio, reciting numbers and letters engraved on the pistol. Looks at Jack.

"Registered to you, Spanky." Her words drip with disappointment and disrespect. She sniffs the pistol. Breaks open the cylinder. "Three spent rounds."

Jack hasn't been told about his right to remain silent yet, but he knows all about it.

"Guess you haven't broken any laws," Laura Pepper says. "but something ain't right, Spanky."

"Sooo…." She gives him time to make a spontaneous statement against his own interests.

Jack has never appreciated constitutional amendments as much as now.

IT'S NO EASIER TO GET back in the drainage ditch the second time, and the water is rising. Only a couple of inches since Laura Pepper let him off with a derogatory nickname and a warning. Exactly the right depth to slop over the tops of Jack's shoes—one more pair of size eleven flaws in his plan.

He tries to think of a good explanation for going back into the ditch just in case Laura Pepper comes back and catches him in the act.

"Well, it's like this, see…." Another missing pet? A dog this time? It really doesn't matter because he'll be dragging a homemade body bag filled to the brim with dead son-in-law—if his quest is successful.

It's hard to stay focused with so many horrible and fascinating things going on in the rising water. A group of rats struggle to climb aboard a rotten limb. A snake swims by and picks a straggler off. A potbellied pig washes past—probably the one that was in front of Richard's temporary tomb. How many can there be?

A twisted mass of black cat fur joins the pig. Old friends on their way to a zombie reunion at the Northwest Thirtieth overpass.

By the time Jack makes it to the chain-link trash barrier, the pig, the cat, and all the rats are nowhere to be seen, and the water is up to his knees. A dead doe and her fawn sprawl on a mountain of plastic bottles and aluminum cans beside a sack of Niger potatoes and a bloated Chihuahua with a rhinestone collar. Like a *Discover Oklahoma* documentary gone terribly wrong.

Plenty of green trash bags. How many of them contain bodies? They look bright and shiny in Jack's flashlight beam, stacked in two neat rows along the outer edges of the chain link barrier, as if by the hand of the patron saint of garbage men.

The illusion of intelligent design. Jack saw a special about it on NOVA. The program ended before he reached his fifth Budweiser, so he remembers most of it. The final segment is mostly a blur, but he's pretty sure they decided nothing was planned, even though it looks that way.

The stacks of bags do look that way. Jack plays his flashlight beam along the chain-link barrier. A family of dead raccoons is caught at the top, posed like a horror show diorama with their legs poking through to the other side. Drowned in the process of climbing to safety over the rising water. How soon before it rises that high again?

A carload of loud teenagers drives over the Northwest Thirtieth overpass. They shout obscenities that are nowhere near as profane as the ones in the rap music blaring from their radio. The bass causes sympathetic vibrations in Jack's chest and in some of the plastic bottles in the pile at the foot of the chain-link barrier.

The water in the drainage ditch surges against Jack, cold and nasty, all the way up to his crotch. It lifts the cans and bottles and shifts the stacked trash bags just enough to send them tumbling around him. The illusion of intelligent disaster.

Jack shines his flashlight at the trash bag avalanche, as if that will hold them back. They bounce off his shoulders and settle in the stream of water that is below his knees again, moving to ankle level. The illusion of intelligent rescue.

A large, familiar-looking lawn bag remains at Jack's feet as the water sweeps through the mountain of bottles and cans under the barrier. The lawn bag is inflated like a weather balloon. Filled with gasses, Jack imagines, and fluids that make the drainage ditch water seem clean by comparison. He grabs the plastic cinched end and starts dragging.

He should open the bag and check inside, but the weight is right, and the gas inside is right. He takes some time to push against the plastic with his hands, the way Helen Keller explored Annie Sullivan's face in *The Miracle Worker*. But Jack is no Helen Keller, and the bag is no Annie Sullivan. He wonders if he's dragging something besides Richard back to his car, something just as dead and just as rotten.

He loosens the plastic cinch so he can see if there's a second lawn bag inside of this one. If that's not proof enough, Jack can try hand-exploration again. Maybe he'll be more like Helen Keller through a single layer of plastic.

A rush of gas hits him in the face as the bag deflates. Jack gags and reaches inside, with the same enthusiasm a veterinarian has as he reaches into the vagina of a pregnant cow. Nasty, but there's no alternative. Jack feels a shoe. He feels another shoe. It comes off inside the bag, and he feels a foot—exactly the way Helen Keller would do it.

The foot jerks in his hand.

Damn! This seems like a good time for a prayer, except Jack can't remember anything but, "Now I lay me down to sleep." He says it with his eyes closed because that seems more religious. He doesn't open them again until he hears a growling sound.

The whole bag lurches back toward the Northwest Thirtieth overpass. More growling, but at least it's not coming from inside the bag. More lurching. To hell with Helen Keller, it's time to use the flashlight.

A coyote backs away, but not very far. It holds a human hand in its mouth. The human hand is attached to an arm that is attached to a body inside the bag.

"Shoo!" No effect at all.

"Get away!" Jack pretends he's about to throw a rock at the coyote.

The animal drops the hand. Mangled fingers, one of them has a golden wedding band. Jack wishes he had a bowling ball, but he settles for another pretend rock.

The coyote snarls and lunges for the hand. Two fingers down the hatch. Three fingers. No more wedding band.

Jack takes a running step at the coyote and aims a toe at his target the way he's seen place-kickers do in college football games. He can't make up his mind whether this is a brave or foolish act until he misses his kick, his other foot slides out from under him, and he lands on his ass, looking up at a coyote with bits of fingers stuck in its teeth.

"Good doggie."

Flattery is getting Jack nowhere, so he backs away while the animal consumes the rest of Richard Daniels's left hand. Jack's flashlight flickers and goes out, but he really doesn't want to watch what's happening to the stump that's being gnawed away by an animal that has picked up a taste for human flesh.

"Now I lay me down to sleep." All Jack has going for him now is the power of a child's bedtime prayer. His hand brushes against something hard and plastic. A whiffle ball bat, Jack can tell by the feel of it. Too light to be good for anything except a threat he can't back up. Maybe God is getting back at him.

Jack stands with the bat in his right hand. The flashlight felt heavier, but he already dropped that in the water. Storm clouds overhead separate around a full moon as bright as a thirty-watt, environmentally-friendly, fluorescent light bulb.

"Thank you, God." Jack raises the whiffle ball bat. He screams and charges the coyote. The scream doesn't sound manly enough to scare a wild animal that is eating a dead man, so Jack hardens his warrior yell with the only German words he can remember.

"*Donner and Blitzen!*" Thunder and lightning—also the names of two of Santa's reindeer. It does the trick.

The coyote backs away, probably more disgusted than frightened. It turns and scampers up the wall of the drainage ditch leaving Jack to wonder how in hell he'll get Richard's body up that wall.

24

SITTING IN THE FRONT seat of his car feels pretty good to Jack Bailey. He listens to the garage door close behind him and waits for inspiration to come his way. That's how Jack usually gets his best ideas, like a case of hiccups. No explanation. One pops up and then another, and they keep on coming until something scares them away. Something like remembering there's a body in his trunk.

"Calm down, Jack," he tells himself. In a whisper, out of respect for the dead.

"Time to make a plan." In a slightly louder voice.

Jack tenses the muscles in his face as he tries to think of a brilliant solution to his problem. It reminds him of when he learned to wiggle his ears when he was ten. He wiggles them now to build his confidence. The left ear first, then the right, then both ears at the same time. A talent no one can take from him.

"It'll happen." Still an inside voice, but it's taken on a shrill edge, like when he used to lie to Ellen.

Waiting for ideas in his garage isn't so bad. Much better than waiting in the back of a police car while a cop reads a list of rights like they are the warning label on a bottle of headache medicine. Definitely better than waiting in the Oklahoma County jail with a drunk cowboy who thinks you look like an old girlfriend. Or beside a drainage ditch after you've dragged your son-in-law's body to the top—after it's already too late to change your mind about tampering with evidence at a murder scene.

Did Mary really kill Richard? Could there be another explanation? An elaborate practical joke gone terribly wrong? A long and difficult suicide? Doubt takes hold at the back of Jack's mind and works its way into chest pains and rapid breathing. Feels like a heart attack coming on, but this is no time for a medical emergency. Not a good idea to call 911 with a body in the trunk.

He should have talked to Mary first. He should have had a plan. He should have figured something better to do with Richard's body than stuff him in the trunk of his car and wait for an epiphany.

Mary. One more thing Jack needs to figure out. He hadn't noticed if her car was parked on the street in front of his house. It certainly isn't in the garage. That's a good thing, he tells himself, because he doesn't want to talk to her about crime scenes and bodies. But where the hell is she, anyway?

The light on the automatic garage door opener goes out and leaves Jack sitting in darkness as profound as the depths of a coal mine. No longer a pretty good place to wait. Fumes of incompletely burned gasoline compete with the odor of decomposition. The gasoline is losing. Jack wants to check his Breitling Chronograph Emergency watch to see how much time he's wasted sitting in his car, but he's not sure which button activates the light, and he's afraid he'll accidentally summon first responders. He promises himself he'll never buy another complicated watch, even if it's a good deal on Craigslist. He promises himself he'll never try to hide another body, either.

Perhaps it's a prayer. He's already sitting in the dark, feeling guilty and hopeless. The evidence of mortality is locked in the trunk of his car. It couldn't hurt, especially if he could come up with something more impressive than "Now I lay me down to sleep."

"I didn't kill him," he reminds God in a respectful whisper.

"The Ten Commandments are silent on concealing a homicide." Lawyerly, the way Gloria Allred would argue her case before the Lord.

"Further affiant sayeth not." Instead of amen. Jack has been watching too much *Court TV*. He counts to sixty since he can't see his watch in the dark.

"One Mississippi. Two Mississippi." Nothing.

He counts to sixty, one more time without the Mississippi's, giving God at least one minute and forty-five seconds to make up his mind. A cricket chirps in the darkness, but there's no voice from the cosmic region above the garage door opener, which means heavenly help is not on the way. Jack figures God has a clean-hands policy.

So how does a civilized, depressingly sober, mostly law-abiding man dispose of a body—not to mention a murder weapon—without divine intervention? He's seen it done thousands of times on police procedure documentaries. Of course documentaries are only made about crimes that have been solved. Jack doesn't want to be in one of those.

Part of Richard is gone already. His left hand is well on the way to being coyote shit by now. No fingerprints. The digested DNA is too disgusting for complicated forensic procedures except on the set of *CSI New York*. But turning the rest of Richard into coyote food doesn't hold much promise.

There's no nearby ocean to dump him in, no highway waiting for the cement trucks to arrive, no sausage grinder, no unattended crematorium, and the body in the trunk of Jack's car will get easier to discover with every passing hour.

He sits in the dark, thinking about an urban legend—a dead man decomposes in a Corvette, generating an odor that can't be removed, and a sale price lower than the cost of a set of tires. All made up, but the story is becoming more believable as the odor of Richard leaks through gaps in the rubber seal of Jack's trunk left behind by bored assembly line workers.

"Burial," Jack says loud enough so Richard will know he hasn't been forgotten, on the off chance that spirits really exist and they hang around their bodies, building up grudges. Jack isn't superstitious under ordinary circumstances, but these circumstances are anything but ordinary.

It doesn't pay to take chances with the supernatural when you are about to do nasty things to a human body. He's already hidden Richard in a drainage ditch, allowed a coyote to eat one of his hands, and crammed him in the trunk of a not-so-late model sedan. Jack knows that most successful killers do something extreme to the body, like cut off the fingers and pull the teeth to make identification difficult. Jack has pliers and pruning shears in the garage. A kitchen garbage disposal might eliminate the most identifiable Richard parts, but there's still a hundred and seventy pounds of rotten human meat to dispose of.

Jack looks over his right shoulder and says, "No offense, Richard," in case angry ghosts can read minds. Sitting in the dark, surrounded by the scents of human decomposition and contaminated water has put him in the mood for a case of Budweiser and a leisurely day to drink it.

He opens the garage door with his remote control, hoping that fresh air and artificial light will clear his mind.

Things look less supernatural in the light, but they also look more suspicious—at least to Jack. So, he closes the door again just in case a police K-9 unit cruises by with a cadaver dog in training.

Paranoia? Of course, it is, but the cops are out there, and bodies in trunks are something that interests them. It's reasonable to be cautious.

Jack's got plenty of lawn bags and a shovel or two. There's a garden in the back yard that hasn't been planted since Ellen went away. Not a proper final resting place, but better than the trunk of a car until he thinks of something more permanent.

Jimmy Hoffa has never been found, or Amelia Earhart, or Ambrose Bierce, or Butch Cassidy and the Sundance Kid. Plenty of bodies have never been found. Richard Daniels could join that club, but first, maybe he should spend a little time feeding the worms in Ellen's garden.

"The weed of crime bears bitter fruit." Jack doesn't have the slightest idea where that came from, but he supposes Ellen's garden will be ruined for vegetables from now on. He pops the trunk with his remote as he walks to the back of his automobile, trying to figure out exactly what comes next. He looks in the trunk, hoping the body has miraculously disappeared.

Decomposition fumes surround his face like a cloud of gnats. Jack breaths through his mouth a time or two, but decomp tastes as bad as it smells. How deeply has it penetrated the carpet in the trunk? The body bag is warm to the touch. The air around it feels thick, full of dead molecules too complex for soap and water.

The engine gives off a loud tick as it cools down. The light on the garage door shuts off, leaving Jack in darkness once again. He backs away from his car, feels his way around lawn equipment and metal shelves, and trips over a half-full two-gallon can of gasoline. He bangs his hip on the handle of his lawn mower and bangs his shin on something short, sharp, and unrecognizable. It hurts way more than it should, but he's almost reached the door into the house, where he'll find a light switch and make some interim decisions about the most final thing in the world.

He mumbles curses under his breath and wishes he had shut his trunk so he wouldn't have to contend with the rising odor. People say it's a smell you never forget. Jack hopes that isn't true.

The doorknob turns as he touches it. The door eases open. A rectangle of light pushes into the garage. A woman is silhouetted in the center.

"Mary?"

A shapely silhouette. Jack doesn't want to have a thought like that about his daughter, but there it is.

The silhouette matches Mary's height perfectly—and her weight and her posture and the way she holds her hands—but Jack's feelings are decidedly unfatherly. The kind of feelings a man denies when testifying before a jury of his peers.

The shapely silhouette leans forward. Her hand rises. A finger points. A perfect imitation of the hand on an American Express bill that tells cardholders to *pay this amount.* The finger's shadow touches Jack's open trunk.

"What stinks?" Ellen's voice. That explains everything.

Ellen flips the overhead light on. She pushes past Jack and walks across the garage to his car.

"Wait! Don't! Stop!" Jack tries to shout orders, but it sounds more like pleading.

"Please, Ellen!" That doesn't work, either. It never worked.

Ellen stares into the trunk, doesn't recoil from the smell, and doesn't cover her mouth in disgust. Her eyes light up as if she's seen something beautiful, the way she looked when Mary was born. She turns to Jack who is standing at the open door to his house with his arms at his side, waiting to be knocked over like a bowling pin.

"Jack, what's this?" The wonder in her voice reminds him of Mary's first trip to Disneyland.

"Well...." How do you explain a body in your trunk to an ex-wife who is back home for the first time after two years? You don't tell her it's her son-in-law Richard, who she might have had an affair with once upon a time. You don't tell her you think Mary killed him and you're hiding the body.

Jack tells her, "It's kind of hard to say."

"I'll bet." Ellen reaches into the trunk, which makes Jack gag a little.

"Please don't." He doesn't remember walking across the garage, but here he is, standing beside Ellen, looking into the trunk of his car as if they are inspecting an exceptionally interesting spare tire.

"Mary's gone to stay with a friend," Ellen says. "She's afraid Richard will show up—before she's made a decision. You know? I'm supposed to tell you."

Ellen points at the stump of an arm protruding through a hole in the body bag.

"Coyote gnawed it off," Jack tells her, as if he were describing a broken plumbing fixture he hadn't gotten around to fixing.

She touches the bag, smiles at its warmth, and examines it with her fingers, the way she might check to see if a cantaloupe is ripe.

"Who is it?"

Ellen's smile looks good, even under the fluorescent lights in Jack's garage, standing in front of an open trunk containing the mutilated remains of her son-in-law.

"You can tell me, Jack. You can tell me anything." She puts an arm around his waist. She pulls him close, as if she hasn't spent the last two years pushing him away. She plants a wet kiss on his cheek, leaving a saliva spot the size and shape of her lips.

Jack wonders if Ellen's saliva will absorb the odor of decomposition. He wraps an arm around her shoulders and tries to pull her away, but she won't budge. He tries to close the trunk with his free hand, but Ellen grabs the lid.

"I didn't know you had it in you, Jack." Her eyes are open wide, shaped like two identical glass almonds, surrounded by facial tissues that look as if they've never felt the strain of worry. Her pupils dilate, the way they used to in their college days before she decided Jack Baily wasn't enough for her. Before she decided she needed something more and went out to find it.

"Who is it, Jack? Who did you kill?"

Jack feels a tremor run through Ellen's body, starting at her ovarian equator and moving toward the poles. He'd felt tremors like that before when they made love, the prelude to an orgasm that always slipped away in the final moment.

Things will be different now. Jack is sure of it. If he can take her this far just by standing here, surely he can take her all the way—if it comes to that. And Jack is thinking it might come to that.

"Trust me, Jack."

Jack will never do that again, but Ellen doesn't need to know.

"How did you do it?"

Jack reaches into the spare tire well, where the pistol is hidden. He presses the gun into Ellen's hand. Kisses her on the lips. Jack isn't good with lies, but he's not telling any. Ellen's tremors increase as she touches the murder weapon. She strokes the barrel, as if she were teasing a penis into an erection.

No teasing is necessary for Jack. He's there. He's already thinking that the dead man in his trunk can wait until tomorrow. The dead are patient. Erections are not. He pulls Ellen away from the trunk and slams it shut.

"I have to dispose of the body," he tells her.

"Jack." She says his name as if it is a complete thought. The consonants are thick and juicy. Her breath is warm and full of musk that overrides the odor of Richard's body.

"Let's go inside," Jack says. "We can figure things out tomorrow."

They walk past the den, where a woman on the television says, "Alligators. Can you believe it?"

"Something on the DVR," Ellen says. "I hope you don't mind." She puts the gun in Jack's hand and turns the barrel toward her heart. Her breathing quickens. "I'll find out how it ends another time."

Jack doesn't understand Ellen's reaction to the murder, or the murder weapon, but men have never really needed to understand. He slides his hand across her bottom. She doesn't object, not even when he gives it a little smack.

The voice on the television fades as Jack leads Ellen to the bedroom. Something more about alligators, but Jack doesn't care. Ellen sways under his touch as he walks her to the bed where they shared unsatisfying sex for years after Mary was born. Things will be different tonight, even if he hasn't got the slightest idea why.

"My Jack turns out to be a killer."

"Yeah," Jack tells her. He hopes the one-word answer will make him sound tough and aloof.

"I always knew you were a dangerous man, Jack. I just forgot it for a little while."

"Right."

"Will you forgive me, Jack?" She hands him the pistol. "Or will you kill me?"

"Have to wait and see." Jack slips the pistol into his waistband, the way he imagines a killer would, and starts undressing Ellen.

25

A boy forgets about his mother when he finds naked pictures of his wife on his brand-new cell phone. Posed and pretty as the barely legal girls on Internet porn sites. There's even a short video—a dance Mary trusted the old, original Richard Daniels not to share.

"All mine," Danny tells himself, now that Richard number one is dead.

The best thing about the video—besides Mary's breasts—is her eyes looking from the screen right into Danny's soul, telling him without words—*Now I belong to you, asshole. Don't blow it.*

He should shut the video down because he's getting a signal that means low power but every time his fingers move toward the controls, he notices something he hasn't seen before. Something he didn't know existed until this moment. Maybe it's the twitch of a muscle or a shadow hardening the lines of a curve, or the way Mary coordinates lip movements with shifts in posture. The way she holds her hands, as if she's pretending to reach out of the phone and touch his body with fingertips that can read his mood like a pretty blind girl reading braille elevator buttons.

Danny Riley never expected things to work out this way when he left the rez. So many things he never knew. So many things he never suspected. So much magic in such a tiny screen. One more dance, he promises himself. Then he'll turn it off and preserve his batteries along with his sanity.

The Navajo believe too much of anything is bad—even things like the prettiest girl in the world dancing naked on a telephone. So, Danny will quit watching just as soon as he regains control of his fingers. But that may take a little longer than he planned because he notices Mary is speaking to him as she dances. It's easy to overlook silent words with so many other things going on. He'll turn the video off, all right, but first, he's got to figure out what Mary's telling him.

"Richard." That's the first word, followed by three more he can't be sure of.

Then there's "Love." That's one's easy, but other words come quickly. Words that look incredibly seductive to the brand-new Richard Daniels. Probably his imagination because Mary isn't the kind of girl who'd talk like that, even dancing naked on the telephone.

He'll watch it one more time. Just long enough to translate Mary's secret message. If he can re-activate the analytical part of his brain.

THE PHONE VIBRATES INTENSELY AND repetitively, like pulses of electricity. As if Mary's naked spirit is trapped inside trying to get out. Danny has heard the vibrations before, even felt them in his pocket, but they catch him by surprise. He can't remember what to do next until a caller ID rectangle covers Mary's breasts.

There's her name and number, just like on the contacts screen. Does she know he's watching her video? Danny Riley never had a telephone as smart and devious as this one, but the Richard Daniels part of him takes charge.

"Hello, Mary!" Spoken too loud and way too fast. Like a salesman who wants to sell a car that's on fire before the buyer sees the smoke.

"*Richard.*" Slow, deep voice, the way women sound when they are half way between two disastrous decisions.

"*I'm back home, Richard,*" Mary tells him. "*You can come back too—if you are really through with meth.*" A strong intake of air that sounds like static.

"Meth." He doesn't say it like a question. It's not a statement either, just a word he throws out there to keep from saying, "I'll do anything for you, Mary." Because even though it's true, and even though it's probably what she wants to hear, he knows deep in his Danny-Riley-broken heart she won't believe him.

"Sure," he says as if there's nothing to it. No problem breaking a meth habit for the girl he loves, even if he's got a history that proves he can't do it.

"I'll try real hard, Mary." He drools a little when he says her name because, somehow, the video of her dancing naked is working again.

"I'll try to be a better man," he says. "I'll try to be straight." That might be part of the Boy Scout pledge. Danny never was a Boy Scout, and the original Richard Daniels probably wasn't either.

"*This is your last chance, Richard. Your very last. Don't come unless you're sure.*" She ends the call as her image on the screen blows him a kiss.

"I'm sure, Mary." Her dance keeps him interested for another two minutes, but that is long enough because he has the real thing waiting for him now.

And he knows the secret of moonflower moth magic, which is sure to win her love if all else fails. There's a dead one in his glove compartment resting beside the truck title and proof of insurance. A perfect place to keep it because that's what magic is—insurance. When all else fails, a half-breed Laguna boy has magic.

Moth magic won't take him back to Mary's house. Magic ants and pieces of umbilical cord are no good for trips through Oklahoma City streets. Urban navigation requires a different kind of magic. Electronic magic from satellites that fly overhead like invisible ancient gods ready with information for men like Danny Riley, who hasn't fasted or spent hours in a sweat lodge getting ready. Shortcut magic, on sale by the minute from AT&T.

Mary's address is right there on his proof of liability insurance, covered by sparkling scales from the wings of his dead moonflower moth.

Liability insurance. That means somebody else pays if Danny Riley hurts someone. He thinks about that for a moment before he finds an application on his home screen that sounds like it might work. *Scout,* like the Indian guides who escorted white invaders deep into tribal territories.

"TURN LEFT ON COUCH DRIVE." A strict female voice orders him over the phone's tiny speaker. *"Stay in the right lane. In four hundred yards, turn right on Robert S. Kerr."* But construction barriers make that impossible.

"Sorry," he tells the satellite voice.

She doesn't answer. She doesn't give different directions. At first Danny believes he's broken some kind of ritual he doesn't understand, but it's only the batteries going dead. As dead as the original Richard Daniels. The son Nelva Riley liked best of all.

26

"FEED A DEAD MAN to the alligators." Ellen looks at Jack like he's just come up with the general theory of relativity.

"Brilliant." She kisses him with her mouth open. It's the third time this morning. She tastes like grapefruit juice and mint-flavored dental floss.

"Came to me last night." Jack doesn't say he thought of it during sex. Men think about all sorts of things during sex that women don't need to know about. Like imagining your wife is the girl in the Taco Bell commercials. Like figuring out who was the greatest quarterback of all time. Like alligators in the southeastern corner of Oklahoma.

"Can you believe it?" Jack repeats the words of the *Discover Oklahoma* girl behind the BLOCKED CALL rectangle the night Ellen called.

His brilliant idea came shortly after Ellen mounted him in a reverse cowgirl position—that looks a lot more comfortable than it feels—while he pointed a pistol at her head. With the safety off and the hammer back. Her idea.

Jack thought about feeding Richard to the alligators at the precise moment Ellen said, "Oh, God!" An answer to the prayer he mumbled in a garage after the light went out.

Ellen dances around the kitchen, wearing one of Jack's old T-shirts that doesn't quite cover her, while he tries to decide if there's time for sex one more time before she figures out he's not a killer, just a man who takes out the trash for their daughter. Even if it's felony trash, he's still not a killer. Not dangerous, the way Ellen likes her men.

"Can we use this?" Ellen has found a meat cleaver in the knife drawer. "For the body, I mean?"

"Why not?" He sits in one of his kitchen chairs and drinks coffee while he watches Ellen sort through implements suitable for dismembering a corpse. She looks sexy while she does it—that's for sure—but Jack hasn't got the slightest idea why.

Ellen is the dangerous one. Ellen will get him into trouble he can't get out of. It's only a matter of time. And once Ellen figures out Jack didn't kill the man in the bag, or if she learns the identity of the corpse, everything will change.

She's found a butcher knife with a blade long enough to, "stick right through a man." Ellen sits on Jack's lap. Puts the knife in his hand. Places the point under her chin. "You can do anything you want, Jack. Anything at all." She moves her chin so the knifepoint makes a little nick.

"Just enough to draw the blood. You see?" She catches a drop on her fingertip and rubs it on Jack's lips.

"You see?" She kisses him. Runs the tip of her tongue over his lips. Smiles at the taste.

Like a vampire, Jack thinks. Like a goddamned autoerotic vampire.

"No harm done," she says. "Never any harm in a little blood."

She settles into him like a five-hundred-dollar lap dance. He knows what is coming next, but Ellen doesn't look like the bedroom is on her mind.

"Anything you want, Jack." She moves her lap dance to the kitchen table and leans back on her elbows, like the dessert after a dinner that left Jack feeling hungry.

"You're the man with the knife, Jack. Know what I mean?"

Jack knows exactly what she means. He's never understood the relationship of sex and violence until this moment. Now he gets it, totally.

"Whatever is on your mind," Ellen tells him, knowing exactly what's on his mind, because Jack is the marionette, and she is the puppeteer, and there is no way he can cut the strings with the knife she placed in his hand.

She pulls a string, and Jack stands up.

"What's on your mind, Jack?" Ellen lies back, totally receptive, the way a Venus flytrap is receptive to an insect.

"Alligators," Jack says.

The butcher knife sparkles under the kitchen lights like a magic wand in a Disney animation. Ellen smiles as he waves it in front of her face.

She holds her arms out—an invitation Jack can't refuse.

"Alligators." The word blends in his mind with making love to Ellen on his kitchen table. He spends a moment wondering if this is how fetishes begin, then turns his thoughts back to alligators and knives and sex because it's far too late to change things.

Chapter 27

WILMA DANIELS SITS IN her easy chair, facing her front door so she'll be ready when Tommy Bracken comes to call. She's got a pistol tucked in the seat cushion beside her. The knife in her ankle sheath is sharp enough to slice bread, or go all Lorena Bobbitt and cut a man's penis off.

How would Tommy Bracken like it if she threw his pathetic little thing to the dogs? She could hang it on her key chain like a good luck charm. Keep it as a souvenir of a very good day, like the scalps Cheyenne warriors took at Little Big Horn. She considers all the savage possibilities, but Wilma Daniels knows she won't do any of those things. She's Cherokee, the most civilized of the Five Civilized Tribes. Cherokee warriors never collected ears, finger bones, or scalps. None of the glamorous, gory things that left such a colorful stain on history—more's the pity.

Wilma is the only one in her family who understands the breadth, depth, and unfortunate limitations of Cherokee tradition. Her son, Richard, is dead, and his son, Ricky, doesn't care. She strokes the handle of her knife. The ancestors wouldn't like it, and Tommy....

That weird bastard might like it just fine.

He eats Wilma's abuse like chocolate cake and always asks for more. She feeds it to him carefully, a teaspoonful at a time. The way women have managed men since Adam and Eve. Give them a little bit of what they want, but always hold some back because men lose interest fast once they get everything. And men like Tommy are dangerous when they lose interest.

She strokes the knife handle a little more. Says, "Maybe later, asshole." Practices the phrase a couple of times until she has the tone just right. It'll go perfectly with an open-handed slap—a nice skin-on-skin smack like an exclamation point at the end of a sentence. It's the little details that keep Tommy coming back.

She draws the knife, fogs the blade with her breath, wipes it clean on her blouse, and looks at her reflection in the chrome. The lines at the corners of her mouth and eyes would be enough to send most men running, but not Tommy.

He's not looking for a young girl with an empty space inside her head and a hollow spot in her belly just right for filling up with babies.

Tommy Bracken isn't like that, bless his heart. Tommy wants an older woman who knows how to make him cry. Someone who won't stop hurting him, even when he wants her to. Wilma likes the little whimpering sound he makes when she gets serious. The way her grandson whimpered when she told him, "Time for another lesson, Ricky," and went to fetch the teaching stick.

The knife handle feels smooth and cold in Wilma's hand, the way she feels about Tommy—a little bit of hatred, a little bit of lust, a lot of satisfaction when she sees him squirm. She slips the blade into its sheath—no good letting Tommy see it when he walks in the door. Wouldn't want to get his expectations too high.

Wilma Daniels is the only person on earth who isn't afraid of Tommy Bracken. He's killed at least two dozen men, up close and personal. Looks into their eyes so he'll know the moment their spirits break free. Gives them messages when there's time. So they'll remember him when they get to the other side.

Once Wilma understood Tommy Bracken's special wants, he belonged to her. He loves the way fear smells. Loves the way it trembles in his hands. Loves the delicate squeaky sound fear makes when it reaches the saturation point. But what Tommy Bracken really wants is the firsthand experience. He wants to feel terror circulating in his blood. Wants to feel sticky-sour sweat coating his skin. Wants to feel his testicles draw up inside him.

Men are sick bastards, each and every one. Wilma takes four mini-swigs from her metal flask of sipping whiskey. Jack Daniel's goes down easy, whether she drinks it fast or slow, but it's only 10 a.m., and Tommy might take advantage if she starts off drunk. No telling where that would lead.

She opens a pack of Marlboro filter tips and holds one between her lips so when he comes in he'll see it—so much better than a knife. She'll make him light it. Make him hold the match until it burns his fingers. Smoking is the kind of nasty habit Tommy loves because it kills one breath at a time.

Wilma thinks about the *Bible* she used to read sitting in her easy chair. A long time ago, when her boy Richard was alive, Richard's daddy came around now and then and shared her with Tommy Bracken.

"John Horse." She likes to say that name every now and then so she'll remember how it sounds. She looks at the finger where her wedding band used to be. The empty circle is all she has left of the only man she ever loved for real. Still misses that ring after all these years. John Horse, not so much.

She checks several times every day to see if the ring has come back. But she's too old and too civilized to believe in magic. Wilma works her right hand between the cushions of her easy chair and wraps her fingers around the grip of her pistol the way she used to wrap them around John Horse's penis—that she never once thought about cutting off and throwing to the dogs.

Well, maybe once, when Tommy Bracken decided he wanted Wilma Daniels all to himself and John Horse said, "Okay."

She hears a faint knock on her front door but doesn't say, "Come in."

Doesn't say, "It's open," or "Just a minute please," or any of the things people ordinarily say when someone's at the door. Because she knows it's not a Jehovah's Witness or a neighbor who wants to borrow a cup of sugar, and robbers never knock.

She'd like it if a robber came in the front door. Someone she could shoot for real, under circumstances her tribe would approve. A bona fide home invader whose blood could drip between the floorboards of her living room while his spirit made the trip to wherever spirits go.

Wilma stares at the widening space between the door and the jam. Says, "the Darkening Land," to remind herself of the Cherokee name for heaven—or hell. To remind herself that she's a member of the Long-hair Clan, responsible for keeping tribal memories alive and passing them on to the next generation. And it's too late for her to do that because her son, Richard, is already in the Darkening Land. One of the men Tommy Bracken killed indirectly with that special brand of meth-amphetamine he sold—Cherokee Ice.

Today, Tommy is a Mexican. Does the accent perfectly, as if he just waded across the Rio Grande.

"*Hola.*" He gives Wilma a timid wave and calls her, "*Mi hija.*"

My daughter. That means he will try to be the boss. Wilma won't let that happen, but Tommy already knows. It's part of the scene he has worked out in his mind, from his dramatic entrance to the shuddering orgasm that will bring it to an end. Not a happy ending exactly, but as close as Tommy Bracken comes. And nothing for Wilma except for a sense of satisfaction. She is only along for the ride, like a designated driver. The way it has always been for Wilma Daniels, except for the years she was with John Horse.

Tommy's eyes are on the Marlboro dangling from her lips. Unlit. Better to keep it that way for a while, until she decides how things are going to play. She doesn't know exactly why Tommy likes Marlbo-ros so much. Marlboro filter tips—not the 100s. Lots of men like to see women smoke, but for Tommy, it absolutely, positively must be a Marlboro filter tip. He can spot another brand from across the room. Thank God he's not fixated on a mentholated cigarette.

Tommy smiles like a field worker from Chihuahua whose boss has paid him exactly what he's due—no bogus charges for damaged lettuce or transportation. No threat to call immigration. His pants are stained at the knees as if he's spent hours doing stoop labor. His shoes are scuffed and dusty. His posture is erect. He wears a silver crucifix around his neck. His English moves up and down a Spanish rollercoaster, so it comes out sounding like a poem, even though the grammar is seriously crippled.

Perfect disguise. Even Wilma might not recognize Tommy Bracken from a distance. If she saw him across a crowded street, she'd look away before he approached her seeking work.

"Ain't you got no one to cut your grass, missus?" Tommy reaches into his pocket and retrieves a kitchen match. He holds it in his right hand and strikes it with a thumbnail, filling the air with the scent of brimstone. He walks to Wilma carefully so the draft from the open door won't extinguish the flame. The walk is perfect. As if he's stepping over rows of crops, as if his bones have been fed a steady diet of corn tortillas and beans.

Tommy can be anyone and everyone. A cop, a lawyer, a hired killer. People believe he has a gang of men doing his bidding, but Wilma knows it's only him. Disappearing here, reappearing there, exactly where he needs to be to do the next methamphetamine transaction.

Today he is an undocumented immigrant worker with an erection. Wilma can see it tenting the worn pants that look like they were pulled out of a Goodwill dumpster. Wilma doesn't know exactly what Tommy has in mind, but it's clear his plans are big.

He pushes the match toward Wilma's cigarette, but his smile is much too wide. Tommy Bracken looks like he's in the mood for ordinary sex. That's how things end sometimes, but only on Wilma Daniels's terms.

When Tommy Bracken's close enough, she kicks him in the groin.

"A little love tap, Pedro." She grabs his wrist as he doubles over. Pulls the match flame to her Marlboro. Blows smoke in Tommy's face and holds his hand steady while the flame scorches his fingers.

Things are going well. She stands up, holding her pistol in her left hand, still holding Tommy's wrist with her right. Gives his wrist a little more pressure. Enough to make the bones pop, but his hand is frozen around the burning match. The flame licks his fingers, the way Wilma's tongue used to lick John Horse's ear.

Tommy's got to pay for a lot of things that aren't his fault and a lot of things that are—Wilma's missing wedding ring, Wilma's dead son, Wilma's no-good grandson, the leaky roof on Wilma's house the Cherokee tribe hasn't gotten around to fixing.

When Tommy sinks to his knees, she lets go of his wrist, slaps him across the face, and points the pistol at his head. She can't remember if there is a bullet in the chamber, so she keeps her finger off the trigger.

Tommy smiles at her, the way he always does when she brings him to his knees.

"Anything you want me to tell Richard," he says. "Say it before you kill me."

Richard's name is almost enough to make her do it, but she won't give Tommy Bracken the satisfaction.

"No trip to the Darkening Land today," she tells him, " but it's gonna be more than a little whuppin'."

Tommy still has his smile, which means Wilma is right on script. Doing everything Tommy Bracken wants, exactly as he wants it. Maybe she'll change her mind and kill him after all.

TOMMY STANDS NAKED IN WILMA'S kitchen, stuffing his undocumented immigrant drags into her garbage can. His Mexican accent fades into television English, one vowel at a time.

"Pack a suitcase. Everything you'll need for a few days in Oklahoma City." He has amphetamine business to take care of there. Won't say exactly where or what.

Wilma asks, "Does this have something to do with Ricky?" even though she knows the answer.

Since Ricky got out of rehab, Tommy makes regular visits to Oklahoma City. Checking the boy out, to see if he's clean enough to have a place in the Bracken organization—John Horse's place.

Ricky is a disappointment to Wilma. Hooked on Cherokee Ice, like his no-good father. Men in the Daniels family were all no good. Just like every man who's ever lived. But Ricky Daniels is blood, and blood is everything.

"What you want with Ricky?"

Tommy removes the teaching Stick from where Wilma keeps it hanging in the kitchen. Left there from when the boys in her care needed a little guidance. He carries the stick to Wilma, laid across his open palms as if it is a sword and she is the queen of England ready to dub him Sir Tommy Bracken. He kneels and hands it to her.

Wilma knows what he wants because Tommy is completely naked, and naked men can't hide their thoughts.

"Maybe later, asshole." Punctuated with a slap. That will have to do for now.

SITTING IN THE FRONT SEAT of his lemon yellow 1965 Mustang, Tommy Bracken doesn't look the least bit submissive or Mexican. His smile has turned into a flat line across a white man's face. The joy has left his eyes.

Wilma can't figure out why Tommy never bruises. No matter how hard she hits him, he never shows a mark. Even when she draws blood, the cuts magically disappear, so there's no sign of violence. No wonder the local Cherokee think he is a witch.

"What are we doin', Tommy?" She wants to ask where Ricky fits into all of this, but she doesn't want to say her grandson's name out loud.

"Where are we going to stay when we get to Oklahoma City?"

No response. Kind of bossy for a submissive. He's all dressed up like a big-city gangster. Expensive jacket—even though it's springtime and already way too hot in Oklahoma. Tommy's classic Mustang doesn't have air conditioning. Doesn't have anything that didn't come stock in 1965.

"Exactly the way it came off the assembly line," Tommy tells Wilma, like he does every time he takes her for a ride. He thinks everything was perfect back in 1965. Things have gotten a little worse every year since then.

"Sixty-five's when they got the Mustang right. The Corvette too. And that's when music hit its prime."

It's a three-hour ride from Tahlequah to OKC. They keep the windows open, so he turns the radio up loud.

"Tube radio," Tommy says. That's the only kind of electrical entertainment because he doesn't want anything in his car but original equipment.

"Like a virgin." Tommy pats the dashboard so Wilma will know he means the car and not the Madonna song. His Mustang's got a girl's name. "Charlene." Tommy uses the car's name at least a dozen times between Tahlequah and Prague.

"Charlene just got detailed. Can you tell, Wilma?"

And, "Charlene uses multigrade oil now." Better for her, even if they didn't have it in 1965, so he makes an exception.

And, "Charlene's got brand-new leather upholstery." Pats the seat beside Wilma's leg like he's fondling a cheerleader's ass.

Wilma pulls a Marlboro out of her pack and lights it, just to make Tommy nervous.

"Please don't smoke inside Charlene." There's a little quiver in his voice, like the kind he gets when Wilma squeezes his nipples, but Tommy isn't having a good time. There's no pretense in his fear. He's not following a script that leads to an orgasm at the end of a one-act play.

"I mean it, Wilma." The voice of a killer this time. The same tone he uses when he tells the men he kills exactly what he wants them to say when they get to the other side. Wilma wonders what kind of message he'd send with her. She'd bet anything it would be something for his mother.

Hi, Mom. Having a good time. Wish you were here. Men like Tommy are all fucked-up by their mothers. She thinks about the baggage her boy Richard carried to the Darkening Land. She thinks about the baggage her grandson Ricky is still carrying around in this life.

She tosses her Marlboro out the window and watches in the side view mirror as the sparks explode on the pavement. Reads the message etched in glass. *Objects may be closer than they appear.* Ain't it the truth.

Wilma leans over the front seat and pops her suitcase open. It's an old-fashioned leather thing, left over from when Richard was alive. The interior smells like dirty socks from the methamphetamine her boy used to pack inside and transport to a dealer outside of Albuquerque.

Every tweaker from Fayetteville to Phoenix wanted Tommy's brand of Cherokee Ice. Richard was the delivery boy.

Cherokee Ice was mellow. Richard Daniels said so, and he knew firsthand. His boy, Ricky, smoked it, too, until he got busted and sent to compulsory rehab. Now? Who knows?

Wilma holds her breath while she sorts through her underwear, looking for the metal flask full of Jack Daniel's that she distinctly remembers packing along with the 9mm Glock semiautomatic pistol that Richard used to carry on his trips to *the land of enchantment.*

Richard's suitcase. Richard's pistol. Underwear that smells like a tweaker's bedroom. Wilma curses herself for being a sentimental old bitch.

Well… not old, exactly.

She finds her hip flask but leaves the inside of the suitcase in a mess. Tommy tells her, "Close that thing, Wilma. It's stinking up my car."

"That stink is all that's left of Richard," she stares hard at the side of Tommy's face until he feels the sizzle on his skin.

He turns to look at her just as she takes a sip of Jack. Room temperature, just the way she likes it. She takes a second sip and lets out a noisy, satisfied breath so full of whiskey molecules the inside of the car smells like a tavern even though the windows are open.

"Cut that out, Wilma." Tommy's head jerks back toward the road. He brakes and looks for a speed limit sign. There never are any in Oklahoma City. He's just exited off I-40, headed through the busiest part of town.

"Can't have open containers in the car." Tommy has that quiver in his voice like he gets right before a whuppin'.

"Maybe I should get the teaching stick," she tells him. She could crack it across his knuckles while he finds his way through the maze of construction barricades that seem to be a permanent fixture in downtown OKC.

"I'm serious, Wilma." Tommy makes a hard turn into an alley. His head whips back and forth the way Richard's used to do when he'd reached the paranoid stage of meth intoxication.

Wilma screws the lid back on her flask, kicks off her shoes—the red strappy ones that Tommy says go perfectly with Marlboros—and runs her toes over the handle of her ankle knife. A girl can't be too careful.

"Got a trunk load of Cherokee Ice," he tells her. "Last batch I have until I get me a new cook." He says that to remind Wilma that his old cook was John Horse. To remind her that John Horse disappeared six months ago without a trace and maybe she could disappear too.

Wilma looks at her reflection in the metal whiskey flask. The convex side makes her nose look big. The concave side gives her crossed eyes. She wants another sip of Jack but doesn't want to push Tommy Bracken over the edge. People who do that disappear the way John Horse did. Or they're found dead, like Richard.

Or, if they're lucky, they get arrested, like her grandson Ricky. Get sent to compulsory rehab where men like Tommy Bracken leave them alone until the state of Oklahoma says they're cured.

"Ricky." Funny Wilma should think of him.

"Fuck, Wilma! Put that goddamned flask away."

She glares at him.

"Please, Wilma." Tommy's voice has got that whining pitch that makes Wilma want to slap him.

"Too much at stake to get pulled over now," he pleads with her. "Life sentence worth of Ice in the trunk. You see that, don't you?" He barely misses a dumpster as he pulls out blind on a street that borders a construction site.

Wilma's pretty sure the OKC bombing museum is somewhere near.

The whole area was bulldozed after that and rebuilt the way people are supposed to be built brand-new when they come out of rehab. Maybe it'll work that way for Ricky. Usually doesn't, though. Usually, boys like Ricky get hooked up with their old crowd and start in using like they did before they learned the Serenity Prayer.

"How come you're keeping track of Ricky?" Wilma's fingers start working the cap on her flask again. The Mustang is moving slowly, so Jack Daniels's fumes fill the car again, too thick to blow completely out the open windows.

Tommy's mouth is open, but no words are coming out. He licks his lips. Adjusts the rearview mirror the way Richard used to do when he thought the dope police were after him.

"Give Ricky a chance." Wilma knows the no-good little half-Laguna bastard will probably blow it, but Ricky is still blood, and Tommy is a lowlife killer who doesn't really give a damn about anybody.

Ricky worked as John Horse's assistant cook for a little while. Family business, Wilma supposes. He's got John's blood in his veins but he's got Wilma's too, and her boy Richard's. The Cherokee look after blood. All Indians do that.

"That boy's too dumb to be a meth cook." Wilma takes another drink. Bigger than she should because thinking about losing Ricky the way she's lost everybody else has made her thirsty. "Undependable, useless. What they call an underachiever." The whiskey cracks Wilma's voice when she finally lands on the perfect un-word.

"Shit, Wilma. You've really done it now." Tommy's pulling into one of the empty sites where the ground has been leveled but no buildings have been started yet.

"Let me do the talking now."

Two swallows of Jack Daniel's ago, Wilma would have understood what was happening right away, but her mind is stuck on Ricky now. Always a disappointment. Always a burden on poor old Wilma Daniels who couldn't beat Cherokee ways into him no matter how hard she tried.

"It's that thick Pueblo hide," she tells Tommy, as if he knows exactly what she's thinking.

"Step out of the car, please." It's a woman cop. Kind of pretty in a young, white, slutty sort of way. Wilma watches her strut up to Tommy's car like a whore at a Shriner's convention. The police uniform clings to her body like it is wet. Her curves look good in blue.

"Skippy, is that you?" The lady cop makes Tommy nervous, but Wilma is pretty sure he's already thinking of how her handcuffs will feel double-locked around his wrists. Wondering if she'll call for male backup to search him or do the job herself.

"Thought I recognized the car. Who's your lady friend, Skip?" She's all the way up to the driver's side window, leaning over, peering in to see what kind of probable cause is lying in plain view. Not asking Tommy to step out of the car again because her eyes have already settled on Wilma's flask, and her nostrils are flexing.

"Laura Pepper." Wilma reads the lady cop's nametag. "Stripper name." She knows she's stuck a sore spot with Officer Laura Pepper when the policewoman's smile turns into a snarl.

"Fuck, Wilma." Tommy's hand comes up from the space between his bucket seat and the console, holding a black-something as square and compact as a billfold full of credit cards. He touches the edge of the square black thing to Officer Laura Pepper's temple. There's a sizzle like the sound effects in old-time Frankenstein movies, and Laura Pepper collapses in the dirt beside Tommy's pristine 1965 Mustang.

"Now I'll have to get new tags," he says. "Maybe paint the car too, and yellow is the factory color."

Tommy sniffs the metal prongs on his stun gun. "Smells like victory." He gives Wilma a clever-boy smile that makes her want to break his nose.

He makes a spark flash across the electrodes like a jagged lightning streak. "Still got charge." He opens the car door, but first, he shoves Officer Laura Pepper aside with his foot. He puts the stun gun in his seat and fumbles under his jacket for a pistol.

"Her eyes are open, Wilma. Do you think she can still hear?"

Tommy wants to send this female cop to The Darkening Land with a message. Wilma's tempted to let it happen, just to see what he has to say that's too important for a simple prayer, but she is a Cherokee, and Cherokee never would stand still for cold-blooded murder. Not like Apache or Lakota or any of those savage tribes that gave the Indians a bad name.

She pulls the knife out of her ankle sheath and presses the point against Tommy Bracken's leather bucket seat. "Tommy. Get your ass back in the car."

"Wilma, please. Not Charlene." He holds his hands up, but the pistol is still in one of them. His finger is inside the trigger guard. Wilma doesn't know much about guns. Doesn't know about safeties and calibers and things like that, but she does know that bullets come flying out of the business end, and that is pointed at the sky for now.

"Drop the gun, Tommy." She puts the tiniest nick in Charlene's bucket seat, so Tommy will know she means business.

"Shit, Wilma. It ain't good for pistols to throw them in the dirt." But Tommy does. A gentle toss. A thump when it hits the ground.

"Now get in the goddamned car." So far, Charlene is barely injured, nothing that can't be covered up with lemon oil. Wilma flexes the muscles in her forearm, getting ready to drive the blade deep into Charlene's interior stuffing. Maybe even nick a spring.

Tommy slides behind the wheel and puts his hands at the ten o'clock and two o'clock positions. "What about the lady cop, Wilma? What about her?" Whining like a little boy who's about to get a whuppin'—or something worse if Wilma can think of it. Her free hand finds Tommy's stun gun. As quick as a left jab, she touches the electrodes to his neck and pushes the trigger.

"Ozone and burned chicken," she tells the convulsing man, who is still holding onto the steering wheel. "Don't smell like victory at all." She holds the trigger down until the charge is gone. Drops the stun gun. Places the cutting edge of her knife over the burn marks. Two cauterized pits as if Tommy has been bitten by an electrified vampire.

His eyes are open, like Officer Laura Pepper's, so Wilma will be able to watch the change when his soul breaks free. All she has to do is drag the blade.

224 JOHN T. BIGGS

"Tell Richard I still love him," she whispers in Tommy's ear. "Tell him I won't let nothin' happen to his boy."

But Wilma only drags the knife hard enough to make a scratch. Too civilized to inflict a mortal wound. That's always been a problem for Cherokee.

She grabs her suitcase and steps out of the car. It shouldn't be too hard to find a cab in this part of Oklahoma City. She tries not to think about the two unconscious people in the empty lot. Tries not to wonder who will wake up first and what will happen after that.

Wilma figures it'll be Tommy. He got the smallest charge. He'll drive off if he's thinking straight, as fast as he can, in case a pesky good citizen reported him while he was out. Probably won't kill the lady cop with the slutty name, but with Tommy, you never know.

Wilma smiles at the possibilities. The ancestors would approve.

28

D ANNY RILEY TRIES TO think of himself as *Richard Daniels.* In italics, the way it's printed on the truck title in his glove compartment. It doesn't help. He looks at the picture on his Richard Daniels driver's license. His face is a perfect match.

"Richard Daniels." He says the name out loud and tries to make it stick. He looks at the name printed on all the official documents Danny Riley never had. *Richard Daniels,* Richard Daniels, Richard Daniels, RICHARD DANIELS. It doesn't matter how it's written, Danny Riley is still the same boy who left the reservation.

"Dead ringers," he tells the DMV photograph.

The whole damn thing is mysterious in that peculiar Native American way Danny Riley knew so well back on the rez. He compares his thumb to the lines and swirls on the miniature black thumbprint on the back of the license. They look similar, at least under the interior overhead light of the only truck he's ever owned.

There's a paper wasp nest between the camper and the cab. He noticed it when he pumped gasoline and paid for it with two of Richard

Daniels's twenty-dollar bills. A white man would spray the nest with poison and knock it down, but Danny leaves it alone because—who knows—it could be one of those sacred things holy men talk about. Like a cottonwood tree that's been struck by lightning or a piece of rock that's shaped exactly like a frog or magic ants that give you visions.

White people go to psychologists when they start having thoughts like that, but Indians sit in their wasp-infested pickup trucks and consider the mysteries of life.

The wasp nest is the size of a clenched fist, full of angry insects that never got to choose where they are now—exactly like Danny Riley. He loses a few of them every time he moves the vehicle. Some find their way back when he stops long enough to eat or shower at a Love's gas station or sleep in the camper shell that smells like dirty socks packed full of cotton candy. The wasps' sense of direction is perfect and impossible.

How mysterious is that?

Danny's sense of direction is tangled in the city streets. Everywhere he looks, there are signs that should tell him where he's going, but somehow never do. It's been three days since he found Richard Daniels's body lying on the kitchen floor of Mary's house, and he still can't find his way back.

Mary. Unbelievably pretty. Unbelievably white. Unbelievably his—like the driver's license, the proof of insurance, the registration, and Richard Daniels's truck.

Danny never had a real, live girlfriend before. Unless he counted Sarah Benally, and that was just a time or two in the backseat of a car. Now he has a full-blown relationship—slightly used, but that doesn't really matter—a wife. Or maybe she's a girlfriend. Things happened so fast he's not certain, and he sure as hell wants to get back to her and find out.

He places his right hand over the amulet bag hanging directly over his heart—the way Navajo Code Talkers do when saying the "Pledge of Allegiance" to the flag. He wants to give thanks to somebody—or something—for Mary.

"Thank you soooo much." Doesn't sound like a regular prayer, but this isn't a regular situation, and the *Greatest Mystery of All* will know he's grateful.

"Really, really grateful," he says out loud. Just in case everybody's wrong about God's mind-reading powers.

Richard Daniels's unidentifiably mutilated body must have been taken away by now. Otherwise, Mary wouldn't be calling him, would she? Wouldn't be moving back into her house unless the blood is all cleaned up and the cops have gone off to wherever cops go to look for murderers.

But Danny Riley can't find his way back to Mary's house. The address on the proof of insurance in his glove compartment—repeated on his previously-owned driver's license—is clear enough, but how to get there is a mystery. A wasp could solve it or a homing pigeon or even a stray city cat, but Danny can't.

People are free with directions that take him farther from his goal with every turn. Deception with a smile. Deception so cleverly disguised, even the deceivers believe it. Who can Danny Riley trust in a city full of Cherokee?

Black people? Maybe some of them are trustworthy Black Seminoles like John Horse.

Danny could identify tribes that lived around the rez. Navajo, Hopi, Zuni, Apache—no problem. But Oklahoma Indians are all mixed up. Some of the black Oklahomans are mixed up, too, so he concentrates on the blackest ones.

They turn away when he says, "*Chehuntamo.*" Hello in Seminole, like John Horse taught him. He checks his smile in the rearview mirror. Looks sincere, friendly, honest. No nasty piece of fast food lettuce stuck between his teeth. Clean face. Clear eyes.

So maybe the truck is scaring them. He parks it at a construction site and sets off on foot. Near the county jail, where people are more dangerous and less afraid.

"*Chehuntamo.*"

The black man doesn't look away when Danny greets him. "You know John Horse?"

Always good to establish relationships first. That's how people did it on the rez. Let everybody know you have friends and relatives, so you couldn't be a witch looking to work some corpse magic.

This black man is not afraid of witches. He's not afraid of anything. He wears a red cap with the bill twisted at an odd angle. His pants are large and baggy, like he's lost a lot of weight. He wears a red jersey with the name of a sports team printed across the front. He holds his arms like he has a gun concealed where he can get to it in a hurry.

Lots of room for guns inside that pair of giant pants.

"You a Seminole?" Richard smiles like white men do on cable news.

"The fuck?" The black man's hands make mystical signs while he rants a string of words Danny doesn't understand.

A spell?

No, this black man is just pissed off about something. Way pissed off. He puffs himself up like an angry bad-luck cat and spits on the sidewalk.

"*Chehuntamo* is all I know." Danny reaches into his back pocket for his driver's license so he can show this pissed-off Seminole Mary's address.

The black man draws a pistol. Fast and artistic, like in old-time television cowboy movies. Smiling, like he can't wait to see a puddle of blood soak into the dirt. Like he can't wait to hear a soul fly out on a dying breath. John Horse never once looked like that.

Another rant filled with blurry words Danny can't understand, peppered with "cocksuckers" and "motherfuckers." The black man holds his gun sideways as if he's aiming at someone in a right-angle universe.

Danny warns him shooting an automatic like that will get him a face full of hot brass. "I've seen it happen." But this black man does not want marksmanship advice.

He doesn't want to shoot Danny either. That's clear because of how hard he pretends to be holding back. He doesn't want to shoot Danny, but he might anyway because he has the gun out and will look like a coward if he puts it away without killing somebody.

There are lots of people watching, as if bullets cannot hurt them.

Lots of people who didn't want to give Danny directions but want to watch him die. The black man with the gun, the sports jersey, and the baggy pants does not think of them as witnesses until Danny reminds him.

"Some of them have cameras." At least, that's what Danny thinks they are. Telephones—like the one that took naked pictures of Mary—are ready to capture a murderer in the act.

The black gunman tips his cap to a steeper angle that will show up better on YouTube. He adjusts his pistol position so the cameras will catch the recoil. Ready for his 15 KB of fame that will go viral if he can think of something clever to say just before the blood and gore.

Richard Daniels has already died from bullet wounds. Danny Riley does not want to go the same way.

"I think that's a TV camera over there."

The gunman turns to get a better look. When he turns back, Danny is gone. Dropped and rolled like a flaming Balance brother. Quiet as a clockwise dust devil. Under a pick-up truck parked illegally by a fire hydrant and out the other side. He sits in front of an oversized tire. Listens to the armed black man on the other side brag about what he almost did.

"Be afraid, motherfucker." Good diction. Deep, the way Darth Vader said, "I am your father, Luke." Volume turned all the way up. Making the most of words because that's all he has now that Danny Riley has gone invisible. Good to know reservation magic works beyond the four sacred mountains.

Police sirens set off howling dogs in the apartment building beyond the bail bonds operations. By the time cruisers arrive, Danny is visible again, and everybody else has disappeared.

THE POLICEWOMAN WHO TASED THE man named Jack in the art museum café is the first. Other black and whites arrive and line up in the street, completely blocking it.

"You." She points an accusing finger at Danny. "Did you call the police?" Her nametag says, Corporal Laura Pepper. There are two stripes on her shoulder, and the flap on her sidearm is unsnapped. Her police accessories are within easy reach, and she looks anxious to use them.

Male cops file out of their cars and walk over to the confrontation. Slow and belligerent, as if they are on their way to a mandatory drug test.

"I don't have time to fuck around," she says. Lots of saliva, as if the word, "fuck," tastes like a lemon drop.

Danny shrugs instead of talking. It's best not to use words with this policewoman, even though he could tell her who killed Richard Daniels. He could say, "The murderer is an African American dwarf with a semi-automatic pistol and a disrespectful name." She'd want to know the name for sure, but Danny can't remember it exactly.

Little Bro. Little Bitty. Little something.

Best not to put the idea of murderous African dwarves into this policewoman's mind. She'll tie the information into knots and weave it into a blanket of guilt that will cover Danny Riley head to toe. Trouble always starts with a few simple words. Every Indian knows that much.

He shrugs bigger, like there is an exclamation point at the end of his gesture.

"Haven't I seen you before?"

Another shrug.

"Naked. About the time the old Tri Delta house exploded and fogged the campus with methamphetamine."

The male cops form a semi-circle behind Laura Pepper. A crescent moon of blue men with overhanging bellies arrange themselves so each has a perfect view of Laura Pepper's ass while she faces Danny Riley. They smile and wait for her to do something stupid. They cross their arms so everybody will know how tough they are and how fast they'll jump in when Corporal Laura Pepper finally goes too far.

"You spit in my eyes," she says. "Surely you remember."

Something the old original Richard Daniels did? Something the brand-new innocent *Richard Daniels* would rather not discuss.

"Not me."

Nothing much a cop can do with a two-word denial. Danny thinks she didn't get a good look at Richard Daniels's face because women are hard-wired to keep their eyes trained on exposed penises when one's around.

Danny holds both hands up, as if he's being robbed. Best policy for an Indian when he's surrounded by white people wearing guns. Officer Laura Pepper looks at the palms of his hands. Steps forward. Touches one of them. Sniffs the air.

"No burns," she says. "No ammonia smell." Disappointed, but there's still an outside chance for an arrest. "Any drugs or weapons on you?"

"No,"

"Mind if I search you, just to be sure."

The cops behind her chuckle and elbow each other. They want to watch Laura Pepper's breasts bounce while she engages in a foot pursuit. They want to see Danny take off running, faster than a bolt of lightning. Faster than Corporal Laura Pepper, who'll come back from the chase exhausted and sweaty and pissed off because her overweight brothers in blue won't be any help. Danny can tell all of this just by the way the policemen stand, the way they hold their mouths, the way they run their hands around their belts, making sure their shirt tails are properly stowed.

"I mind," Danny tells her. Quiet and polite. Not like a confrontation, but he knows that's how she'll take it. He doesn't elaborate because she's angry enough already. Doesn't talk about probable cause because she knows without him saying anything.

She looks at the sidewalk around Danny's feet. In this part of town there's always something. Points at a clear plastic envelope on the ground. A skull and cross bones is printed on it in red—the psychology of the heroin branding. Nothing promises quality like the symbol of a deadly poison.

"Did you drop that?"

The wind is already moving the heroin bindle out of Laura Pepper's reach. She puts a foot on it.

"Not mine," Richard doesn't have to tell her that because she already knows.

"Probable cause." She turns him around. Holds his hands together in a complicated finger grip that all cops seem to know. Tells him, "You're not under arrest."

Doesn't say, "yet," because that's understood.

A string of words blasts out of all the police car radios at the same time. Jumbled words and numbers, impossible to understand—except the part about, *"Shots fired!"*

Danny's back is turned away from the male cops, but he hears them shuffle off. He hears their police cars start, hears rubber tires squeal on the street, and hears Corporal Laura Pepper say, "Shit."

She already has a cuff closed on Danny's left wrist but takes it off in less than a second.

"Your lucky day, asshole." Police version of catch and release. Waiting for Danny to grow into a trophy-size criminal. Meanwhile, there's a shooting and Laura Pepper doesn't want to miss out.

"Catch you later." Laura Pepper winks at Danny. Conspiratorial, flirty, as if they have a future. Sometime when there isn't a real crime going on.

Danny holds his hands behind his back in the pre-handcuff position while he watches the departing police cars weave around bail bonds businesses and taverns. They head north, the Navajo direction of bad luck and death. Where else would Oklahoma policemen go?

"It really is your lucky day, Richard." The voice comes from behind him—jittery cadence, run-together words.

"Hey there, Toad." Danny is not surprised to see the man with the tattooed face and the split tongue. The first time he met the strange man with backward writing on his forehead, Danny received ten thousand dollars. The second time, he found Richard Daniels's body. Something will happen this time too. He is sure of it.

Toad licks his upper lip. The split ends of his tongue move independently. He taps his chest with his closed fist. Flashes a peace sign. It looks more like a threat than a greeting.

"Need the rest of my Cherokee Ice."

A Richard Daniels promise that Danny Riley is expected to keep. Toad holds the peace sign for a couple of seconds. Closes his fingers together like a pair of scissors. Smiles like he's just invented the wheel.

"Last batch was so full of visions, it's got the whole damn town talking to Elvis."

"Cherokee Ice." Danny likes the nice crisp sound of the words. Likes the way they end with a faint whistle that skates into a pitch human ears can barely hear. He figures Cherokee Ice is some kind of methamphetamine because what else could get a man like Toad this excited?

Danny considers telling Toad he doesn't know anything about Cherokee Ice, but he thinks about it for a while. Indians don't speak unless they are very sure, and how can Danny Riley be sure when so many unexpected things came with his new identity—Mary, a driver's license, the pickup truck with the wasp nest, and the camper shell that stinks too much to sleep in.

The camper smells a little like a meth lab. He walks back to his truck in silence. Reservation quiet. Toad follows him, filling the air with gossip.

"Little Bits thinks you're some kind of ghost."

Little Bits, the disrespectful name Danny couldn't remember. Toad's split tongue turns the *Ts* into *THs*, so at first, Danny isn't sure exactly what he said. By the time he figures it out, Toad has moved on to Little Bits's new bodyguards.

"Two white killers with Italian names. You know—professional, hard guys with names that end in A's and O's. Big as the last one. Maybe bigger. Armed to the teeth."

According to Toad, Little Bits has doubled the number of coins on his Mercury dime anklet. He wears two silver crucifixes now. One with Jesus' eyes open. One with them closed. Toad's gossip is as hard to follow as a rabbit running from a coyote.

"Tommy Bracken called me. Willing to do business. Looking for John Horse. Thinks I might have found him."

Then something about Mary's mother.

Then something about the president of the United States.

Then something about needing, "more of that Cherokee Ice that's got everybody wondering if John Horse is back in town."

Lots of wasps have found their way back to Richard Daniels's truck.

"Ought to get rid of those." Toad is still a white man under all that ink. Still thinks the way a white man does about killing inconvenient things—spiders, wasps, armadillos, Indian witches.

"They might come in handy later on," Danny tells him, letting him in on the Native American thought process.

"How could insects come in handy?"

Toad will never understand the value of mystery, but then Danny will never understand either. People aren't supposed to understand supernatural things.

"Hard to say. Think you could take me back to Mary's house?" White men like Toad don't know about holy things, but they know all about city streets.

"I'm kind of lost," he tells Toad's back because the tattooed man with the split tongue is trying to open the door to the camper shell and isn't having any luck.

"This where you keep it?" Toad's hands run over the aluminum doorframe like a pair of squirrels trying to break into a bird feeder. It doesn't take him long to figure out the camper shell is warped so he has to lift the door and pull to trip the latch. He sniffs the air that's heated up while Danny was off looking for Black Seminoles.

"This is it all right." Toad smiles at the meth stink the way hunters smile over a fresh pile of scat. Takes a deep breath, followed by two more. Tries to pull enough amphetamine molecules out of the atmosphere to get a buzz.

"I'm kind of lost, you see." Danny raises his voice just short of a shout, hoping volume will make up for the lack of details about why he can't find his way around a city he's lived in for years. "So, if you could drive me...."

But Toad is already inside the camper, throwing things around as if the world will come to an end if he doesn't find what he's looking for in the next few seconds. Toad has the devotion to time shared by every ordinary white man, even though he doesn't look ordinary at all. Even though his only watch is a tattooed image of one on his left wrist. Both the minute and the hour hands are stuck on the Roman Numeral XII. The fulcrum balancing morning and afternoon—the minute between night and morning.

"Eureka!" Toad hops out of the camper smiling like he's just discovered something that's going to change the world. Danny hopes it's a *Rand McNally Road Atlas*, but Toad is waving around two military green pouches with "U.S. Army" stenciled on the flaps. Exactly like the one buried in the Queenie grave.

The dirty socks/cotton candy smell wafting from the pouches stirs up the wasps.

"ShitGoddamnFuck!" Toad slaps one on his neck, but not before it's planted its stinger.

"Damn, that hurts!" He turns to show Danny the damage. A big red circle with a black dot in the center where the stinger penetrated. While he's complaining, two more wasps land on his neck and bury their asses in the swollen zone.

"F-u-u-u-u-u-k." The Doppler sound of Toad running down the street away from Danny Riley and the wasps. Toad, getting smaller and smaller until he's just a tiny dot on the horizon, farther than his cries of pain can travel. Toad will not help Danny find his way back to Mary's house.

The jingle-thump sound of one dwarf with a Mercury dime anklet and two white thugs with Italian names closes in behind Danny Riley.

"Well, well, well." Little Bits's voice is different when he isn't in panic mode, but Danny knows it's him.

Two silver crucifixes, just like Toad said. Two Italian killers. A pistol in Little Bits's left hand pointed at Danny's chest. Not an automatic like the one that killed Richard Daniels. This one is a revolver. The hammer is pulled back. The barrel ends in a hole that's as big and black as the pupil in a meth addict's eye.

"Silver bullets," Little Bits says. "You won't rise up this time." The Italian killers stand behind him in a V-formation, like a pair of geese following their miniature leader to the Promised Land.

Danny wonders if he'll get out of this one alive. Wonders if his spirit will be able to find its way to Mary's house. He casts his eyes around, looking for a way out. They settle on a pair of dead wasps—the ones that stung Toad—lying on the pavement.

Maybe this is one of those spirit things reservation holy men are always going on about. Can't hurt to check it out. He bends over and plucks them off the cement like a pair of lost contact lenses. He pops them into his mouth because he can't think of anything else to do, and thinks of acacia ants and moonflower moths and mysterious things that have happened to him all his life—that will keep happening only if magic rescues him.

The Italian thugs make retching sounds. "Fuck, boss. This Injun's crazy."

Danny doesn't know which thug said that. The pair of white killers are completely interchangeable, like Danny Riley and Richard Daniels. The wasps break into a crusty pulp between his molars and burn a little as the juices ooze down his throat. He crosses his arms on his chest as if he is an Apache warrior instead of a half-breed Laguna who doesn't really know much about being an Indian, much less about magic.

Nothing but repulsed expressions coming from the Italians and Little Bits. The dwarf's cowboy pistol is drawing circles in the air. Clockwise circles. Danny takes it as a sign of good things to come. Why not?

"So, we gonna kill this red-skinned prick or what?" one of the Italians asks.

"Sure." But first, Little Bits wants to know, "Why the hell are you eating dead bugs, Richard? Some kind of Two-Heart witch magic?"

Danny hopes so, but so far, nothing's happening, except his heart is beating faster, like it always does when someone's about to kill him. And he feels a little queasy, like maybe wasps don't digest as easily as ants and moths. Like maybe they don't digest at all.

There's a tickle on the side of his neck right above his jugular vein. Like a live wasp is crawling there getting ready to do to him what her sisters already did to Toad. He's pretty sure the sting is coming. One more problem for a man who's just about to be shot with a silver bullet. There's no way to brush the wasp off without breaking his bulletproof Indian warrior pose that is the only thing holding the gunmen back.

Danny wonders what Apache warriors did about nausea because when the stinger sinks into his neck, he gets sick. Projectile vomiting sick. A stream of *Exorcist*-colored vomit covers Little Bits, like a liter of split pea soup shot out of a water cannon. Who would have thought Subway sandwiches would be so colorful coming out?

Green goo covers the African American dwarf's eyes, spoiling his aim as he fires a silver bullet into the wasp nest on Danny Riley's pickup truck.

Danny feels the burn of the wasp toxin for the time it takes his heart to shift into overdrive. The nausea clears. Poison tumbles through his drug factory enzymes and winds up in his brain, where it's a lot different than it started out. Danny Riley suddenly understands that bullets aren't nearly as dangerous as wasps.

His wasp-sisters' poison doesn't turn into visions inside Little Bits's hired killers. They have their pistols out, squeezing shots off this way and that, filling the air with projectiles that fly off to lodge in buildings and automobiles and maybe an innocent bystander or two.

Clouds of nitrate-flavored smoke don't hinder Danny or his wasp-sisters at all. Gunpowder residue tastes as sweet as nectar on his lips. It doesn't burn his eyes or dull his vision. Everything is crystal clear, broken into a thousand pieces. Washed in rainbows, as if Danny is gazing at the world through a cut diamond lens.

Danny Riley knows he is not a wasp, as much as he knows anything, but he is moving too fast to think about it clearly. Faster than thoughts, faster than all the reasons a man can't move this fast. Faster than Little Bits can take aim through the haze of smoke and vomit and superstition.

The African American dwarf empties his revolver of silver bullets and tries to make one land in Danny, who is moving around him the way a swarm of hornets attacks a marauding bear.

Danny snatches the pistol out of Little Bits's hand. Throws it at one of the Italian killers. Hits him square in the face. Knocks him out as he fires his pistol one last time and shoots his partner in the knee.

Little Bits takes off running down the center of the street, screaming for one of his two silver Jesuses to save him from witches and wasps.

Danny is behind the wheel of his truck. Doesn't remember how he got there. Catches up to Little Bits. Nibbles at him with the bumper of the GMC truck. Nudges his evil dwarf ass and then speeds up so Little Bits is stuck on the grill like an insect, wondering what is coming next, knowing it isn't good.

Police sirens howl in the background. Ambulances collect wounded Italian thugs, who don't look dangerous and professional anymore, while Danny Riley drives his truck away from the scene as fast as he can.

He's already forgotten the shoot-out. He's already forgotten the stinger in his neck and the African American dwarf who never wanted to be on Danny's grill but now is praying to stay there a little longer.

Danny Riley knows things about wasps that nobody in the world has ever guessed. Wasps don't know where they are going. They just go. They don't love life, but they live it fast. Too fast for memories to hang on. Too fast for fear, too fast for hate, too fast for love, too fast for anger—but there is something like anger circulating through them like blood. The only time they lose it is when they sting.

Danny hears a thump as something falls off his grill and lands between his front wheels. Doesn't remember what it is, but that doesn't matter now. It's gone. He drives through a blur of reality and hears voices that Richard Daniels might have heard in life, but Danny Riley never did. It sounds something like a GPS voice. Strict and female. "Turn left. Go straight ahead. Faster. Faster. Skid the tires. Slide around the corner. Stop."

The wasp haze lifts, like a cloud of teargas in the wind. Moisture droplets form in the corners of Danny Riley's eyes and evaporate like pools of gasoline before they become tears.

His neck feels like it's on fire. Vaguely remembers getting stung was the answer to a prayer. How long ago?

There is Queenie's grave with the tipped wooden cross. There is the vegetable garden with the hanging scarecrow. There is Mary walking out her front door. Behind her is an older woman, pretty in that noble, savage way white artists always portray Native American women.

Richard Daniels knew her. That much is certain. Mary looks at the bullet holes in his camper shell but doesn't say anything about them.

"Richard." She twists her mouth into an insincere family photographic smile. "Grandma Wilma Daniels is here for a little visit."

Danny Riley hears Richard Daniels whisper in his ear, "Bitch!"

29

JACK KEEPS THE POLICE car centered in his rearview mirror.

"Following us," he tells Ellen. "Been following us since I turned onto Mudline Road." Three miles until they reach the Red Slough Wildlife Management Area. A lot can happen in three miles.

"Mudline Road." Ellen says the name with the phoniest peckerwood accent Jack has ever heard. "Sounds like a country-and-western song." She tells him not to worry. "Cops follow people. That's what they do on Mudline Road." She hums a few uncertain notes like she's trying to remember a tune.

"It's like that cop was waiting." The way Officer Laura Pepper was waiting, Jack remembers. Waiting at the edge of the drainage ditch when he went in to retrieve Richard's body. Jack knows Laura Pepper can't be driving the police car that's following him now, but he won't be sure until he gets a closer look.

One driver. No passenger. A green uniform with a County Mountie hat, but he can't tell if the driver is a man or a woman. His left front tire drifts over the centerline as he adjusts his rearview mirror for the third time in sixty seconds.

Ellen says, "County cops are no big deal," but Jack thinks all cops are a big deal when the trunk of his car smells like a sewage treatment plant because there's a body in it. Even if that cop is not the tenacious Laura Pepper with her Taser and her handcuffs and her ability to shoot a cat out of midair.

There's no speed limit posted on Mudline Road. It must be forty-five at least, so Jack slows down to forty, pretending he's an ordinary citizen with too many points on his driver's license, a misdemeanor criminal instead of a felon.

"Should have changed the body bag." Jack wanted to, but Ellen told him it's no good touching nasty things more than necessary.

She told him, "We'll drive with the windows down," like she was an old hand at feeding bodies to alligators. She'd smiled and kissed him, and tucked the pistol in his waistband with his Hawaiian shirt pulled over it. "Where you can get to it real easy, just in case."

Just in case.

The police car flashes its blue lights, and for a few seconds Jack considers running.

"He's probably calling it in. Checking my registration, so if anything happens, the cops will know I was involved." Jack pretends it's not the blood and the violence and the fact that one man always loses in a two-man confrontation, and it probably wouldn't be the cop.

"You worry too much, Jack." Ellen lifts his Hawaiian shirt and reminds him the gun's still there. Reminds him there are plenty of hungry alligators in the Red Slough with enough appetite for two dead men. She puts her hand around the pistol grip, squeezes, breathes a little harder, and gets that faraway look in her eyes that tells Jack her sexual pressure cooker is about to reach a boil.

"Maybe he hasn't called it in at all," Ellen says. "Maybe you won't even have to kill him."

"A penny for your thoughts." Jack feels the right front tire of his car sink into the shoulder as he pulls over, so he doesn't pull over very far.

Maybe he has a bad brake light or a loose license plate. Maybe he was speeding and the cop will write him a ticket and won't ask to look in the trunk where something smells dead enough to attract vultures. Maybe he won't see the butcher knife or the meat clever under the passenger side floor mat or notice the metallic bulge poking at Jack's Hawaiian shirt like a strangulated hernia.

The McCurtain County cop steps out of the car and takes a few seconds to shake the kinks out of his arms and legs.

"Morbidly obese." Ellen pronounces the words with great precision.

The cop's belly is as large and flaccid as a weather balloon. It droops over his belt, which—Jack would bet anything—has a Western buckle. The policeman confirms this by lifting the belly momentarily and letting it flop again. It continues jiggling all the way to the driver's side window of Jack's car. A case study in harmonic motion.

"Howdy, y'all." The cop repositions his belly again and leans his chubby forearms across Jack's open windows. So his hands are inside the car, where they can grab Jack in an instant.

In a McCurtain County minute. Jack figures that's about how much time he has left before Ellen pulls her butcher knife, or tells Jack to "Shoot the morbidly obese son of a bitch."

But all she says is, "Howdy, officer."

Ellen doesn't tell the cop a blowjob is available for the asking. She doesn't tell him he can touch her breasts or hold her panties in his sweaty fingers, but somehow that all comes across in her down-home greeting.

Jack watches the County Mountie's pupils dilate and constrict in a rhythm that would be perfect for a country-and-western song about something that is about to happen on Mudline Road.

Jack tries to say, "Howdy," but he loses his way before he makes it to the last syllable.

"How...."

"A regular Injun greetin'." The cop smiles. Chipped teeth. Stained fillings that used to be white but now are the color of urine. "Y'all goin' to the slough?"

He doesn't ask about the smell coming from the trunk or the suspicious bulge in Jack's Hawaiian shirt, or the pretty woman who is fucking him with her eyes.

"Well, yeah," Jack says. "How did you know?"

"Nowhere else to go on Mudline Road." The cop tips the brim of his Mountie hat back a little so he can get a better view of Ellen, who manages to look incredibly nasty and innocent at the same time.

She asks, "Were we speeding, officer?" A touch of the Old South in her voice. A hint of a simpler time when women like Ellen didn't know any better than to sleep with men like…. She leans forward, showing him her cleavage while she reads his nametag.

"Officer Lester Harjo." She says the cop's name like it's an offer to commit lewd acts.

"Will y'all step out of the car for a minute?" Official now. He retreats a step. Readjusts his paunch. Puts his hand on the butt of the six-shooter that he wears in a Western holster slung low like Wyatt Earp's.

Jack slides out like a mouse that's crawling into a room full of cats, and Ellen struts around the car like a New York runway model who's pretending to be a whore. Jack is wearing jeans and a Hawaiian shirt. She's wearing a sheer white blouse and a black miniskirt. The way Ellen's skirt moves on her body screams, "Thong or nothing. Take your pick." None of this is lost on McCurtain County Officer Lester Harjo.

The cop wipes his nose, the way people do when they are nervous. He looks unaccustomed to anxiety. He looks like this may be the first case of nerves he's ever had, and he really needs a Xanax.

"Y'all was drivin' way too careful," he tells Jack while continuing to look at Ellen. "And the young lady don't look dressed for the slough." He lifts his belly again. Holds it up for a count of three. A show of strength? Long enough for Jack and Ellen to appreciate the silver and gold Western buckle with green agate inlaid in the shape of Oklahoma. He lets his belly down slowly.

"Thought I'd pull y'all over and check things out."

Ellen stands in a way that suggests her legs would fit around Lester

Harjo perfectly. She touches her lower lip with one manicured finger-nail. The color stirs a memory in Jack.

"Milani Neon-Red," he says. A police officer was present when he learned that information.

Officer Lester Harjo looks at Jack for a second but decides Ellen is more interesting.

"Thought I'd subject y'all to my own personal lie detector." He crosses his arms over his massive belly, shifting its bulk six inches farther south. He stands pigeon-toed, the way fat men do, tips his head forward so the shadow of his Mountie hat hides his eyes, and stares at Jack for thirty seconds, then at Ellen for much longer.

Four McCurtain County minutes, according to Jack's Breitling Chronograph Emergency watch.

Jack watches Ellen too. He's never seen a woman do so much with so little effort. A subtle shift of her hips, a ripple of abdominal muscles, a smile that suggests complete satisfaction, a breathing rhythm that dares onlookers to match it. All these things summon memories of things Jack—and Officer Lester Harjo—have only done in dreams that happened when they were sixteen years old.

"Damn." Lester Harjo starts to lift his belly once again but then decides to let sleeping dogs lie. "I need a cigarette. Y'all enjoy the slough."

As the cop sits behind the steering wheel of his cruiser and fishes a cigarette out of his pack with a very shaky hand, Ellen says, "Told ya. County cops are no big deal."

THE RED SLOUGH WILDLIFE MANAGEMENT area is a network of gravel roads, dirt trails, and algae-filled channels that are too complicated for the GPS on Ellen's cell phone.

"Doesn't look all that managed," she says. "Doesn't look as pretty as the pictures either."

Jack tells her, "It's a perfect place to dump a body."

There are signs that warn visitors of rattlesnakes, Africanized bees, fire ants, and alligators, but there aren't any visitors as far as Jack can see. The roads and channels wind around each other like a nest of breeding snakes. Bridges with gates across them. Yellow caution signs with no further explanation. Fields of limestone fossils that look like prizes in prehistoric boxes of Crackerjacks. Blue-tailed lizards scamper in front of Jack's car, pursued by predators invisible to the human eye. A dragonfly the size of a sparrow crashes into his windshield and bounces off.

"Turn here," Ellen points at a pair of ruts in the grass that look like a dozen other pairs of ruts they've already passed. "This looks like a good place to find an alligator."

"Good as any," Jack agrees. The odor of the channels is even worse than the decomposing body in the trunk. A pair of vultures circle a spot just over the next hill. "Lots of killers probably dump their bodies here."

He concentrates on keeping his tires inside the ruts and suppresses the desire to tell Ellen everything. Richard's name takes shape on his lips, and he chases it away with a fake coughing fit. Guilt, Jack supposes. Even though he hasn't really done anything to feel guilty about. His conscience perches on his shoulder and harasses him the way Jiminy Cricket nagged at Pinocchio. Maybe he can dump his guilt here in the Red Slough along with Richard's body.

The ruts take them between swampy channels, around dead trees, past a lone coyote that doesn't look at all intimidated by the presence of humans in the slough.

"Richard says coyotes are an omen," Ellen tells him. "He's always going on about visions and omens."

"Maybe because he was Native American," Jack says.

"Was?" Ellen rolls her window up. The smell is equally bad outside and in.

"Was?" she asks again as she turns the air conditioner on.

Past tense. A slip of the tongue. The kind of slip that gives the dead man in Jack's trunk a name.

"Putting him behind me." Jack pulls into a barren section of red hardpan next to a pool of swampy water the size of a Walmart parking lot.

"I don't think so," Ellen says. "Mary still loves Richard. I think she'll take him back."

Jack doesn't tell her there's no way that's going to happen unless they bring her a bag of alligator turds from the slough. How long does the reptilian digestive process take, anyway? How long until there is no DNA, no dental forensics, no sign that Richard Daniels ever was?

"I think I see an alligator." Jack uses his master control to roll Ellen's window down again. He sits there for a few seconds before he kills the engine because what if it won't start again? What if he and Ellen are stuck in the Red Slough until they become alligator food like Richard? They sit in the car, listening to cicadas rattle like a billion BB's rolling down marble stairs.

"Look!" Ellen points to a reptilian snout pushing its way onto the shore.

"Not as big as I expected." The gator pulls back into the water as Ellen opens her door. The cicadas go quiet, like nature has just gone on a five-minute break. Then everything starts up again.

Four alligators crawl onto the shore. Three more follow them. None is more than five feet long, but seven medium-size gators should be plenty for one partially decomposed son-in-law.

"Feeding time at the Red Slough." The alligators don't react when Ellen gets out of the car, or when she pulls the body bag onto the hard pan parking area. But they pull back when she starts to work with the meat cleaver. Ellen looks a lot more dangerous than alligators.

Jack stands well away from the action as Ellen tosses bits and pieces of Richard into the gator pond. The reptiles plunge back into the water and sweep floating chunks of meat off the surface like a vacuum cleaner. Big pieces, small pieces. If Ellen throws them in the water, the gators eat them in a matter of seconds. They ignore anything that lands on solid ground.

Lots of splashing and thrashing. The gators look a lot bigger when they are eating.

"They don't eat humans, so I'm told." Jack quotes the *Discover Oklahoma* narrator who told him about this place from behind a BLOCKED

CALL rectangle on the night he heard Mary firing pistol shots over the telephone.

The night Ellen contacted him for the first time in two years.

Now Jack and Ellen are here in the Red Slough feeding Richard to the alligators. The whole thing has a mystical symmetry Jack hasn't considered until now.

Things get even more mystical when a coyote comes 'round and slurps up pieces of Richard that are lying on the ground.

It's the closest thing Jack has had to a religious experience since an evangelist minister saved his soul during a Baptist crusade when he was just a boy.

"Right after I learned to wiggle my ears." Jack thinks he might have to explain that, but Ellen is busy disinfecting her hands with Purell and wet wipes and rinsing them with Evian bottled water.

"I think our work is finished here," she says.

The coyote has disappeared. The gators have gone to the opposite side of the swamp to digest their dinner. The cicadas have added a pulsing rhythm to their song.

Jack asks Ellen if she wants to say some words. "That's what people do in the movies."

She says, "*Bon appetite.*" A perfect imitation of Julia Child. She looks at the alligators basking in the sun across the swamp. She follows the vultures circling in the sky. She swats a biting insect neither of them can identify. She says, "Thanks for bringing me here, Jack. This is about the best time I ever had."

There's nothing left to say, so Jack and Ellen are quiet enough to hear a low-pitched alien noise that doesn't quite blend with the insect sounds.

"Droid." Like the voice of a Red Slough god making an accusation.

Jack is ready to confess everything, promise never to break the law again, and sacrifice a goat if necessary, but Ellen says, "I have a text."

She takes the time to toss the meat cleaver and kitchen knife into the alligator pond. "Evidence, right, Jack?" She retrieves her purse from inside the car and searches for her cell phone.

"It's from Mary." She shows the screen to Jack. *Strange visitor came today. Drop by when you can.*

"Can't hear gunshots on a text," Jack says. Ellen smiles, the way she always does when he mentions gunshots or murder or any other kind of violence.

30

GRANDMA WILMA DANIELS SITS in the most comfortable chair in Mary's living room, as rigid as a paraplegic Marine. She carries no weapons, as far as Danny can see, but if looks could kill, he would already be mortally wounded.

The thumb and index finger of her right hand pinch and explore the ring finger of her left as if they might discover a clue that will lead her to the missing wedding band.

"Ain't felt right since my boy took it." That was twenty years ago, but the memory still draws blood.

She sits up straighter—*Richard* hadn't thought that was possible—and recites a list of bad events in her life, starting with the ugly name her parents chose for her, ending with the shamefully high price she paid for a fifth of Jack Daniel's only yesterday. She taps her toe against her suitcase where the bottle is stored between her socks and underwear.

"People always done me wrong." Her attention locks onto the finger once again. Not the most recent wrong, but the most important.

"Tommy Bracken's offered me a ring, but...." Wilma Daniels smiles at her finger. It wiggles in response. "Tommy." She scans the room and looks at every piece of furniture, as if Tommy Bracken could be hiding there.

"Sneaky, that's what Tommy is." According to Wilma, Tommy Bracken has a way of turning up when you least expect him. "Invisible as a goddamned chameleon. Nobody sees him coming until it's too damned late."

She fixes her attention on Mary for a moment, as if *Richard's* wife might be Tommy Bracken's cleverest disguise.

"Loves me more than anything," Wilma says. "Loves me more than that old Mustang he's polished like a diamond. Ain't right I should have to stand between him and a half-breed bastard Richard put inside some Laguna whore." Checks her ring finger again to see if her missing wedding band re-appeared while she wasn't looking.

"Blood is blood, I guess. Even worthless, half-breed blood." She turns her killer look Danny's way again. How would Grandma Daniels feel if she knew two half-breed bastards came out of Nelva Riley?

Twins, like in the Navajo legend—Monster Slayer and Born to Water. Do Cherokee have a twin legend? Danny is afraid to ask. Afraid Grandma Daniels might suspect he's not the Richard she remembers. Not the one she feels a need to protect even though she hates him.

"Didn't I take him in? Ain't that enough?" She reaches into her purse and withdraws a silver flask with a screw top that comes off after a brief struggle.

"Medicine," Wilma Daniels explains. "Cousin Jack."

Danny watches her Adam's apple bob like a cork on a lucky fishing line. Four swallows, naturally, a sacred number for every Indian tribe in the world. Even Cherokee like Grandma Daniels respect the number four, and they've given up on just about everything else.

"Come here to protect my Ricky." Wilma screws the cap back on her flask and smiles like an alpha chimp in a Jane Goodall documentary. "Even if he ain't worth a damn."

Danny scoots his chair back a little. He looks for an emergency escape route, just in case. Grandma Wilma Daniels is in her early fifties. Pretty, in a stern schoolteacher sort of way. All muscle and sinew, packed onto a female shape that's more suited to assault than reproduction, bristling with anger, the way a saguaro cactus bristles with thorns. Wilma Daniels looks strong and quick, even after finishing off half a flask of Jack Daniel's.

"Cousin Jack is the best doctor ever." She thumps the flask, the way a fruit vendor checks the ripeness of a watermelon. "Got a full fifth in my suitcase. Ought to last till my business here is done."

She checks her wristwatch. Thumps it the way she did the flask. When the hands don't move, she sighs and takes another four swallows. Smaller and quieter this time. She screws the cap back on and places the flask back in her purse. Looks at it tenderly, the way a mother looks at her sleeping child.

Did she ever look at her grandson like that?

Mary asks, "Can I put your bag away, Miz Daniels?"

Wilma is too busy playing with her ring-less finger to answer. She looks at Danny as if she's noticed him for the first time.

"Where's your eye patch, Richard?" Claps her hands together and stares at him hard enough to burn away a layer of skin. She holds her left hand out, palm up. Extends her ring finger like it's an obscene gesture. Her eyes jerk as they move back and forth between Danny and Mary, trying to keep track of both of them.

Cops watch for that jerky motion when they do a field sobriety test. When they ask a suspect to follow the path of an index finger from one peripheral vision border to the next. Danny learned all kinds of police procedures in his reservation days. From watching Nelva's boyfriends get arrested. From sitting in the back of Sarah Benally's Navajo Tribal Police car, waiting for a new erection to replace the one he'd just used up.

Danny says, "Nystagmus."

That's what Sarah Benally would call Wilma Daniels's jerky eyes. It's the first word he's said to her since she took a seat in Mary's living room and started emptying her Cousin Jack flask four swallows at a time.

Wilma squints at his left eye like she's trying to read a message written in small print.

"How'd your eye come back, Richard? Momma wants to know."

Danny watches her like she might turn into a snake.

"Don't make me come over there." Wilma Daniels crosses her arms under her breasts.

Danny has never seen a pair of breasts like that on a woman Wilma's age—well-shaped, a little on the large size, but floating over her crossed arms like a pair of helium balloons. He tries to chase the image from his mind, but it won't budge. He puts his hand over the amulet bag underneath his shirt, pushes it against his heart, and takes comfort from the familiar things inside—an empty shell casing, the tooth of a timber wolf, a circular glass box of hallucinogenic ants, and Wilma Daniels's wedding band.

The gold feels thick and hot to the touch, even through the leather of the amulet bag. As thick and hot as the bourbon fog Wilma Daniels exhales as she accuses him.

"Why'd you take it, Richard? Why'd you give it to that whore?"

Nelva Riley, the Laguna whore who knew Wilma's only son just long enough to get pregnant and blind him in one eye. Danny knows part of the story—Nelva's side of it. She told him when she handed him the ring.

"Something from your father," Nelva told him. "Every boy needs something from his father. This is all I have."

Now he knows his father's *something* once belonged to Grandma Wilma Daniels, and Grandma never stopped wanting it back.

"Can I get you something to drink, Grandma Daniels?" Mary asks. "Something besides... medicine?" Her smile is as even as two years in braces could make it, white from toothpaste that bleached her enamel and left her breath as fresh as Wilma Daniels's is sour.

Wilma puts her ringless left hand over her eyes and rubs them through her eyelids.

Danny wants to comfort her, but Wilma Daniels is too full of hate. Her arms are as tense as rabbit snares. He doesn't dare place a hand inside the deadly zone.

"Sorry, Ricky." Wilma Daniels doesn't look sorry at all. She looks like there's so much rage inside her that her clothing is about to catch fire. "I know you didn't take my ring."

Danny's hand is over his amulet bag again, pushing against the ring that Wilma Daniels doesn't know is there.

"It's just... you look so much like my boy." Her face softens into something close to grandmotherly. But Wilma's compassion has a very short lifespan. "Before your whore mother took his eye."

Wilma takes four more swallows from her metal flask and divides hostile stares between Mary and Danny. Wet breathing noises. No talk at all.

Danny never expected so much silence from a Cherokee. Nelva told him, "Oklahoma Indians talk all the time. Like white people, maybe worse."

But Grandma Wilma is doing well with her Indian ways. Too well for Mary.

She asks, "Grandma Daniels, can I show you your room?"

And, "Grandma Daniels, can I get you something to eat?"

And, "Granma Daniels...?"

"Are you still awake?" Danny finishes Mary's question because Grandma Wilma Daniels has won the battle of Indian ways.

Her eyes are open. Have been open—now that Danny thinks about it—since she stopped talking. Way too long between blinks. A small stream of tears trickles from the corner of her left eye—the one her boy Richard lost to Nelva Riley shortly after he gave her Wilma's wedding band.

"She's dreaming about my father," Danny says. Sure of it, the way he's sure it's bad luck to kill frogs or say the name of a dead person when you are all alone at night.

He touches the stream of Wilma's tears with the tip of his little finger and tastes it.

"Jack Daniel's and vinegar," he tells Mary. "I think she's passed out. I don't think she can hear us now."

"Let's move her bag into the guest room," Mary says. "Where she can be more comfortable when she's ready to sleep... you know, sleep for real."

Danny holds his left hand over his amulet bag as if he's about to take an oath. He takes a step toward Grandma Wilma's suitcase. Puts his weight down carefully so the floor won't squeak. Deciding if it's safe to get close to her—one step at a time.

"I'll open the front door," Mary says. "Let some fresh air in."

She doesn't say, "Let the Jack Daniel's smell out," but Danny knows that's what she means.

The sun has set since Grandma came to visit. The last residue of sunlight hangs over the trees like a fire inside the cumulous clouds over the western horizon. Mary's door is lined up perfectly with the setting sun—exactly the opposite of how it would be on the rez. The red light from the sunset covers every square inch of Mary's living room. Shadows stretch out on the interior walls like spirits of the night waiting their turn to rule the world.

Danny reaches for Grandma Wilma's suitcase slowly, the way a clever mouse sneaks a piece of cheese out of a trap without triggering the spring. When he touches the handle, Grandma Wilma's hand shoots out. Like a rattlesnake striking a rabbit, her fingers close around his wrist. Too hard to be a grandma's hand. Too fast. Too painful. As if her fingertips have turned into teeth injecting his arm with poison that will fill his mind with visions as it stops his heart.

"Don't touch my suitcase, you little cocksucker." Wilma Daniels licks her lips. Getting ready for a full-fledged frontal attack that is sure to involve biting and scratching and maybe murder before she's finished. Danny finally understands why a coyote will gnaw his leg off to free himself from a trap.

Grandmothers aren't so scary back on the rez. They are matriarchs, elders who are obeyed because they are the most respected, most loved members of the family.

"Grandma?" Maybe if Danny identifies himself, she won't eat him. Blood is blood, after all. Indians don't kill their relatives, do they? Not even Cherokee.

She squeezes harder. Twists his arm a little. Puts so much pressure on the bones Danny's fingers start to tingle.

Mary watches silently from the open door.

The red light shining through the screen turns a deeper shade, like venous blood spilled on the ground where a hunter made his kill.

Danny knows something is about to happen soon. Grandma Wilma will make her choice—to let her grandson live or kill him on the spot. All he can do is wait.

Strains of a Mexican song drift through the door. *Cielito Lindo*— Lovely Little Sky. Danny heard it many times back on the rez.

"That's him." Wilma loosens her grip on Danny's wrist. Almost as comfortable as a handcuff.

The singer rolls out a string of Spanish words that blend perfectly with the color of the setting sun.

"That's my Tommy." She eases the pressure on Danny's wrist. Constricted vessels expand, filling his cold hand with pins and needles.

"Take me to him, Ricky."

Wilma Daniels is on her feet before Danny can step back. She stands on his foot. Pushes against his chest with a pair of breasts caged in a brassier that must be made of solid steel. She tosses his hand aside. He's not worth hurting any longer. Not while Tommy Bracken fills the air with Spanish music.

"Take me to him, Mary." Finally acknowledging Mary is in the room. Ready to listen when Mary says, "Okay."

She takes Grandma Daniels by the hand and leads her out the door, all the way to the drainage ditch that separates her property from the Hispanic singer the way the Rio Grande River separates Texas from Mexico.

The walls of the ditch are sloping concrete. Rocks and trash are strewn across the bottom. A small trickle of dirty water winds around an old bowling ball, a tricycle, and the skeletal remains of something that looks like it might have come from another planet. Graffiti on the sloping walls tells the story of class struggle, mottled by lichens and stains from deteriorating moss.

"Richard" lets Grandma Daniels hold his hand again, although by this time, he knows better. The three of them stand in a line beside the drainage ditch and watch the man on the other side perform while the sun dips below the horizon.

He comes to the final words and stops. Looks at Wilma Daniels. Smiles. Blows her a kiss. "*Hola, señora.*"

Wilma shouts, "You leave Ricky alone." Pokes her chest out. No sign of Cousin Jack's visit at all.

"Ricky's got no business with your Cherokee Ice." She stares across the chasm. Swallows noisily in regular intervals, like a time bomb counting down to doomsday.

"You know what happens when you don't listen, Tommy." She lets go of Danny's hand long enough to point an accusing finger.

Tommy's breathing quickens in anticipation. He smiles and blows her another kiss. He understands Wilma's threat completely, and he isn't the least bit afraid.

Her grip tightens on Danny's hand again. It tightens even more when Tommy Bracken tells her, "*Quiero, mi corazon.*"

"It's what won't happen you need to think about," Wilma Daniels scolds. "What won't never happen if you don't leave my grandson out of it."

The smile tumbles off Tommy Bracken's face. Without it, he no longer looks Hispanic. He steps backward into the shadows that have turned from grey to black.

"Is that really Tommy Bracken?" Mary pulls her hand free of Wilma's. Shakes the blood back into her fingers. Flexes them to see if they still work.

"He looks like someone else," Mary says. "He looks like Skip, the process server."

"Hi, Skip," She waves her injured hand.

Skip salutes her. He turns and walks away between the trees that grow along the edge of the drainage ditch. One step, two steps, and he's gone. No crunching of broken leaves. No sound of feet dragging through the grass. Maybe he's stopped. Maybe he's turned around, watching them from the darkness that has fallen over the world like a blanket.

Green reflections of a pair of wild eyes hover three feet off the ground in the darkness where Tommy Bracken disappeared. A brown muzzle eases into the ambient light from the moon and stars that are visible now that the sun is gone.

Insect noises Danny hadn't noticed until now come to a complete stop as the coyote steps into the place where Tommy Bracken stood.

"Skin-walker," Danny whispers. He never expected to see one off the reservation.

"Shoo!" Wilma Daniels finds a rock, but by the time she's ready to throw it, the coyote is gone. Exactly the way skin-walkers disappear— so Danny has heard.

Venus shines through the branches of the trees like the headlights on a distant airplane. The full moon hangs above it, yellow and luminous.

Danny watches its reflection shimmer in Wilma Daniels's eyes as she tries to find the coyote in the shadows.

"Didn't I tell you, Ricky? Didn't I tell everybody?" Wilma slurs her words a little. She leans heavily against "Richard" and tells him, "Take me inside, please."

"Got to rest," she says. "Got to be ready when Tommy comes."

Danny steers her across the yard, past the Queenie grave. Past the hanging scarecrow over the tomato cages where moonflower moths are hovering. One of them lands on Mary's shoulder. Another lands in her hair. They spread their wings in the moonlight like spirits of Mary's ancestors, gathering to protect her.

"It was Tommy killed that damn dog of yours," Grandma Daniels says. "I didn't have no part in that except bringing him into our lives."

"Sure thing, Grandma." Just like Danny's wolf back on the rez. Grandma is as innocent as Nelva.

Mary ignores the moths hovering around her. She holds the door open, ready to be inside again with the door closed against Mexican folk singers who look like process servers and may be murderers. "Let's go inside, Grandma," she says.

No response. Wilma Daniels watches the full moon turn from luminous yellow to luminous white. "I see John Horse's face there." Draws a circle around the moon with her pointing finger. "Does that mean John is dead?"

"No, Grandma," Danny tells her. "He's not dead." He doesn't tell her John Horse is on the rez with Nelva, who's also very much alive.

"'Course he's not." Wilma turns her attention to Mary's tomato garden. Moonflower moths. Tomato cages. A beam of moonlight as straight and rigid as an icicle. At the end of the moonbeam is a dull reflection the exact size and shape of the semiautomatic pistol that killed Richard Daniels.

Grandma shoves Danny aside and runs to it. Still drunk, but agile now. Down on her knees and up again, inspecting her find. She holds the weapon up for the man in the moon to see.

"John Horse is up there, looking out for me." She checks the weapon over in the moonlight. "A little rusty, but the slide works, and there's a bullet in the breach."

Danny isn't surprised that Grandma knows her weapons.

Strains of "Cielito Lindo" come from the other side of the drainage ditch again. Soft and slightly out of tune. Grandma Daniels points her pistol at the song. Takes it in a double-handed grip, the way policemen stand when they shoot perpetrators on television.

Grandma doesn't pull the trigger. Her hands drop slowly so the pistol is pointing at the ground.

"How do I kill somebody who loves me for somebody who never will?" She lets the pistol dangle at her side. Walks past Mary back into the house. Takes a seat beside her suitcase again. "Mind if I smoke?"

Mary does, but Grandma lights up anyway. "Get me an ashtray, will you, Ricky?"

A few deep breaths of Marlboro smoke raise Wilma's mood from depression to smoldering rage again. Danny figures that's as good as it gets with Grandma Daniels.

She points her cigarette ash at Mary. "Your little girl's got a way with bugs."

Mary notices the moth perched on her shoulder. Walks to her front door and brushes it into the darkness.

Grandma says, "Think I saw a black widow web in that garden where she grows pistols too." Talking about Mary like she isn't there. Without saying her name, the way Navajo talk at gatherings on the rez. No good identifying a person for marauding crooked spirits who might have a family grudge. No good giving a ghost somebody's name. Maybe Cherokee weren't so different after all.

"Black widow?" Mary looks at her garden, as if anyone could see a spider in the darkness.

Perhaps she can. As far as Danny is concerned, his brand-new wife has unlimited possibilities. If only he could be alone with her. With Mary and the moonflower moths and without Grandma Daniels and her skin-walker boyfriend.

"Black widow!" Mary says it louder this time, so maybe Wilma Daniels will talk to her directly. "Those are poisonous. Maybe I should spray."

Wilma Daniels coughs, the way people do who've smoked cigarettes and drunk whisky for thirty years. A deep cough, full of wet gravel on the verge of breaking loose.

"Spiders are good luck," Wilma says. "Black widows especially." She takes a two-second long drag on her Marlboro, burns the tobacco all the way to the filter, and lights another. Hungry for the cancer-causing smoke. Hungry for the feel of the filter between her lips. "Back when the world was first made, nobody had fire." Wilma's smoky words hover in a well-defined layer just below the ceiling. Mary tries to fan it away, but all she manages is an artistic ripple in the cloud.

"The only fire was on an island in the middle of a lake," Wilma says, "and nobody could figure out how to get some and bring it back."

According to Grandma, a spider finally saved the day. A spider so small it could walk across the delicate skin of the water and carry a tiny coal to the Cherokee. "That's why the black widow has a red spot on its belly." Grandma burns another Marlboro to the filter. "Never know when a spider's going to save the day again."

"Lots of tribes have spider legends," Danny tells her. "The Pueblo say Grandmother Spider wove the whole world out of nothing."

"Savage nonsense," Wilma Daniels tells him. She lights a third Marlboro in as many minutes. Blows a smoke ring into the low-hanging cloud above her head. Watches it until it drifts away. She blinks—the first time Danny has seen her do that—once, twice, three times, and her eyes stay closed.

Danny takes the burning cigarette from her hand. He reaches into his amulet bag and finds her ring. Grandma Wilma Daniels stays asleep while he puts it on her finger. Her hand closes into a fist—so there's no going back. A piece of his history is under her control now. He wonders if that's a terrible mistake.

"Leave her there," Mary says. "She looks so peaceful."

"Yeah," Danny agrees. "I don't think she's that way very often."

31

EXCEPT FOR HAVING GRANDMA Daniels asleep in the living room, Danny Riley's day is off to a perfect start. He says, "Awesome," three times while he's deciding whether to take a shower or let the scent of Mary linger.

Grandma snorts loud enough to hear through a hollow-core door that is the only thing standing between her and Danny's naked body—decision made.

A shower is the perfect way to kill time until Grandma's finished waking up. He sniffs the brand-new shower curtain as the water washes evidence of Mary down the drain. It triggers a memory he can't quite place. Something that happened a long time ago? He's pretty sure it involved Mary, so it can't be all that long ago, unless…. It's Richard Daniels's memory, formed before Danny's twin was murdered in this very house.

Too damned supernatural for a young man who just had one hell of an "Awesome" night with a girl who is at least a thousand times too good for him. Danny finds a bath brush in the shower with bristles stiff enough to make his skin tingle the way it did when Mary ran her nails over his back. Not hard enough to leave marks—but almost.

The Richard Daniels memory won't wash away, even when Danny Riley's mind is full of Mary and lavender soap. He figures sharing someone else's memories is one of those mysterious things that happens between identical twins. And keeps on happening even after one of them is dead because they share a common soul. Two hearts and one spirit, linked by the scent of a shower curtain.

"Awesome." That word keeps popping out of him like a string of hiccups. Maybe it will go away when Danny finally leaves the shower and faces Grandma Daniels.

He hadn't thought he could make love to Mary with Grandma in the house. Thirty feet away, snoring in that jittery, entitled way only people over forty can pull off. Hard to keep your mind on business with Grandma running through your mind, even when that business is something you've been really interested in ever since you turned thirteen.

Mary knew tricks that steered Danny back on course. Tricks he hadn't imagined would work so well, and he'd imagined quite a lot of things over the last few years. Some of them he wouldn't care to talk about—especially to Mary—but she knew them anyway.

Exactly where he wanted to be touched. Places he'd never been touched for real, except during strip searches after a couple of legal misunderstandings back on the rez. Cops didn't do it like Mary—not at all.

And she did that little whispering thing. Warm moist air pushing words he couldn't quite understand all the way to parts of his brain that had been passed down from the dinosaurs and were still working fine. Thank you, Charles Darwin.

Mary knew how to turn her body so the parts of her he wanted more than anything were right where he wanted them to be. Her skin was smooth, stretched gently over muscles that moved in a rhythm he'd been trying to recall ever since he came out of the birth canal.

Making love to Mary changed things for Danny Riley. Balanced him on the knife-edge of time. Carried him through the universe at a speed so fast that all his troubles were left behind—Nelva Riley, back on the rez, and Richard Daniels, whose spirit is already in the afterworld, and his body is—who knows where?

But Grandma Daniels is still asleep in the living room. Her snores sound like an argument between two feral pigs as she moves into her early wake-up stage, one labored breath at a time.

"Awesome."

The weirdest part is all the things Danny knew about Mary when the time was right. The way his fingers found exactly the right spot to make her tremble. Where to put his hands. Where to apply pressure. When to breathe in that broken stutter that comes just before everything is over.

He hadn't known any of those things when he made love to Sarah Benally. That was good but not nearly as intense as last night with Mary. No enhancements. No hallucinogenic ants or moonflower moths, just Danny and Mary, moving through nuances that undoubtedly took months to learn. Months Danny hadn't been around.

How many Richard Daniels memories does he own? He steps out of the shower and dries himself with one of Mary's towels. Looks at a trapdoor in the ceiling that leads to the attic. The hiding place for more memories that are barely out of reach.

Grandma Daniels smacks her lips the way old people do when they're about to wake up and make your life miserable. Danny remembers the Wilma Daniels wake-up-snort almost as well as he remembered how to lead Mary around every obstacle between foreplay and the finish line.

"Ricky! Where the fuck are you, Ricky?"

And that doesn't seem awesome at all.

Danny rushes into his clothing as fast as Superman changed into his Clark Kent drags inside glass-paneled phone booths before the age of cellular technology. So many things have changed so quickly, but Grandma Wilma Daniels is just the way she's always been. So full of hate and misery that some of it slops over onto everyone she passes.

She's already out of the easy chair as Danny opens the bathroom door and fills the hallway with lavender-scented steam.

"Hi, Grandma."

She moves around the room, exploring every knick-knack, every chair, every lamp, like a spider checking out her web while she waits for a careless fly.

Grandmother Spider.

Wilma Daniels bumps against her suitcase. Looks at it for an angry moment but can't think of anybody to blame. Finally notices the wedding band on the ring finger of her left hand. It sparkles in the morning light as she removes it and checks the inscription inside.

"Wilma Daniels." She frowns, as if her name has left a sour after-taste. Puts the ring back on. "Where'd it come from, Ricky?"

She twists the ring as if she's unscrewing a cross-threaded bottle cap that's gotten loose but won't come off. Its reflection in her eyes wavers like a pair of tears working up the nerve to fall.

Danny's cell phone vibrates in his pocket. Charged and returned to him by Mary after he was tired and spent and satisfied. He doesn't remember putting it in his pocket, but his hand finds it there. He checks the screen.

Nelva Riley. He touches *Ignore*. Smiles at Wilma Daniels the way he imagined his twin brother smiled when he knew something Grandma didn't.

Wilma Daniels scratches at her wedding ring, testing its reality with her fingernail. "Goddamn, Ricky. There's no such thing as magic."

But Wilma isn't sure enough to pick a fight. She looks up as Mary walks into the room. She explores Mary the way a pathologist evaluates a tumor under a microscope, trying to decide between a simple excision or something more radical.

"How about you?" Wilma extends her left hand so Mary can inspect the ring up close. Wiggles her fingers as if she's teasing a declawed cat.

Danny steps between them, takes Wilma's hand in his, inspects the ring in silence for a few seconds, and asks, "How does that make you feel?"

"Who the fuck are you, Dr. Phil?" Wilma jerks her hand away and curls it against her chest as if she's had a sudden stroke.

"Thought I'd feel better once I had it," Wilma says. "Maybe it'll take a while." She sits in the easy chair again. Crosses her legs so Danny and Mary can see the knife in her ankle sheath. "This fucking place needs dusting."

She points her ring finger at a perfectly symmetrical spider web between an end table and a floor lamp. It sparkles in a beam of sunlight that's found its way inside. Rainbow colors. Magic colors. The silk fibers vibrate with the voices in the room.

Mary starts to sweep it away, but Wilma tells her, "Let it be." She touches the tip of her tongue against her magic wedding band. Flattens her lips into a neutral expression. Not happiness, exactly, but Grandma Daniels isn't as angry as she used to be.

"Let it be, for now."

Compassion, Danny realizes. Compassion for a spider. Maybe the ring is magic.

Chapter 32

AFIRM KNOCK AT THE front door makes Wilma jump. She curls her legs into her chair and wraps her fingers around the handle of her ankle knife.

"Don't open it!" Her voice carries the hint of a tremor. "Please!"

Danny is already moving toward the door. He puts his hand on the knob and hesitates for a moment while he considers what it would take to scare a woman like Wilma Daniels. When the knock rattles the door again, he opens it.

Wilma struggles to her feet, like a spider that's slid into a sink and can't get out. She sits down hard when she sees it's Jack Bailey standing in the doorway.

Jack doesn't look happy to see *Richard*.

"What the fuck?" He takes a clumsy retreating step. Slips and falls but reaches backward and catches himself before his butt hits the ground. His Hawaiian shirt crawls high enough to expose the pistol in his waistband.

Danny's turn to take a backward step.

Jack crawls away, belly up, like an animal that's been turned inside out. His arms give way and send him sprawling on his shoulder blades.

The woman with him says, "For God's sake, Jack." She shrugs at Danny, the way people do when a family member does something inexplicable. "Sorry, Richard." Deepens the shrug. She smiles. Exactly like Mary until her lips harden at the edges.

Mary's mother. Danny knows without a doubt. Another Richard Daniels memory? She's pretty, the same way Mary is pretty, but older, harder, and much more dangerous. She shifts her body in a way that says, *You can have me if you want.*

The spirit of the original Richard Daniels whispers, "Watch out!" from the other side. Danny listens for more, but there is nothing. He extends a hand to Jack Bailey, ready to duck at a moment's notice because the last time the two men were this close, he got a bloody nose.

"I thought you were...." Jack props himself up on his elbows and takes a second to cover his pistol with the hem of his shirt. He breathes so fast all the extra oxygen clouds his mind.

"Alligators." He bites his lower lip, as if he's just made a shameful confession.

Danny feels a delicate hand on his shoulder—Mary's touch—feels her body radiating heat next to him.

"Get up, Dad. You're acting silly."

Everything is quiet while Jack Bailey sorts things out. So quiet they can all hear Wilma Daniels breathing like an asthma attack in the easy chair. Her wheezes are punctuated by the metallic sound of a wedding band clinking against a hip flask.

"Not Tommy," she says. "Not yet, anyway." The smell of Tennessee sipping whiskey follows those words. "Get the fuck inside, you're letting in the flies." The whiskey mellows Grandma Daniels's breathing but not her mood.

Jack Bailey is on his feet, picking bits of gravel out of his palms. He dusts his pants off, checks the pistol in his waistband, and touches Danny on the shoulder tentatively, the way he'd check to see if a wire is carrying an electric charge.

"Good to see you, Richard." Eases himself through the door, as if his son-in-law is an improvised explosive device.

"Sorry, guys." Mary's mom looks like she's had lots of practice apologizing. She brushes against Danny as she passes him and lets her hand trail across his belly while Mary leads Jack inside.

"Not that chair!" Grandma Daniels shouts a whiskey-saturated order. Taps her wedding band against her flask as if she's sending a message in Morse code. "Black widow lives there."

She points at the web. Exhales cloud of Jack Daniel's forcefully enough to make it vibrate.

"Let Ricky sit there," she says. "Spiders like Indians. Even Laguna."

Wilma picks seats out for everyone. Mary is in a corner, as far away from everyone else as possible. Jack and Mary's mother are on the couch.

"Ellen!" Wilma snaps the name out like she's disciplining a naughty puppy. "We met at the wedding. Remember?"

Ellen blushes. Something Danny is sure doesn't happen very often.

Jack Bailey puts his hand under his Hawaiian shirt, reminding himself he holds the power of life and death. He stares at a spot between the spider web and "Richard," as if he's having trouble deciding which one he should step on first.

Wilma takes another swig from her flask, completely in charge of the room, until another knock on the door chokes her in mid-swallow.

Mary is on her feet before Wilma can stop her. Ready to fill her house with people. Lots of targets for Wilma Daniels's anger. The more, the merrier. She doesn't notice that Wilma isn't angry anymore, but Danny does.

Grandma Daniels has pulled her legs underneath her again. She wraps her arms around them, like a late-term fetus that knows things are only going to get worse.

"Toad!" Mary doesn't sound exactly glad to see Richard Daniels's old druggy friend, but she steps away from the door and makes a grand-entry gesture.

Toad shrugs. Runs the split ends of his tongue past his lips. "Hope we're not intruding."

We?

Toad steps into the living room. Wilma hasn't assigned him a place to sit, so he leans against the wall. Mary stands at the open door, looking confused.

A tiny person comes in next, wrapped in gauze and adhesive tape like a mummy. Two walking casts. One arm in a splint. He wears two silver crucifixes around his neck and a string of coins stretched around one plaster-coated ankle. The miniature mummy's nose is hidden under a nasal splint. His one visible eye finds Danny.

Brown iris with an African eyelid. The sutures in his lips are crusted with blood and coated with petroleum jelly so they don't crack when he talks.

"I'm gonna kill you, motherfucker. Soon as Tommy says I can."

"Little Bits!" Danny doesn't recognize him exactly, but who else could it be?

There's a semiautomatic pistol in Little Bits's one good hand. He grunts as he points it at the man who ran him over with a truck. It looks like he's about to pull the trigger until someone who isn't in the room yet orders him to, "Stop!"

Little Bits jingles as he tries to catch his balance.

Wilma Daniels takes a final swig of Cousin Jack. Screws the lid back on her flask and says, "Fuck you, Tommy."

Her voice breaks halfway through Tommy's name, as if she is unsure—for the first time in her life—exactly who is the meanest person in the room.

The famous Tommy Bracken holds both arms up as he makes his grand entrance—a compromise between an unconditional surrender and a victory sign. He walks over to Wilma Daniels and kisses her on the cheek. Holds his face within slapping distance, but Wilma doesn't take the bait. She pulls her knife instead. She shows him the blade, but it's trembling too much for a proper threat.

"You leave my Ricky alone." She doesn't say please, but everybody in the room can see it in her eyes.

Richard Daniels's cell phone vibrates in Danny's pocket. The spider web next to his chair vibrates in sympathy, as if a fly is caught in the fibers. A black widow climbs into view. A big female, the size of a murderer's thumbprint. Big so she can eat her mate after she's gotten what she needs.

"Grandmother Spider."

She turns her eight eyes toward Danny Riley's voice. Shows him the red spot on her belly.

Wilma Daniels looks at Danny too. Her knife doesn't tremble when she turns the point his way. The problem with spiders is they never know exactly who to kill. She pops out of her seat. Quick, dangerous, full of venom. Nothing like an ordinary grandmother. Everything like Grandmother Spider.

She stares at Danny for a moment, then turns her attention to Tommy Bracken.

"Blood is blood," she tells everyone in the room. "Even if it's tainted."

Tommy shrugs. "John Horse is gone. I need a new cook. One that has the knack for Cherokee Ice." He points at Danny. "Toad tells me this one does."

Toad says, "Sorry, Richard. You know how talkative I get on speed."

Little Bits jingle-limps to Tommy's leg. Tugs on his pants like a five year old who needs to go to the bathroom but can't get Dad's attention.

"Got to let me kill somebody, Tommy." He points his pistol at Danny, then at Ellen, then at Toad. Holds it there because nobody could be sentimental about a man like Toad.

The phone vibrates in Danny's pocket again. The black widow shakes her web. She turns a full circle in precise ten-degree jerks, taking in every possible threat.

Wilma Daniels holds the knife in her right hand like it's a magic wand that can solve every problem she's ever had. She picks at her recovered wedding band with the thumbnail of her left hand, trying to remember why she thought it was important. The only thing she knows for sure is, "Blood is blood."

Jack Bailey stands. His right hand strays to the pistol-shaped lump under his Hawaiian shirt. Everybody in the room knows what he's thinking before he's made up his mind.

"Hold on, Jack." Danny reaches his open hand toward the spider web. "Time for a little John Horse Magic."

The meth cook's name puts all the violence in the room on hold. It won't last long, so the magic had better work.

The black widow climbs onto Danny's fingers.

"What the fuck?" Little Bits has turned his pistol in Jack Bailey's direction, but his eyes are on the spider as Danny carries her to his lips.

"You gonna eat that thing?" He remembers what happened the last time Danny ate an insect.

Danny holds the black widow to his lips. Makes a kissing sound until it lunges and bites him in the tender red zone full of blood vessels that spread the toxin through his system. His magic John Horse enzymes will do the rest.

Not as painful as a wasp sting. More like a shot of Novocain that fills his face with soda pop tingles. Bubbles of black widow energy explode in Danny's brain, then in every muscle of his body. He stands up fast because his spider senses know that Little Bits's pistol is pointing at him, and the miniature killer's finger is already closing on the trigger. Danny feels the heat from the muzzle flash. Watches the slug fly past him into the wall. Hears it pass through the other side and lodge in a stud in another room. Feels the copper pipes vibrate throughout the house, as if the wood frame building is a web filled with insects all ready to be wrapped in silk cases and saved for leaner times.

While Little Bits jingles into another shooting position, Danny grabs Wilma Daniels and kisses her on the lips. Mouth open. His tongue probes hers, pushing modified black widow toxin where he knows it will do the most good. She is almost at the killing stage already, and spider kisses work very fast.

Danny hears Little Bits cursing as he levels the pistol for another shot, but spiders have perfect timing. He lashes out with his foot before the African American dwarf's stunted finger can apply a lethal amount of pressure to the trigger and kicks the pistol out of Little Bits's good hand, which isn't quite so good after the kick.

Danny watches the pistol spin in the air and follow a ballistic arc directly into Jack Bailey's hands.

A perfect, double-handed catch—unexpected, even in Danny's spider-enhanced brain. This is the most mysterious part of reservation Magic.

The pistol fires. A slug passes through Little Bits and disintegrates as it hits a nail in the living room floor. Danny reaches out and catches the ejected brass cartridge in mid-air, pops it into his mouth, and swallows it.

Hot, but eating the brass seems like a very spidery thing to do.

Jack Bailey drops the pistol. Ellen smothers him with kisses and promises him more if they get out of this alive.

Tommy Bracken looks at Toad and says, "Guess I need a new Oklahoma City distributor." He waits for an answer, but before he gets it, Wilma Daniels's spider kiss has taken hold. She drives her knife into Tommy's shoulder and rakes the blade across his face as he falls to the floor beside the pistol Jack Bailey dropped.

"Fuck you, Tommy Bracken!" Wilma twirls the knife between her fingers like a baton, her black-widow senses tuned to maximum efficiency. She talks about stabbing Tommy in the eyes and then in the balls and then in the heart, but she won't do that until he's sufficiently unhappy. The thing is, Tommy doesn't look unhappy about any of her threats.

Wilma picks up the pistol beside Tommy. She holds the gun in one hand and her knife in the other, weighing the relative cruelty of each weapon.

Danny looks at the black widow that has remained on his fingers during all of this. She doesn't look so big after he's seen Wilma Daniels in action. He flips the spider onto Tommy Bracken's face.

"That's for Queenie." His wolf and Richard's dog blend together in his spider-toxin-soaked mind.

Tommy doesn't look happy at all about the spider bite, but Wilma Daniels does. She looks happier than Danny—and probably Richard Daniels—has ever seen her. Danny sits in the spider chair again, watching all the action, because that's what arachnids do when their jobs are finished. Mary stands beside him. Wants to kiss him, but he tells her, "It's not a good time yet," because the toxin is still on his breath and in his brain.

Jack Bailey fiddles with his watch.

Ellen kisses him some more. Puts a hand in one of his pockets. Whispers something in his ear that makes him smile, but he keeps pushing buttons on his Breitling Chronometer Emergency timepiece.

Danny reaches into his amulet bag and finds the brass cartridge with the burned-in fingerprint he's kept all these years. Now he knows why. He tosses it on the floor. That will confuse the crime scene investigation, which will occur now that one man has been murdered and another will probably die.

He doesn't have to wait long until the door is pushed open and a policewoman walks in, pistol drawn. He expected more police, but he expected them much later.

Maybe spider time runs at a different speed, like Indian time. He watches the black widow scurry across the floor and disappear under his chair.

"Nobody move." The voice of Corporal Laura Pepper.

She checks Little Bits's pulse through his gauze bandages. Tells everybody, "This one's dead."

She nudges Tommy Bracken with the spit-shined toe of her uniform boot. "You've been a bad boy, Skippy." She steps on the fingers of one of Tommy's hands and grinds them until the bones pop.

Tommy smiles a little when she snaps her cuffs around his wrists so tight they cut the circulation off.

Wilma says, "Looks like Tommy's got a new girlfriend."

Danny's phone vibrates once again. He reaches into his pocket before Officer Laura Pepper can tell him not to.

Nelva Riley's name and number are displayed on the screen.

He touches the exact center of a rectangle that says, *Ignore*. But he's never been able to ignore Nelva for very long.

Chapter 33

OKLAHOMA PLAIN-CLOTHES POLICE DON'T look anything like reservation cops, even through Danny Riley's spider haze.

He counts, "Two of them," through the living room window. "Detectives, I think." He's seen men like this in police shows on satellite TV. Rumpled suits, five o'clock shadows, go-to-hell expressions on their faces. No black and whites, other than Laura Pepper's, but he hears sirens.

The policewoman cuffs Toad and seats him on the couch beside Ellen and Jack. He looks nervous, but as far as Danny can tell, Toad always looks that way. Tommy Bracken lies sprawled face down on the floor. His hands are cuffed behind him. His fingers are starting to turn blue. A tremor begins at Tommy's feet and travels toward his head like an earthquake spreading from the epicenter.

"You okay?" Laura Pepper nudges Tommy.

He answers her with a string of gibberish ending in a word that sounds like, "Mommy."

"Sick bastard." Laura Pepper turns Tommy's head to the side. "So he won't drown in his own vomit."

Danny thinks that's probably a good idea because Tommy's gibberish is starting to sound like a cat choking up a hairball.

When the retching noise tapers off, Danny asks her, "Are we under arrest?"

So far, Laura Pepper hasn't pulled out a Miranda card or ordered anybody to assume the position, but every now and then her hand strays across the third set of handcuffs hanging on her utility belt.

"I called it in." Her lips flatten into an angry, straight line as she looks out the window. "The gold shields will decide."

She glances at the flask of whiskey Wilma has turned up several times already and the pistol in Jack Bailey's waistband that almost doesn't qualify as a concealed weapon, but she clearly has other things on her mind.

"Homicide detectives. Two of them." Laura Pepper confirms Danny's guess. She turns toward the door and waits… like a soldier facing an enemy with an overwhelming advantage. She doesn't say a word when the two men walk into Mary's house without knocking.

The boss cops throw hard looks at all the potential perpetrators in the room then focus their attention on Laura Pepper, as if she's the most serious troublemaker in the place.

They walk around her in opposite directions, like a pair of coyotes circling a steel trap. They poke at Little Bits's body. They frown at Laura Pepper's handcuffed prisoners. They flash badges but don't introduce themselves.

Laura Pepper rests her hand on the grip of her sidearm.

Danny steps in front of Mary, just in case.

One detective teases the pistol and the brass cartridge next to Tommy Bracken into separate plastic evidence bags. The other asks Laura Pepper, "The sick fuck on the floor—he the shooter?"

She forces Tommy to his feet. Grabs his hair and turns his face so they can see it straight on and in profile, like a mug shot. His eyes roll up in his head so only the whites are showing. A stream of yellow drool the thickness of honey drips from his chin.

"Looks like a face out of Lindsay Lohan's family album," one of the detectives says. The other fakes a laugh that sounds like a recording from a circus funhouse.

Laura Pepper lets Tommy go and watches him slump onto the floor.

The detectives don't ask why the dead dwarf is wrapped up like a mummy or why Tommy looks so bad. Danny figures Little Bits and Tommy must have been wanted dead or alive.

"Fuck all," one boss cop tells the other, then turns to Laura Pepper. "Put the drooler and the tattooed prick in your black and white. Get everybody else out of here."

The detectives turn away from Danny, so he can't tell which one is talking, but it really doesn't matter so long as no more sets of handcuffs are coming out.

LAURA PEPPER STANDS IN THE front yard "with all the goddamned civilians." She doesn't look too happy about it, but as far as Danny can see, the only thing that makes her happy is the sound of handcuffs snapping into place.

He can hear the conversation in the house, but it's hard to tell how things are going. The detectives have decided "the sick fuck" was the shooter because he was closest to the gun. Laura Pepper will get credit for the arrest because the poor bastard might die before they get him to the station, and there'll be hell to pay. "The tattooed asshole" will have warrants, and "the dead midget mummy" is sure to have an arrest record of one kind or another.

Any problems—and it looks like there might be plenty—can be blamed on "the bitch cop," who had the bad luck of being first to the scene of a brand-new quirky murder. Their voices are raised in the half-angry, half-excited way people talk about presidential elections that didn't go the way they were supposed to. Every other sentence ends with, "Fuckin' A."

Two more black-and-whites crowd down the one-lane street that leads to Mary's house. The sound of sirens mixed with the sound of metal against metal. The cops park their cars side by side, blocking the street completely, and argue over whose fault the accident is.

Lots of shouting and flashing blue lights. Nobody pays any attention to the handcuffed men in the backseat of Laura Pepper's cruiser. Danny asks her, "Think you should call for an ambulance?" He points at Tommy Bracken, so maybe Officer Pepper will notice how sick he is.

She opens the back door of her cruiser and rolls the window down, ignoring Toad completely but asks Tommy, "You okay?"

The cut on his face has started to clot, but it seeps a little blood when he smiles and lolls his head back onto the seat.

"Want me to loosen those cuffs?"

Tommy smiles a little wider and bleeds a little more. His lips move, but no sound comes out, like an actor in a silent movie about dying of a spider bite in the backseat of a police car.

Danny feels pretty much back to normal, except for a little spot on his lip that is sore as hell. But Tommy? That was a big spider, and the bite was so close to the brain, and he doesn't have any holy man enzymes.

Danny thinks maybe he should tell Corporal Laura Pepper that Tommy was bitten by a black widow, but she doesn't seem in much of a mood to talk. His attention is diverted by the interesting sound his phone makes in his pocket. A text from Nelva. *We're in OK City. Can't find you. Need address.*

We. That means John Horse is with her. As Danny tries to figure out what to do next, a cloud of Jack Daniel's vapor settles in over his left shoulder. Wilma puts an arm around his waist. At first, he can't tell if it's a sign of affection or an attack, but then she takes the phone from his hand, reads the message on the screen, and says, "Now ain't a good time for visitors. Text her back, Ricky. Tell her the cops are here."

Wilma takes a sip of Cousin Jack, a little something to help her face the fact that the Laguna whore isn't dead. How much more Jack Daniel's will she need when she learns John Horse is with Nelva now? Probably more than her little hip flask will hold.

"My Richard was a lyin' prick, God rest his soul." She taps her ring against her flask. It sounds hollow. Way too empty for Danny to consider giving her any more bad news.

Wilma screws the lid back on, done drinking for now. She sets her flask on the top of Laura Pepper's black and white. Walks over to the uniformed female cop as if they are long-lost friends. "That's Tommy Bracken in the backseat of your car. Most wanted dope dealer in Oklahoma." The gangster looks unconscious, but he stirs when Wilma says his name. His eyes are dilated, as if he can't find anything in this world worth focusing on.

"Those detectives in the house don't know shit," Wilma says. "I reckon Tommy will be good for your career, whether he dies or not."

"Tommy shoot the midget?" Laura Pepper looks like she is starting to remember police procedure. Thinking she ought to search all the goddamned civilians in the yard since the detectives don't seem interested.

"Probably did," Wilma says. "Everything happened so fast." She spreads her arms as if she's trying to get them all the way around the biggest lie she ever told.

She looks at Jack Bailey. "I might have wiped the fingerprints off the pistol. You know, a woman my age cleans things when she's nervous."

Jack looks a lot less nervous now that he isn't being accused of killing an unarmed man. He holds his watch up for everyone to see. "Good thing I had this baby."

"Breitling Chronometer Emergency watch," he says. "Got it for three thousand five hundred nineteen dollars and twenty cents on Craigslist. Retails for ten thousand."

Laura Pepper walks over to Jack. Twists his wrist more than necessary to get a good look at his watch. Makes a point of ignoring the pistol under his Hawaiian shirt.

"What the hell are you talking about, Spanky?" She makes a face like she smells something unpleasant. Like gunpowder residue that she won't say anything about because there are two macho detectives who would take over her case if they had the slightest idea who was cuffed in the backseat of her cruiser.

Jack shows her the series of buttons he pushed to signal first responders.

"Up to a hundred klicks." He says. "That's short for kilometers." In case there's someone on the planet Earth who doesn't know that.

"That's really fucked." Most women don't use the word fuck nearly as often or as comfortably as Laura Pepper. "Because I was responding to a complaint of a 1965, yellow Mustang blocking a neighbor's driveway when I heard gunshots." She points at Tommy Bracken's classic car. Its yellow paint is barely visible through the trees.

"Not my ten thousand dollar watch?"

Wilma Daniels moves to Jack's side, as close to his disappointment as possible.

"No way," Laura Pepper tells him.

"No fucking way," Wilma Daniels agrees.

Ellen comforts Jack Bailey with a kiss.

Mary walks over to her father and takes the hand Laura Pepper isn't twisting. "It's still a nice watch, Dad."

Danny snaps a picture of Wilma, Jack, and Corporal Laura Pepper with his iPhone. He sends the photos off to Nelva Riley along with a text. *Family pictures. What do you think?*

Tommy Bracken makes a noise like a lung-shot deer in the backseat of the police car beside Toad, who leans against the door as far from the dying man as he can get.

Danny steps over to the car. Laura Pepper watches but makes no move to stop him. He reaches into his amulet bag and removes Queenie's tooth. Puts it into Tommy Bracken's shirt pocket. "Say hello to Queenie for me."

The blood seeping from the cut on Tommy's face looks as black as his fully dilated pupils. A drop trickles off the edge of his chin and drips into the pocket onto Queenie's tooth.

"Tell her I still think of her," Danny says. Two different Queenies, but it really doesn't matter.

Tommy Bracken's left eye stays dilated, but his right pupil constricts until it is the size of a period at the end of a death sentence. His spirit leaves his body, the way they always do, with his dying breath. It rides out on a pair of Spanish words—*Cielito Lindo.*

The constricted pupil dilates until it matches the other one—two black pools covered by a film of tears, thickened by spider venom and evaporation, and reflecting colors like oil on water. Red, blue, green, and yellow. The rainbow colors at the border of the spirit world.

Another text from Nelva. *Family is the most important thing. That's what the Laguna people say.*

Everything John T. Biggs writes is so full of Oklahoma that once you read it, you'll never get the red dirt stains washed out of your mind. The tribes play a significant role. No authentic discussion of the state is possible without them. Traditional Native American legends are reworked and set in the modern era, the way oral historians always intended.

One of John's stories, "Boy Witch" took grand prize in the 80th annual Writer's Digest Competition in 2011. Another won third prize in the 2011 Lorian Hemingway short story contest. Sixty of his short stories have been published in one form or another, along with several of his novels—*Shiners, The Owl of Death Row, Sacred Alarm Clock*, and *Clementine: A Song for the End of the World.*

Facebook: John T. Biggs
Twitter: @biggspirit

www.johnbiggsoklahomawriter.com